Chilean Poet

Chilean Poet

A Novel

ALEJANDRO ZAMBRA

Translated by Megan McDowell

Viking

VIKING
An imprint of Penguin Random House LLC
penguinrandomhouse.com

Originally published in Spain as *Poeta Chileno* by Editorial Anagrama, Barcelona, in 2020
First English-language edition published in North America by Viking, 2022

Page 339: Cover of *La montaña mágica* by Thomas Mann. Reprinted with permission
of Editoria y Distribudora Hispanoamerica, S.A. (EDHASA), Barcelona.

Page 340 : Cover of *Poemas* by Emily Dickinson.
Reprinted with permission of Tusquets Editores, Barcelona.

Owing to limitations of space, text credits may be found on page 359.

The author would like to thank the Cullman Center for their support in the writing of this book.

The author and the translator would like to thank Anthony Careli for his reading
and comments on the poetry translations.

LIBRARY OF CONGRESS CATALOGING-IN-PUBLICATION DATA
Names: Zambra, Alejandro, 1975– author. | McDowell, Megan, translator.
Title: Chilean poet : a novel / Alejandro Zambra ; translated by Megan McDowell.
Other titles: Poeta chileno. English
Description: New York : Viking, [2022] |
Identifiers: LCCN 2021038783 (print) | LCCN 2021038784 (ebook) |
ISBN 9780593297940 (hardcover) | ISBN 9781101992180 (ebook) |
ISBN 9780593492505 (international edition)
Subjects: LCSH: Poets, Chilean—Fiction. | LCGFT: Domestic fiction. | Novels.
Classification: LCC PQ8098.36.A43 P6413 2022 (print) |
LCC PQ8098.36.A43 (ebook) | DDC 863/.64—dc23
LC record available at https://lccn.loc.gov/2021038783
LC ebook record available at https://lccn.loc.gov/2021038784

Printed in the United States of America
1   3   5   7   9   10   8   6   4   2

Book design by Daniel Lagin

For Jazmina and Silvestre

There is no house, no parents, no love:
there are only playmates.

—ALAIN-FOURNIER/JORGE TEILLIER

A method for writing
should also be a method for living.

—FABIÁN CASAS

I. Early Works

I t was the time of apprehensive mothers, of taciturn fathers, and of burly older brothers, but it was also the time of blankets, of quilts, and of ponchos, and so no one thought it strange that Carla and Gonzalo would spend two or three hours every evening curled up on the sofa beneath a magnificent red poncho made of Chiloé wool that, in the freezing winter of 1991, seemed like a basic necessity.

In spite of all the obstacles, the poncho strategy allowed Carla and Gonzalo to do practically everything, except for the famous, the sacred, the much feared and longed-for penetration. Carla's mother's strategy, meanwhile, was to feign the absence of a strategy. At most she would occasionally ask them, trying to chip away at their confidence with almost imperceptible irony, if perhaps they weren't a little warmish, and they would reply in unison, their voices faltering like a couple of terrible acting students, that no, in fact, it really is freezing cold in here.

Then Carla's mother would disappear down the hall and turn her attention back to the TV drama she was watching in her room, on mute—the TV in the living room was loud enough, because Carla and Gonzalo were watching the same show, which they weren't all that interested in, but the unspoken rules of the game stipulated that they had to pay attention, if only so they could respond naturally to Carla's mother's comments when she reappeared in the living room, at uncertain and not necessarily frequent intervals, to arrange flowers in a vase or fold napkins or carry out some other task of questionable urgency. Then she would glance sidelong toward the sofa, not so much to look at them as to make them feel that she could see them, and she'd slip in phrases like, *Well, she was pretty much asking for it*, or *That guy's a few cards short of a deck*, and then Carla and Gonzalo, always in unison and scared stiff, practically naked under the poncho, would answer, *Yeah*, or *Totally*, or *She's so in love.*

Carla's intimidating older brother—who did not play rugby, but whose size and demeanor could easily have gotten him drafted to the national team— usually came home after midnight, and the rare times he arrived earlier he locked himself in his room to play *Double Dragon*, though there was still the risk he would come downstairs for a salami sandwich or a glass of Coke. Luckily, when that happened Carla and Gonzalo could count on the miraculous help of the staircase, in particular the second—or penultimate—step: from the moment they heard its strident creak until the instant the older brother landed in the living room exactly six seconds went by, which was long enough for them to get situated under the poncho so they looked like two innocent strangers weathering the cold together out of simple solidarity.

The futuristic theme song of the evening news marked, every night, the end of the session: the couple would go to the front yard and play out a passionate goodbye that sometimes coincided with the arrival of Carla's father, who would flash the Toyota's headlights and rev its engine, either as a greeting or as a threat.

"This little romance is lasting a bit too long, if you ask me," he would add with an arch of his eyebrow, if he was in a good mood.

The bus ride from La Reina to Plaza de Maipú took over an hour, which Gonzalo spent reading, though it was hard in the dim light of the streetlamps, and sometimes he had to content himself with catching a glimpse of a poem when the bus stopped on an illuminated corner. He was scolded every night for coming home late, and every night Gonzalo swore, without the slightest intention of keeping his word, that from then on he would come home earlier. He went to sleep thinking about Carla, and when he couldn't sleep, as often happened, he thought about her and he masturbated.

To masturbate while thinking about one's beloved is, as we all know, the most ardent proof of fidelity, especially if one jacks off to fantasies that are, as a movie trailer might put it, based on a true story: far from getting lost in unlikely scenarios, Gonzalo pictured them on the same sofa as always, covered by the same chilote poncho as always, and the only difference, the only fictional element, was that they were alone, and then he entered her and she embraced him and delicately closed her eyes.

The surveillance system seemed inviolable, but Carla and Gonzalo trusted that their opportunity would soon present itself. It happened toward the end of spring, right when the stupid warm weather was threatening to ruin everything. A screeching of brakes and a chorus of howls interrupted the eight o'clock calm—a Mormon missionary had been hit on the corner, and Carla's mom hightailed it outside to gossip, and Carla and Gonzalo understood that the moment they'd yearned for had arrived. Counting the thirty seconds the penetration lasted and the three and a half minutes they spent cleaning up the drops of blood and assimilating the insipid experience, the entire process took a mere four minutes, after which Carla and Gonzalo went, without further ado, to join the crowd of curious onlookers gathered around the blond youth who lay on the sidewalk beside his mangled bike.

If the blond boy had died and Carla had gotten pregnant, we would be talking about a slight tipping of the world's scales in favor of brown people, because any child of Carla's, who was pretty dark, with even darker Gonzalo, could hardly have turned out blond, but none of that happened: the incident left the Mormon with a limp and Carla withdrawn, so sore and sad that for two weeks, making ridiculous excuses, she refused to see Gonzalo. And when she finally did, it was only to break up with him "face-to-face."

In Gonzalo's defense it must be said that information was scarce in those wretched years, with no help from parents or advice from teachers or guidance counselors, and without any assistance from governmental campaigns or anything like that, because the country was too worried about keeping the recently recovered and still shaky democracy afloat to think about such sophisticated First World issues as an integrated policy on sex education. Suddenly freed from the dictatorship of their childhoods, Chilean teenagers were living through their own parallel transitions into adulthood, smoking weed and listening to Silvio Rodríguez or Los Tres or Nirvana while they deciphered or tried to decipher all kinds of fears, frustrations, traumas, and problems, almost always through the dangerous method of trial and error.

Back then, of course, you didn't have billions of online videos promoting a marathon idea of sex; while Gonzalo had seen publications like *Bravo* or *Quirquincho*, and had once or twice "read," let's say, a *Playboy* or a *Penthouse*, he had never seen a porno, and as such had no audiovisual material that would help him understand that, any way you looked at it, his performance had been disastrous. His whole idea of what should happen in bed was based on his ponchoistic practice sessions and on the boastful, vague, and fantastical stories he heard from some of his classmates.

Surprised and devastated, Gonzalo did everything he could to get back together with Carla, although everything he could do amounted only to calling her every half hour and wasting his time on the fruitless lobbying of a couple of duplicitous intermediaries who had no intention of helping him, because, sure, they thought he was smart, kinda cute in his own way, and funny, but compared to Carla's countless other suitors they found him lacking, a weirdo outsider from the periphery that was Maipú.

Gonzalo had no other option than to go all in on poetry: he locked himself in his room and in a mere five days produced forty-two sonnets, moved by the Nerudian hope of managing to write something so extraordinarily persuasive that Carla could not go on rejecting him. At times he forgot his sadness; at least for a few minutes, the intellectual exercise of fixing a crooked verse or finding a rhyme took precedence. But then the joy of an image he found masterly would be crushed under the weight of his bitter present.

Unfortunately, none of those forty-two compositions held genuine poetry. One example is this completely unmemorable sonnet that must nevertheless be among the five best—or the five least bad—of the series:

The telephone is red as is the sun
I couldn't sleep, was waiting for your call

I look and look for you but find no one
I'm like a zombie walking through this mall

I'm like a pisco sour *sans alcohol*
I'm like a lost and twisted cigarette
Ne'er to be smoked, this treacherous Pall Mall
Abandoned in the street so sad and wet

I'm like a wilted flower in a book
I'm like a threaded screw without a drill
A dead dog sprawled beside the road—don't look
But I'm just like that sorry-ass roadkill

Everything hurts, from feet to face to eye
And nothing's certain but that I will die

The only presumable virtue of the poem was its forced adherence to the classical form, which for a sixteen-year-old could be considered praiseworthy. The final stanza was, by far, the worst part of the sonnet, but also the most authentic, because, in his lukewarm and oblique way, Gonzalo did feel like he wanted to die. There's nothing funny about mocking his feelings; let us instead mock the poem, its obvious and mediocre rhymes, its schmaltz, its involuntary humor. But let us not underestimate Gonzalo's pain, which was real.

While Gonzalo was battling tears and iambic pentameter, Carla was listening over and over to "Losing My Religion" by R.E.M., a contemporary hit that she claimed perfectly summed up her state of mind, though she only understood a few of the English words (*life*, *you*, *me*, *much*, *this*), plus the title, which she connected with the idea of sin, as if the song were really called "Losing My Virginity." Though she did go to Catholic school, her torment was not religious or metaphysical, but rather absolutely physical, because, all symbolism and shame aside, penetration had hurt like hell: the very same penis she used to furtively, happily put in her mouth, the same one she stroked daily and pretty creatively, now seemed to her like a brutal, deceitful power drill.

"No one is ever going to put another one of those in me, never. Not Gonza or anyone else," she told her girlfriends, who visited her every day, contrary to what Carla herself wanted; she proclaimed to the four winds that she wanted to be left alone, but they still kept showing up.

Carla's girlfriends could be divided into two camps: the angelical, boring, and larger group of those who were still virgins, and the scant motley crew of those who were not. The virginal group was divided, in turn, into the smaller subset of those who wanted to wait until marriage, and the bigger, more fickle subset of the *not yets*, to which Carla had belonged until recently. Among the non-virgins, two in particular really stood out, and Carla referred to them, with irony and admiration, as "the leftists," because they were, in nearly every sense, more radical or maybe just less repressed than anyone else Carla knew. (One of them insisted Carla change her favorite song, since she felt that the Divinyls song "I Touch Myself," also a hit in those days, was more appropriate to the current situation than "Losing My Religion." "You don't choose your favorite song," replied Carla, right as rain.)

After considering the abundant advice from both sides and giving special preference to the opinions of the leftists, Carla decided that actually, the most reasonable thing was to erase her first sexual experience as soon as possible, for which purpose she logically, urgently, needed a second one. On a Friday after school she called Gonzalo and asked him to meet her downtown. He was beside himself with joy: he ran out to the bus stop, which was very unusual for him, because he thought people who ran in the street looked ridiculous, especially when they were wearing long pants. The bus he caught had no empty seats, but even standing he still managed to reread a good number of the forty-two poems he'd brought with him in his backpack.

Carla greeted him with an eloquent smack on the lips and told him, straight up, that she wanted to get back together and she wanted to go to a motel, which was something she herself had refused to do for almost an entire year, alleging indecency, lack of money, illegality, bacteriophobia, or all of the above. But now she assured him, in a somewhat exaggeratedly sensual tone, that she did want to, that she was dying to go.

"I heard there's one near the craft market and I got some condoms and I have the money," said Carla in a single rapid-fire phrase. "Let's go!"

The place was a sordid hole-in-the-wall that smelled of incense and reheated grease, because you could order fried cheese or meat empanadas delivered to the room, as well as beers, pichuncho cocktails, or pisco and Cokes, all options that they refused. A woman with dyed-red hair and blue-painted lips took their money and of course did not ask for ID. As soon as they closed the door to the tiny room, Carla and Gonzalo took off their clothes and looked at each other in astonishment, as if they had just discovered nudity, which in a way they had. For some five minutes they limited themselves to kissing, licking, and biting, and then Carla herself put the condom on Gonzalo—she'd practiced on a corncob that very morning—and he slowly slid inside her with the restraint and emotion appropriate in a person who wants to treasure the moment, and everything seemed to be going swimmingly, but in the end there wasn't much improvement, because the pain persisted (in fact, it hurt Carla even worse than the first time), and the penetration lasted about as long as it would take a hundred-meter sprinter to run the first fifty meters.

Gonzalo half opened the blinds to look at the people heading home from work with a slowness that seemed fantastical from afar. Then he knelt down beside the bed and looked very closely at Carla's feet. He had never before noticed that feet had lines, that there were lines on the soles of feet: for a full minute, as if he were trying to solve a maze, he followed those chaotic lines that branched into invisibility and thought about writing a long poem about someone who walks barefoot along an endless path until the lines on their feet are completely erased. Then he lay down beside Carla and asked if he could read her his sonnets.

"Sure," replied Carla, distracted.

"But there are forty-two of them."

"Read me your favorite."

"It's hard to choose. I'll read you twenty."

"Three," Carla negotiated.

"Five."

"Okay."

Gonzalo started to read his sonnets in a solemn singsong, and although Carla wanted to think they were good, the truth is they said nothing to her. While she listened, she thought about Gonzalo's neck, his chest, which was smooth as a sheet of ice but so warm, about his graceful, nearly visible skeleton, his eyes that were sometimes brown, other times green, and always a little strange. She thought he was beautiful and it would have been great if she also liked the poems he wrote, though in any case she listened respectfully, with a smile that was meant to appear serene and relaxed but actually just looked melancholy.

Right as Gonzalo was starting in on the fifth sonnet, the sound of moaning began to filter in from the room next door, through the thin partition wall. The unsought intimacy with those strangers produced a disparate effect in them: Gonzalo felt something like gratitude for the privilege of gaining access to a true porno, live and in person—real, crude sex, with a pounding bed and semi-synchronized grunts, which surely corresponded to some truly memorable thrusts. For Carla, on the other hand, such proximity was disturbing at first, and she even thought about banging on the wall to ask for a little discretion. But then she started to focus on those moans and speculate about whether the stranger so enjoying herself was on top or on the bottom or in one of those weird positions her classmates drew hastily on the blackboard during breaks. The idea of grunting like that, like an invincible champion at the French Open, seemed magnificent, and yet, for the moment, impossible, because the moans she was hearing were from pleasure, and though at times pain and pleasure can mix together, that was not Carla's case—what she felt was purely and exclusively pain.

With the sudden desire to cry out louder than her neighbor, Carla sat on top of Gonzalo and started to lick his neck. He grabbed her ass in both hands and felt his full erection return instantly, and it seemed inevitable that they would do it for the second time that day, the third time in their lives, and it would erase or at least take the edge off the memories of the previous times. Gonzalo tried to put another condom on himself, and although he proceeded with an almost dignified fumbling, those additional seconds were enough to make Carla desist, and the skirmish ended instead in routine and efficient mutual masturbation.

Gonzalo lay his head between Carla's breasts and would have fallen asleep if it weren't for the racket in the room next door, where the neighbors were still going at it like rabbits or crazy people or maybe crazy rabbits. He picked up the remote control, thinking it was almost time for their show. They'd both ended up getting into it, which was only natural, since the show wasn't bad and was nearing its finale. But Carla, who had been staring at the ceiling for about ten minutes now, took the remote from him and not only turned off the TV but also removed the batteries and threw them against the wall. A silence fell that had little of silence about it, because the neighbors were still, as a literary theory professor would put it, in medias res.

"It can't be," Gonzalo said then, with sincere incredulity. "It's too much."

"Too much what?"

"You don't hear it? They're going too long. I don't think that's normal."

"As I understand it, that *is* normal," said Carla, trying to tone down her emphasis. "As I understand it, *that's what normal is.*"

"Seems like you know a lot about sex," stammered Gonzalo, trying to hide his shame. She didn't answer.

When the panting in the room next door finally subsided, Carla and Gonzalo still had over an hour of motel time left, but they didn't feel like doing anything. Gonzalo looked at Carla's lovely back and caressed some faded tan lines left by the alternation of different bathing suits, which descended from her shoulders and formed a kind of inverse tattoo.

"I'm sorry," he said.

"It doesn't matter," said Carla.

"I'm sorry," Gonzalo repeated.

They retrieved the batteries for the remote and caught the last few minutes of their show. Then they walked toward Alameda talking about the episode they'd just watched. And that was one of the sad scenes of the afternoon, of the week, maybe of their entire relationship: Carla and Gonzalo holding hands, headed toward Alameda, talking about the TV show. They were like two strangers searching desperately for a subject in common; it seemed like they were talking about something and were together, but they knew that really they were talking about nothing and were alone.

Gonzalo faked a stomachache so he could visit Dr. Valdemar Puppo, who was not a psychiatrist or psychologist but rather the very same pediatrician he had always gone to. Though he tended toward euphemisms and prevarications, the patient tried to be clear: the problem was with penetration. During foreplay he could contain himself, but as soon as he entered Carla—he didn't specify that this had only happened twice—it was impossible. The doctor let out a slobbery and humiliatingly long cackle full of masculine complicity.

"It happens to everyone, bud, though I have to admit it's never happened to me," said the man, caressing his belly with both hands as if he'd just devoured a wild boar. "Penetration is overrated. You're just nervous, champ."

Always in that forced, odiously youthful tone, Dr. Valdemar Puppo recommended that Gonzalo relax, and he told him all about the distraction technique, which he summarized in a vague and vulgar way:

"When your pecker's good and hard, think about your grandma," he said.

Gonzalo understood what he meant, but he also couldn't help but literally think about his grandmother, and thus about sadness, because the old lady had only recently died.

The advice was good, when it came down to it. The lovers had sex again in the same motel and at a couple of parties and even in Gonzalo's attic, flanked by shining spiderwebs and possibly a few mice, and the distraction technique, which Gonzalo referred to as "the Puppo technique," tended to work: of course, he didn't actually think about his grandmother, but about women he found ugly, although his idea of ugliness included categories that were, so to speak, moral. The repulsion inspired in him, for example, by ex–Minister of Education Mónica Madariaga, or the singer Patricia Maldonado, or Lucía Hiriart de Pinochet herself, was much more ideological than physical, given that—with the possible exception of Mrs. Maldonado—they were not objectively such ugly women.

In any case, atrocious as these ladies seemed to him, at some point their skin, presumably rough, coarse, and slack, would recede before Carla's smooth back or perfect thighs—reality overcame imagination, and Gonzalo, much sooner than later, would get off. The key, he realized then, was to concentrate on more abstract or neutral or pleasant matters that would bring a more lasting distraction, like paintings by Kandinsky or Rothko or Matta, or certain beginner-level chess exercises, or the conquest of outer space, or some very serious and dramatic poems by Miguel Arteche that he didn't like at all but had had to analyze in school ("Golf," "The Idiot Child"), and he even achieved notable results thanks to the cruel method of imagining a man with Parkinson's trying to eat an artichoke.

Although the sex was growing more frequent and slightly less painful, Carla was no longer sure about staying with Gonzalo. She tried to convince herself that she was more in love than ever, but the truth is she had left behind the fantasies of their early days: the idea of spending years or her whole life with Gonzalo now seemed to her increasingly daunting.

That summer, one of the leftists invited Carla to Maitencillo, and although she could have asked to bring Gonzalo along, Carla decided she would rather spend the time thinking about their relationship. And that was pretty much what she did during the nine days she spent in Maitencillo: she ate breakfast, lunch, and dinner thinking about the relationship, she stretched out on the sand to take long naps thinking about the relationship, she played volleyball or paddleball or caballito de bronce thinking about the relationship,

she drank Fanta mixed with beer and danced frenetically to hits by Techno-
tronic while thinking about the relationship, and even the night when she let
a muscular Argentine kiss her and grope her ass and breasts, she was thinking
about the relationship, and though it may sound a little hard to believe, the
truth is that while she was sucking the Argentine's dick, Carla was also, in a
way, thinking about the relationship.

The story of the fling with the Argentine was told, commented on, and analyzed by many semi-present witnesses, and it was going to reach Gonzalo's
ears any minute. Overcome with remorse, Carla decided to confess her infidelity, including the blow job, which acted as a mitigating factor because it
served as proof that she had refused p-in-v sex. Although—cards on the
table—she hadn't refused out of faithfulness, but because the idea of being
penetrated by a member that was a couple centimeters shorter than Gonzalo's, but considerably wider in girth, just seemed horrible.

For the next six months, their relationship was fueled solely by guilt.
There were days when Carla was afraid Gonzalo would take his revenge, but
other times she wished he would, because if the score were even at least she
could recover her dignity. Which, of course, she had never really lost, even
if Gonzalo did occasionally torment her with hostile or self-pitying comments.

Going against his faithful nature, Gonzalo decided to respond to insinu-
ations from Bernardita Rojas, a girl from his neighborhood with whom he
felt a nebulous bond, given that his last name was also Rojas. They weren't
related, of course, it was a very common last name, but she greeted him as
if they were; really, it was her way of flirting. ("How's it going, cuz?" she'd
say, and her nostrils would flare like a bad actress trying to express emotion.)
He thought Bernardita Rojas was unique, because she didn't wear her bangs
frozen with gel into the shape of a threatening wave, as nearly all of her peers
did, Carla included; it was as if all teenage Chilean girls had gotten together
and agreed to pay homage to Hokusai's *Great Wave*. Another thing that attracted him to Bernardita Rojas was that she always carried a book by Edgar
Allan Poe, which she reread with the kind of devotion other people showed

as they deciphered *A Lover's Discourse: Fragments*, *Open Veins of Latin America*, or *Your Erroneous Zones*.

The false Rojas cousins went to see *Night on Earth*, and although the implicit idea of going to the movies was to make the most of the darkness and fool around a little, they found Jim Jarmusch's film so entertaining that they just stared hypnotized at the screen.

"I had a great time," Bernardita told him afterward, while they were waiting for the bus.

"Me too," Gonzalo replied, distracted.

On the way home Gonzalo thought about Winona Ryder—he imagined her at the wheel of a Lada taxi, waiting for a green light at some Santiago intersection while she chewed gum and smoked and listened to Tom Waits. Tired of her seatmate's monosyllabic replies, Bernardita abandoned any attempt at conversation and started to reread "Ligeia," which was her favorite Poe story. Gonzalo watched her read for a few minutes, the city at dusk as a backdrop, and then he did feel like he wanted to kiss her. He tried to, but she rebuffed him with her characteristic tight-lipped smile.

"I'm reading," she said.

"Read me a little," replied Gonzalo.

"I don't want to," said Bernardita, who nevertheless put the book between them so Gonzalo could see it too, and they rode the rest of the way with their heads together, almost embracing, reading Poe's story.

They reached the corner where they had to part ways, and now Bernardita accepted a quick kiss, without much tongue. Gonzalo walked home weighing the possibility of continuing with his revenge until it was more or less symmetrical. He wasn't convinced, so he decided to take the matter up with Marquitos, a slightly older redhead who worked in the corner store, and who owed the diminutive of his name to his short, almost dwarf-like stature. Night was falling as Gonzalo helped Marquitos close up shop, and they settled at the counter with two cold one-liter bottles of Escudo beer.

"Your girlfriend is a lot hotter than Bernardita," Marquitos told him, after considering the dilemma for a few seconds. "Why would I lie to you— your girlfriend is much, much hotter."

This was a tic of Marquitos's: "Why would I lie to you, ma'am, these are the best watermelons of the season," he'd say, for example, or maybe, "I fell asleep, boss, why would I lie to you," and sometimes he would also use the formula in bland phrases like, "Why would I lie to you, it's cold out."

"Yeah, I know, but she cheated on me," said Gonzalo.

"But you're ugly, Gonzalo, really ugly."

"What does that have to do with it? What difference does it make if I'm ugly?" replied Gonzalo, who didn't consider himself ugly (and wasn't).

"Look, the thing is that your girl is crazy hot. Your girl is the hottest of them all." It sounded like Marquitos had been holding that comment back for ages.

"What's your deal, asshole?" said Gonzalo, surprised and annoyed.

"Sorry, but it's true. Friends have a responsibility to tell each other the truth, right?" Gonzalo hesitated two seconds before nodding, seemingly meek. "Why would I lie to you: your girlfriend is a rich cuica snob, but she's really hot. And she's too good for you. She's too much for you, man. I don't know how you got her to give you the time of day. If you break up, you'll never get a girl even half that hot."

"I don't want to break up with her," said Gonzalo, as though thinking out loud.

"But she's gonna catch on to you. Women see everything," said Marquitos, with the air of one who knows.

Marquitos went to get more beers, and he also got out a loaf of bread and offered some slices to Gonzalo.

"So, what do you like most about my girlfriend?" Gonzalo asked, in an artificially serene voice.

"You really want to know?"

"Yeah."

"You're not gonna get mad?"

"No, Marquitos, take it easy. How could I get mad about something like that?"

"You're gonna get mad, man."

"No, bro, it's okay. I'm just curious."

"I don't know, man, everything. Her tits are just right. And that ass—please. Your girl's got some ass. She's a luscious piece of ass, I guess you know that. And her face."

"What about her face? Go on, tell me, I'm not mad. . . ."

"I'm saying this with all due respect, but I mean, the face on that girl . . . why would I lie to you, bro, your girl's got the horniest face, know what I mean?"

Gonzalo had no choice: an uppercut to the eye, two stomach punches, and a kick to the balls ended his friendship with Marquitos for good. He left the shop sad and disconcerted and also worried, for the first time in his life, about his supposed ugliness. He blamed his stubborn acne, although by that point, since he'd had it since he was eleven, he just considered it part of his face.

"What's wrong, cuz?" Bernardita asked him that Friday.

"Why?"

"You look like something's wrong."

"I look like my face is wrong," said Gonzalo, attempting a joke.

They went to the plaza and talked for a long time, and Gonzalo told her everything, or almost everything. Before saying goodbye, Bernardita looked at him as if he really were her cousin, or maybe her brother, though she was also angry: she'd known he had a girlfriend, she'd seen them together more than once, but she thought they'd broken up or were breaking up, and of course it bothered her to be nothing but a means for revenge. Still, the next morning, she rang the bell at Gonzalo's house, set down a package, and ran away: it was a shoebox that held a newly cut aloe vera leaf, a razor, a hand-written note with instructions for treatment, and a map where Bernardita had marked the locations of ten aloe vera plants at various points around Maipú.

Gonzalo got into the habit of cutting a leaf off a plant every afternoon, and before he went to bed he'd spread its pulp over the many problematic areas of his face. If anyone had asked him why he was carrying that razor around in his backpack, he would have replied that he needed it for self-defense, which was ultimately true, because he needed it to ward off ugliness.

I t had all been so natural at first, so pleasant and fun, thought Gonzalo, thinking back to his first encounter with Carla, almost three years ago now, on the way out of an Electrodomésticos concert—it was a brief flirtation that seemed inconsequential, because they talked for less than five minutes, but Gonzalo gathered his courage and asked for her phone number, something he had never done before. When she said no, he begged her to at least give him the first six numbers, and she thought that was so funny that in the end she gave him the first five.

The next day Gonzalo sat down in front of the yellow pay phone on the corner with a pocket full of hundred-peso coins, and he started dialing in ascending order (from 00 to 04). Then he decided to change to descending order (from 99 to 97), then he let himself be guided by his gut (09, 67, 75), and he got so mixed up he had to start writing the numbers down in the same notebook where he drafted his poems. The process dragged out for days and it seemed infinite, as well as wasteful—the corner pay phone had turned into a kind of slot machine and Gonzalo a crazed gambling addict, not to mention a thief, since his allowance plus the change from bread runs wasn't enough, and he had to dip into his parents' wallets daily. When discouragement set in, Gonzalo pictured Carla as she was pulling her hair back into a ponytail. He'd been left with that image: Carla raising her arms to tie up her pitch-black hair, her elbows bony, the shape of her breasts discernible under her green shirt, and a smile that showed the slight gap between her front teeth, which was very common but struck him as unusual and beautiful.

When he was almost convinced that his endeavor was doomed to fail, Gonzalo hit the jackpot with the number 59. On that first call Carla was pretty unenthusiastic—she couldn't believe he'd been so persistent—but they started to talk every day for a few minutes, almost always the time afforded by two or three coins, and then, months later, when the phone lines were finally installed as far as Gonzalo's house, they talked for at least an hour every day. The plan to meet up was ever more serious and yet Carla kept putting it off, because she thought she might like Gonzalo less in person. But from the first Saturday morning when they met up and made out, there were no more doubts.

They used to glow with satisfaction as they spoke of the origin story that Gonzalo now remembered with sorrow. Even as he insisted on idealizing his relationship with Carla, he understood and reluctantly came to accept that they no longer had such a good time together and they no longer laughed so much and that, maybe because of the infamous penetration, their bodies no longer harmonized. ("I never should have put it in her," Gonzalo said one morning out loud, involuntarily—his classmates burst out laughing, and from then on they called him "Señor Sorry.")

Gonzalo wasn't surprised that Carla was an object of unanimous desire. By that point he was used to seeing how nearly every man (including, sadly, Gonzalo's own father) stared at her shamelessly, and also how some women had trouble hiding the envy or perhaps the desire Carla awoke in them. Gonzalo wasn't a jealous person, though after the fling with the Argentine and the incident with Marquitos he thought he should be, that in a way he had a duty to be jealous. But he didn't want to be jealous or possessive or hostile. He didn't want to be like everyone else.

Going against the grain of all those superficial teens so dedicated to cliques and the cult of physical beauty, Gonzalo had found an oasis of pure companionship with Carla. To say or imply, as Marquitos had, that Gonzalo had "gotten" Carla and should make every effort to keep her and cling to her was to understand nothing about the nature of love. But the really offensive part was that Marquitos had called Carla a rich snob, because she didn't talk like a cuica or dress like a cuica—or she sort of did, she was cuica compared to Gonzalo or Marquitos or Bernardita Rojas, but compared to a cuica from Vitacura or Las Condes, she wasn't a cuica at all.

There were obvious differences between Carla and Gonzalo to which neither of them was blind: private Catholic school in Ñuñoa versus a public boy's school in downtown Santiago; big house with three bathrooms versus a small house with one; daughter of a lawyer and a dental technician versus the son of a taxi driver and an English teacher; traditional La Reina middle class versus Maipú middle class (lower middle class, Gonzalo's father would say; emerging middle class, said his mother). Neither Gonzalo nor Carla, however, thought that the social divide really separated them, and the differences in fact fed their mutual interest: the idea of love as a fortunate and random encounter, bolstered by the enduring notion of finding one's "other half."

Marquitos's poisonous words reappeared with the insistence of a mosquito at midnight and settled into what Gonzalo considered the most fragile zone of the relationship, which was Carla's obvious disinterest in poetry. She loved music, she'd been an amateur photographer ever since she was little, and she was always reading some novel or other, but she thought poetry was childish and overblown. Gonzalo, however, like almost everyone, associated poetry with love. He had not won Carla over with poems, but he had fallen in love with her and with poetry almost simultaneously, and it was hard for him to separate them.

Things took a more serious turn when Gonzalo decided he would study literature. He'd been sure for some time that he wanted to be a poet, and although he knew the profession didn't require formal studies, he thought that a degree in letters would divert him the least from his goal. It was a brave, radical, and even scandalous decision that Gonzalo's parents opposed tenaciously, since they thought it seemed like a waste: with a lot of effort and frankly inexplicable talent, their son had become an outstanding student at what was supposedly one of the best public schools in Chile, and as such he could and perhaps should aspire to a less reckless future. When Gonzalo mentioned his plans to Carla, expecting blind and loving support, she reacted instead with indifference.

At that point, Chilean poetry was to Gonzalo the story of some great and eccentric men who liked their wine and were experts in the ups and downs of love. Infected by that mythology, he sometimes thought that in the future Carla would be nothing but that distant girlfriend of his youth who hadn't known how to appreciate the budding poet he had been (the woman who, in spite of the many signs, had not taken the measure of the man in front of her—and had even cheated on him!). To be sure, Carla didn't seem like the right travel companion for the difficult road he wanted to go down; sooner or later, Gonzalo conjectured, the relationship would end and she would start dating some civil engineer or some dentist or some novelist. Gonzalo projected the breakup for the medium term, although sometimes he surprised himself thinking, in advance, about the words he would say to her then: he imagined a sophisticated speech that would proceed gradually toward the need to—he liked this expression—"part ways," and at first he would blame fate or destiny, but if she got too worked up he would take all the blame on himself and be done with it.

One morning they played hooky and walked in silence through bustling downtown Santiago until they reached Paseo Bulnes. They usually sat on a bench across from the bookstore to smoke and kiss, and then they'd turn down Tarapacá, and after eating a couple hot dogs they'd play a few rounds of pool—she always won—or go into the Normandie art house theater. This time, though, it was clear that the script was different: Carla just wanted to walk, they weren't even holding hands, and she was staring up at the thick clouds as if she wanted to dissolve them with her eyes. She'd planned a long preamble, but instead blurted out this succinct sentence:

"My feelings have changed, Gonza."

Those words, as severe as they were elegant, hit Gonzalo with a heretofore unknown violence. As we know, he was somewhat prepared for a breakup, but in his head it was always him who broke up with her.

During the following weeks he alternated between denial and spite, which took the form of fanciful masturbations—he punished his ex by imagining sex with Winona Ryder, with Claudia Di Girólamo, with Katty Kowaleczko, and even with an aunt of Carla's whom Gonzalo was mildly attracted to.

As for Bernardita Rojas, one afternoon he ran into her right beside a monumental aloe plant that grew by the entrance to Villa Las Terrazas. The first thing Bernardita did was touch his face, which, thanks to the miraculous treatment she'd recommended, was partially recovering its bloom. He thought he had nothing to lose, so he went right in for a kiss, but she dodged him.

"We're friends, Cousin Rojas," Bernardita told him, unequivocal.

"No, Berni, we're not really friends."

"We are friends. We're good friends," she said again.

"But we're not *such* good friends," Gonzalo said again.

The conversation was significantly longer and more idiotic. They didn't reach any conclusion.

"I just want to be friends," insisted Bernardita when they said goodbye.

"Well, I already have friends," said Gonzalo. "I have too many friends. I don't need any more."

Soon Gonzalo abandoned his onanistic vindictiveness and sank into indolence, as well as the Los Prisioneros album *Corazones*, which suddenly seemed like the soundtrack to his entire life. He became averse to any kind of conversation, even with himself—that is, to writing. He almost never came out of his room, but the most worrying thing, at least for those in his immediate surroundings, was his radical refusal to bathe.

Finally, one morning, reviving what had been a frequent punishment in his childhood, Gonzalo was forcibly deposited under a stream of freezing water. At first he reacted the way anyone would to such an intense humiliation, but he soon found a certain pleasure or novelty in soaping his body meticulously, and he spent about an hour under the water—which back then was considered an inexhaustible natural resource—in a kind of reconciliation with cleanliness. He got dressed quickly and made the most of the sunny day, lying in the scraggly grass of the plaza with his notebook. He didn't dive straight into poem-writing, but instead lingered in a preliminary state, debating a matter he had long put off: the choice of a pseudonym.

The idea of adopting a pseudonym was cheesy and unpleasant, but he felt obligated to do it, because although he had only read a few random poems by Gonzalo Rojas—and found them magnificent, it must be said—he was aware that the man was one of the most renowned Chilean poets in the world, and in fact had just won the National Prize for Literature, plus another prize that was apparently very important in Spain. His name, then, was already taken, and the option of using his mother's last name, Muñoz, wouldn't work either, because there was another poet, much less well-known than Gonzalo Rojas but blessed with an aura of vanguard and mystery, named Gonzalo Muñoz. And the option of signing his name as Gonzalo Rojas

Muñoz, he thought, would be like saying, *Not* that *Gonzalo Rojas*; it was like admitting defeat from the get-go.

He considered following the example of Pablo de Rokha, born Carlos Díaz Loyola, who had invented a last name that meant something on its own, but he could only come up with inanities like Gonzalo de Vil or Gonzalo de Port or Gonzalo de Clame (which he did like a little). Then he turned toward the option of finding a pseudonym in other literary ecosystems, as Gabriela Mistral and Pablo Neruda had done—and after all, both had won the Nobel Prize. After ruling out the silliest options (Gonzalo Rimbaud, Gonzalo Ginsberg, Gonzalo Pasolini, Gonzalo Pizarnik), he consolidated a short list with the names Gonzalo García Lorca, Gonzalo Corso, Gonzalo Grass, Gonzalo Li Po, and Gonzalo Lee Masters, but he couldn't decide on any one of them. Night was already falling when he thought of the pseudonym Gonzalo Pezoa, which would allow him to pay homage, simultaneously, to the Portuguese poet Fernando Pessoa (who he hadn't read but knew was great) and the Chilean poet Carlos Pezoa Véliz (who he liked a lot).

Seven months after the breakup, Carla started to receive letters from Gonzalo sent through certified mail. They were long, funny letters based on the fictional premise that their relationship hadn't ended, but that he was off traveling to remote places like Morocco or Istanbul or Sumatra, and even some nonexistent locales. He had a special talent for inventing carnivorous flowers and wild animals, as well as for relating natural disasters. Gonzalo signed those beautiful letters with his name, but the poems he attached were signed, instead, with his brand-new pseudonym.

Gonzalo's newest poems didn't adhere to Western forms; instead of sonnets or ballads he had turned to writing haikus, or rather some short poems that he called haikus. (Gonzalo never did connect his sudden passion for haikus with his premature ejaculation problem.)

The first letter featured this simple and perhaps beautiful poem:

> The wind in the trees
> you drew with your
> eyes closed.

This verse included in letter number three was less memorable:

> Betrayal of morning
> imprecise noontime
> in the middle of the night.

In some poems, the contemplative serenity characteristic of the haiku was conspicuous in its absence, as in this one from letter number nine:

> All the leaves of autumn
> have fallen. And it's still autumn,
> goddammit.

At letter number twelve, a failed urge toward experimentation emerged:

> A call, a groan
> a loco analog zoo
> long ago: a croon

This erotic moment comes from letter number fourteen:

> Those moles on your
> left thigh
> I devoured.

In his final letters the humor tended to fade, as proven by this somber, insolent, perhaps desperate poem:

Where your blood was
there was I,
inside.

    There were seventeen letters in total, and their addressee read and re-read and loved them, but she was nice enough or smart enough not to encourage any false hopes. She didn't feel resentment or anger or anything like that, but her relationship with Gonzalo now seemed to her like a serious waste of time. Several of her girlfriends had recently broken up with their respective boyfriends, and one of them had the idea to organize a sort of exorcism in which they would collectively burn photos and keepsakes. The project evolved into a veritable barbecue: onto that charcoal drenched with lighter fluid went dozens of notes, letters, postcards, tickets to movies, pools, and concerts, plus a few beleaguered teddy bears, all of it burning before the girls' rapt eyes. At first Carla didn't want to participate, but eventually she gave in to the peer pressure and ended up feeding all the letters and mementos from her relationship with Gonzalo, including a pocket edition of *Siddhartha* he had given her, to the bonfire.

The city of Santiago is big and segregated enough that Carla and Gonzalo could have lost touch forever, but one night, nine years later, they saw each other again, and it's thanks to that reencounter that this story will grow into enough pages to be considered a novel.

II. Step-Poet

I t was almost four in the morning, "Stop!" by Erasure was playing, and the two-hundred-plus enthusiasts crammed onto the dance floor were all dancing with everyone, or else no one was dancing with anyone. Carla saw him first, lost over by the bar, and since it was a gay club she assumed Gonzalo had come out of the closet, which surprised her at first, and even momentarily annoyed her, but after thinking about it for a few seconds she thought she should have realized, that in a way she'd always known and it explained a lot of things, though if someone had asked her what exactly it explained, she wouldn't have known how to answer. She went over to him, affecting a light, elegant sashay, anticipating astonishing and conclusive confessions. Gonzalo pounced on her and tried to lead her to a corner where they could talk, but it was hard to move amid the feverish throng, so they stayed on the dance floor, tangled up in that happy simulacrum of anarchy.

"I'm not gay!" shouted Gonzalo as he realized the possible misunderstanding, and he received some withering glares that were somewhere between skeptical and disappointed, and maybe Carla was also a little disappointed, because she had gotten as far as imagining telling her girlfriends that her first boyfriend, the first man she'd ever slept with, the one she referred to with affectionate sarcasm as "the poet," was gay, and she'd even thought of one of her guy friends who might be interested in him.

"Me either!" replied Carla, just in case, although in those blundering years of collective ignorance, it was still a new idea that homosexuality was not exclusively the province of men.

It would be an insult to dancers and choreographers and to university dance professors to say that Carla and Gonzalo danced, because what really happened was that they didn't stand still, and that lack of stillness took the form of a succession of muddled movements. In any case, Carla shook her shoulders with relative grace and synchronicity, which created the false impression of stability and as such of sobriety, while Gonzalo employed a step that, well executed, could be described as fake-drunk, but in this case it wasn't necessary to fake it, and so, strictly speaking, Gonzalo didn't dance but was as motionless as someone so drunk could be—he stumbled and grabbed Carla by the waist as though clinging to a mast, and then he fully, boldly, embraced her. She felt like she should rebuff him, but she wanted and maybe needed to hug him back, because it had been a long time since anyone had embraced her with such intensity or urgency, or because on receiving Gonzalo's body she felt a rush of familiarity, or because that hug took her nine years back in time, or who knows why, we just have to fully rule out any stupid ideas like that she never got over him—she managed to get over him almost right away—and we can also rule out the influence of alcohol, which of course did influence them, but by then, in the full-on dawn of the twenty-first century, the cynical move of blaming it all on the booze was passé.

Carla caressed Gonzalo's long hair, something she had never done before, because during the years they were together he invariably wore his hair short, the "regulation length" his school required—that is, two fingers above his shirt collar. The hug moved to the music, and now "Can't Get You Out of My Head" by Kylie Minogue was playing, but they looked like they were dancing to a bachata by Juan Luis Guerra or one of those steamy hits by Chichi Peralta, though at times it also seemed like they were dancing a kind of waltz, as if they were a pair of lovers unaccustomed to seriousness or solemnity or glamour who were just trying to dance a waltz with dignity.

In a matter of minutes they went from erratic, libidinous dancing to groping and slobbering on each other in the men's bathroom. When they entered the only cubicle, which luckily was available, there was a moment of hesitation, a brief pause of good judgment during which Carla managed to think, What the hell am I doing here? and Gonzalo was about to propose that instead of locking themselves in that foul bathroom they go back to his place, but they both knew that stopping to talk would break the spell. Given the choice between stammering out the words and phrases typical of a reunion and the possibility of an irresponsible, frenetic, and really difficult-to-justify fuck, they both preferred the latter.

Carla dug her teeth into Gonzalo's neck, which he meekly offered up to her like a dying man, but a dying man still alive enough to fumble for Carla's ass, an ass that he remembered or thought he remembered, though now it seemed more shapely, more ample and firm. He knelt down, and while he kissed between her legs he took off her panties and put them in his pocket as a trophy. She also knelt down, and then Gonzalo stood up and even had the courtesy to help Carla with the complicated mechanism of his belt. She started to suck him off voraciously. With her right hand she held his penis and with her left she untied Gonzalo's right boot, and then she switched hands to also untie the left, and, keeping Gonzalo immobilized with effective licking, she took off both his boots and his pants and underwear, and, although she herself wasn't clear that this was her plan, she threw his briefs into the toilet and flushed.

The briefs were a light blue pair with dark blue trim that he'd just received for his twenty-sixth birthday, a gift from the very friends who had dragged him to the club that night—friends, by the way, who were obsessed with proving to Gonzalo that heterosexuality was something like a chronic but curable disease. When he saw his favorite drawers—which, aside from their design, were really comfortable—stuck there in the toilet, Gonzalo was overcome by a fit of laughter, and then Carla, who was kneeling with his penis throbbing in her mouth, started cracking up too. Then Gonzalo also threw Carla's panties into the toilet and flushed, and the two of them went on flushing the toilet several more times, doubled over with laughter, as if they were high instead of drunk, although really they seemed more like two little kids playing a game.

"Let's do this right," she said suddenly, straightening her skirt and smoothing her hair.

Gonzalo wanted to do it right or all right or just okay or even badly, but he wanted to do it right now, and he almost convinced her, because they went back to kissing and groping and they would have proceeded in that vein if not for the intervention of a drunk guy who pounded on the stall door and bellowed:

"Hey, the bathroom is for everyone, you aren't the only ones who want to fuck!"

Sans panties and sans briefs, respectively, Carla and Gonzalo went out into the Bellavista night. They still had the giggles and a generous reserve of horniness, and there were clearly a thousand questions they should have been asking each other, but they opted instead for the partial silence of the night. They passed a group of punks finishing off a bottle of pisco halfway across Pío Nono Bridge and Gonzalo took Carla by the hand. She thought it seemed like an old-fashioned gesture, comically gallant, though she did like to walk holding hands with Gonzalo, or rather to remember what it was like to walk holding his hand. The punks didn't even glance at them and Gonzalo started to let go of her hand, but she held on to his.

"I like that club, it's the only place where I can dance in peace and be safe from the creeps," said Carla when they got to Plaza Italia and neither of them knew what to do.

"I like it because it's the only place where I really feel desired," joked Gonzalo, though it wasn't clear that it was really a joke.

They should have said goodbye, it was perfectly possible for everything to stop right there, an episode to be filed under the heading of "crazy nights," but then Gonzalo said he lived three blocks away, and Carla agreed to go with him. While they silently walked those three blocks, which were really more like six, night became day.

Whenever dawn caught him in motion, Gonzalo tended to feel like there was some kind of link between the birth of the light and the very fact of moving forward, as if the walker were somehow responsible for the dawn, or the other way around: as if the dawn generated the movement of feet over sidewalk. He was about to say this to Carla, but he wasn't sure he could explain it, he was afraid of getting tangled up, and he felt like anything he said could spoil that beautiful senseless morning.

Inside the apartment, everything happened with a quick sort of calm. As soon as the door closed they went right for it, without a condom, and she hung on to his neck and they stumbled to the bed. While Gonzalo licked Carla's nipples he thought that maybe her breasts were bigger now and he liked that and also thought it was strange, though there was nothing strange about it, he thought, as though answering himself, because bodies change, of course bodies change: her hips were in fact wider, her legs a little less smooth, and she was maybe less thin than she'd been nine years ago.

Gonzalo is a different person, Carla was theorizing for her part, while he thrust slow and hard; at least now he's a person who's good in bed. She felt the imminence of orgasm and at the same time the anachronistic fear that Gonzalo would ejaculate right away, and her pleasure receded, but the imminence returned a few minutes later and then she did have an orgasm, either a double or a very long one, she didn't know.

Gonzalo zeroed in on Carla's belly button, unsure that he remembered it precisely—it seemed to have turned slightly outward. He moved down between her breasts until he had it in front of him and he kissed and licked it deliberately, or rather he kissed and licked it with the purpose of looking at it deliberately, and he thought, tentatively, imperfectly, that it was a new belly button. A little lower, two centimeters above her pubis, Gonzalo found the faint scar from an operation.

Carla got on all fours and he went back to pounding hard, in sync with both of their moaning, and he looked at her back and waist, where there was something like an archipelago of stretch marks, and then he remembered— he had just seen it, but it was already possible to remember it—her belly button, her scar, her larger nipples, and her breasts that were noticeably slacker, and other stretch marks he thought he'd glimpsed, as well, around her breasts, and he put into mental words what he already knew, what he was resisting accepting, because it was an irrevocable and terribly powerful phrase, capable of ruining everything: Carla has a child.

He got distracted, just as he used to back in the days when he applied Dr. Valdemar Puppo's technique, though this time it was completely involuntary: he no longer needed to think about world peace or planetary music or magnetic fields or *Pilgrim's Progress*, for years now he'd managed his timing without any issues, and yet he felt himself enter an undesired fugue state that didn't entirely annul the present, because the thrusts and moans continued and his dick was every bit as hard, but at the same time he saw a distinct image of a seaside emerge and he imagined himself walking there with a beach umbrella and building sandcastles and even buying an ice-cream cone and pan de huevo and giving a swim lesson for Carla's son, a faceless child who soon reappeared in a bedroom saturated with color, sprawled out asleep while Gonzalo picked up the countless toys scattered over the floor.

They kept on screwing while he imagined that Carla's son behaved like a holy terror, that he wouldn't listen to anyone, got bad grades, that he was sullen and rebellious, that he threw tantrums too often and said: You're not my dad. He saw himself in the living room of a house that was too bright, where Carla waited for the faceless child to stop playing with his cereal and finally finish breakfast, and then the three of them rushed out toward the metro station. The boy pulled free of his mother's hand and ran ahead or fell behind; he walked at a different pace, at his own rhythm, until the three of them joined the crowd that filled the train car, and then Carla and the boy got off and Gonzalo stayed on the train for several more stops, and then he walked alone, very quickly, then ran several blocks so he could make it on time to an indefinite, shitty job, the worst job imaginable, a job that he'd never wanted but had to hold on to because he had a child, because he had a son, because he had a son who wasn't even his.

Carla had another orgasm and lay back satisfied and exhausted. Gonzalo, who hadn't ejaculated, sensed that he was going to lose his erection and he didn't want Carla to realize, so, after a brief pause, he moved back down between her legs and tried to focus solely on giving her pleasure, but he couldn't help but picture yet another scene, this time in a park where he was playing soccer with Carla's faceless son. What a typically masculine idea: a father and son or someone who seems like his son playing ball in the park. The son tries to play well but the ball bounces off every which way, and the father cheers for his supposed progress, practicing positive reinforcement; the boy hasn't made a goal, the boy could not make a goal, the boy isn't yet fully clear on the concept of a goal, but the father says or shouts or proclaims that the boy has made a goal and cheers exuberantly anyway. The father subtly and authoritatively explains how to kick the ball, because the father knows about those things. The father lets the son win, because to be a good father you have to let your children win. Being a father consists of throwing the match until the day when the defeat is real.

Carla was about to fall asleep with Gonzalo's mouth between her legs. He stretched out beside her planning to sleep as well, but after five minutes she stirred and started to masturbate him and suck him off. Gonzalo resisted for a few seconds, because by then he was totally flaccid, but she kept going and he felt a little desperate, almost sure his erection wasn't going to return— it seemed really unlikely to return. Carla kept jacking him off with the tip of his dick in her mouth, and although he never got as hard as he'd been a little earlier, he finally came. She swallowed all the semen and they fell asleep tangled in the gray sheet.

Gonzalo woke up two hours later. The sunlight flooding the room made it seem like they were outside, but a thin block of opportune shade protected Carla's face. He looked again at her cesarean scar, her wider areolas, her darker nipples, and he confirmed the stretch marks on her breasts. He didn't want to look at her that way, and yet, at the same time, a certain sense of authority emerged in his head, as if sleeping with someone or having slept with them meant you acquired the right to look coldly at their body. And yet his gaze wasn't cold—it was meticulous, but it wasn't cold.

While he walked to the mini-market, his happiness did battle with the ominous feeling that he had locked Carla up—but she wasn't locked up, she was asleep, and a sleeping person is always free, in a way. He bought bread, two different kinds, and eggs and blackberry jam, because there had always been blackberry or alcayota jam at Carla's house when it was time for tea— they'd always had tea before settling in under the red poncho to watch their show. Suddenly he had a clear memory of Carla licking blackberry jam from her front teeth. He walked quickly back to the apartment. I locked her in, I wanted to lock her up, he thought again, because if he'd left the door unlocked nothing would have happened, any thieves who broke into that minuscule apartment would only be disappointed by the utter absence of loot—no TV or computer, and of course no jewelry or cash, just a blender and books and a bunch of half-filled notebooks. And some cassettes and CDs and a tattered black coat. In any case, if those thieves knew what they were doing at all, they'd be able to pick the lock without much effort using an everyday wire. And if they came right now they'd be met with the surprise of a naked woman in the bed, conjectured Gonzalo, starting to get alarmed now, so he ran up the stairs like a superhero trying hard to make it in time, and when he saw that Carla was still asleep and naked he felt like he was the thief and she the helpless inhabitant of that apartment. But she could never live in such a small place. Why not? Again: Because she has a son, because she has a son, because she has a son.

He lay down carefully beside Carla, and while he finished off a roll he tried to read some poems by Jaime Sáenz, by Marianne Moore, Luis Hernández, Santiago Llach, Verónica Jiménez, Jorge Torres. He couldn't concentrate: they were poems he liked, ones he knew well, but now they were playing the role of frivolous magazines in a waiting room. He looked at Carla's slightly aquiline nose, her somewhat rounded face, no moles on the right cheek, nine on the left; he sheepishly remembered having written a poem comparing that cheek to a handful of dirt after an earthquake. And then he had the thought that he liked Carla now just as much as the person he'd been at sixteen had liked the person she'd been at sixteen.

He had thought he was prepared for when she woke up, thought he knew what to say to her, but when Carla woke up there wasn't time for many words. The first thing she did was ask him what time it was and if she could take a shower. Two minutes later she was back, wrapped in a towel printed with MAZINGER Z, the only one Gonzalo had in the apartment. He gave her some briefs that she didn't like and she asked for a nicer pair, so he brought her the cardboard box where he kept his clean clothes, of which there weren't many. Carla chose a pair of red Italian boxers.

"They almost fit," she said, looking at the wall as if there were a mirror there.

Gonzalo asked her if she wanted to eat something. She replied that she was starving, but she had to go in twenty minutes. While Carla got dressed, he made coffee and scrambled eggs and put bread in the toaster.

In the living room/dining room/office there was a table, two chairs, and two bookshelves that weren't enough for all the books. Carla peered at the spines with tentative curiosity. It was the smallest apartment she had ever seen, and nevertheless she liked to imagine Gonzalo's happy, disorganized life there, his anonymous, autonomous, brave trajectory. He had gotten what he wanted, at the end of the day; he'd studied what he wanted to study and he lived in the company of his books and his countless notebooks, surely scrawling poems better than the ones he'd written in adolescence.

"Looks like you're still a poet," she said.

"Yes," replied Gonzalo, who thankfully didn't even remotely consider reading her a poem, and he held back the long-winded response, which anyway could have been summed up briefly: He still wrote every day, with disciplined passion, but he didn't like anything he wrote. That would have been the short answer.

Gonzalo poured jam into a bowl and offered it to her.

"There was always blackberry or alcayota jam at your house," he said.

It was one of the sentences he had pre-planned, and he'd imagined a long and melancholic conversation in which they would exchange remembered details from those years. He thought they had a lot to talk about—he remembered so many things, some because he treasured them, because he had wanted to remember and did, but he also could have filled the silence with a thousand inconsequential images that had stuck in his abundant involuntary memory.

"Maybe so," she said. "I don't remember."

"We always ate bread with jam. Your mom put it in white porcelain dishes with animals on them. Lions, elephants. And a giraffe."

"I do like blackberry jam. Sure, I've always liked it," said Carla, who avoided engaging—she didn't have time for nostalgia.

Gonzalo wanted her to stay. And he wanted, at least, to touch her. To touch her shoulder, her hair, maybe, but it seemed impossible to get close to her. Because she was in a hurry, but not only that: Carla had quickly constructed a distance that was only growing.

"What's your son's name?" Gonzalo asked her out of the blue.

He had wanted to annul that distance with a warm and casual phrase, and yet it came out sounding like a question posed by a detective or a public functionary or a nosy neighbor. He didn't ask her if she had a child, he took that for granted. And he also took it for granted that her child was a boy. He'd thought that if he said it like that, so abruptly, he could demonstrate that he was willing, as he thought he was, as he *was*, to start or restart something. He'd thought these words would say that he didn't mind if she had a son. That he was ready for anything.

"Who told you?"

"No one."

Carla felt the oppressive scrutiny of many eyes. "Your body is the body of a woman who has given birth," someone said, maybe Gonzalo, maybe another man, a stranger; she felt that Gonzalo was the spokesman for a committee of men who gazed at her pitilessly, with mocking curiosity, though there were also some women who inspected her and mocked her or felt sorry for her: *We looked over all the marks on your body, we compiled all the information provided by the marks on your body, and we reached the conclusion that something ruined it, probably a son. It was surely a son who destroyed your body forever.*

She felt exposed, accused, and mistreated, and nevertheless she met Gonzalo's gaze and felt like kissing his eyelids and the circles under his eyes and biting his nose. She ate her toast slowly so the silence would last longer, so she wouldn't be obliged to reply. And she finished her toast and still hadn't answered.

"I don't have a son," she said finally. "I have a daughter and her name is Vicenta."

It was a lie, because she was the mother of a boy named Vicente. She lied instinctively, maybe to keep Gonzalo from being the star pupil who gets all the answers right. At that moment she decided she would never see him again, so she wouldn't be forced to explain that lie.

"How old is she? Three?" Gonzalo asked.

"Six."

"What about the dad?"

"You seem to know everything," said Carla, not even trying to hide her sarcasm. "What do you think happened with the dad?"

"You're not with him anymore."

"Affirmative," said Carla.

"Vicenta is an original name," said Gonzalo, to cut the tension. Really, he thought it was horrible.

"It's a weird name, but I like it."

"And is Vicenta with her dad now?"

"No," said Carla curtly. "Her dad doesn't exist anymore. Vicenta is with my mom. And I have to go."

She hugged him the way she would a friend, and left.

Carla hadn't even given him her phone number, and Gonzalo tried fruitlessly to track it down in the following weeks, until it occurred to him to call the same number as always, the same one whose two last numbers he had once guessed, a number he still knew by heart, because it was still the one he had dialed most in his life. Carla herself answered—she still lived in the same house, but now it was just her and Vicente. The call at times felt tense and anachronistic, because the days of long phone calls over landlines were past.

"I want to see you," said Gonzalo for the umpteenth time, toward the end of the call, with no choice but to go for broke.

"I don't want to see you, but I want you to do me up the ass," she said with delightful vulgarity. "And for you to do me up the ass we have to see each other."

So, their two first dates were just hookups. On the third date they talked a little more, mostly about Vicenta—Carla told him about the dresses she bought her daughter, about how much the girl loved her pink room with its walls covered in pictures of fairies and princesses, and how Vicenta was, everyone said, the spitting image of Carla. On the fourth date, at an Italian restaurant, Gonzalo turned up with a gift for Vicenta: a doll with intricate black braids, which in any case Vicente liked a lot. Only on the fifth date, at Gonzalo's apartment, did Carla confess the truth, but, out of an abundance of caution, she did it after the sex, because she thought he might get mad or wouldn't understand. Gonzalo didn't get mad and he did understand and he even, without really knowing why, apologized.

"And is he really six years old? Did you lie about his age too?"

"Do you have any whiskey?" Carla asked, with a slightly deeper intonation.

"Just red wine."

"That'll do."

While Gonzalo uncorked a bottle she put on her underwear and shirt, as if possessed by a sudden and belated modesty. She downed the glass of wine in one gulp and asked for a refill immediately, apparently needing all the alcohol before she could get the next sentence out. She brought her hands to her face as if her eyes hurt, and said:

"Vicente is your son. I was pregnant when we broke up, but I figured there was no point in telling you."

The silence that descended then was very long. Gonzalo was stunned, moved, in a certain way hurt, but also almost excited. It would take many adjectives to describe what he felt. He had the sudden image of a son of an indeterminate age, almost a teenager, and he imagined receiving the boy's hostile and icy greeting, and then he felt very stupid when Carla couldn't take it anymore and burst out in a guffaw that instantly became a laughing fit.

"So it's a joke," said Gonzalo, in a tiny voice.

"Of course it's a joke, Gonza," said Carla, who was coughing as she tried to recover her seriousness. "Vicente is six years old, I didn't lie about that. And of course he's not your son."

Those words, so unequivocal, sounded offensive to Gonzalo. And of course he's not your son, he repeated mentally, as though registering a somber and painful piece of information.

"What I wanted to tell you is that I didn't care if you had a son, that I was willing to go all in," Gonzalo explained later.

"And are you still willing to go all in?"

"Yes," he said, without hesitation.

They agreed that the sixth date would take place at a Peruvian restaurant near Carla's house. Gonzalo arrived right on time to pick her up, and she asked him to wait outside. It was clear that she didn't want him to meet Vicente, at least not until the relationship was serious, though she herself wasn't sure she wanted anything serious; she didn't know if she was willing to go all in herself. Gonzalo spent five minutes gazing at the facade of the house, a little anxious, as if he were being forced to turn the pages of a high school yearbook. It was exactly the same image he had in his memory, except the lemon tree now took up almost the whole front yard: he thought it looked like an adult stuffed into a baby's crib. He was still taking it all in, his pose that of a painter projecting a future work, when Carla came back outside and told him he'd better come wait in the living room, because the babysitter was running late.

In place of the large leather sofa where they'd settled in so many times back in their poncho days, now there were two armchairs and a giant gray futon awash in green and blue throw pillows. The walls were still white, but it was a white that to Gonzalo seemed colder or more absolute: whiter. He remembered the reproductions of famous paintings that used to hang on the main wall—Velázquez, Van Gogh, Carreño—now replaced with photographs by Sergio Larraín neatly framed but badly printed. Instead of hanging lamps there were standing lamps, and the rug with black and red arabesques that used to lend the place a funny solemnity had given way to the chilly red brick floor. Gonzalo felt like he had entered a museum he knew well, but that had been completely remodeled—a museum that, in a way, he was also part of.

Perched on the edge of an armchair, Gonzalo looked like what he was, a suitor, lacking only the bouquet of flowers. He heard Carla and Vicente's voices coming from the second floor as they carried out a task that was ambiguous, indecipherable, but also encouraging, somehow: a kind of indirect welcome. Then the voices went quiet, and Gonzalo felt he knew that silence of honking horns, barking dogs, and robins. He was slow to notice Vicente, who had been standing there for a while on the stairs, looking down at him.

A tall boy, thin and large-headed with huge, wet, black eyes, who was eating or more like devouring a handful of something: that was Gonzalo's first image of Vicente. The child descended the stairs with coy, tentative steps, and his mother's suitor greeted him with that somewhat exaggerated and pathetic cheerfulness characteristic of people who aren't used to kids. Vicente didn't answer but looked at him mischievously, then came closer to ceremoniously offer a little of the food he held in his hand, which Gonzalo didn't know was cat food: into his mouth, out of pure politeness, went the presumed cookies or cereal, and he nearly vomited right there. The boy produced the sophisticated smile of a consummate prankster.

In those days Carla had been doing battle for some time with her son's addiction to cat food. At first she'd been worried not about the boy, but about the mysterious thinness of Darkness, a black cat with startling, enormous, disproportionate fangs whom Vicente had insisted on adopting. The obvious theory was that some other cat was stealing Darkness's food on the sly, but it took some doing for Carla to discover that the other cat was really Vicente, because the boy went about it cautiously and even had the presence of mind to brush his teeth immediately after his daily feast of cat food. Far from suspecting, Carla even bragged about how good her son was when it came to brushing his teeth, and it was only when his teacher informed her that Vicente brought cat food for his daily snack and even promoted its consumption among his little classmates that she understood the boy's sudden passion for oral hygiene. She tried to make him quit his habit cold turkey, but Vicente refused to eat anything else.

The doctor explained to Carla that it was fairly common for children to develop an affinity for their pets' food, especially cat food—dog food addicts were less frequent, since dog food was harder and apparently much less appealing to the human palate. The doctor said there was nothing strictly toxic or harmful in cat food, though of course it wasn't the most balanced or nutritious cuisine in the world. The only real danger, he explained, came from the cat's germs, so it would be best to keep him from eating out of Darkness's bowl. She would have to wean the boy little by little from his addiction, decreasing his ration the same as if he were hooked on chocolate or cotton candy or the intoxicating fragrance of glue.

And so, every afternoon, along with his vanilla milk and bread with avocado, Vicente received an ever less abundant handful of Whiskas. It was a rationing plan that also included his flavor preferences: starting with salmon Whiskas, which was far and away his favorite, they moved on to beef, which he liked less, and then to chicken, his least favorite, which was odd, because when it came to "real" foods, Vicente preferred chicken to beef and beef to salmon.

"These days I just give him a little of the chicken-flavored," Carla explained to Gonzalo that night, over a ceviche sampler at the Peruvian restaurant. "And I hope in a few weeks I can get him all the way off it."

"I mean, it wasn't disgusting, but it took me by surprise, I was expecting something sweet," said Gonzalo.

Then, almost without pausing for the change in subject, he added:

"I know you didn't want me to meet Vicente."

"I didn't want you to, but maybe that's how things have to happen," replied Carla, as though talking to herself.

"How?"

"Without thinking. Without thinking about them so much."

During the following weeks, on walks in the park and over pistachio ice cream dipped in chocolate, the rough draft of a family began to be written, but neither of them was sure whether that draft could eventually become a book. Although Gonzalo was the more enthusiastic of the two, they both behaved like the kind of writer who, rather than getting tangled up in paralyzing disquisitions, just keeps barreling ahead, trusting that abundance of material will translate, down the line, into some reasonably good pages. There was no need to reread or revise or print or change the font size, because they had a good time and laughed a lot, which was all they wanted, especially Carla, who'd been around the block and back again: she had naïvely stuck by a regrettable character who had made her the mother of a boy who in turn had made her into something like a solitary, voluntary slave—a boy she adored, but whose arrival had obliterated her idea of the future, an idea that, to tell the truth, had never been fully formed, or was formed indistinctly, with touches of fantasy, and had never felt urgent to define. Constrained by the facts, her new idea of the future was significantly more precise and did not, theoretically, include love, at least not in its most turbulent/destabilizing/passionate iteration, nor was she looking for a father for her son or anything like that. Quite the opposite: she imagined herself alone, maybe with some lover who came and went, but mostly focused on her work and her son, hopefully in that order. For now she didn't even have a job, per se: from nine to five she acted as a secretary at her father's law office, and even though it wasn't all that unpleasant to answer the phone or coordinate meetings or update files, and her salary wasn't bad, being her father's secretary was for Carla a daily humiliation that at times felt deserved and almost always felt irreversible.

Gonzalo's arrival on the scene shook up her plans. She didn't think she was in love with him, but she would have been incapable of stating the contrary. She had no doubt about this: she needed his company, she wanted him beside her, as close as possible, and he didn't resist, not at all. So maybe, if someone had forced her to decide whether she was in love with him, she would have said yes, even if only to justify her decisions, which were always lightly shaded by doubt. And that sounds pretty bad, sure, but it's okay, because everything is like that, everything has shades.

As for Gonzalo, not only would he have declared his love for Carla, he would have shouted it from the rooftops, though at times he thought or feared that this unexpected family life would permanently bury his own projects, which in any case were no longer as idiotic or spectacular as in his adolescence. The university had given him a couple of scholarships but he'd still had to take out loans, and after he graduated he worked whatever jobs he could find—phone operator, waiter, mailman, ghostwriter for illiterate students, pamphlet writer at a pharmacy chain—before joining up with a test prep school, where instead of talking about poetry he spent his time teaching tricks and shortcuts to use when taking university entrance exams. He still envisioned trips and books, but his primary dream was to get a job that was related to literature, and he also hoped to depend less on the miraculous but bloodthirsty credit card he'd finagled by crying in the face of a distracted or compassionate or perhaps negligent account manager. He still aspired to some imprecise sort of relevance, and his love of poetry remained intact, but he no longer dreamed of becoming a Pablo Neruda or a Pablo de Rokha or a Nicanor Parra, or even, let's say, an Oscar Hahn or a Claudio Bertoni: he aspired to be considered a good poet, that's all. He aspired to have his poems appear in anthologies—maybe not in all of them, but in some, in the good ones.

When Gonzalo started sleeping over at Carla's it was really hard to have sex, or rather—the expression he used, in an attempt to be funny—*quality* sex. Carla had let her son sleep in her bed for years, and though she'd started to reeducate him a few months before her reunion with Gonzalo, it was still an ongoing process. The boy would come down in the middle of the night and settle in between his mother and Gonzalo like the sword that separated Tristan and Isolde. The all-out Oedipal struggle included grunting, kicking, hitting, and even headbutting, but the hostilities were suspended in diurnal hours, because practically since day one Vicente had seen in Gonzalo a formidable playmate, something like a fun friend who, as if he had no family of his own, stayed too long at their house and even slept over—Vicente always seemed surprised when Gonzalo stayed to sleep. The upgrade to a king-sized bed only served to redraw the battlefield: if the surface of the mattress were a map, Vicente represented something like a small and belligerent Mediterranean country, a minor nation that was nevertheless the subject of constant debates between the great powers, because the disputes, at times, grew heated.

Though it was true that, in the abstract, Carla was even more interested in sex than Gonzalo, he complained that she didn't do anything to make it happen. The greatest point of contention was Carla's radical refusal to put a lock on the door or even to close it completely, because she honestly thought that if she did, she might not hear it if her son cried out for her.

Except for the rare instances when Vicente spent a night with Carla's parents (they now lived in a large apartment in Ñuñoa) and a few morning escapes to motels (much nicer ones, it should be said, than the motel of their first encounters), Carla and Gonzalo were doomed to have sex in a tense and monastic silence and in pretty uncreative positions. Unfortunately, the second—or penultimate—step, the same one that back in the days of the poncho had acted as their sentinel, no longer worked. Or rather, it worked better than ever, because supposedly steps shouldn't creak, and their trusty step, inexplicably, had stopped creaking. When, almost exactly a year after they reunited, Gonzalo officially moved into Carla's house, the first thing he did was loosen that board a little, but the results of the repair (or disrepair) were subpar: the step seemed to have definitively adapted and refused to emit its characteristic sound. Gonzalo tried out a wide variety of screws on all the boards of the stairs, with no success. He spent one Saturday morning making a collar with bells that Vicente happily hung around his neck. "My son is not a cat," said Carla, scandalized, and with an odd certainty given the boy's dietary preferences. Then Gonzalo taped the collar to one end of the step, but he found that even if an adult were to tap dance or stomp out a cueca on that blasted step, the bells only emitted a timid little tinkle, entirely insufficient as an alarm.

In a more or less desperate search for a solution, Gonzalo fantasized about the possibility of the boy staying at his father's house some weekends. Strictly speaking it was the simplest solution, but Carla wasn't even willing to discuss it with León. It had been years since they'd seen each other and they rarely spoke on the phone: laconic emails, plus the not always punctual paternal deposit of a paltry sum of money in the maternal savings account, were the only forms of interaction.

The airtight protocol for avoiding each other had been established early on. On visiting days, Carla drove to León's parents' house and honked the horn five times in a row as a signal for Vicente's grandmother to come out and get him. Then León would return him at seven in the evening to that same house, where Carla pulled up at eight and again honked the horn five times so the grandmother would bring the boy out to the gate, where she greeted Carla with a calculatedly scornful raise of her eyebrows. When Gonzalo showed up in this story, the protocol even improved, because it became his job to take the boy to his paternal grandparents' house.

One morning, without talking it over first with Carla, Gonzalo decided to propose an arrangement to León. Breaking with all tradition, he got out of the car with Vicente, rang the bell, and insisted on waiting for his presumed antagonist, who hadn't arrived yet. Vicente went out to the yard to play with Adamo, a whiny and insufferable wiener dog. Gonzalo watched them out the window and thought that Vicente must be the most beautiful boy in the world, and that Adamo must be the world's ugliest dog. It was unclear what time León would arrive, but Gonzalo was prepared for a long wait: his backpack held a voluminous anthology of contemporary French poets and a 1.5-liter bottle of mineral water, since he assumed the boy's grandparents wouldn't even offer him a glass of water. After half an hour León's father appeared with a glass of Bilz soda and a plate with three graham crackers, and though the old man didn't even say hello, to Gonzalo that gesture was courtesy enough.

León was surprised by Gonzalo's unexpected presence, but he also found it funny. He sliced up a salami while the two of them spoke, and at first they talked more about how good that salami was than about the schedule of visits. León was enjoying Gonzalo's nervousness, while Gonzalo didn't really know how to direct the conversation, the purpose of which was clear to León: he knew how to spot a poor guy who just wanted a halfway decent sex life. Less than a quarter of the salami remained by the time Gonzalo finally came out with a proposal.

"Every other weekend," he said, trying to sound tough and sensible.

"No way, buddy," said León. "One weekend a month."

"How about three days a month. One Saturday or Sunday, and then a Saturday and Sunday."

"You mean, two weekends a month, one partial and the other full?"

"Exactly," said Gonzalo, hope drawing up the corners of his mouth.

"Not a chance, my friend, that won't work for me. One weekend a month. Take it or leave it."

"Okay, but from Friday to Monday. You pick him up at school on Friday afternoon and you drop him off again on Monday morning."

"It's a deal, my man," said León.

As an addendum, maybe because he wasn't entirely sure he had won, León brought up the always controversial matter of extra expenses: he declared that they would no longer share the cost of clothes or school textbooks or Vicente's extracurricular activities, which in any case were limited to some pretty cheap swimming lessons.

To Carla, the idea of her son spending an entire weekend at León's house was horrible—it was an exhausting argument and their first really serious one and also the first that Gonzalo won, contending that it would be good for the boy to get to know his father better ("to find out, really and truly, who his father is," was his winning phrase). Carla had to resign herself to the idea of her son deep in an endless marathon of hamburgers and Cartoon Network. Gonzalo knew he would miss Vicente too—he was beginning to love the boy like his own son, or the way he thought he would love a son of his own—but of course he was euphoric.

The first weekend without Vicente adhered strictly to the plan Gonzalo drew up in advance. On Friday night they went all out on a sexual encounter that involved some pretty predictable costumes but ended up being truly memorable; on Saturday they had sushi in bed for lunch, spent the afternoon watching season two of *The Sopranos* on DVD, and took long baths as they waited for (1) her gay friends + his gay friends, and (2) her single girlfriends + his poet friends (who were all single heterosexual male poets) to arrive. The idea was to try to fix them up, which worked quite well in (1) and very badly in (2).

By the end of the night they were pretty sloshed, and morning found them asleep on the futon. Although Sunday (which didn't really get going until two in the afternoon) was dominated by their hangovers, they adored that dose of irresponsibility, and they also enjoyed playing host. By that point they were bored with all the hot dog parties, picnics, and barbecues that had come to characterize their social life as a family.

The only one not pleased was Darkness, who hated the invasion of friends and Vicente's prolonged absence, and who did not seem to approve of the sudden lasciviousness that prevailed in the house. At seven in the evening, after a leisurely screw befitting of convalescents, Gonzalo got up to go to the bathroom and was suddenly met by Darkness's eyes staring at his dick. His first reaction was to cover himself, as if shamed by the animal's gaze, but then he burst out laughing and even swayed his hips so the cat could observe his dick and balls in movement, and then he danced and sang a sort of tarantella for about a full minute under the cat's watchful eyes. Carla joined in the dance, and if anyone had seen them they would have thought that this was happiness: to dance naked in the living room, with no music, endlessly.

One year later, in March of 2003, Carla was finally able to go back to school. At first she thought about returning to psychology, but instead she decided to sign up for photography at an institute, because it was a short program, and also because her hobby of taking pictures was one of the few things that had remained constant in her life. Her father didn't love the idea, but he ended up agreeing that Carla could leave her position as the firm's receptionist and take on the more ambiguous post of part-time assistant. Gonzalo's support was key, because he managed to coordinate his hectic schedule as a traveling teacher—he now worked at three test prep schools and taught a university intro to lit course—with the even more demanding routine Carla kept up, dividing her day between the law firm and the institute, where she took classes almost every evening and on Saturdays. Nearly all of Vicente's contact with his mother consisted of bleary and fleeting conversations over breakfast.

Up until then, Gonzalo had stuck to the comfortable role of older brother or indulgent uncle or live-in clown. His first months as Vicente's caretaker were, as such, disastrous. When he helped with homework, Gonzalo felt like he too was a child being forced to do homework. Some things were easy—he had a certain talent as a chef, and even took an interest in the arduous process of learning how to iron (he'd often say that ironing a shirt was much harder than writing a sestina). But overall, supervising the boy's behavior was an uphill battle: Vicente behaved like a sly, capricious squirrel, or like a veteran prisoner determined to challenge the inept new guard. Even more difficult were those days when the boy, for no precise reason, abandoned his proverbial joy and became a maudlin little dinosaur—Gonzalo would resort to the demagogy of pizza and try to talk to him, but received only a wan, solipsistic smile in return.

The most difficult thing was to fill or mask Carla's absence; he'd manage it for a while, but the closer they got to bedtime, the more inevitable his defeat became. Getting Vicente to sleep was a real challenge, because the boy had a supreme capacity for play, and because the stories Carla usually read him lost their allure in someone else's voice: they were just an excuse for the bonds of affection, for the treasured routine of intimacy.

"I don't want you to read to me," Vicente told Gonzalo one night. "I'll just get to sleep by myself. Or I'll read to myself. I know how to read, I've known for a while now."

"I know. But you won't go to sleep that way."

"I'm not going to sleep, but I want to be alone."

It wasn't a provocation. For Vicente, Gonzalo's presence at the foot of his bed functioned as a parody. It was better to skip that scene entirely.

"I'm not going to read to you," said Gonzalo, "but I am going to stay here until you fall asleep."

"What for?"

"To keep you company."

"Cut my nails, then."

"Your toenails?"

"Yeah, I just bite my fingernails off."

"You shouldn't bite your nails."

"But I do."

Vicente had never before asked anyone to cut his toenails, and they didn't really bother him, but they were so long they almost wouldn't fit into his shoes, so it needed to be done. Gonzalo got nervous—he had never cut Vicente's nails or anyone else's, and really, he wasn't even satisfied with the way he cut his own.

"You want me to teach you how to cut them?" he asked.

"No. I want you to cut them for me."

Gonzalo started in on his surprise task with superstitious caution. Vicente's little feet seemed formidable to him. Why don't toes have a name in Spanish, he wondered, like they do in other languages? They're just called *dedos de los pies*, the fingers of the feet. It suddenly seemed incredible and maybe a little unfair that it hadn't occurred to anyone to give them their own name. Gonzalo thought about this even while he doubted it—maybe he just didn't know the Spanish word for the fingers of the feet.

"I'm still going to tell you a story," he said when he was almost finished.

"Tell me a joke instead," said Vicente.

"I can tell you a story that's also a joke. A funny story."

"Tell me a joke instead."

"Okay. A psychic meets another psychic on the street and asks him: 'How am I?'"

Vicente let out an exaggerated laugh, like he was in a captive audience, though it was unclear whether he understood the joke or not.

"Tell me another one," he begged.

Gonzalo knew a lot of jokes, he'd always been one for telling jokes, but right at that moment he couldn't remember any. Plus, he was dying for a smoke.

"Okay, but wait for me a minute, I'll be right back," he told him.

It was almost ten at night, and Carla usually got home at nine-thirty. What would happen if she didn't come back? Gonzalo wondered while he smoked in the front yard. He always imagined the worst; he was more or less an expert in dreaming up horrible scenarios, in part because he felt like by anticipating pain he avoided it. There's never an earthquake when we think there's going to be one, and when we drive along imagining awful accidents nothing bad ever happens. And when someone is late enough for us to start thinking they're never going to return, they suddenly arrive and then it's almost impossible to tell them that for a few seconds, mid-cigarette, we believed they wouldn't come back—it sounds excessive, it *is* excessive.

Just then, as if to confirm this theory, Carla got home and headed straight up to Vicente's room.

Gonzalo stayed in the yard, lit a second cigarette, and went on thinking about what would happen if Carla never came back, if she were to die. He imagined Vicente was a teenager and the two of them were still living in that same house, after several years of acute sadness. He imagined them keeping each other company, sometimes talking about soccer or literature or problems of the heart, forever united by the habit of mourning. He even had a vision of them painting the house: Vicente was fifteen, eighteen years old, and taller than Gonzalo. One sunny morning they picked up their brushes and went out front to paint. They took a break to share some cheese sandwiches and drink lemonade. And they listened to the news on the radio. And they smoked or coughed or whistled, their clothes paint-spattered and their shoulders sore.

He was trying to convince himself to do the dishes when Carla came into the kitchen.

"Vicente doesn't want to go to sleep, he says you owe him a joke."

"I'll be right there."

He went up the stairs two at a time, pleased. Darkness was dozing at the foot of the bed, and when she saw Gonzalo she yawned maybe too long and started licking her fur with singular enthusiasm. Vicente was, in effect, wide awake.

"One solitary man meets another solitary man on the street and he doesn't say hi, because they're both solitary," Gonzalo finally improvised.

"That's not a joke."

"It is a joke," says Gonzalo. "A bad joke, but it's a joke."

"And what else?"

"That's the end."

"Boring."

"Okay, when he gets home he remembers that other solitary man and he regrets not having said hi, and he wants to see him again."

"And does he?"

"Yes, but a few days later, when they happen to run into each other again."

"Where?"

"On the beach."

"What beach?"

"An empty beach."

"What's the beach called?"

"Solitary Beach."

"And is it full of solitary people?"

"No, every day just one of them goes. But this morning, by chance, two went."

"And now they do say hi?"

"Yes."

The story was much longer, or maybe there were several stories with the same protagonists:

"Solitary Man One invited Solitary Man Two to play solitaire, but since solitaire is a card game you play alone, they decided to sit at different tables, each with a deck of cards, without talking or making eye contact, though every once in a while they acknowledged each other by mentally raising their eyebrows.

"Solitary Man One and Solitary Man Two argued over which of them was One and which Two, and logically neither of them wanted to be Solitary Man Two, because the existence of a Solitary Man Two presupposed the existence of a Solitary Man One, whose solitude, as such, was more complete.

"After a long courtship, Solitary Man One decided to marry himself, and the only guest he invited to the wedding was Solitary Man Two, who was still single."

Vicente howled with laughter, the story went on for almost an hour, and it seemed like the kid would never fall asleep. And the storyteller was so euphoric at his surprising, resounding, and indisputable triumph that he also had trouble, later on, falling asleep.

Sometimes Gonzalo hated not exactly that Vicente wasn't his son, but that he'd met him so late. He felt like he'd started a TV show in the middle of the season; it seemed enjoyable and understandable, but then certain details would suddenly reveal that no, those first episodes he'd missed had included all the keys to the story. It seemed to him that Vicente was already formed, completely made, for better and for worse: he was already, latently, who he would be in the future. Carla told him all about the days of endless diapers, the exhausting tantrums, the abundant whims and fears, and Gonzalo kept quiet but thought that if he had been around back then, everything would have been different. Other times he thought, with absurd and effusive melancholy, that in a way it was his own fault he'd arrived late.

Raising Vicente was a beautiful challenge, but through vacillations, mistakes, and stories of solitary men, he rose to it. They went out every afternoon, sometimes to the movies (they saw *Finding Nemo* four times) or to the paddleboats at Intercomunal Park, or just to buy something. At the supermarket, where they went every Saturday, they chose products without thinking about price or quality: they picked the detergent with the most attractive colors or the bleach brand with the funniest name. They didn't have an excess of money, but they bought all kinds of things: caramel, Nutella, cheeses, cold cuts, and a bunch of cereals and exotic imported fruits they didn't even like that much.

The stroll through the toy section was, naturally, the highlight of every shopping trip, because the kid got much more out of Gonzalo than his mother usually granted him. One day, though, inexplicably, Vicente didn't want anything: he perused the whole aisle sunk deep in hermetic speculation, and although at one point he seemed to choose a basketball, which he dribbled skillfully for a few seconds, in the end he announced with a pretty violent or defiant listlessness that he didn't want that ball or anything else. Gonzalo didn't understand what was happening, but he decided not to ask—better to pretend he hadn't even noticed the boy's anomalous behavior.

"I heard Santa Claus isn't real," Vicente blurted out while they were waiting in line to pay, in a tone that was trying to be casual, as if he were commenting on an interesting news item he'd seen on TV.

Only then did Gonzalo notice that, though it was only the beginning of November, the store was already full of Christmas decorations.

"People sure say a lot of silly things, don't they?"

"But a lot of people say it."

"Why do you call him Santa Claus?"

"Because that's his name."

"But you used to call him Viejito Pascuero."

"*Viejo* Pascuero. I never called him *Viejito*. And Santa Claus is his real name."

"He's also called Papa Noel. And Saint Nicholas, I think. In Chile we call him Viejito Pascuero. I don't know what he's called in other countries."

They were putting their items on the belt, and it was clear they were following a routine: they took the largest packages from the cart first and organized them so they could build a pyramid.

"Have you heard it too?" asked Vicente.

"That Viejito Pascuero doesn't exist?"

"Yeah."

"A lot, since I was a kid. Ever since I was your age I've been hearing that darned rumor, and I'm sick of it."

"But what do you think?" asked Vicente.

"I know him, he comes here to shop," the cashier interrupted, in solidarity.

"Really?" asked Gonzalo.

"Sure," said the cashier.

"You mean, he buys his gifts here?" Gonzalo sounded excited.

"Of course not, and he doesn't come in dressed as Viejito Pascuero, either. He's too famous, just imagine. He comes in wearing sunglasses and a ski mask, so no one will recognize him or ask for his autograph. He dresses really simply, in blue jeans and flip-flops. He buys his whiskey, his cheese, his antacids, and he leaves. The other day he also bought a fan, for the heat."

Vicente peered at the cashier gravely, anxiously. She smiled at him. A green band partially hid her hair, which was also green, almost the same color.

"So, are you two brothers?" she asked.

"No," replied Gonzalo, hesitant.

"What are you, then?"

The cashier was asking just to make conversation, to change the subject, to flirt a little. At twenty-eight years old Gonzalo looked young, but not young enough for someone to doubt that he was the father of an eight-year-old boy. They could have been brothers, it's true—they did look a little alike: they were both dark, thin, and tall, with large eyes—Vicente's were larger, and his hair was also blacker and frizzier than Gonzalo's. On comparing their features, perhaps, disparities emerged; the shape of their faces, especially Vicente's more pointed nose. Looking closely at them, an expert might have posited that they were not father and son, but people don't tend to look closely at anyone, and on seeing them together, everyone thought or assumed that they were. Miss Sara, for example, who had been cleaning their house twice a week for a year, had recently overheard them talking about "Vicente's dad," and had thus learned that Gonzalo and Vicente were not father and son. She couldn't believe it, she said, they looked just alike, and even laughed at the same things.

"What are you, then?"

The cashier's question still hung in the air after twenty seconds, an extraordinary amount of time to spend preparing such a seemingly easy response. Gonzalo was paralyzed; he didn't want to answer, but he sensed the boy's eager eyes on him. He felt his responsibility to answer.

"Friends," Gonzalo finally said. "We're friends."

The cashier responded with a cautious smile, and didn't ask any more questions.

Friends, Gonzalo ruminated in the car, overcome by a sorrow he would have liked to either decipher or dismiss out of hand. He thought he should have told the cashier that he was the boy's father or uncle, or simply that she shouldn't meddle in other people's affairs. But we have to use the words, he qualified to himself then, searching for a light note, or at least a freeing one. The word *stepfather* and the word *stepson* are so ugly in Spanish— *padrastro, hijastro*—but we have to use them. We have to use them or maybe invent others.

Vicente was staring out the window at the power lines—he liked to think they were like scratches on the sky—but Gonzalo let the idea that the boy was hurt or disappointed grow larger in his mind. The trip from the grocery store to the house was only about ten blocks and they had driven it a thousand times, reciting tongue twisters or imitating birds or listening to the Beatles or Los Bunkers or the songs from the program *31 minutos*, but that day nothing seemed easy to Gonzalo.

At the last stoplight before their house, a woman of about fifty years old lunged at the car and started washing the windshield. Gonzalo searched resignedly for some coins while the woman proceeded with a skill that was mechanical, frenetic, and also somewhat solemn. As he always did in those cases, Gonzalo handed the coins to Vicente so he would be the one to give the tip.

"She's not going to make it," said Vicente, suddenly interested, but the woman did make it, of course, it was her job: she finished a second before the light turned green, and Vicente reached out his hand to give her the tip. She looked at him in surprise, offended, and didn't accept the change: her enormous eyes communicated a deep befuddlement.

I know her," Carla said that night, when Gonzalo described the scene.
They were lying in the grass in the backyard, barefoot, drinking white wine to celebrate Carla's perfect grade in Lighting II.

"How do you know her?"

"You've never seen her? I see her almost every morning when I come out of the metro. She's the crazy lady who's always on the corner of Providencia and Eliodoro Yáñez."

"But it wasn't at that corner. It was right here, two blocks away."

"So the crazy lady can't change neighborhoods?"

"She didn't seem crazy to me," said Gonzalo, in the tone of one willing to admit he was wrong. "She was offended, I think. I don't know why. I mean, sure, she spends all day on the corner cleaning windshields and someone gives spare change to a kid to give to her. So he can learn about compassion, about charity. It's horrible. Or maybe not horrible, but humiliating."

"But you didn't mean anything bad by it," said Carla sweetly.

"But it's humiliating."

"She was a skinny lady, with wavy hair? Really skinny?"

"Yeah."

"With bulging eyes, right?"

"Bulging eyes, like crazy people in cartoons?"

"Big, very expressive eyes," said Carla. "Dark green. I think it's the same crazy lady from Eliodoro Yáñez. She's known for that."

"For her eyes?"

"No, for cleaning windshields and not accepting payment. She does it for free. Just for fun."

"For fun," Gonzalo mimicked her. "I don't see the fun of cleaning windshields at a stoplight. Everyone looks down on you. It must be shitty to work at a stoplight."

"I think the jugglers and acrobats have a great time," said Carla. "And the hip-hop dancers."

"They're awful jobs!"

"I'm kidding. Clearly that woman is crazy as a loon."

"Well, I don't think she's crazy. Maybe she just didn't understand, or she was annoyed it was a kid giving her the change. Or maybe for her it's the driver who should give the handout, not the person in the passenger seat," said Gonzalo.

It took him a few seconds to realize it, but he had just committed a grave mistake. For a few months, with the goal of making his outings with Vicente into memorable moments, Gonzalo had been letting him sit in the passenger seat on short trips, which was something Carla had expressly forbidden.

He didn't have much to gain in that argument, as was often the case when he fought with Carla, who was able to control her voice so that not even the most unfair recrimination sounded excessive. Gonzalo was ready from the start to accept full guilt, and his silence was that of the punished, of the penitent. Carla started in on a lecture about commitment, trust, and responsibility that included data and citations of studies and news items about horrible accidents; as the cherry on top, she even invented a convincing statistic about exactly how many kids are killed every year riding in passenger seats. It really didn't seem like she was exaggerating: listening to her, it was almost impossible not to be persuaded that letting a child ride shotgun was only slightly less cruel than beating him upside the head or leaving him in the desert to die.

Gonzalo knew he deserved the sermon, and nevertheless, when Carla's lips formed the word *betrayal*, which seemed so unfair, so out of place, so extreme, his guilt instantly evaporated.

"I'm so sorry for taking care of Vicente every single day," said Gonzalo.

"It's times like these it's clear you're not his father," retorted Carla.

Gonzalo looked at her with astonishment and contempt. He grabbed his hair with his left hand, and with his right he tore up an abundant clump of grass.

"I'm a much better father than that lame-ass, ugly, mediocre mother-fucking pusillanimous sack of balls who stuck his dick in you."

The sentence felt a bit ungrammatical and was a pretty stupid outburst, but almost all its assertions were pretty fair. León's lameness was undeniable, and the worst part was that he thought he was great fun, if not outright fascinating; his daily routine was full of obvious little jokes and obsolete gallantry. Gonzalo, on the other hand, was much more fun and passionate, and although at times he was overcome by fits of timidity or seriousness, in general he knew how to get other people's attention without steamrolling them. Above all, he knew how to have a conversation: listen, wait, go, accelerate, stop.

Neither León nor Gonzalo could have competed in a beauty contest, not even at the neighborhood or municipal level, and nevertheless Gonzalo's advantage was also indisputable on this point, because the six-year age difference between them was evident—neither of the two worked out, but time was on Gonzalo's side, and León was particularly haggard for a man of thirty-four. Gonzalo's zits, for one thing, had completely disappeared, while the marks on León's skin recalled the surface of the moon, and his fatness seemed irreversible. Vicente's beauty was, on his father's side, hard to understand: seeing them together, you could catch a glimpse of the similarity, but you'd also have to suspect that the boy's mother must be—as in fact she was—a knockout.

When it came to *mediocrity*: Gonzalo was no hero and didn't believe himself to be one; on the contrary, he carried with him the woes of lost struggles and unfinished battles. But he still came out far ahead in this round too, because he wasn't the best teacher in the world and nor was he shaping up to be an important poet, but he tried bravely and soberly to be something like a father to Vicente, while León, who was a lawyer, did not dedicate himself to noble causes of any kind, but rather tried to make money, and didn't even excel at that. As a father, it would be generous to call him mediocre.

As for the word *pusillanimous*, it didn't apply; León wasn't pusillanimous, at least not clearly or not all the time. Although they had only ever spoken that one day over salami, Gonzalo had noticed that León said *less* when he meant *fewer* (he said "less people," as nearly everyone does, including even some announcers on TV and radio), and that he said *myself* when he just meant *me* or *I* (ditto). They weren't such terrible mistakes, but they particularly irritated Gonzalo. So maybe he accused León of being pusillanimous for the mere pleasure of saying a word that León would have had to look up in the dictionary. But León wouldn't even have bothered to look that word up in the dictionary. There are people who, when they hear a word they don't know, simply burst out laughing.

The expression *sack of balls* is unnatural, and for that reason gives the phrase a certain force. Gonzalo came out with that insult because in addition to hurtful, he wanted to be original. *Sack of shit, asshole, dickwad, raisin dick, son of a bitch, shit for brains,* or older phrases like s*hit whistle* or *sleazeball* would have been less offensive than that expression, unused and thus effective.

The truly damning part was definitely that grand finale, *who stuck his dick in you*, which brought jealousy to the forefront and insinuated that Carla was some kind of whore. Still, the accusation held a trace of childishness, as if Gonzalo had only just found out how babies are made.

Carla didn't reply. She was silent, thoughtful. And as she took a bite of broccoli with mayonnaise, she decided she would stay silent indefinitely. Gonzalo poured himself a double whiskey that he downed in one gulp, just the way bad actors down fake drinks in movies. And he did feel, in a way, like the suffering protagonist in a film. He slammed the kitchen door even though he abhorred that habit, and he took the bottle with him outside, where there was a detached spare room—referred to in the family as "the little room"—that he used as a study.

They believe themselves generous because they pay two hundred bucks a month, but they've never done homework with their children, who love them anyway and include them in all their drawings. Even if they don't show up. Because sometimes they just don't show up. Biological fathers, divorced fathers, part-time dads, they're all the same shit. Sometimes they don't show up and it's fine. They've been given that guarantee. They can disappear and they'll still be waited for, forgiven, welcomed, and any delay, any complaint, anything at all can be fixed with a bag of popcorn or a few devious teddy bears.

The kids get bored to tears at the stadium watching those long, slow games. While the fathers scream their heads off at the refs, their kids spend the ninety minutes absorbed in their chocolate bars and caramel corn and candied peanuts. Then, almost bursting with sugar, the kids get happy meals at McDonald's and their fathers take the opportunity to down some burgers of their own, double or triple or even with bacon, and chug some oversized cups of watery Coke. And then, their fingers still slippery with french fry grease, these noble men turn to slurping their sundaes with caramel sauce and ordering countless espressos while their kids dive dolefully into those stupid pools of multicolored balls.

From time to time they glance at their kids while they chat with selfless single mothers or affectionate caretakers who are maybe older sisters but are clearly underage. And maybe they even take a book to McDonald's, the sons of bitches, to reinforce their aura of being serious, responsible, even sensitive men. Maybe they quote Ernesto Sábato or Rubén Darío or they hustle a discourse on Roque Dalton and recommend *The Dark Side of the Heart* or *Dead Poets Society*, which are not their favorite films, because these fuckers go in more for *Lethal Weapon* or *Speed*, but they know which movies work for sweet-talking. Their children serve as the perfect bait to attract girls who are ever more stunning and naïve. Girls who are ever younger and less inhibited and more obliging, who prize the presumed effort, the feigned selflessness of these occasional fathers, and are hopeful, caught up in the promise of a future that will last two months if they're lucky.

Those fleeting girlfriends accept everything willingly, with unquestioning resignation, and they never get tired of listening to the refrain of the Sunday dads, because from so much repetition the speech takes on form and coherence and above all rhythm and dramatic flight—they talk about the impossibility of planning a future together, of changing, of committing, because they already have a son and he's the only thing that matters, they already have a child who is everything. They talk about how they'd give their lives for that kid, and how every morning, when their strength fails them, they think of that child's smile and how that's what they're working for, it's why they breathe, why they're seriously thinking about quitting smoking, quitting drinking, it's why they've almost completely given up cocaine, why they're planning to get their colons checked out, their cholesterol, prostates, everything.

They've been blessed, ennobled, legitimized by the perfume of experience, but they don't know anything about anything. They are parasites, inoperable tumors, mere faces posing for the cameras: radiant, relaxed, tanned, psychoanalyzed, well rested, carefree; they're victimizers disguised as victims, because these days it seems like they weren't the ones who insisted a thousand times, in every tone of voice and accompanied by fits of rage and bouts of shoving, on aborting. It seems they weren't the ones who searched for filthy clandestine clinics at reasonable prices. Apparently they weren't the ones who, not only on the few days when they half-heartedly perform their role, but also the rest of the time, feel that their children are a burden, the prolonged consequence of an irreparable fuckup.

And while they speechify and inspect cleavage—they've developed the skill of looking simultaneously at tits and eyes—there are other men, some poor fuckers, who raise their kids for them twenty-four hours a day. Men who were dumb enough to fall in love with the women they themselves happily discarded. Men who tidy the house and even cook and wash dishes with degrading enthusiasm. Ridiculous men who avoid sugar, salt, and saturated fat. Men tame as lambs, worried about saving water, ridiculously anxious about the planet's future, and resigned in advance to the many criticisms of their hyperbolic, ungrateful, cruel women.

Gonzalo scrawled all of this in a Word file and tried to give it the shape of a furious and arbitrary poem—a poem that had little or nothing in common with the ones he normally wrote—until the words simply ran out. He sat looking at the screen like a TV viewer refusing to believe the electricity's gone out. The rumble of the garbage truck startled him, and he stood up, lit his umpteenth cigarette, and looked at his books distantly, almost with curiosity, like they belonged to someone else. Then, as if manifesting an unformed thought, he grabbed the Spanish dictionary and looked up the word *padrastro*. He read the first entry: "The husband of one's mother by a later marriage." The second said, straight up, "Bad father." The third was one he didn't know: "Obstacle, impediment, or inconvenience that hinders or does damage to a thing." Even the fourth meaning, rather technical, struck him as humiliating: "Small piece of skin that separates from the flesh immediately around the fingernails, causing pain and discomfort; hangnail."

Goddamned dictionary, motherfucking Spanish Royal Academy, he thought. *Who* was the bad father, the obstacle and impediment, just *who* was the one who hindered, who did damage? Shouldn't he be off living in a perfectly furnished bachelor pad where he could sleep with half of Santiago, where he could fuck girls a whole lot hotter than the ones Vicente's dad probably fucked? Didn't he *deserve* that, in a way?

Motherfucking Spanish language, he thought again, out loud this time, in the scientific tone of someone confirming or identifying a problem. No Spanish word that ended with the suffix *-astro* meant or could ever mean anything other than contempt or illegitimacy. The calamitous suffix -*astro* "forms nouns with pejorative meanings," said the *RAE Dictionary*: *musicastro, politicastro*: inept musician, unskilled politician. The same source defines the word *poetastro* simply as "bad poet."

"What does your padrastro do?"

"My padrastro is a poetastro." He imagined Vicente giving that reply.

The problem isn't exclusive to the Spanish language, he discovered later, as he reviewed the pile of foreign language dictionaries at the end of the bottom shelf. He also searched online, and wrote down on some Post-its, as if he needed to remember them forever, the words *stiefvater, stefar, stedfar, padrastre, patrigno, ojczym, üvey baba, beau-père, duonpatro, isäpuoli*, and he even laboriously transcribed the words in Arabic, Chinese, Russian, Greek, Japanese, and Korean. Then he spent half an hour searching for the Mapuche word for *padrastro*. He couldn't find it.

The English word *stepfather* seemed so much nicer, finer, and more precise than the word *padrastro*, marked by that stupid pejorative suffix. "The husband of one's parent when distinct from one's natural or legal father," said the *Merriam-Webster Collegiate Dictionary*, quite simply. And the *Larousse* defined the beautiful French word *beau-père* by distinguishing two meanings, neither of them disparaging: "*Père du conjoint*," and "*Second époux de la mère, par rapport aux enfants issus d'un premier mariage*." Gonzalo found it a very fine detail that in French the roles of *father-in-law* and *stepfather* coincided in one word (though there was no love lost between him and Carla's dad).

It was four in the morning, but he still decided to call his friend Ricardo, a know-it-all linguist. He was in luck, because at that hour the specialist was drunk enough to casually accept the call. Ricardo talked to him about *The Elementary Structures of Kinship* by Claude Lévi-Strauss, and cited an array of other studies. Gonzalo asked him if the word *stepfather* existed in Mapudungun.

"For the Mapuches," Ricardo told him, suddenly using professorial diction, "the chau is the mother's companion, no matter if he's the biological father or not. *Chau* is the name of a function, the father-function."

"And how do they distinguish the father from the stepfather?"

"That's the thing—they're not interested in distinguishing them."

"And does the divorced chau change his title?"

"No. Well, I'm not sure, but I don't think so. That is, if you were once a chau you go on being one, even if there's another chau in your place."

"So a kid could have two chaus."

"Sure. Or more."

Gonzalo thought it was a pretty fair rule, even a great one. He decided that he would carry out an exhaustive investigation and then interview speakers of a wide variety of languages, and ask them . . . he didn't really know what, he couldn't quite articulate or catch sight of the crucial question. But there is one, and I will ask it, he thought. And he also decided that he would start right now on a letter to *El Mercurio* about the various words that designate "the husband of the mother with respect to her children."

An essay, maybe, but a letter to the editor? How long did it take him to remember that he wasn't remotely the kind of person who writes letters to *El Mercurio*?

He nodded to sleep at his desk. And that was where he woke up, in the middle of a cozy puddle of drool, just before dawn. He went to the bedroom and climbed into bed, lying as far away as possible from Carla, who was asleep with her right hand clutching the sheet.

Sunday transpired as expected: Carla and Gonzalo didn't speak to each other, they avoided each other, and the only words they uttered were addressed to Vicente or the cat. Only after lunch did Gonzalo remember his padrastro project, and it seemed to him, in effect, like nonsense. From the second floor came the hypnotizing music of *Super Mario World*, which Gonzalo interpreted as a summons because they usually played that game together, Vicente as Mario and Gonzalo as Luigi. Gonzalo himself had brought the console home—a classmate from his master's program had traded it for the complete works of Cervantes, of which Gonzalo had two. By that point the Super Nintendo was almost obsolete—Vicente's friends all had Nintendo 64 or PlayStation.

He went up to the boy's room and sat down beside him, and they immediately returned to the two-player game they had saved. For a couple of minutes, Gonzalo silently watched Mario's dogged attempts to save the princess Toadstool.

"Hey, you remember that lady at the cash register?" Gonzalo asked in a forced opening tone. The question was almost rhetorical—the incident had just happened, it was impossible Vicente wouldn't remember.

"Yeah," said Vicente, absorbed in the rhythm of the game. (Mario risked his neck to collect some gold coins.)

"The one who asked if we were brothers, I mean."

"Yeah," Vicente replied, with something like boredom.

"And what did I say?"

"That we're friends."

"And it's true, we are friends," Gonzalo began.

"It's not true," Vicente interrupted.

"Why not?" asked Gonzalo with a sudden, alarmist fear.

"Because she was right, we *are* brothers," said Vicente, with the hint of a smile on his lips.

Anyone would have seen there was a joke coming, but Gonzalo, who was pretty desperate, was incapable of anticipating it.

"I mean, right now," said Vicente. "We're brothers. I'm Mario and you're Luigi."

"Aaaah," said Gonzalo, relieved.

Mario fell off a cliff and Gonzalo wasn't sure whether it was a slip-up or Vicente had done it on purpose. Gonzalo picked up his controller—for which he used the old-fashioned term *joystick*—to continue Luigi's journey.

"I am your stepfather. And you are my stepson. It sounds ugly in Spanish."

"Yeah."

It was very strange to have this conversation while Luigi was leaping over dinosaurs, so Gonzalo paused the game.

"But we have to use the words. Even if we don't like them. The word *padrastro* sounds bad, but it's the word we have. There are other languages where the word is nicer. And in Mapudungun there is no word for stepfather. Both of them, the father and stepfather, are called the chau."

"Chau? Like goodbye?"

"Yes."

"But how do people know who's the stepfather and who's the father?"

"They don't care, it's the mother who matters. The chau is the man who is with the mother."

"What if they're lesbians?"

"Well, then I suppose they're both mothers."

Gonzalo wanted to sound convincing, though he wasn't at all sure his drunk friend had provided him with reliable information. He touched his sparse beard exaggeratedly, like an intellectual.

"Do you want me to call you *dad*? Or *chau*? That would be weird. Hola, Chau."

"No," Gonzalo said emphatically. "You call me whatever you want, it's your decision. Maybe *padrastro*, which in other languages isn't such an ugly word."

"How do you say it in English?"

"Stepfather. And in French it's *beau-père*."

"Oh. You know French?"

"No, but I know that word. *Beau-père* means 'good father.'"

Really it was more like "beautiful father" or "lovely father," though perhaps what he said worked better to demonstrate his point, which had to do with the concept of a *good father*: Vicente had two dads, and one was good and one was bad or mediocre and it turned out that the bad or mediocre father was the true father, the biological one.

"But do you want us to speak in French?"

"No. What I want to tell you is that this is our language. We have to use the words, even if we don't like them. And if we use them enough, maybe they'll start to mean something different; maybe we'll manage to change their meanings."

This last phrase, so hippie, was not one he'd planned to say. It just came out, maybe triggered by the hopeful cadence he tried to imprint on his words when he spoke to the boy: suddenly, a surprising faith would appear, a lurking, latent enthusiasm. Vicente looked at Gonzalo in silence, fully focused on the conversation.

"The next time someone asks, I'm going to say I'm your padrastro, and you can say that you're my hijastro."

"Okay, Padrastro," said the boy in an almost solemn tone. "Want to keep playing?"

"Yes."

The silent treatment seemed endless. It had happened before, but this time, breaking with custom, Gonzalo held firm, convinced he shouldn't have to apologize, and he even enjoyed it a little whenever he heard Carla let slip a sigh or some involuntary phrase that betrayed her willingness to reconcile. They were ten days in when Mirta, Gonzalo's mother, called to beg them to come to a party she was hosting in honor of the lech. Gonzalo wanted to either go alone or with Vicente, but Carla insisted on joining them.

The lech was Gonzalo's grandfather and of course he had a name, but it's better to deprive him of that privilege. He had somewhere between twenty and thirty children—maybe the old guy kept count, but no one dared ask, because it was also possible he had no idea of the number. Absolutely all of his children had reason to hate him, especially Mirta, whom the lech had abandoned when she was four years old—all she remembered was that her dad had left and then come back a few months later, but only to take all the furniture in the house away with him, except the beds. When Mirta was little she used to run into him in the street, and sometimes she would hear things about him, news of the births of his other children—generally two or three a year—or his sporadic jobs—head of an auto repair shop, bolero singer in a diner, taxi or bus driver, horse race gambler (which wasn't a job but was his most frequent occupation)—and more or less every two years he would reappear in all his glory and settle into the living room to dole out opinions and vehement declarations of love, though of course he never came close to apologizing, and he nearly always, by dint of promises and conventional flattery ("Baby, I know it's too late, but I've realized you're the love of my life"), managed to stay over. The next morning, the lech himself headed out to the corner store, and in a jiffy whipped up what he called a "breakfast of champions" that included a glass of orange juice, dobladitas with butter and jam, pancakes with dulce de leche, and a long time spent telling astonishing stories that Mirta and her mother listened to, paralyzed with emotion. And maybe the old man stayed another night, but never three in a row. This was what the lech understood paternity to be, and he received the sweeping approval of a world in which seducing and impregnating women left and right was a well-regarded method of proving one's manliness.

Gonzalo had seen the lech only once, when he was seven years old. One day the old man had shown up out of nowhere with his most recent daughter, who was then four.

"Gonzalo, this is your aunt Verito," the lech said, laughing hysterically.

The visitors had stayed until after midnight. Mirta had to lend her little half sister a sweater. Then they took off in the old man's beat-up bucket of bolts.

Gonzalo found his mother's invitation odd. She herself had made the effort to contact the lech and get the phone numbers of many of her half siblings, nineteen of whom had RSVPed for the luncheon. But the most surprising and egregious thing was that Mirta had spent all her savings to pay for the meal and rent the house where the family reunion would be held. Gonzalo's mother didn't have money, she never had; for some time she had been supplementing her meager teacher's salary by giving evening English classes at small businesses. Officially, her lifelong dream was to travel to a country—any country—where people spoke English, and that's what she was saving up for. And yet, apparently now her dream was to honor the lech. Gonzalo thought the lech's children should indeed get together, not to pay him homage, but to shoot him or kick him in the balls or at least give him a good beating, crowned with a generous shower of loogies. He didn't want to go, but Mirta begged him ("He *is* my father, after all"; "A father is a father").

It was a long trip to Talagante, and Carla drove and Gonzalo stared out the window at the fields of almond and walnut trees, while Vicente played a game that involved blinking between utility poles. As they approached their exit, Gonzalo fantasized about the possibility of continuing on down the highway until they reached the ocean: it would be great to get out of the car a hundred kilometers later and stroll down the beach under the reasonable end-of-spring sun. He pictured them going into a restaurant to eat some shellfish stew while they slowly downed a bottle of white wine. He thought about suggesting it to Carla, but then he remembered the silent treatment.

The reunion was a mega-event, with a dozen cars crowded along the dirt driveway that led to a half-hectare parcel of land, dominated by some slender eucalyptus trees and a giant, almost disproportionate swimming pool. Gonzalo greeted everyone with feigned naturalness. The guests said their names, provided some clues to distinguish themselves, and introduced their children, who explored the house or chased each other through the grass or headed straight for the pool. Carla and Mirta stood near a small chicken coop and talked as if they were great friends, though they had never really gotten along. Vicente stayed with Gonzalo. In situations like these he usually stuck with his mother, but this time he thought Gonzalo would be more fun.

The patriarch kept them waiting, and at times the dominant feeling was that he wouldn't show up at all: every one of his kids looked immensely nervous, as if their father had never disappointed them before. Gonzalo and Vicente played a discreet game of guessing which people were the lech's children and which their respective companions. None of his kids was over five-foot-five; they were all pretty dark-skinned; thinness predominated; sons outnumbered daughters and they all still had abundant hair; and although the blazing sun called for dark glasses, it was still possible to note the preponderance of eyes that were nearly black and tended toward the small. Of course, none of the lech's exes participated in the party, because by that point half of them hated him wholeheartedly, and the other half were dead.

The old man finally did turn up, walking with firm steps and holding a guitar in his right hand by the neck as if it were a cane, though of course he

didn't lean on it, it was more like a part of his body. He was with his youngest child, who was no longer Verito, but rather a burly fourteen-year-old boy
with short hair and a military bearing. By then the potatoes and ribs were
ready and everyone ate in the yard, vying for the lech's attention with varying
degrees of artfulness.

After lunch, Gonzalo's father carried a rocking chair out to the picnic
area so the lech could sit down and hold forth. The old man loosened his
flannel tie with some difficulty and unhurriedly gave thanks for the invitation, before coming out with a piece of news that no one present was aware
of: he'd just been diagnosed with gallbladder cancer. The prognosis was still
uncertain, but soon he would probably have to undergo surgery, and then
would come radiation and chemotherapy ("la quimio," the lech called it, and
it sounded weird, as if he were referring to a new girlfriend). The outlook
was not hopeful.

"Most likely I'll soon be off to a better place," he declared with theatrical resignation.

Gonzalo thought of those bums who fake epileptic fits on buses, con-
vulsing on the floor for a while before jumping spryly up to vociferate their
sad stories and get off the bus with their hands full of bills to pay for their
imaginary medications. But no one questioned the veracity of the news. Several of the lech's progeny who were crowded around the old man burst into
tears, including Gonzalo's mother.

"Please, Dad, let us help you pay for treatment, we can take up a collection," begged one of the sons who looked most like the lech. Gonzalo thought
he must be a plant.

"I don't know, why waste your money?" replied the lech, but they all
insisted and gestured to each other that they could figure out how to collect
the money later. "Well, now, we didn't come here to be sad," the lech added
then, gallantly. "If I die today, I'll have lived eighty-two very full, very happy
years. And the best demonstration of that is this splendid day with all my
children and grandchildren."

"They didn't all come," said Gonzalo, just to rain on the parade, and
Mirta shot him a withering, reproachful glare, a look he hadn't seen on his
mother's face in decades.

"Well, not all of them, but most," said the lech, who proceeded jovially to take out his guitar and launch into a rendition of "Como la cigarra." His interpretation was impeccable, with a voice that was full and beautifully deep and accompanied by pristine guitar chords.

When he came to the verse where the narrator talks about being forgotten by everyone and going to his own funeral "alone and crying," he sang it with an extra emphasis that seemed to allude to his current circumstances, and he reinforced the emotion with a strange, intermittent arching of his abundant gray eyebrows, as though he were possessed by a sudden tic.

Then it was his offsprings' turn. The old man had taught them all the same songs when they were little; luckily only some of them wanted to sing, or else it would have been endless. The situation was ridiculous and pathetic, as though they were auditioning for a starring role, each performer striving to become the favorite child of a really shitty father.

Vicente and Carla had thus far stayed beside Gonzalo, but then the boy got bored and headed to the pool with his mother, who sat with her feet in the water while she slowly sipped a glass of red wine.

"Who's your dad?" a little girl with braces and some showy green water wings asked Vicente.

"My dad's not here," he replied casually. "I came with my mom and my stepdad."

Carla was unaware of her partner's conceptual dalliances, but when she heard her son use the word *padrastro*, she understood that something had changed in Vicente's relationship with Gonzalo. It wasn't the first time the boy had used the word—he had already debuted it with his classmates. He'd decided to adopt it right after his conversation with Gonzalo, more out of necessity than obedience: he needed to name the person with whom he shared a large part of his life. He needed, above all, to clarify that the man was not his father.

Moved, Carla looked toward the picnic area to find her son's stepfather among the spectators of the guitar show, but she didn't see him, because he was kneeling down with his hands over his face while he listened to Mirta sing "Debut y despedida," by Los Ángeles Negros, the same song two of her half siblings had already sung.

Gonzalo felt his mother's humiliation in his own flesh, though she herself looked proud, defiant even, because she sang the song best—if it really had been a contest, she would have made it to the final round.

The afternoon wore on to the sound of guitar strumming until at last people's attention dissipated, and the juicy pineapple cake—the old man's favorite—was served up. They moved into the living room, where Mirta sat down on the main sofa beside the lech with a heavy laptop on her lap, and began to take diligent notes in an Excel file—its cells elegantly color-coded—of all the lech's grandchildren's names and their respective birthdays.

"You there, sir," the old man called to Gonzalo, who pretended not to hear. "Hey, there!"

Mirta whispered her son's name into her father's ear.

"Gonzalito!"

Vicente instinctively moved closer to Gonzalo and took his hand. It was an odd and unusual gesture, as if he wanted to offer help, though when a child takes an adult's hand we assume it's the child who is seeking protection. Carla also came over. They both went with Gonzalo as he walked slowly to appear before the patriarch.

"You judge me, don't you, kid?" said the old man.

"Yes," said Gonzalo. "Of course I do."

"I can tell. I've been watching you."

"So what?" Gonzalo's voice sounded adolescent.

"I don't judge you for judging me," the old man said in a magnanimous tone. "I always think of you. At your birthday and at Christmas. Gonzalo. Gonzalito. Good ol' Gonzalo. I always ask about Gonzalo. It's not my fault if no one gives you my messages."

Gonzalo was going to retort with one of about two hundred ironic replies that came to mind, but he saw his mother watching the scene anxiously, as if she had in fact spent decades not passing on the old man's messages. He limited himself to a skeptical laugh and he picked up Vicente, who at eight years old was too big to be held, but who cuddled up anyway, as if he were sleepy. The old man kept talking.

"Mirtita tells me you're a poet. Go on, then, recite us some poetry."

"I'm not a poet, you heard wrong," said Gonzalo, trying to hide his embarrassment.

"Oh come on, don't be shy now, give us a poem, I'll accompany you on the guitar." The old man strummed out the opening chords of "Lágrima" by Francisco Tárrega. "I met Neruda and Pablo de Rokha and all the great Chilean poets. Once, I sang at a peña and Neruda was there, and afterwards he came up to congratulate me, and he gave me his scarf as a gift."

Everyone listened to the lech with all the attention afforded to a leader. Vicente, still in Gonzalo's arms, was expectant.

At that moment Gonzalo felt the boy's weight—twenty-five kilos that were breaking his back—but he didn't want to put him down. He thought confusedly that at that moment carrying Vicente was his responsibility.

"You heard wrong, sir," Gonzalo repeated, before carrying the boy out to the yard.

He overheard the old man asking his mother about Vicente: "That kid's awfully cute—is he a grandson of mine?"

Half an hour later, they were the first to leave. When it was time to say goodbye, Gonzalo hugged the lech. It was an unexpected gesture, seemingly meant as reconciliation, but actually he did it so he could say something into the old man's ear.

"What did you say to my father?" Mirta asked him as she walked them to the car.

"Nothing," said Gonzalo evasively.

"'Bye, Step-Grandma," Vicente interrupted opportunely.

"Why would you call me that?" asked Mirta, irked.

"Because you're my stepdad's mom, so you're my step-grandmother," replied the boy.

Gonzalo's father also came out to say goodbye.

"'Bye, Step-Grandpa," said Vicente.

"'Bye, Step-Grandson," was the cheerful reply.

"'Bye, step-family!" shouted Vicente from the car window as they rolled away.

On the return trip it was Gonzalo who drove, and Carla and Vicente rode in back, curled up together.

"What did you whisper in his ear?" Vicente asked for the umpteenth time, as they merged onto the highway.

"I told him I loved him," said Gonzalo.

"You didn't say that, because it's not true," said Vicente.

Gonzalo tried to focus on the road. He imagined that fat drops were falling from the sky and he had to activate the windshield wipers; his eyes followed the phantom rods as they swished over the glass.

"Come on, what'd you say?" Carla asked too.

She never expected Gonzalo to reply seriously, and she meant no harm. But he felt it was absurd for her to pressure him, especially when they were still officially mad at each other.

"Fine, I'll tell you what I said," announced Gonzalo as he passed a truck around a curve. "I told him that I don't believe he has cancer, but I hope he does have cancer and that it advances quickly and he dies tomorrow and no one goes to his funeral."

Carla let out a nervous sigh.

"That's a lie, no way Gonzalo said that to his grandfather," she assured the boy, who was looking at her expectantly.

"He's not my grandfather," said Gonzalo. "He's my mother's father. He's a son of a bitch who abandoned my mother and all those nitwits at that party. He's a lazy, cruel, horny motherfucker who doesn't deserve anyone's respect."

"Control yourself, please," said Carla.

Ten minutes went by during which Carla tried to explain to Vicente what Gonzalo had meant to say. Vicente could discern the threatening air of truth that permeated the scene. When they went inside, all three were dispirited. Gonzalo hugged first Vicente and then Carla. He apologized and thanked them for going with him. He said he didn't wish death on anyone. And that he really did think the old man didn't have cancer, but he was probably wrong. He said that everyone has the right to be forgiven. (He said this so many times he sounded like a priest.)

"So, are you really a poet or not?" Vicente asked him later, over dinner.

The boy truly didn't know. He knew Gonzalo was a teacher and that he read a lot and he wrote stuff, but writing stuff didn't sound the same as writing poetry, and writing poetry didn't sound the same as being a poet.

"I write poetry, yes."

"So why'd you say you didn't?" asked Vicente.

"I didn't want to be forced to recite a poem."

"But you can recite a poem for us, right?" asked Vicente. "Just for us."

"Yeah, come on," said Carla, in the same eager tone as Vicente.

"The poems I write aren't for reciting, they're for reading in silence," said Gonzalo.

"Lame," said Vicente.

"Maybe it is lame." Gonzalo wanted to imprint his words with lightness and energy, but he couldn't avoid a trace of dramatics. "It's just that I'm not like my grandfather."

"You're never going to leave us," said Vicente, as though playing at guessing what was coming next, though those weren't the words Gonzalo had planned to say—really, he hadn't planned to say anything else.

"Never. I'll never leave you," he said anyway, and he felt the vertigo of decisive words.

That night, Carla and Gonzalo consummated their reconciliation like perfect bonobos, and only after the sex, exhausted and with dawn approaching, did they start a prolonged and not at all analytical competition of apologies that finally ended in a tie, and created the feeling that all the contained violence had been the result of a simple misunderstanding. Still, Gonzalo had won, because Carla had been imagining life without him for weeks, and she thought she had behaved like an idiot.

During the hot, hectic days that followed, Carla took her final exams at the institute and Gonzalo corrected his students' verbose essays, and they hardly had any time left over to plan for the holidays.

A dults all get together and agree to lie to kids," Vicente said bitterly,
the morning of December 24.

"Do you think that's really possible?"

"Yeah."

"Gimme a couple minutes," said Gonzalo.

Vicente reluctantly finished eating his scrambled eggs. Gonzalo returned
with a giant tome of Chesterton's, and he read this line to Vicente:

> Personally, of course, I believe in Santa Claus; but it is the season
> of forgiveness, and I will forgive others for not doing so.

"It's just one book," said Vicente. "It could be a lie. And I'm sure there
are other books that say he doesn't exist."

"Chesterton says there are people who believe in Santa and people who
don't believe, and that he believes. And he's an adult." Gonzalo thought it
was funny to lift Chesterton up as a representative of adulthood. "Do you
know who Chesterton was?"

"A writer."

"A great writer."

"Did he win the Nobel?"

"No," Gonzalo admitted.

"So Neruda was better."

"I don't think so."

Vicente remained sullen, so Gonzalo tried another argument. "Did you realize that your mom and I were mad at each other for a few weeks?"

"Yeah. How could I not realize that? I'm almost nine years old."

"Have you noticed how your grandma fights with your grandpa all the time, during the whole lunch?"

"Yeah."

"Have you noticed how the United States fights with Cuba and Russia and Iraq and the whole world? And Chile fights with Argentina and Bolivia and Peru, and Peru fights with Ecuador?"

"They do?"

"Well, but you *have* noticed how adults spend a lot of time fighting."

"Yeah."

"And do you think those same adults who spend their whole lives fighting with each other, just like that, are going to all get together and agree to lie to kids on Christmas?"

Vicente looked very serious, thoughtful.

"You're right," he said, and he walked away with a hesitant smile.

After this brilliant and trenchant argumentation, Gonzalo rushed out to the supermarket. The plan was for Carla to get Vicente out of the house and return at three in the afternoon, leaving Gonzalo a margin of several hours to hide the bicycle and the other presents, though they didn't know exactly where, since they could assume that, spurred by his suspicions, the boy would search the house and all its closets.

It was only their third Christmas together, but already they had something of a tradition: they left a drink and a piece of fruitcake beside the Christmas tree, and a few minutes before midnight they went for a walk around the neighborhood to try to catch a glimpse of Santa's sleigh in the sky, and to reinforce the illusion they would point out the reindeer droppings on the ground (which was really dog poop—the neighbors all agreed not to pick it up for a couple days). When they came home, Vicente would see the empty glass and the bites taken from the fruitcake, and of course the profusion of presents.

There were always a lot, because aside from the real presents, Carla and Gonzalo would have all their groceries wrapped; in addition to generating the impression of abundance, this served to let the boy know that a head of lettuce or a can of tuna or three nice ripe tomatoes were worthy Christmas gifts. The false presents had tags that clearly stated they were for Vicente from Santa Claus, so that the boy thanked the imaginary being not only for his toys, but also for artichokes or watermelons or cereal and even for things he found repugnant, like kiwis or eggplants.

Gonzalo spent an eternity at the supermarket, mostly waiting to have the fake presents wrapped. (The gift wrappers hated him with all their hearts.) He wanted to buy the bike there too, but he wasn't won over by any of the models they had left, so he had to stop at a department store, where he looked around nervously until he found a blue bike that fit his expectations and budget. It was another half hour before someone helped him, and then there were problems with his card, and then he hit traffic. By the time he got home, charred by the heat—he detested air-conditioning—and dying of hunger, Carla and Vicente were already back, and the newly rescued Christmas joy was again in danger.

Five minutes before midnight, they went out to look for Santa Claus. Gonzalo went back as always, with the excuse that he'd forgotten his wallet. He downed the glass of cola de mono and gobbled the fruitcake, which was pretty stale, and instead of presents he left a giant letter on one of the Christmas tree's branches; then he ran to catch up with Carla and Vicente. The boy always thought he saw Santa's sleigh, but this time it took him longer than usual, and in fact, as they were heading home, only Carla and Gonzalo said they'd definitely seen it; Vicente said he wasn't sure, and that the reindeer droppings looked suspiciously like dog poop.

When they got home they found the glass empty and the plate scattered with crumbs, but no presents. There was only one step leading into the house and it wasn't very high, maybe thirty centimeters, but in his letter, printed in Comic Sans MS 24 font, Santa explained that his back was too bad to go up steps carrying so many presents. The three of them went running out to the car, where, in effect, they found the bicycle and all the other presents. Vicente radiated joy. During the following days he told everyone he saw all about Santa's bad back.

By the next Christmas Vicente had stopped believing in Santa Claus, but he decided to pretend he still believed. Out for revenge, he asked for so many things that Carla and Gonzalo had to explain to him that, even though Santa was in charge of buying and transporting the presents, a few days later he sent an invoice to the parents, who had to pay for it all with a credit card.

I n April of 2005, they discovered the cat was missing her upper right fang. They thought someone must have hit her, but she didn't seem hurt and she looked tremendously funny. They decided to take her to the vet, but the next day Darkness was nowhere to be found. Vicente even had time to put up posters around the neighborhood, but late that evening he found her at the back of the wardrobe: she had also lost her upper left fang, and a mixture of blood and saliva was dripping from her mouth. Beneath an orphan sock she was using as a pillow or mattress, they found her two lost fangs.

The vet told them they needed a specialist's opinion. So the three of them set off for Colina, site of the office of the only cat dentist in all of Santiago. They stopped at a store on the way to buy a cat carrier so Darkness could travel more comfortably.

Dr. Dolores Bolumburu was an enormous woman about fifty years old, with hair dyed a rigorous black and eyes that were very light, almost sky-blue. After a quick examination of Darkness's teeth, the specialist ordered a biopsy and said that, no matter the results, it could be necessary to remove all the cat's teeth; she would have to start, specifically, by pulling the teeth next to the lost canines ("They're called canine teeth, not fangs," she noted), and only as she was performing the operation would she know if it was necessary to remove them all or only some. It wasn't a problem for the cat to lose all her teeth, she could eat perfectly well without them, said the doctor.

"And what happens if we don't operate?" asked Gonzalo.

"It's unclear, it'll depend on the biopsy. Basically, it's possible that Blackie here—"

"Darkness," Vicente corrected her, with all the zeal of a language teacher.

"It could happen that Darkness will lose her teeth gradually and her quality of life will decrease exponentially," Dr. Bolumburu said categorically.

"You mean we have to surgically remove all the teeth that are going to fall out anyway," said Gonzalo, with veiled sarcasm.

"Yes, but it's better to excise them and facilitate an immediate recovery."

While her assistant took a sample for the biopsy, the doctor drew up a painstaking estimate for the surgery. Carla and Gonzalo looked at the figure incredulously. They didn't even have to confer before agreeing it would be madness to pay for the operation: it cost 552,000 pesos. They would have been able to consider it, as those were days of relative prosperity: Carla still needed a few classes to graduate but she was already getting gigs shooting weddings and graduations, and although she was about to quit her job at her father's firm, she was still receiving that income. Gonzalo's situation was even more auspicious: because he'd gotten a permanent contract at a university, he no longer had to clone himself just to fill his various positions, and aside from his endless student loan payments, he now had almost no debt. But it wasn't a matter of money, it was the principle of the thing: even if Darkness's life had been in real danger, they would not have paid for the operation.

They walked in silence down a pebbled path toward the car. Darkness weighed almost five kilos, but Vicente insisted on carrying her cage, and he talked to the cat in the quiet, condescending tone people used with him whenever he was sick.

"So when's the operation?" Vicente asked when they reached the car.

"Soon," replied Carla.

"Tomorrow?"

"Wait for me here, I need to use the bathroom," said Gonzalo, and he went back into the clinic.

He drank a cup of water and paged through an intimidating copy of

Animal Science Journal while he waited for the doctor. He never haggled, he detested the habit—he would rather go into debt—but on this occasion he felt it was his duty to at least try.

"I need you to do the operation for half that estimate, ma'am." He called her ma'am in order to deny her the title of doctor. "Even half is too much."

"That's impossible," replied Dr. Bolumburu.

"You have no idea what that cat means to my son." Gonzalo thought the status of biological father would help his cause.

"That's what the operation costs," Dr. Bolumburu said dryly. There was a slice of lemon pie on her desk and she seemed anxious to devour it. "Read the estimate carefully. It's all detailed there."

"I already read it and it seems to me like armed robbery. You think we're a couple of idiots."

"Please lower your tone, Mr. Rojas."

"Then you lower your estimate, Mrs. Marlboro."

"Bolumburu."

"This is extortion, you're the only cat dentist in Santiago, maybe in all of Chile."

"And proud of it," the woman said. "I also work with dogs, rabbits, and ferrets. I'm sorry, but I'm busy now, I can't help you."

"You know you're robbing us."

"If you don't have the money to pay for a pet's dental health, which is of the utmost importance, you simply should not have pets."

"How about a meaningful discount? Two hundred thousand less?"

"Impossible. The estimate reflects the real costs of the procedures and—"

"Just cut a measly hundred thousand?"

"This is not a negotiation, Mr. Rojas. I only have a few minutes of calm before the next patient, please leave."

"Bloodsucker."

"Ingrate."

"You're a bad person."

"You're ugly."

Gonzalo picked up the doctor's lemon pie, took a greedy bite, and was about to throw the rest against the wall (he planned to aim for a diploma from Utrecht University), but it was truly delicious, so he finished it as he ran back to the car.

"The operation will be in June. It's a long way away," said Gonzalo as he licked his fingers and buckled his seat belt.

"What month is it now?" asked Vicente.

"April," replied Gonzalo. "It's several months away."

"What day in June?"

"June first."

"Why don't they do it right away?"

"Because Darkness has to get ready for the surgery," said Gonzalo.

"And because it's not so easy to schedule the operating theater," Carla added astutely, and the conversation turned toward why the surgical site was called a *theater*. On the way home, they reinforced the idea that the surgery was not urgent.

Although he had just turned ten years old, Vicente was still hanging on to the imprecise chronology of childhood. For him, there was one long day that stretched from Monday to Friday, and another, shorter day that was the weekend, and of course there were the milestones, like winter vacation and national independence holidays, family birthdays, Christmas, and summer, which were still his only truly stable coordinates. Imaginarily delaying the operation was a ploy that could well have worked, because the meaning of June was imprecise: heaters, leaky roofs, syrupy sopaipillas, sweaters, anti-biotics, boredom.

But it didn't work, because Darkness's illness worried Vicente like nothing ever had before. So, on that Wednesday, April 6, 2005, Vicente became completely and irreversibly aware of chronological time. Before he went to bed, he took possession of a calendar with photos by Cartier-Bresson that had been in the kitchen for years, and after a quick editing process with colored markers, he'd adapted it for the countdown. That evening, with much fanfare, he announced that there were fifty-five days until June 1, and from then on he continued crossing off days and announcing the timeline: every morning he struck out the new day and barked the countdown in the voice of a carnival announcer. And he talked a lot about the operation, particularly with the cat, but also with everyone else. It was his only topic of conversation.

Carla and Gonzalo got the biopsy results—they had to bribe the doctor's secretary—but were incapable of deciphering them; still, they chose to believe the operation wasn't urgent, and they kept waiting for Vicente's chronological fixation to wane. Twenty days before the deadline they almost told him the truth, but they lost their nerve, and before they knew it there were ten, then five days until the supposed operation, and they still kept putting it off. It wasn't until Tuesday, May 31, at eight o'clock at night, after a supper that included some succulent, buttery pastries with the goal of sweetening the news, that Carla and Gonzalo told Vicente that the operation wasn't going to happen. They explained that at the last minute, after taking stock and trying—desperately, unsuccessfully—to find a solution, they had come to the sad conclusion that paying for the surgery was impossible. It was a maudlin conversation that for a few minutes seemed on its way to doing the trick, but then they made the stupid mistake of mentioning the exact amount.

"The operation costs five hundred and fifty-two thousand pesos, Vicente, it's too much," said Carla. "With that kind of money we could buy about five new TVs or go on vacation in Buenos Aires for a whole week."

"But we don't need more TVs, and I don't care about Buenos Aires."

"It's more than four times the minimum wage," explained Gonzalo, confident the conversation would veer off toward the concept of a *minimum wage*.

"Five hundred and fifty-two thousand pesos, son, is what Miss Sara earns from us in fifty days," added Carla.

"Even more, fifty-five," said Gonzalo, as if that precision were necessary. In any case, Vicente perceived it as a final thrust of the knife, disloyal and cruel. In this kind of discussion, Gonzalo would normally have adopted an indulgent or less inflexible position than Carla's, but this time there were no shadings: they acted together as the enemy band.

"It's almost a thousand dollars," insisted Gonzalo, his computer open, "nine hundred and forty."

"And a thousand dollars is a lot of money," emphasized Carla, more alert, because of course to Vicente a thousand dollars sounded like very little money.

Gonzalo tried to repair his unnecessary mistake by calculating the amount in Colombian pesos.

"Vicho, in Colombia it would be 2,227,489.80 pesos, imagine that," he said pitifully.

"Who cares about Colombia! Who cares about Colombian pesos!"

Vicente went to his room weepy and infuriated. He didn't want to sleep, the last thing he wanted to do was sleep. In one corner of the yard that was protected by an awning, there was a pile of old newspapers full of inserts and advertisements much more voluminous than the newspapers themselves. Vicente went down at midnight, carried the whole bundle to his room, and was up until three in the morning looking at all the ads from department stores and pharmacies. That afternoon he continued his search online, and his old abstract idea of money started to become vertiginously concrete. This was how, in just a few months, Vicente came to be fully aware of not only chronological time, but also of the value of money.

"Stop the car, Mom," he said the next morning on the way to school.

"Why? What for?"

"Stop," he repeated.

"What for?"

"So I can stand in front of it and you can run me over," said Vicente, on the verge of tears.

That was Vicente's state of mind, but he didn't give up the fight: on Tuesday afternoon, for example, he fired Miss Sara. Though it was of course unrealistic for him to be the one to fire their maid, his explanation was pretty persuasive: Carla and Gonzalo loved her, but they weren't in a position to go on paying her, and since they couldn't bring themselves to fire her, they had given him that unpleasant mission.

"I love you, Sara, I love you a lot, this isn't personal," said Vicente guiltily. "You can take the blender if you want."

"I already have a blender. I'm still paying it off but I have one, and it's better than yours," responded Sara, who of course didn't believe the farce, but was still concerned enough to call Carla at work and tell her.

It wasn't easy to punish Vicente, who was more or less a model child and whose grades were good, at least in the subjects that interested him. Luckily, it was time for a leonine weekend (as they now called them), which wasn't exactly a punishment for Vicente, but neither did he think it such a prize to spend all that time with his father.

"You've missed all my birthday parties," Vicente said to his father, imitating the singsong of a reproach. It was true, though León did usually give him belated presents, and once had even bought a cake and brought in some kids from his building to act as extras in singing an inharmonious rendition of "Happy Birthday." Vicente wasn't at all interested in reproaching his father, but he smelled opportunity.

"You owe me half a million pesos, which is less than it would have cost you to organize ten birthday parties."

"Doesn't that seem like a little much?"

"It's a steal," replied Vicente, perfectly prepared for that objection. "There's the cake, the party favors, streamers, hats, balloons, the piñata, candy for the piñata, snacks, beers for the parents."

"What parents?"

"The parents who come too early to pick up their kids. You have to at least offer them a beer, right? It's only polite. And they'll usually drink two or three while they wait and chat. Plus the plastic cups and plates. All that adds up to over fifty thousand pesos. And I'm not even counting the clowns. Clowns can't be cheap. Multiply that fifty thousand by ten."

"So you're cutting me a deal."

"Yep."

Vicente had been talking about money all weekend and adding things up on his father's scientific calculator, though he'd refused to tell León why. Finally, though, he came out with it.

"So you need cash?"

"Yes."

"I don't have a penny, son, I'm tapped out."

"Then I want the collection."

Vicente was referring to the extensive selection of toy cars that his father kept locked in a glass cupboard in the living room. There were almost four hundred models of all sorts that León had hoarded since childhood—he wouldn't let Vicente play with them, which at first the boy had found as disappointing as it was incomprehensible, but over time he got used to gazing at the little cars through the glass as if they were fish in an aquarium. The collection was León's favorite conversation topic when his son was at his house.

"Do you have any idea how much that tiny little green car costs?" he'd say, for example, pointing at a Matchbox Jaguar race car, made in England in 1957.

"No. How much?"

"A lot," León would say. "And more every day. When I die, the collection will be yours"—he had told Vicente this dozens of times—"and you'll be able to continue it. Or maybe, if you're not interested, you can sell it, you'll make a fortune."

Though Vicente had a good imagination, he had never believed the collection was really that valuable. In his current situation, though, he figured that even if he sold them off singly for really cheap, he could make enough money to pay for the operation. He never thought that León would roundly refuse. It was the first time he had the feeling or maybe the certainty that his father was a jackass.

"You're selfish, Dad," was what he said instead. "At least give me some, maybe fifty."

"No. The collection is valuable as a collection, don't you get it?"

"If Darkness dies, I'm going to come over here and smash the case in with a hammer."

"It's just, that's my whole life in there," replied León, unfazed, as if he were used to that kind of threat. "I've collected those cars all my life. They have a lot of sentimental value. I can't just get rid of them."

"I want to go home," said Vicente.

"Hang on," said León, going for his checkbook.

He wrote a check out to his son for 55,200 pesos, knowing that it would be problematic, if not impossible, to cash it. He conscientiously marked the option "check to bearer."

"This is ten percent of the money for the operation. I can't afford any more."

To get an idea of what was in store, Vicente asked his father to show him how much was ten percent of the pallid hamburger he was about to eat. León cut it into ten symmetrical pieces and Vicente ate one of them, thinking that there was a long way to go, but it was possible. Maybe in an attempt to stimulate his courage, he chugged a full glass of Coca-Cola and let out three timid burps.

On Monday afternoon, Carla stared incredulously at the check.

"The kid has to go with his legal guardian to cash it," said Gonzalo, who had already called the bank.

"Why are you thinking of cashing it?"

"I'm not, but I want to understand León's intentions."

"León's intentions are always to screw with people," said Carla. "I can't believe Vicho managed to get any money out of him."

"What about your parents? Did he ask them?"

"I don't think so. Vicente knows how they are. Maybe they'd lend him money, but then they'd make him work a thousand years at the firm to pay it back," said Carla grimly.

After discussing it all afternoon, they decided they would in fact cash the check, if only to screw with León right back. The next morning, they let Vicente miss school and took him to the bank. On the way they tried to tempt him into spending the money on CDs—his incipient musical taste was disconcerting, ranging from metal (Pantera) to emo pop (Kudai)—or at least donating it to charity, like to the Telethon or to help children with cancer. Vicente seemed not to hear them; he didn't even look at them.

"Let's get a juice and keep talking about it," said Carla as they left the bank.

"And where are we going to get the money for that juice?" asked Vicente, on the warpath. "If you plan to spend my money on juices and ham-and-cheese sandwiches, my answer is no."

"Of course we're going to pay for it, sweetie, like always," said Carla, and she tried to hug him, but Vicente resisted. "It's just juice."

They didn't go for juice, and the afternoon was a cacophony of difficult and unfinished conversations.

Vicente searched the house, thoroughly and surreptitiously, for things that he could sell. He found a lot of books, of course, and he thought—perhaps correctly—that Gonzalo wouldn't even notice if he took some. He found a bag of winter clothes that his mother only used when they ran out of kerosene for the heaters. He found ten horrendous paintings of maritime scenes perpetrated by his maternal grandfather in his downtime. He found a VCR, a pile of cassettes, two fishing poles, a portable toilet, three old cameras, and a slide projector. He found a wedding dress compatible with a four-month pregnancy. He found a small box with a lock whose combination he easily guessed (123), which he thought must hold money or jewelry, but held only a disappointing (to him) rubber duck, which was really a waterproof vibrator in the shape of a rubber duck.

After planning numerous thefts, however, more out of pride than shame or guilt, Vicente decided not to steal anything, and to only sell the things that belonged to him—not some, but all of them. He figured he could live exclusively in his school uniform—he could wear it even on weekends, he didn't need anything else.

He made a list that at first he planned to photocopy and distribute, but then he realized the news couldn't reach the ears of his potential customers' parents, at least not right away, so he simply showed it discreetly to his classmates subject to a confidentiality agreement. All his clothes, all his toys, all his books went up for sale at reasonable prices, which he deduced using catalogs. If the business was successful, he would earn even a little more than the 496,800 pesos he needed.

The first two days were a bust, with zero signs of interest. On the third day he cut his prices in half, but still nothing happened, and things went on that way until the next week, by which time his prices were frankly laughable. Then Vicente managed to sell three magnifying lenses, a microscope, some basketball shoes, and the first five volumes of the Harry Potter saga. He handed over the merchandise with a mixture of pride and sadness, and though he was well aware that the amount he earned was ridiculous (8,250 pesos for the lot), he felt satisfied. Soon there was interest in the pricier items on the list: the bike, at a humiliating 15,000 pesos, and his bed frame with a twin mattress + bedding (he saw no problem with sleeping on the floor), at the low low price of 34,500 pesos. Vicente considered these deals closed, but just as he was putting the final touches on his detailed plan to get the bed out of his room without arousing suspicion, the secret leaked and Carla learned of her son's commercial activities. Aside from scolding him and making plans to take him to a psychologist, she didn't know what to do. Gonzalo also spoke to the boy, but got nothing out of him except a prolonged scowl of contempt.

"That damned kid," Gonzalo said later, while they were trying to concentrate on a very slow film.

"Don't talk about him like that," Carla chided him. "It was our mistake. We should have explained it all from the beginning."

"I didn't get to go to the dentist because my family couldn't afford it."

"Are you comparing yourself to Vicente or to Darkness?"

"We should have told him you just can't spend that kind of money on a fucking cat."

"I don't understand why you're so angry."

The stepfather was given the task of parleying with the parents involved. He had no problem annulling the sale of the bed, but the father of the boy who wanted to buy the bike insisted on going through with his deal, claiming he really wanted to contribute to the poor little cat's operation. The conversation was so unpleasant that Gonzalo decided to honor the sale, if only so he could stop arguing with that old cynic. He drove over himself to deliver the blue bike, the same one he had bought just a year and a half before, to its new owner.

Encouraged by this modest win, and also a little dazed from the popularity the small scandal had won him, Vicente hung up signs all over school and designed a zine with abundant material about Darkness, and two fake interviews in its central pages. ("CATS ARE INFERIOR BEINGS," Carla declared, and the headline of the interview with Gonzalo was even more damning: "DARKNESS'S LIFE MATTERS DIDDLY-SQUAT TO ME.") Thanks to these maneuverings, Vicente landed the more or less immediate support of most of his class. There were twelve volunteers from Five B who contributed cakes, pies, cuchuflíes, and lollipops that they sold during recess over the course of three weeks. The close of the campaign was a moment of relative glory and the results not all that insignificant (15,286 pesos), though he was still nowhere close to reaching his goal. Vicente had collected 93,736 pesos; that is, he was still 458,264 pesos short.

A few weeks later, when Vicente finally realized he would be unable to collect all that money, he tried one last time to convince Carla and Gonzalo. It was a convoluted conversation, tense and fruitless, and afterward Vicente exploded with rage and got out his stepfather's clippers and shaved off all of his hair. At recess the next morning, he goaded the bullies from the rival class until an unequal battle erupted, replete with punching, kicking, and spitting. He ended up with a black eye and a bloodied face, and on top of all that the school principal decided to suspend him for three days.

It was the start of a calculated rebellion: overnight, Vicente became sullen, cantankerous, and insolent. Just like those teenage stars made reckless by fame, the once affable and introspective child turned into an indefensible miscreant who got into every kind of trouble. To wit: the throwing of spit-balls and apple cores; theft of lunches, pencil cases, barrettes, erasers, balls, and sneakers; compulsive nickname invention; signature forgery; adulteration of grades in the grade book; premeditated use of permanent markers; faking of coronary illnesses; trafficking in water balloons and firecrackers; plus extortion, nudism, wall drawing, and the treacherous detonation of whoopee cushions.

Vicente vented his discontent at school but abandoned his public persona at home, because, beyond the frustration and resentment he was feeling, he didn't want to ruin behind closed doors a world that he otherwise liked. School was a stage, which makes sense, because school is always a stage, while home was a kind of greenroom where he momentarily rested from the recurrent scandals he had decided to instigate.

His two months of systematic scholastic rebellion were reflected in the lapidary personality report that Carla and Gonzalo received in shame at the end of the second term:

Regularly attends classes	Never	N
Demonstrates punctuality in all school activities	Occasionally	O
Is respectful	Never	N
Tells the truth	Occasionally	O
Is honest	Never	N
Responsibly completes homework and school tasks	Never	N
Recognizes errors and finds ways to correct them	Never	N
Accepts constructive criticism	Never	N
Takes care of his/her personal hygiene and presentation	Occasionally	O
Participates in class	Never	N
Respects his/her physical integrity and that of others	Never	N
Demonstrates a can-do spirit	Occasionally	O
Controls his/her impulses	Never	N

Shows initiative and creativity	Never	N
Cooperates/shows solidarity in benefit of others	Never	N
Is integrated in the course group	Never	N
Properly represents the school in all his/her activities	Never	N
Cares for his/her belongings and environment	Never	N
Acts in accordance with established norms	Never	N
Demonstrates respect for the national culture and values	Never	N

What a useless document, in any case. How is it possible that these personality reports, with their ham-handed design, riddled with redundancies and generalizations, real methodological aberrations, have been used—and still are—to stigmatize who knows how many generations of Chilean children? And just how qualified, anyway, was the teacher in charge of choosing all those misleading adverbs?

Enrique Elizalde had made a name for himself playing on the left-hand side in the youth teams of Santiago Morning, at first as an old-school forward—some of his crosses led to truly spectacular goals by a fifteen-year-old Esteban Paredes, future record-breaking scorer in Chilean soccer—and later as the kind of fullback, more industrious than brilliant, who runs tirelessly up and down the flank over the full ninety minutes. The coach could well have called him up to the premier league, but he didn't, and the young player got frustrated and turned to pisco and compulsive fornication, to the point that, after a few years of living it up and now with three kids by two different mothers to feed, Elizalde retired from soccer for good and tried to get his life on track by enrolling in a second-rate university, and though he had to repeat Cellular Biology, Physiology of Exercise, and Theory and Practice of Coaching (twice), he still managed to receive a degree in health education. Not even he could believe it when he found a full-time job with a decent salary at a laidback school in Ñuñoa, though he wasn't thrilled when he was assigned a supervisory role: all he wanted was to saunter through the halls of the school dressed in a tracksuit with a whistle dangling from his neck, and order laps around the field and sets of squat jumps, push-ups, and sit-ups. Coach Elizalde soon developed a reasonable phobia of parent-teacher meetings, but what he most hated about his new job was sitting down at the end of term in the teachers' lounge to calculate averages and fill out those stupid personality reports, which didn't interest him in the slightest except when they served as a vicious means of revenge.

Vicente had behaved terribly, no doubt about that, but Elizalde's evaluation was far from fair. For example: during those months the boy had been suspended often, at least two days out of every week, so that he was incapable of attending school *always*. Thus, instead of recording that Vicente *never* attended classes regularly, the teacher should have noted that he attended *occasionally* or *usually* or even *always*, because strictly speaking the kid *always* went to classes when he wasn't suspended. It's understandable for the teacher to declare that Vicente was *never* respectful, because almost all the teachers had suffered his insolence, but then it's surprising he would consider that Vicente *occasionally* told the truth but was *never* honest, which seems contradictory in any light. Though we could argue over whether telling the truth and being honest are exactly the same thing, it would be a philosophical discussion for which the teacher—and this must be said without mincing words—was entirely unprepared.

And while we're at it, just what is that bullshit about "respect for the national culture and values"? Assuming it refers to dancing cueca in September or singing the national anthem on Monday mornings or compulsorily playing the Los Jaivas song "Todos juntos" on the recorder, what difference did it make, really, if Vicente refused to stomp around like an idiot in that sexist, vulgar dance of feigned sensuality, so unimaginative and overrated? And wasn't changing every one of the national anthem's lyrics, objectively speaking, a demonstration of "initiative and creativity"? And wasn't it more interesting and groundbreaking if instead of "Todos juntos" Vicente tried to play the Nirvana song "Lithium" on the recorder? The teacher, moreover, lied outright when he affirmed that Vicente *never* participated in class, because really he *always* participated, that was precisely the problem, that he participated in class *too much*, which often kept the teachers from participating at all.

———————

"You know I'm not like that, Mom," said Vicente when Carla confronted him with the report. "You guys forced me into this. If you paid for Darkness's surgery, my problems at school would be over like *that*."

They were gathered in the living room in the pose of family-having-a-serious-conversation, when something totally unexpected happened:

"We're going to do the operation this Saturday," announced Gonzalo.

"What? Why?" asked Vicente, disconcerted, hopeful, and moved.

Carla didn't understand either, but she hid her confusion.

"Do you have the money you saved?" asked Gonzalo.

Vicente nodded.

"We're going to pay the rest," he said, putting an end to the matter.

On the appointed day the three of them set off in the car not to Colina but to a clinic nearby. Vicente protested, but they explained to him that they'd found another veterinarian specializing in feline dentistry, an eminent young doctor who had just set up an office in Ñuñoa and was willing to do the operation for 120,000 pesos.

Vicente never suspected the trick. His brief season in hell had not entirely stripped away his innocence. Moreover, part of the story was true: the doctor was young and he did have a newly opened veterinary office. He wasn't a dentist, but he agreed to star in the ruse in exchange for that 120,000 pesos, which he could really use.

The vet looked Darkness over and asked them to wait outside for the duration of the operation.

"This little kitten is like new," he told them an hour later, showing them some X-rays of another cat. "It turned out I didn't need to remove all her teeth. I only took out the pieces from her gums, as you can see in the image."

They couldn't see anything clearly in the image or in Darkness's mouth; the cat got angry when Vicente tried to inspect her.

"It'll take her two weeks to recover, and you'll have to give her baby food in the meantime," announced the vet.

"You used to eat cat food, and now the cat's going to eat human food," joked Carla, and Vicente gave her a long, wide grin.

The kid was in charge of feeding baby food to Darkness, who was delighted with the treats, especially the chicken and the pureed beans with noodles.

Gonzalo helped Vicente study for his final exams—in addition to his bad behavior, he was in danger of having to repeat the grade, since during his faked madness he had drawn boobs, dongs, and butts on all his quizzes. They studied until late, two or three hours a night, especially in English (the exam consisted of singing "Sweet Child O' Mine" a cappella), which in the end Vicente barely passed. But it was still too late: Enrique Elizalde himself had the task—which he found quite enjoyable—of confirming that, in light of his failing grades in math and science, Vicente would have to repeat fifth grade.

It's not so bad to repeat a grade," said Gonzalo. "People make a big deal out of it, but I would have liked to repeat."

The two of them were walking to school. They had never gone on foot before because the walk took a good forty-plus minutes, but this was Vicente's debut as a repeater. Gonzalo thought that under the circumstances it made sense to pause within that landscape they usually only saw through restless car windows.

"Don't lie to me, Gonza. I know you're trying to make me feel better, but it won't work." Vicente was walking, as always, a little more slowly than Gonzalo, but suddenly he hopped a few times, as though leaping imaginary puddles, to catch up with his stepfather.

"I'm not lying. It's just that later on there's no going back, there's no more time to stop. I grew up in a world where you couldn't repeat. And now you can. It's almost like a prize. We should celebrate."

Vicente was too nervous to smile. At the school entrance he waved with sad complicity to his classmates from the year before. Gonzalo walked to the metro stop thinking about how he really would have liked, at some point, to repeat.

"So as not to feel the horrible burden of time that breaks your back and bends you to the earth, you have to be continually drunk." Gonzalo thought insistently about Baudelaire's words while he drank coffee and ate a brownie in the university cafeteria. He had less than an hour to prep a class, but he decided not to do it; like almost everything in his life, his classes turned out better when he decided to improvise. Instead, he spent the time writing a kind of letter, intending to give or read it to Vicente:

Time hems us in. Time fattens us up, gives us wrinkles, gray hair, and canes. We can't stop it, turn it backward or forward. And nevertheless, repeating a grade is, in a way, to stop time: to freeze it, to momentarily cheat the future, to cheat death.

We take it easy and go back over subjects we already know. We can finally linger: finally, we can doubt, go deeper, laugh at our wounds and heal them. When we repeat we move at our own speed, willing to get lost, take detours. Without fear. Without fear of fear.

We already know the plot. The exam questions arise in our memories like warm, famous melodies. They are songs we don't like, but still we know the lyrics by heart. We look at our teachers, listen compassionately, generously, to their lessons, because they are also—we now know—repeaters. We repeaters lose the hateful drive to succeed. Failure gives us back our nobility and joy.

Almost without realizing, we do things a little better. Or we decide to make mistakes again. Because we can repeat again, over and over. We have won the freedom of playing the same game until we've had enough and are drunk with happiness; using the same words as always, we put together poems no one will ever understand, not even us, but we read them out loud a thousand times and a thousand times we experience the same sober delight.

Those who kept going—the studious, the tame, the obedient—shoot us envious looks at recess, because they know they weren't wise enough and they missed out on the priceless opportunity to repeat; the ones who didn't repeat gave themselves over, irreversibly, naïvely, to the stupid game of timeline and anxiety. We repeaters inhabit another time, legendary and new.

Carla loved the letter, but naturally she objected to that bit about how "we can repeat again, over and over." Gonzalo ultimately agreed and decided not to show it to Vicente. Only then did he comprehend that reuniting with Carla nine years later had been, in almost every sense, like repeating a grade. He said as much that night, very late, when they were both pretty drunk, and then they repeated, for the umpteenth time, the ceremony of tearing into each other in bed, a ceremony that they wanted to go on repeating indefinitely; they were completely amenable to the eternal repetition of a life that, especially on nights like that one, captivated them: high on sex, beautified by belly laughs, they were even capable of savoring words that opened up and intermingled as if they were newly learned: *ritual, routine, redo, rite, route.*

Over time the sound of the days is lost, and it becomes difficult to remember precisely how daily life sounded, what the idea of silence was, the repertoire of sounds included in white noise: the sneezes, coughs, sighs, and yawns, the cars and trucks going by, the sporadic cries of vendors and preachers, the capricious hum of the refrigerator, the distant sirens, the alarms and the birds that imitate alarms, the melodies whistled or hummed, the rattling of doors in their frames, and even the words, the sentences fully articulated in tones that didn't disturb the silence. Everyone talks to themselves, for example. They never get that right in movies. It always seems unbearable if someone talked to themselves in a movie. We all talk to ourselves, but if we saw someone doing it in a movie, we might even leave halfway through, indignant, and go home and say out loud, to no one, to ourselves: What a terrible movie.

Gonzalo, Carla, and Vicente talked a lot to each other, of course, but they also talked to themselves. Or rather, Gonzalo talked to the computer screen and to the mirror and to the pressure cooker and all kinds of appliances, while Carla talked to the mirror, the plants, and to no one, and Vicente talked to no one, though when he did it seemed like he was talking to the cat. All three of them always talked to the cat, but talking to the cat is not talking to yourself. And all three could distinguish perfectly well when the others were talking to themselves, and there weren't any misunderstandings, it wasn't even necessary for anyone to clarify that they were talking to themselves. And maybe that's what people mean when they talk about happy families.

They always smoked in the front yard. They always replaced the burned-out light bulbs and the remote control batteries immediately. They usually respected traffic signals. They occasionally used toothpicks.

They always bought powdered cinnamon and garlic and merquén. They usually had heartburn. They usually had hopes and misgivings.

They always refilled the ice cube trays immediately after emptying them. They usually ate their eggs scrambled, occasionally hard-boiled, never with lemon or soft-boiled.

They always bought marraqueta bread rolls, they usually hollowed them out, occasionally they used the crumbs to play war.

They usually changed the sheets and their expectations. They occasionally played rummy and dominoes. They never defragged the hard drive. They never cleared the leaves from the gutters when they should. They never fell asleep with the TV on.

Usually Gonzalo went to the stadium with Vicente, and occasionally also with Carla, to watch Colo-Colo, a team that in those days usually played great and won, and occasionally trounced their opponents.

Gonzalo and Carla usually went to the protests, and they occasionally brought Vicente, who was always the one who yelled the most and had the most fun.

Usually Carla and Gonzalo slept in an embrace. They usually had sex four times a week, and the same child who used to always come downstairs to sneak into the big bed now never did.

Usually Carla got on top of Gonzalo, usually she had an orgasm, usually more than one, occasionally more than two. Always, after making love, she went to the bathroom, usually to pee, sometimes to look at herself in the mirror.

Occasionally, Gonzalo did her in the ass. Carla sucked him off usually in the morning, when they came back from dropping Vicente off at school and they had a good half hour before leaving for work.

Usually, while she sucked him off, she masturbated. She usually swallowed his semen, though occasionally she liked him to come on her face, and always when that happened she would say, laughing hard, that it was good for the skin.

Usually Carla thought she would live for a hundred years, like she was somehow indestructible, but occasionally she caught herself thinking about death.

Usually Carla thought that if she died, Gonzalo would go on living with Vicente. Gonzalo also thought that.

Occasionally they talked about having a child; it was usually Gonzalo who brought it up. "Another child," he said, usually, but occasionally he called it "a child of my own."

Usually Carla thought that if Gonzalo died, she would spend some years in mourning and seclusion, but would eventually start a new life with someone else.

Usually Carla completely forgot that Gonzalo was not Vicente's father. And that also happened, occasionally, to Vicente himself.

Usually Carla thought she would be with Gonzalo for the rest of her life.

Usually Gonzalo thought he would be with Carla for the rest of his life.

Carla occasionally thought that at some point in an imprecise future, she would like to sleep with other people. Occasionally she let colleagues flirt with her.

Occasionally Gonzalo fantasized about sleeping with his students or with other teachers. He occasionally thought that someday, in the medium term, he would do it.

Carla usually thought that if she caught Gonzalo with another woman she would go crazy with rage, but in the end she would forgive him.

Gonzalo usually thought that if he caught Carla with another guy he would go crazy with rage, but in the end he would forgive her.

Usually Carla wanted to be where she was and who she was.

People say that's what happiness is—when you don't feel like you should be somewhere else, or someone else. A different person. Someone younger, older. Someone better.

It's a perfect and impossible idea, but still, during all those years, Carla generally wanted to be exactly where she was. Gonzalo too. And Vicente too; Vicente especially wanted to be exactly where he was, except on the weekends he spent with his father, when he missed his room, his house, his family.

One night Gonzalo dreamed he was on a plane, in the middle of a long, possibly transatlantic flight, his forehead pressed to the window: he couldn't see much more than the inchoate darkness of the night sky, and yet he kept watching for a length of time that in the dream seemed endless, until he felt a terrible urge to pee—he had to get past two nearly identical guys who were drooling and snoring as though in sync with each other, but he managed, pretty miraculously, to jump over without waking them.

Trying to keep his balance, he walked toward the green light that indicated the bathroom was free, but when he opened the door there was a woman sitting on the toilet, her underwear around her ankles and her knees pressed together. She didn't seem surprised, and her body made no movement that betrayed a desire to shield herself.

"This is the women's bathroom," the woman said pleasantly.

"Bathrooms on planes aren't like that," replied Gonzalo, who was not convinced that those approximate, imperfect words expressed what he wanted to say.

"You went to an all-boys school," guessed the woman.

"What does that have to do with it?" Gonzalo had the impression he knew her.

"Do you think it's natural to separate men and women, as if they were incompatible?" The woman's tone approached hostility but maintained, never-theless, a casual, unconcerned inflection.

"That's what I'm saying, this bathroom is for both men and women."

"You don't understand a thing, Gonza. While I finish, you pee in the sink like you used to. I don't think it's gross," she said.

He woke up in the middle of the night with an uncontrollable urge to pee. As he tried for the ten steps that would take him to the bathroom he still retained some images from the dream, which he found funny and extrava-gant, especially because he had never taken a long plane trip. Of course, he didn't pee in the sink, as he in fact had done a few times as a teenager. He was still half-asleep, it was hard to aim his stream, and it skewed off crazily. He thought about cleaning up, even glanced at the bottle of bleach in one corner, but he was dead tired, and instead went back to bed and fell asleep instantaneously.

Carla woke him up before six o'clock, when it was still dark out. Gon-zalo remembered he had missed the toilet and thought she was waking him up to reproach him.

"I know what you're going to say." Gonzalo cleared his throat.

"What am I going to say?" Carla didn't sound angry, not at all.

"That I missed the toilet."

"And what are you going to tell me?"

"That it's not easy to aim straight. The first squirt, especially, is hard to control."

"And what else?"

"What else what?"

"What else am I going to say?"

"That I should pee sitting down. How hard can it be for me to sit down to pee. And I'm going to tell you that it's tradition, men don't pee sitting down. And you're going to tell me that I have a really crude idea of masculin-ity. And I'm going to tell you that peeing standing up doesn't have anything to do with my idea of masculinity."

"You're right, I was going to tell you all that, but later," said Carla, raising her right hand to her forehead as if she had a fever. "I wanted to tell you that I woke up half an hour ago and I went to the bathroom and, sure, it annoyed me to clean up your piss, but then I sat down to pee and I took the test and I'm pregnant."

They waited a week to tell Vicente, who reacted with surprising indifference. That night they went to a pizzeria to celebrate and they ordered, as always, a family-sized mushroom pie, but Vicente didn't want to even taste it.

"What's wrong?" asked Gonzalo.

"I don't like mushrooms."

"Yes, you do."

"I did, but I don't anymore," replied Vicente, mysteriously timid.

"So what do you want?"

"An espresso."

Vicente had never tried espresso before, but he thought that, now that he was eleven years old, it was within his rights. He insisted on drinking not one but three espressos in a row, which he sipped ceremoniously and found horrible, though he hid it very well. He got over the aftertaste by devouring a slice of tiramisu.

"You sure you don't want any pizza?" Carla asked him as they were about to leave. "We can ask them to heat it up for you."

"No, thank you," said Vicente, overemphasizing the word *thank*.

He had trouble sleeping because of the caffeine, but maybe even if he hadn't had three espressos plus a strong tiramisu he still would have had trouble sleeping. He went to the living room at three in the morning and found Gonzalo there, also wide awake.

"You want some pizza now?"

"Yeah," said Vicente.

"Are you mad about the news?" Gonzalo asked as he heated up two large slices in the toaster oven.

"I get embarrassed when people ask for the leftovers to go."

"Why?"

"I don't know, I just get embarrassed."

"Well, there was a lot left over. Why didn't you want to eat?"

"Because I wasn't hungry."

"Are you mad about the news?"

"What news?"

"About your new little brother or sister. Which would you prefer?"

"Brother," said Vicente, but he changed his mind immediately: "Sister."

Vicente didn't know what was wrong with him either. He liked the idea of a sibling, or at least he thought he should like it. For some reason he was incapable of imagining that brother or sister. He slept awhile and woke up to the ferocious purr of the cat beside his left ear. He thought that maybe Darkness would sleep, in the future, with that new brother or sister, and suddenly he was sure it would be a sister. It was a very concrete, very visual, very powerful thought. He went back to sleep. In the morning his reticence had turned into enthusiasm. A sister, he thought: awesome. Nonchalantly, he went in and declared to Gonzalo and Carla that he was happy.

"Still, I can't decide what to name the baby," he added in a troubled tone.

"You can't name the baby," Carla told him seriously, after exchanging nervous glances with Gonzalo. "It's not a pet."

"It's the parents' job to name their children," said Gonzalo.

"I know!" said Vicente. "It's a joke, how can you not realize I'm joking, it's like you guys lost your senses of humor. But I do think it would be better if people got to choose their own names."

"Impossible," said Carla. "A baby can't go without a name. It's illegal."

"They could give it a number in the meantime, and let the kid choose his own name later on," said Vicente.

Gonzalo thought it was a reasonable idea.

"So, do you like your name?" he asked. "It's like the poet Vicente Huidobro."

"Yeah. I would have picked Vicente too. It sounds good. Mom got it right with me, but she could have made a mistake."

"Hopefully we'll get it right with your brother," said Gonzalo.

"It's going to be a sister," Vicente declared.

Even though Carla was only eight weeks pregnant, they liked the exercise of coming up with names, they couldn't help it. Plus, it made sense to start the negotiation, because they weren't at all in agreement. Carla preferred common names, like Carolina, Sofía, Matías, or Sebastián.

"I like Sofía and Matías, but they're cacophonous," said Gonzalo one Sunday morning, two weeks later.

They were coming back from the market, and the boys were carrying the bags, though Carla insisted they at least let her carry the one with lettuce and endive. Vicente had had a growth spurt and looked very thin, but he still hefted his bag of potatoes with dignity.

"I like how they sound," said Carla.

"*Ese día Sofía sabía que Matías tenía una sandía* . . . It sounds bad," said Gonzalo. He thought that Vicente also rhymed with a lot of Spanish words, but he didn't mention that.

"It sounds bad in a book, but not in real life," said Carla.

Gonzalo preferred names that had fallen out of use, ones that were original and literary, like Casandra, Cordelia, Miranda, Horatio, or Romeo.

"If that's what you're into, let's name him Sophocles instead, or Oedipus," Carla retaliated.

"Oedipus. That's not a bad name," said Gonzalo flirtatiously, gazing out at the horizon as if mulling over the possibility. "Or Medea. Oedipus or Medea."

"Remind me who Medea killed?"

"Her children," said Gonzalo, laughing.

"Oh great, Medea, then," said Carla. "Let's make things easy for the kid."

"If you have such a hard time agreeing, I don't get why you won't let me name the baby," Vicente chimed in.

"You're right, help us," said Gonzalo. "Give us ideas. Propose something."

Vicente took his role as onomastic adviser seriously: right away he started a list of girls' names, because he was so convinced he was going to have a sister that thinking up boys' names seemed like a waste of time. His criteria were a perfect blend of Carla's and Gonzalo's, because he tried to think of names that were not very common but were not at all extravagant—classic names that were not currently in fashion. He also interviewed some girls in his class, just to be sure.

"Amparo," he proposed a few days later, confidently, ready with a ton of conclusive arguments to meet any possible objection.

They were eating supper on a strangely luminous day at the beginning of May, and it seemed like the perfect occasion to discuss the matter; instead, an inexplicable silence descended.

"It could also be Aurora, Antonia, or Ana," he added, while he tried to figure out what was happening. "Girls' names that start with A are unbeatable. And Ana is written the same forwards or backwards."

Carla burst out crying and ran to the bathroom. Though she'd wanted to be the one to give him the news, it was Gonzalo who had to tell Vicente that there would be no brother or sister, at least not for the time being. The boy was perplexed, and a couple of hours later, when his wan mother emerged from the bedroom with a bag to go to the clinic, he hugged her harder than ever. They had to explain to him what neither of them had wanted to put into words: that there were remains of the dead fetus left in his mother's uterus. They used the word *curettage*, which seemed more technical or compassionate than the word *scraping*. A babysitter came; Vicente wanted to stay by himself, but he relented.

The gynecologist had scheduled the D&C in a maternity ward, which infinitely intensified the bitterness. In the car on the way there, Carla didn't hear the useless words of consolation Gonzalo said to her. She was focused on imagining some kind of ancient god, vengeful or more like resentful: a failing god, aware of his irrevocable decline, who was using his final ammunition, the remnants of the immense power he had once wielded, to make himself known, to remain faithful to the habit of destruction.

"I want to be alone," she told Gonzalo, in the sweetest tone she could manage as they entered the room. "Go on and smoke, sweetheart. I'll ask them to call you when it's all over."

That's what Gonzalo did while the procedure was being prepared: smoked rabidly and held back his tears, which wasn't easy, because smoking and crying are complementary activities. At some point he remembered the masculine custom of cigars to celebrate births, and he saw himself as a parody of a father with his awful Belmont Light between his lips. He briefly distracted himself with the promise that from then on he would smoke Lucky Strikes or Marlboros.

He went back to reception and looked at the reproductions of old paintings, all alluding to births, that crowded the walls. There were five paintings by Mary Cassatt. Gonzalo stared intently at the image of a woman with her hair in a bun who was cradling a blond baby. Both figures were in profile, facing each other as though hiding from the viewer, as if the viewer were excluded from their joy, condemned to imagine it.

He went out to smoke again, and this time he did cry on the sidewalk. He'd cried very little until then—he felt the impropriety, the illegitimacy of his pain. He thought that the claim to crying belonged exclusively to Carla, as if there were a quota of tears, a preassigned quantity of suffering. Both of them had lost the child, but especially her. He was the one who would console her, that was his mission, his function, his job. Because the insides being scraped were hers.

When they informed him that the procedure was over and Carla would remain sedated for a few hours, Gonzalo ran to find the gynecologist.

"What was it, Doctor?"

"What?"

"The baby, was it a boy or a girl? Do you know? Is it possible to know?"

"What do you want to know for," said the doctor, in a tone that didn't sound like a question.

"I just want to know, is all," said Gonzalo. "I have the right to know."

The doctor smiled kindly and tried to hug Gonzalo, who resisted.

"I don't know," replied the doctor, and he walked down the hall toward the parking lot.

Gonzalo wanted to know, he would have preferred to know, though he didn't understand why or what for. So he could name it anyway, perhaps. He went back to the room and sat down on the sofa bed where he would spend the night. He took Carla's hand at the exact moment when a newborn started to cry in the room next door. Carla woke up, didn't want to talk, and went back to sleep at eleven o'clock. Gonzalo didn't sleep or let go of Carla's hand all night long.

Then came days filled with an even, attenuated sadness that wounded like the echo of a terrible scream. In the evenings they watched films by Eric Rohmer, and sometimes Vicente sat with them for a while in front of the TV, somewhere between interested and bored, aware that watching those movies was nothing but a way of enduring the silence.

One morning they woke up to the news that the lech had died, not from cancer—the treatment had been a rousing success—but from a heart attack while he was playing guitar in a bar on Matucana. Carla had spent nearly a month without leaving the house even to go down the street, but she thought it made sense to return to the world with a funeral. The lech was buried in Memorial Park, which was an expensive cemetery, but among all the mourners they managed to design a sophisticated system of checks, transfers, and IOUs to cover it. At the funeral, two of the deceased's buddies and three of his children—including Gonzalo's mother—took the floor to paint a picture of the lech in uniformly flattering terms.

After the ceremony, Carla and Gonzalo sat on a stone bench in the shadow of a memorious ginkgo biloba.

"Your grandfather was nice, after all," Carla said, just to say something.

"What?"

"That afternoon, when we met him, I liked him in spite of everything. He was a jerk, but I liked him. It's weird how that works."

"What?"

"When you know someone is a jerk, but you like them anyway."

"Yeah. But I didn't like him," said Gonzalo. "He was a player. He seduced people, that's why you liked him."

They walked toward the car in silence, both thinking about the child they'd lost. Gonzalo started naming the trees, as though greeting them: soapbark, Japanese maple, European beech, sweet gum, crepe myrtle, blue pine.

"I didn't know you were a tree expert," Carla said, genuinely surprised.

"I'm no expert. Once, when we were at the park, Vicente asked me the name of a tree and I didn't know it. I felt bad and started to learn them."

"I hardly know any," said Carla, softly.

"And if you don't know the names of the trees, you make them up." While he was driving home, Gonzalo remembered that phrase he'd read somewhere, he couldn't remember where, maybe in an essay on medieval literature. Then he thought about those new cemeteries that had started to inundate Santiago in the nineties: just some plaques sown in the ground the length and breadth of a splendid park, with the grass rigorously maintained, like on a golf course. He hated them, found them false, saturated with illegitimate optimism, and stripped of all nobility or beauty.

"Still, I like the name of this cemetery," he said, as if to himself.

"What?"

"Memorial Park," he said. "I don't like this kind of cemetery, but I like this one's name."

"It's nice," said Carla, to say something.

That night, Gonzalo talked in his sleep. He'd never done that before, or he had but not like that, because it wasn't just random words, but rather whole sentences: he talked so loud that Carla woke up and heard what he was saying: "You don't have the right to ask that of me," was one of the sentences.

The others: "The metro was full, so I walked instead"; "Let me kick it, man"; "It's not hot out"; "I remember, of course I remember."

Carla tried to imagine that dream, whose meaning seemed unfathomable but also, somehow, precise. And although it's absurd to make decisions based on a dream, especially an incomprehensible dream of someone else's, the image of Gonzalo talking in his sleep somehow reinforced in Carla the conviction that she would never try to get pregnant again.

"Nature is wise," her mother had told her when she found out about the miscarriage, and for Carla there were few things less satisfying than agreeing with her mother, but she had to admit that's how she felt at times: her body had made a decision, the right decision. Even Vicente's initial reticence seemed to her, in retrospect, like a warning, a premonition of what was to come.

"We're fine the way we are, you're already a father," Carla told him the next morning. "You've been a great father to Vicente, the best father."

"Thanks," said Gonzalo, surprised. "What about León?"

"León isn't worth shit."

"Should we kill him, then?"

"Yeah!"

"How?"

"With a Colt .45," said Carla, her smile crooked, luminous.

"Better with a machine gun," said Gonzalo, "just to be sure."

"Let's poison him."

"With rat poison."

"Let's decapitate him."

"Let's impale him."

They went on like that for a while, cackling as they imagined the details of the murder and their alibis.

"You talked in your sleep last night," Carla said as if she wanted to change the subject, though she had the ambiguous feeling that, no, they were still talking about the same thing.

"What did I say?"

"A lot of words, full sentences. You don't remember? You can't remember your dream, or that you dreamt?"

"No, not at all. What did I say?"

"A lot of stuff."

"What?"

"I don't remember. Nothing bad, I don't think. I didn't really understand."

After years of using leonine weekends to hold parties or dinners, Carla and Gonzalo became averse to social life. They didn't acknowledge it, but they had both decided not to have guests over for an indefinite period of time—they needed to restore their home before they could share it again. One Friday, however, Gonzalo announced that the poet Salgado was coming over for dinner. ("He's more depressed than usual," he explained.) Carla was annoyed and asked them to go to a bar instead.

Supremely satisfied with her decision, she lay down in the bed to listen to a Juana Molina album she'd just bought. Instead of making the most of her solitude to turn the stereo all the way up, she chose to pummel her eardrums with the headphones of a Discman that was like new, because she'd received it as a gift not long before Vicente was born, when she didn't yet suspect that her relationship to music was also about to change, possibly forever. She switched the remote control batteries into the Discman, then flopped on the bed to listen to the first few songs on the CD, which she liked, but the experience of returning to headphones felt complicated or arduous or absurd—she felt like she was missing something, like she didn't have the right to disconnect that way, like she was exposing herself to some kind of danger. She took them off and put the CD into the stereo while she chopped fruit for a salad. She listened to it twice in a row, and it seemed to her like a new kind of music, intense and strange.

Then she returned the batteries to the remote control and settled in for a marathon of *Friends*, something she couldn't do with Gonzalo, who thought the show was superficial, even though he always laughed at Phoebe's quips and Joey's buffoonery (and he secretly thought that Carla was a tangled mix of Rachel and Monica). Carla had never rewatched the first season, whose episodes she now enjoyed as if she were watching old home movies. They all looked so young, practically kids: she pictured herself in the mid-nineties, even younger than the *Friends* actors, and she thought that back then she'd very likely spent an evening exactly as she was now—lying in bed in only her underwear watching those same episodes on TV, maybe laughing at the same jokes. It didn't feel ridiculous to spend her leisure time the same way so many years later; on the contrary, those thoughts flooded her with an absolute, enigmatic joy.

She watched the first eight episodes of the first season, skipped the ninth—she could never get into Thanksgiving episodes—and was halfway through the tenth, the one where Ross adopts a monkey and Phoebe meets David, when she heard Gonzalo coming back from dinner, the poet Salgado still with him. She reluctantly put on her robe and appeared in the living room, on the warpath. The poet Salgado was Gonzalo's best friend and the one Carla found the funniest, but that night she didn't want to share lodgings with a couple of drunks.

"He really is depressed, he wants to keep talking," explained Gonzalo.

"So give him a few of your antidepressants," said Carla.

"I don't take antidepressants," said Gonzalo, disconcerted.

"I'm sorry, Carla," interrupted Salgado, with the false discretion of the drunk. "I've had some fucking pissy luck lately. I don't understand why things go so bad for me."

"How do things go bad for you?" asked Carla.

"With the ladies."

"I know why," Carla replied. "You have bad luck because you're selfish and fat as hell. Just the thought of sleeping with you would make any woman run for the hills."

Carla regretted the insult immediately and she stayed with the men for a while, doling out useless advice. Although she had never needed to go on a diet, out of pure guilt she designed a very simple one for the poet Salgado, whom no one really called the poet Salgado, because ever since he was a boy he'd been known as Fatty Salgado, to the point that he would refer to himself like that, which in a certain way allowed him to forget his obesity, or to not see it as a problem, because it had become more of a name than a description. (There'd been a period during which he'd lost about twenty pounds, and then people would talk about how thin Fatty Salgado was, which of course didn't mean he was actually thin, just slightly less fat.)

"I'm sorry about that, she didn't mean to hurt your feelings, it's just that sometimes she's a little too honest, that's all, and as you know we've had a rough time of it lately," Gonzalo said later, in a supposedly quiet voice, because he was also pretty wasted. Anyway, Carla could hear everything from the bedroom.

"Don't worry, I know I'm a little on the corpulent side." Fatty had a time of it pronouncing the word *corpulent*.

He'd spent the past hour announcing he was about to leave, but Fatty Salgado was someone who stayed until you threw him out.

"Okay, buddy, time for bed," said Gonzalo.

Salgado stood up unsteadily, and after slapping Gonzalo superfluously on the back several times, he said:

"Here's hoping it works out, brother. Best of luck."

"Thanks, buddy," Gonzalo muttered.

What was it that he was wishing Gonzalo luck on? Carla had no idea. She didn't want to ask him, because she was exhausted and also because she hoped to decipher the mystery on her own, and she spent much of Saturday painstakingly reviewing the range of possibilities. By then it was clear they weren't going to try to have another baby, but then she thought maybe Gonzalo would try to convince her and that was his secret goal. It made sense, because he had been, historically, the one who advocated for the idea, and it was even strange that after only three months he seemed content with or resigned to not having one.

Alarmed by this thought, she asked Gonzalo about his secret outright, what it was that Fatty Salgado had wished him luck on. He replied naturally, convincingly, that he had a book of poems and there was a possibility of publishing it with Wooden Bridge Press.

"I had no idea you'd finished a book."

"I didn't think you'd be interested."

"I am interested. Very. Of course I'm interested. Let me read it, please."

"I'm just going to correct a few things, and then I'll show it to you."

"I want to read it now," said Carla, with sweet determination; she didn't sound domineering, just emphatic.

"Tomorrow?"

"Now."

Over the years, Carla's interest in poetry had not increased—she didn't have time for it, really: every once in a while she picked up a novel by Amélie Nothomb or Yasunari Kawabata or Salman Rushdie, but never poetry, and although at times she thought Gonzalo's poet friends were funny, and although he himself talked about poets constantly, she tended to forget that, in addition to studying and teaching it, Gonzalo wrote poetry. But still, if he was about to publish a book of poems, she wanted to read it, of course she did.

"And is Wooden Bridge the only option?" asked Carla.

"It's the most prestigious poetry press right now," said Gonzalo, as though stating the obvious.

"I hope it works out. How likely is it?"

"They're reading it, they still haven't said anything."

"Did you send it to other presses too?"

"Well, there aren't many options. Communicable Vision is a good press too, but they have terrible distribution, and the folks at No Future Editions are cool, I like them, but their books are awful. And the other presses are ruled by cliques I don't have access to. And that I don't want access to."

This final phrase was fortunate, because it conferred upon its speaker a certain artistic integrity. Gonzalo grabbed the remote control and started to channel-surf at roughly the same speed as his nervous blinking.

"I want to read it," insisted Carla.

"I'll show it to you. Let me correct it a little. It's not finished."

"But you said it was finished. You mean you sent it to that publisher before it was finished?"

"Well, I thought it was finished at the time. Paul Valéry said that a work is never truly completed, but abandoned." That perfect sentence sounded strange in this context, as if Paul Valéry were a pretentious French professor or a judgmental carpenter.

"Okay, but I want to read it now. Go get it, what's the holdup?"

"Fine, but first I have to take a shit."

He picked up his computer and locked himself in the bathroom. He sat on the toilet without pulling his pants down, because it wasn't true that he had to shit. He went through the folders where he stored his poems and hastily reread them all, trying to see them from a distance, through Carla's eyes or a stranger's. He thought they weren't bad, or rather that it would be hard to decide if they were good or bad, which meant they were more good than bad. He also thought they weren't bad, but they were unnecessary. It didn't seem like the world needed those poems. He wanted to write the poems no one had written before, but at that moment he thought no one had written these particular poems because they weren't worth writing.

He was saddened to admit or to realize that his poems would excite no one. Other files held more intense and extreme drafts, versions that encapsulated tentative, unstable emotions, and they were funny or furious or desperate texts, like his diatribe against biological fathers, but he felt they were too raw, dangerously transparent. He was capable of recognizing the purifying flash of rage in others, the warmth of self-assurance, and some of the poets he admired were extravagant, arbitrary, unfathomable. But when he himself wrote, he tried to stay as far as possible from personal expression, from the tyranny of feelings. Rage is not good for writing poems, he tended to think, but that day, as he hid out in the bathroom and reviewed his complete works, he realized he'd been wrong. Rage was good, there was power in rage and beauty in vehemence.

But he didn't have time to improvise anything, so he chose some poems, the ones he thought were the most finished, to assemble the manuscript of his supposed first book. He cut-and-pasted the verses into a file he named "Poetry Book 34," chose the font and size and spacing, and, in a gesture toward authenticity, he flushed the toilet and even sprayed air freshener.

Carla was waiting for him in bed, the TV now turned off. He read her the first twenty poems, which she found unambiguously bad, though she thought maybe she didn't know enough about poetry to have an opinion. It was a compassionate thought, because in fact she was absolutely sure that in spite of her long-standing distance from poetry, she would be capable of recognizing a good poem, a poem that at the very least intrigued her. What she heard was, to her, simply bad, so she decided this: she wouldn't open her mouth.

Gonzalo was hurt by the faint reception, and also afraid of going on with the reading—he had just used what a comedian would call his best material. He figured that although Carla's eyes were fixed on his laptop screen, she couldn't distinguish the words he was reading out loud, and for greater security he turned the computer to the side to obstruct her view even more. Then, betraying every last one of his convictions, he read three of "his" poems that were really poems by Emily Dickinson, translated by Silvina Ocampo, which he knew by heart. Carla reacted immediately. She thought they were strange, she liked them.

"Read me more," she said.

Already in deep, he "read" five poems that were by Gonzalo Millán. They were poems he wished he had written and that were somewhat similar—though not obviously so or maybe obviously only to him—to the poems that he wanted to write, that he was trying to write, except they were unquestionably superior. Suddenly he felt terrible and almost confessed what he had done, but there was no way to admit it without embarking on a long and dangerous explanation.

"They're by far, by far, the best poems you've ever written," she said.

"You like the book, then?"

"Especially the last poems, I liked those a lot. Read me one more," she said.

"I don't have any more."

"But isn't it a whole book?"

"Well, poetry books are short."

"One more!"

"Okay, but it's not finished."

He pretended to read "Kamasutra," which was his favorite poem of Millán's:

The vaccination scar will remain
and the moles on your neck and underarm.
The elastic marks will remain
behind your breasts and on the skin
around your waist, under your navel.
But not the crescent moon,
the wild boar's bite, the broken cloud,
the tiger's claw, the coral and the gem.
The loving traces left by
the art of my teeth and my nails.

Carla asked him to read it again and then Gonzalo thought he'd made a terrible mistake, or an unforgivable mistake within another, even more unforgivable mistake, because Carla didn't have moles on her neck or on her underarm.

"It's truly beautiful, Gonza," said Carla. "It's the best poem you've written. It's simply brilliant."

"It's about an imaginary woman," said Gonzalo, to excuse himself.

"Of course she's imaginary, it's a poem," said Carla. "What do I care if you got inspired by the moles of an ex or whatever? It's a great poem, period. I'm going to remember it forever. It's the best poem you've written. Thank you."

"For what?"

"For sharing the book with me," said Carla. "Still, I like those last poems a lot more. What's the book called?"

"I still haven't decided."

"Call it *Kamasutra*, like that poem. It's great."

———————

Gonzalo felt like he was the worst fraud ever, the king of assholes. He went out to the little room to get the books where the stolen poems appeared, and he hid them in the bathroom alongside some old toys and an ancient and unusable vacuum cleaner, inclined to never read them again. It was unlikely Carla would discover the trick, but Gonzalo wanted to be sure.

And if you don't know the names of the trees, you make them up, he thought later that night, grimly, as he skillfully licked between Carla's legs.

G onzalo started to go to Memorial Park every day, sometimes just for a few minutes or at his lunch hour. The first few days he only took notes, but then he decided to write right there, on the fly, which lent his poems a weight of reality they had never had before. The place still seemed odious to him, but at the same time he was attracted by its consistent and occasionally convincing illusion of lightness, that deceitful sobriety that strove to normalize mystery and mask pain.

He tried to absorb, understand, dismantle the landscape: he looked at the water lilies and hyacinths in the pond, he walked down side paths through the sweet gum trees, he peered at the exquisite gardens on the other side of forged iron bars that marked off the exclusive areas with failed subtlety— stone benches where executive-class mourners could sit comfortably to honor their dead, with easy access to the parking lots to enable quick getaways.

Gonzalo didn't even stop to look at the lech's grave; he was mainly there to observe people. He snuck respectfully into a few funerals, but what most interested him were the short visits by people alone, almost always office work- ers who slipped out for half an hour on their lunch breaks to sit beside their dead and murmur something, maybe prayers. Sometimes the mourners took out Tupperware containers and uncertainly ate whatever they'd brought for lunch: their bleak green bean salads, their disconsolate rice with egg, their severe pasta bolognese. Some days Gonzalo made small talk with the guards or smoked a cigarette by the offices just inside the gates while listening to the

soulless Muzak that played over a speaker at a moderate volume, Beatles or
Simon & Garfunkel songs played on the pan flute, or the Bangles or Radiohead as bossa nova. There were a couple of Sundays when he went with Carla
and Vicente—Carla took a lot of photos, especially of the trees, while Vicente passed the time looking around with voracious curiosity.

In just two months Gonzalo solidified a book that, after thinking about it
long and hard, he decided to call, simply, *Memorial Park*. To mitigate his
fraud, he sent it first to Wooden Bridge Press, who rejected it kindly and immediately, and then he sent it to other presses. Some of them rejected it; others
never replied. When he was starting to give up, the solitary editor of Why Not
Editions wrote him a long message full of baroque praise and grammatical
blunders in which he accepted the book on the condition that Gonzalo finance forty percent of the publication cost.

It wasn't the ideal offer, and yet he was happy. The print run would be
only two hundred copies with no bookstore distribution, but he didn't much
care—he couldn't wait to hold his first book in his hands. He didn't sign it
with the pseudonym Gonzalo Pezoa, which now struck him as childish, or
with both of his last names, which was how he signed his academic articles,
but instead with the new pen name Rogelio González, which was like Gonzalo Rojas backward. Carla read the draft several times and even corrected
some mistakes. (In spite of his scrupulous academic formation, Gonzalo
thought that *belie* was a synonym of *disguise* and that the word *disgression*
existed.) She thought it wasn't bad, though she only liked four of the poems,
and only one of the whole series struck her as truly beautiful. To be sure, she
missed the formidable poems she remembered—Gonzalo explained that they
were part of another, still-unfinished project.

Gonzalo had used credit to pay for his part of the publication, and the editor
assured him the book would be printed soon, though he refused to give an
exact date. ("I don't want to let you down," he said more than once.) Pre-

cisely during that period, when he would lie awake at night thinking about
the publication, Gonzalo received a brisk message notifying him that he
had won a government grant to finance a doctorate in New York. It was fabulous news, though the euphoria immediately mixed with the terror of telling
Carla, which would mean admitting he had applied to that and other grants—
which was what Fatty Salgado had really been wishing him luck on—and
also that he had already been accepted at two universities. Without a word
to Carla, he had filled out forms, gotten certificates and letters of recom-
mendation, and he'd even taken the precaution of using his work address, so
that no correspondence endangering the secrecy of his efforts would be delivered to their house.

It wasn't just Fatty Salgado, but several of his friends who were in the
loop about his project, which was a reasonable one, to be sure, maybe more
reasonable than having a baby: for two years now, the university's program
director and the dean had been insinuating, in ever less subtle tones, that it
was time for Gonzalo to get his doctorate. But doing it in Chile seemed to
him like going backward. Literally: he didn't want to go back to the same
university and listen to the same professors whose speechifying he had already sat patiently through for so many years. Nor did he want to cling to
his position like all those supposedly well-trained academics who had never
even left Chile or learned another language or had children or lived any even
minimally erratic experience, nothing remotely close to an adventure: they
were like big kids with postdoctorates and theoretical backgrounds but no
real experience of the world. He felt contempt for those academics precisely
because he wasn't so different from them. And he didn't want to go on being
like them. Though very soon he would be a published poet, in his heart of
hearts the idea had taken root that he was not a great poet. To say it in the
fundamentalist language that he himself sometimes used, Gonzalo suspected
that deep down he was not a poet, not a true poet. But he didn't want to
resign himself as a professor too. He wanted to grow, and he intuited the
correct direction of that growth.

The same night Carla told him they weren't going to try for another pregnancy, Gonzalo, as he lay awake, decided to apply for the doctorate. At that

moment it had seemed cruel to talk about it right away with Carla, though his idea was to take her and Vicente with him, he had no doubt about that—or he did, but the possibility of going alone functioned rather as a tenuous, brittle fantasy, a somewhat self-destructive flirtation that returned him immediately to his more stable fantasy—albeit with epic trimmings—of the family trying their luck in New York. He felt they were perfectly capable of facing any adversity together. Still, he kept putting off the conversation with Carla, partly because he didn't want to share the period of expectancy, and then the likely failure of his plans—he thought he wouldn't get the grant, or that he would get it only after years of applying religiously.

No one can turn down an invitation to live in New York, he thought the night he waited for Carla perched oddly halfway up the stairs, ready to tell her everything. But he couldn't tell her, he didn't know how, not that night or any of the days that followed. A month passed, a very tense month that was full of misunderstandings: Gonzalo silenced his phone, stayed out late, and though Carla wasn't a jealous person she couldn't help but suspect infidelity. She asked him outright, stoically, like someone walking down the middle of a street just before a hurricane. He assured her she was wrong, he was just nervous about the book publication. She thought that publishing a book must be a terribly stressful thing and she wanted to believe him, but she still tried to read his emails, guessing at a thousand different passwords, until one night, when she saw Gonzalo in bed with his email open, she simply grabbed the computer away from him and locked herself in the bathroom.

She lingered over messages from women whose names she didn't recognize at all, but she didn't find anything beyond trivial flirtations, which she tended to allow herself too ("Your message brightened my whole year," "Sending you a long hug," "Sending infinite hugs"). When she was just about to come out of the bathroom, almost ashamed of her suspicions, from the other side of the door Gonzalo said:

"So what I have to tell you is, we're going to New York." The words sounded ridiculously overzealous.

They sat at the table, face-to-face, and Gonzalo came out with the whole story, lingering over the details, and he said he never planned to go alone, that had never been his intention. He said he wouldn't go anywhere without her and Vicente.

"There are a lot of photos to be taken in New York," he added.

"There are a lot more photos to be taken in Santiago," replied Carla. "All the photos in New York have already been taken. Not in Santiago. Not in Chile."

"I'm sure you'll find work."

"Without speaking English?"

"But you're a photographer, you don't have to speak much," said Gonzalo. "A photographer can work anywhere."

"Sure, I can work as a mime too," said Carla.

They had to interrupt the conversation because Vicente came running down the stairs, went to the kitchen for a knife, and sat down at the head of the table to nonchalantly peel a green apple.

"That's dangerous," Carla told him.

"No, this knife is barely sharp at all," said Vicente. "I want to learn."

"And you don't like the peel?" asked Gonzalo.

"I love it," said Vicente. "I'm going to eat it too, but separately."

They had to wait for Vicente to peel the apple, extremely slowly and with uneven skill. At one point Carla thought he must have overheard them and come to sit down there on purpose, to forestall a fight or something. But he hadn't heard anything, he was just intent on learning to peel apples.

"I'm going to yell at you," said Carla, in a low voice, dryly, when Vicente had gone back to his room.

"What?"

"I'm going to yell at you a *lot*," said Carla, in an even lower voice.

She called Vicente's best friend's mother to ask if he could spend the night at their house. Gonzalo went to drop him off.

Some teenagers were shouting on the sidewalk about soccer or a soccer video game and about a mutual friend who had just come out of the closet: Carla tuned in and out of their conversation while she made dinner and thought over and over about all those omissions, all that time of poisonous stealth; she just couldn't understand Gonzalo's silence, or maybe she understood it for what it was: an act of aggression. A lover would have been so much easier to understand, she thought.

She made salmon with capers and pumpkin puree, and uncorked a bottle of white wine. It looked like a celebration, when it was exactly the opposite.

"Think of Vicente, he'll finally learn some English," said Gonzalo as soon as he got back.

"You didn't talk to me about this because you want to go alone," said Carla.

"I already told you, it seemed cruel to talk about it at the time. Indelicate."

"Indelicate," Carla mimicked him. "This feels a whole lot more indelicate."

"You want me to be transparent," said Gonzalo. "But I can't be transparent. We all have some opacity."

"You didn't talk to me about this because you want to go alone," repeated Carla.

"On Monday I'm going to make an appointment for us to get married." Gonzalo pretended he hadn't heard her. "We have to hurry with the visa applications. We still have several months, but it's better if we get a move on."

"You didn't talk to me about this because you want to go alone," Carla repeated again.

"We'll have to see about Vicente's school too. Tomorrow I'll write to some friends there, to see if they'll help us find a school and an apartment."

"You didn't talk to me about this because you want to go alone," said Carla for the fourth and final time.

They got in bed and stared up at the ceiling, as if searching for impurities in the paint or constellations in the night sky. Their sex was full of rage and desperation; it seemed like both of their bodies were covered in burns. Afterward they said atrocious things to each other, things they felt and others they more or less invented, but that once uttered took on reality and could not be erased or even clarified, explained away. Suddenly Carla fell silent and tried to argue with herself, though she was startlingly convinced that she was completely in agreement with herself.

At four in the morning she went out to the yard and ate a granola bar in the moonlight. She wasn't new to insomnia—she'd been inducted into it very early, at nine years old. Her mother took her to the doctor, who asked a thousand questions and ordered sleep tests. She had to spend a night with electrodes attached to her head and other parts of her body in a room decorated like a bedroom, with stuffed animals, an awful night-light, and dozens of photographs on the walls (all of people sleeping in pleasant positions, except for one skinny old man with a severe expression who looked more dead than asleep). Suddenly her mom appeared with a storybook and sat in an armchair to read to her—Carla's parents had never told her bedtime stories, and it's possible the experience only served to keep her even wider awake. Her mother left at midnight, and the next day, when the people in charge of the exam informed her that Carla hadn't slept at all and the exam had been useless, she was furious. Some months later Carla managed to sleep at night, though she usually woke up after two or three hours, sometimes for just a few seconds, others for the rest of the night. During adolescence, everything changed thanks to pills, though sometimes she dreamed the electrodes were still attached to her or that she couldn't scrape off the wax they'd used to stick them to her head, or that her room was really the bedroom in a clinic. Later, when Vicente was born, she slept badly as all mothers do, but sometimes she even felt that she slept better, because her sleeplessness made sense: she was taking care of someone, teaching him to sleep, telling him stories.

She was incapable of sleeping without pills, but sometimes she decided not to take them so she could remember what she was like, who she really was, like a nearsighted person who decides to leave her glasses on the night table and feel her way through the whole day. That night, for example, taking a pill and sleeping like a log would have been, for her, hypocritical, inauthentic; she needed those additional hours. She had just decided that her story with Gonzalo was over, and she needed to keep thinking until she wiped out any hint of doubt. But she didn't really have doubts. Maybe it was just about understanding whether breaking up with Gonzalo was what she wanted to do or what she should do or whether this was one of those rare occasions when desire coincided with obligation.

"Think of Vicente," what a ridiculous thing to say, come on: she'd been thinking about Vicente for twelve years now, and it would be impossible not to think about him even if she tried. She also thought about the dead fetus and felt like it was still in her belly, that it hadn't been fully expelled, that the D&C hadn't worked. She felt, bitterly, like the scraping was only now being completed. She thought: Vicente needs Gonzalo, he loves him like a father, loves him more than his real father, because Gonzalo raised him; Gonzalo loves Vicente like his own son but now I'm sure that sooner or later he's going to abandon him. And it's better to get it over with now.

She smoked, drank coffee, opened another bottle of wine; at nine in the morning she was still sprawled on the living room floor as though inventing yoga postures, completely awake and destroyed and a little drunk. She went to the bedroom, where Gonzalo was still asleep, his snores like fitful gasps. She shook him awake so she could tell him, without mincing words, to get out.

"I raised Vicente." Gonzalo was walking around the room in his underwear as if looking for his clothes or as if he were cold. "I raised your son. What do you think about that, how I raised your son?"

"And now you don't feel like raising him anymore," said Carla.

"Your son takes after me. It was thanks to me that you got to study. Everything you have is thanks to me."

He repeated the refrain twenty times, flooded with resentment: he felt like Carla wanted to obliterate him, kick him while he was down, kill him.

"I put him to bed a thousand times, two thousand times, I took care of him when he was sick. I drove him to school, I showed him the world, I taught him everything."

He's acting like a man, she thought; he yells the way men who aren't used to yelling yell, he cries the way men who aren't used to crying cry.

"Thanks to me you're not still a sheltered little girl, a brat, a daddy's girl. Your son takes after me, I raised him for you. You can't take him away from me just like that. You can't erase me. I have rights."

The last phrase was ridiculous and maybe that's why it hung in the air for a few seconds, even a full minute, like when a joke cuts a conversation in two. Except it wasn't a joke.

"What rights do you have?" Carla said finally, crying. "Get out of here now, go to New York or go fuck yourself."

Gonzalo took a long shower and went out to buy a mattress, which he set up in the little room outside.

He lived in the little room for two months, practically squatting. Every morning they fought for an hour or two and Carla told him he had to leave, he refused, then went to work or spent the day killing time downtown, and at ten at night, after faking stability fairly well in front of Vicente, he locked himself in the little room to read bad books, because the good ones only reminded him of the complexity of life, while the bad ones soothed him, gave him hope, made him sluggish. He felt completely lost. An earthquake, maybe that's what he wished for: that right then Chile would be hit by the most devastating earthquake in its history, that the house would collapse but the three of them would survive, and for a long time there would be no travel or plans because the future would consist merely of drawing out their survival— finding water, food, housing, and a certain fleeting, cherished joy.

Four days after they had their final blowout—an explosion of scream-ing and crying and erratic accusations—and Gonzalo definitively moved out of the house, he finally received, at his university office, his copies of *Memorial Park*. The first thing he did was dedicate one to Carla. He called her, as he had every day, and she answered with a new voice—an evasive, composed voice he didn't recognize. He asked her to meet him so he could give her a copy, and she congratulated him but said he should mail it instead. Gonzalo went straight to the post office, but his hand was trembling so much he couldn't manage to write the address on the envelope. He tried for ten minutes, ruined fifteen envelopes. He even tried with his left hand, which, oddly, trembled less.

"I don't know how to write," he said to a woman of about twenty who was watching him, first with skepticism and then with veiled pity.

The woman didn't look anything like Carla, but as he was dictating the address to her, Gonzalo thought she did. After mailing the package, he walked quickly through the crowds of downtown Santiago. It was as if he was being chased or was chasing someone or as if he wanted to prove to the world that, though he didn't know how to write, he did know how to walk.

He was panting when he reached the bookstore Metales Pesados, where he greeted one of its owners, the poet Sergio Parra. They had known each other forever, they'd been on speaking terms practically their whole lives, but they weren't friends. Gonzalo gave him two copies of *Memorial Park*.

"Why two copies? You want me to read it twice?" asked Parra, more out of mischief than malice.

"They're for the store," explained Gonzalo, his voice suddenly hoarse. "Or one is for you and the other is for the store. If it sells, let me know and I'll bring you more."

"I'll do that," promised Parra as he placed the book in the poetry section.

To Gonzalo, the possibility that a stranger would page through his book and end up buying it seemed every bit as flattering as it did remote. Still, he got caught up imagining that scene while he ate a tiny slice of baklava for lunch. He walked slowly through Forestal Park, toward Bellavista. He was planning to walk past the club where, six years before, he and Carla had found each other again, but he wasn't ready to close that circle. So he called his father, who claimed to be nearby, but even so Gonzalo had to wait half an hour for him. As they drove to Maipú, he told his father about the breakup and the grant to study in New York. He blurted it all out in a single run-on sentence, followed by a silence interrupted only by brief phrases and monosyllables. It wasn't the same taxi Gonzalo had ridden in when he was a kid—the old Peugeot 404 was now a Hyundai Accent—but he felt like it was, or rather he recalled, with unexpected intensity, those trips in the passenger seat—because back then, if there were no other adults in the car, kids rode in the passenger seat. They were work trips, there was no one to leave Gonzalo with, and his father made him crouch down so potential passengers wouldn't think the taxi was occupied. When someone got in the car, Gonzalo came out of hiding and started chattering away. Maybe back then that's what he was, exactly that and nothing more: a kid who liked to talk.

"Stay with us for a few days," his father said once they were home.

"Don't ask him that, you know he doesn't like it here, he's not from here anymore," said Gonzalo's mother.

It was a sterile, tedious, oppressive conversation. He still had a book in his backpack, but he didn't want to give it to his parents; he felt it was a waste. But in the end, he did. They congratulated him. They congratulated him several times, for the book and for the grant, but they didn't say a word about the separation—it was as if they'd been waiting years for that news. Nor did they ask about Vicente. They had never liked Carla, but supposedly they loved Vicente.

His mother paged through the book with a mixture of pride and distrust. Gonzalo thought he had never seen her with a book of poetry in her hands. They talked about the Memorial Park. They talked about the lech.

"I decided to get closer to my father because I felt like I was losing my son," said Mirta, with a cruelty that seemed so inevitable it didn't sound like cruelty.

He stayed over that night. The next day he got up early, ate breakfast with his parents, and spent some hours alone in the house after they left for work, unsure what to do. He lay down in their bed to watch TV while he tried out misguided theories and rushed conclusions about his life. The book—his book—was on his mother's nightstand. He started to read it. It was the first time he'd read it in print, and at that moment he knew it would also be the last.

He left, finally. He bought an ice cream in Plaza de Maipú. It was two in the afternoon, there were a lot of people on the street, but he walked until he reached a deserted spot. He heard the distant sounds of car alarms and an Amy Winehouse song. He sat down on the curb, leaned against the slender trunk of a plum tree, and lit a cigarette. He felt with absolute certainty that he had lost everything. I've just published a book, he thought. While he smoked and looked at the sky empty of clouds, he thought, joylessly, that he had published a book and he was, finally, a poet, a Chilean poet.

III. How to Become
a Chilean Poet

I 'm gonna eat your sweet pussy," Vicente says in shitty English, because he doesn't speak English, and the few words he knows are ones he learned from watching porn. Pru does know some Spanish, she minored in it in college, but just now she's not speaking Spanish, she's only moaning, most likely in English.

Vicente is eighteen and Pru is thirty-one, and they've just met: only a few hours earlier, after a somewhat tedious evening out with his poet friends at a bar in Plaza Italia, Vicente was waiting for the night bus when he saw a gringa vomiting at the bus stop and approached her, and although Pru's recent past didn't give her much reason to trust anyone, she instinctively trusted this tall boy with immense eyes who, without any questions or introductions, held her hair back while she threw up, and even gave her a shy caress on the nape of her neck, his touch like that of an ally or an accomplice. Pru said *Thank you* in English, and of course he was up to the task of replying with a *You are welcome*, but he chose to say *De nada*, and then they didn't speak any more for the ten or fifteen minutes of a walk to nowhere, because sometimes a person walks just to feel the purifying rush of wind in their face.

A few weeks before Pru had set off on her trip to Chile, a Chilean woman she met through a Belgian friend of hers at an overcrowded Greenpoint bar had assured her that, although Chilean taxi drivers were for the most part fascists, retired military men, and ex-torturers, fortunately or surprisingly they weren't in the habit of assaulting or kidnapping people—worst-case scenario, they'd spout some sexist and/or xenophobic nonsense or take the long route—so when in Santiago it was more or less all right to take a taxi at any hour. So, Pru hailed a cab and gave Vicente a hug and kiss on the cheek that would have been suggestive in the United States, but she'd been in Chile long enough to know that in Chile people are always giving each other hugs and kisses on the cheek, and although Vicente wanted to draw out the scene at least long enough to learn Pru's name, he did nothing to stop her, he said nothing, in part because he *couldn't* say anything that wouldn't sound frankly stupid, since he thought that even asking her name in English would, under those conditions, have an irritating schoolboy ring, and so he resigned himself to watching her leave. But when the driver looked straight at her tits and asked where she was going, as though in fact it were Pru's tits who would answer that question, and when she caught a glimpse of the man's face, a stony, irate face that could perfectly well be the face of a fascist-torturer-murderer, or a rapist's, Pru thought it was stupid to follow the distant advice of her Belgian friend's Chilean friend, a woman to whom she'd spoken for all of five minutes, because, come on, can it really be safe to get into a car driven by a fascist-torturer-murderer-rapist at two o'clock in the morning?

So Pru got out of the car and kept walking with Vicente, who was looking at her as if she were the single most fun person in the world, and he wasn't necessarily wrong, though just then there was no way Vicente could know that Pru was fun, because unless you find it entertaining when someone vomits in the street, nothing she had done up to that point was even slightly amusing. Pru showed him a card with the address of the hostel where she was staying, and now they were no longer walking aimlessly but were aiming for Providencia, for the heart of Providencia as some pompous tour guide might say. They had walked three blocks in silence when Pru again said to him, this time more solemnly and serenely, *Thank you*, and he told her in Spanish not to worry, it was his job, because Santiago de Chile was full of people throwing up on street corners, and every night he went around helping all those vomit exhibitionists, and Pru wasn't sure she'd understood entirely—she knew Vicente was joking, but she didn't quite get the joke. She was going to ask him to explain, but she didn't want to speak Spanish, she didn't feel up to it, she thought she would only trip over her words so she spoke to him in a slow and clear English that to Vicente was only slightly more intelligible than Cantonese, though he looked her in the eye and nodded like the best student in class, or like a not-so-good student, even a bad one, who only makes an effort because he's hot for teacher.

A block before they reached the hostel Vicente signaled to Pru and they stopped at a corner store, where he bought a large bottle of mineral water. They sat down on the curb to share it, and Pru began to tell him, hesitantly at first as though testing the waters, the story of how she had come to be in Santiago, and though her tale was pretty incoherent it didn't matter at all, because her listener was incapable of understanding her, which was ideal, because although Pru needed to speak freely, there was no one in the world she trusted enough to spill everything to. Under the circumstances, this stranger who understood little to nothing was the perfect confidant, better than the most qualified of therapists—she didn't want opinions or verdicts, quite the contrary, she wanted someone to merely listen or bear witness to her story, as Vicente was doing, with no questions or follow-ups, no compassionate gestures, no explicit words of solidarity.

Still, Vicente understood that Pru was talking about her trip to Chile and about San Pedro de Atacama and how on that trip something or maybe everything had gone wrong, and that a boyfriend or girlfriend had betrayed and abandoned her, and that the story he was listening to was sad, though she was trying to tell it as if it weren't. Vicente understood that Pru was laughing at herself and that her tone held something like a delicious humility, but also a certain brashness. He understood that, if he knew English, he would be hearing a variety of rhythms and emphases and dozens of jokes that Pru cracked to defend herself from seriousness. And he thought that if he ever had to tell a sad story, he would like to tell it the same way.

When the goodbye was becoming inevitable, Vicente was the one who set off talking about trips and solitude and the four times he'd flown in an airplane and whatever else came to mind, and Pru understood a lot more than Vicente had of her story. It was still a confused speech and it made her laugh, because it was clear to her that the only thing he wanted was to keep her there, and she delighted in that mixture of eloquence and nervousness, he was like a TV host transmitting live, forced to improvise—an entertaining host, a great host. And everything was fine because she didn't want to turn off the TV either, the last thing she wanted just then was to say goodbye: when the words slowed to a trickle, she hugged him in earnest and wanted the hug to last, and when he felt that considering the depth and duration of the hug it was almost impossible she would reject him, he gave her a shy kiss on the neck. Then she thought that she should not sleep with Vicente or with anyone, but she also thought, more or less at the same time, that she'd had such a bad time of it that she deserved a good screw with that friendly and beautiful stranger she would probably never see again, so she put her right hand on Vicente's ass, and with her left she firmly grabbed his package. That was when he said his first English words to her:

"Do you like it?"

The long kiss that followed still held a hint of vomit, but Vicente didn't care.

"You are really hot," he says now, in shitty English, while he licks Pru's thighs. "You are a really really hot girl. And I'm gonna eat your sweet pussy."

He wakes up at noon, amazed, moved, and anxious: he wants to remember everything, he feels a pressing need to take it all in, not just the details of the hookup, but also, for example, the features of this hostel room, which he didn't even glance at the night before—this provokes a kind of guilty throb in him, because Vicente believes it's the poet rather than the prose writer who has a responsibility to notice absolutely all the details of every lived experience, not in order to relate them later, not so he can shout about them in a story, but to inscribe them, so to speak, in his sensibility, in his gaze: in a word, to *live* them. Then he avidly inspects the emblematic images that decorate the walls: there are posters of Torres del Paine, Easter Island, Valdivia, San Pedro de Atacama, and Violeta Parra, Víctor Jara, Salvador Allende, Joe Vasconcellos, and also a small photo of Barack Obama, which he finds inexplicable, unless it's meant as some kind of welcoming gesture. He makes a mental note as well of the arbitrarily arranged handicrafts from Chiloé, the clay curios from Quinchamalí, some horrible swans made of raffia palm, and those tiny Mexican sombreros that are so common in Chile that an untrained eye might see them as another typical Chilean artifact.

What must the gringa think of all this? Vicente muses as he looks at her lying in bed, half-covered by a red blanket. He really wouldn't mind getting her phone number, but Pru is irrevocably asleep, and her even, tenuous snores betray, it seems to Vicente, a certain helplessness. He looks at the somewhat faded tattoo on the upper part of her back: it's the tangram of a ship, with the pieces slightly separated from each other. He caresses her hair one last time, though it's not exactly a caress, it's just that he wants to touch those blond locks, a little like a hairdresser planning out his work. He closes the door carefully and goes down to the reception desk, where he raises his eyebrows to greet an enormous bearded guy dressed or disguised as a hippie, who looks at him with a sullen expression while he timidly strums a guitar, as if he were just learning to play.

Vicente goes out into the merciless Santiago summer sun, and is about to head home when he gets a message from his father saying he is having lunch in Providencia at one-thirty and inviting him to come along. Vicente thinks about some locos with mayo or maybe some tempting sea urchins and he decides to go. He has over an hour to walk the ten blocks, but his happiness prevents him from taking it slow; people who walk slowly, he thinks, in a grandiloquent inner voice, are tired or wounded, and he feels a devastating joy, a happiness with no counterweight, a fullness that would be hard to convey in words: it would be possible, perhaps, to draw that fullness, on the condition that the drawing never stopped. He arrives too early at the restaurant and orders a glass of water, and though he is starving he doesn't touch the pebre and sliced bread the waiter offers him; better to be prudent, because he has no money and he knows that his father could, at the last minute, as he has on so many other occasions—about fifty percent of the time, in fact—stand him up.

He takes out his notebook, thinking how it's a miracle he didn't lose it in the excitement of the night, and he congratulates himself. He wants to write a poem, or more like the start of a poem, because for him a poem is a thing that one starts and only sometimes finishes. He immediately writes down the image that is hounding him:

zenithal light on the shell of a skin

How he likes that "zenithal light," it's so elegant. And he's been thinking a lot lately about skins and shells and peels. Because everything has a skin,

even skin has a skin, he thinks. And then he writes very quickly, in unintel-
ligible handwriting:

Even skin has a skin

Then he starts a new page where he drafts the poem in different handwriting, one that doesn't seem to belong to his generation of digital natives,
but that also, in a way, does, because strictly speaking, those characters
correspond to a skillful imitation of Times New Roman or Garamond:

even skin
has a skin
even the mask
has a mask
even the darkness
darkens
even the sun
revolves around
the sun

All the lines start with lowercase letters, because that's how poems are
these days, thinks Vicente; starting lines with uppercase letters, especially
the first line, is a sign of aesthetic conservatism.

He leaves the poem for later and starts another page, because he remembers his desire, his obligation to retain details, and he decides to list them
quickly:

—white skin
—walk
—Obama
—reddish forearms
—green eyes
—dirty blond hair

—scar on foot

—remains of dark red polish on toenails

—snoring

—shorter than me but still very tall

—pubic hair less blond almost brown

—noon

—tangram ship back

—flaky elbows

And then, on another page, another list:

—condoms

—anthologies

—letter or legal sized paper light blue

The verb is missing: *buy*. He wants to buy light blue paper, because he's gotten it into his head that his poems would look better printed on blue paper. But the main thing is to use his allowance to get his hands on a new anthology. He wants to own them all: the good, the bad, the monumental, the trifling, the thematic, the historic, the over-inclusive, the exclusionary, the cliquey, those labeled as "handbooks," the regional anthologies, the high school ones, the university ones, the bilingual ones, and especially those that include explanations of poetics, interviews, and a ton of portraits in which the authors look rebellious, dreamy, and beautiful. Anthologies are phone books for young poets, although maybe young poets won't understand the comparison, because they grew up in a world where phone books were falling out of existence. Even so, at Vicente's house there are a ton of phone books piled up on the patio, and so maybe, one of these days, he might write a poem about all those old phone books, especially all those names, all that information that's now pretty useless, all that wasted paper, all those outdated numbers. The condoms: his hookup with Pru reversed a tendency that until then had seemed intractable: every time he left his house with condoms he returned with them unopened, and he was convinced they brought him bad luck. Whenever he slid one into his wallet, he felt it was an act of unbearable naïveté and optimism. And back when he'd been dating Virginia, a beautiful redhead who was nearly bald (by choice), he always went out with condoms—not in order to use them, but as a way of thwarting himself and reinforcing fidelity. Another tendency that his one-night stand with Pru had radically changed, though he didn't know it yet, was his tendency toward sadness. His tendency toward daydreaming was left intact.

"We've started casual Fridays," is the first thing León says. He arrives a little late, but he does show up.

While Vicente devours, finally, the bread and spicy pebre, León opens his laptop and shows his son a meticulous Excel table with the accounts of the company where he works as a realtor. It's not his company, but he still tends to refer to it that way, pompously, affectionately, reveling in the possessive.

"We've consolidated," he says. "This thing is finally making money. That's why we have casual Fridays now."

To make conversation, Vicente asks who it was who decided they no longer had to wear ties on Fridays.

"Everyone, from the CEO down to the interns; we all met and voted, by simple majority."

Then León fakes a cough, which sounds every bit as stupid as those people who cough when they pass a person smoking in the street, but León is a smoker and his cough seems to signal a change in tone; specifically, the shift from relaxed small talk to serious conversation. Vicente knows this, so he takes his time ordering. He looks at the menu wishing he could hide inside it and fall asleep from boredom, because he knows what's coming. Over the years, his father has had very few serious talks with him. León is about to speak seriously now, and since he coughs artificially two more times, it's possible he'll be speaking *very* seriously. But the food takes a long time. It's tacitly quite clear that the serious conversation will begin when the food arrives. It's absurd, thinks Vicente: he should just come out with it, because if he waits for the food before starting the serious talk, at some point he's going to have to talk with his mouth full, or else be quiet to avoid talking with his mouth full, and none of that will look very serious.

When the food comes, in effect, it's as if a director had cried, Action!

"So, where are you going to apply? What are you going to study?" León feels ridiculous as he utters these questions. He feels ridiculous but also proud, because he sounds like a father, because fathers always ask those kinds of questions.

Vicente slowly chews his locos with mayo (and parsley and chopped onion), and looks with vague disgust at the blood sausages sprawled over some gigantic potatoes on his father's plate. And he stays silent, like the moody teenager he no longer is.

Several months ago, when he had just started his last year of high school, Vicente officially announced that he didn't want to go to college. It was a well-considered decision that neither his parents nor his teachers took seriously at the time. But Vicente held firm: he even fought against taking the university entrance exams, but in the end he took them, and when his results came two days ago it was just as he'd feared: he did pretty well, especially in language, and though his math score was disastrous, he could almost certainly choose from among several different options; the problem is that none of them really interest him. His plan for the coming year of 2014 is to dedicate himself to reading and writing, and to find a more stable job. (From time to time he dresses up as Patrick Star, SpongeBob's friend, for a toy store, but they don't always need him—Patrick is a secondary character, after all.)

And so, this is not the first time this conversation has happened. For two months now, almost every morning, it's been his mother's sole subject over breakfast. By now Vicente is used to hearing those long sentences in which the word *future* appears with abnormal frequency, and he's learned to let the pauses grow long. He is an intrinsically polite person and it's hard for him not to answer right away, but he has developed a strategy for this kind of conversation: he sits silently until his interlocutor, annoyed or restless at the absence of an answer, has no choice but to repeat the question.

León extrudes a sausage with the air of an expert and takes a few sips of his red wine, like an indecisive sommelier.

"What are you going to study?" he finally repeats.

"I already told you," replies Vicente apathetically. "I told you like a year ago. I've told you so many times."

"I always thought you were fucking with us."

"No, Dad, I wasn't fucking with anyone. I'm not going to college, at least not now. It doesn't make sense."

There is something endearing in Vicente's voice, an involuntary warmth. Something protective or professorial that, coming from a skinny kid with an incipient beard, circles under his deep-set eyes, and eyelashes only a little shorter than when he was a child, sounds comical.

"You have one day left to apply. What do you have to lose by just applying? Later on we can decide what to do."

"But if I apply and get in, I'm going to feel like I have to go, and I don't want to."

"But I can pay! If you don't get into a public university I can pay for a private one. They're almost all equally expensive in this damned country."

"There's no point in you going into debt to pay for my college. I already told you, I'll go to college when it's free," replies Vicente.

This is an excuse that appeared miraculously, one that Vicente latched on to at first in order to give more meat to his argument, but after he repeated it so much it finally became a conviction. He went to all the demonstrations for free education, and he even had a short-lived starring role as vice president of his school's student federation, and he really does trust in those young leaders like Giorgio Jackson, Camila Vallejo, Karol Cariola, and Gabriel Boric, who are still in their twenties and are now preparing to take their places, in March, in the Chilean Congress. And he also believes—a fair amount less, but he does believe—in the good intentions of the newly reelected president Michelle Bachelet. And he believes that education in Chile should be, as the campaign slogan promises, free and high-quality—although if he is honest, he has to admit that even if education were, right now, free and high-quality, he still wouldn't want to go to college, at least not right away.

"And do you really think all those sons of bitches are going to magically come together and agree to make education free?" asks León.

His indignation is false. If by some stroke of bad luck León was ever elected as a representative or senator or governmental authority and came to belong to that group he now refers to as *sons of bitches*, he would most likely act like one more son of a bitch. There is a tinge of impotence in his tone; sometimes he wants to be like those men of old who pounded the table and got their way. He would like to be able to force his son to study something, anything. The problem is that Vicente is a good son, and León's presumed moral authority is, at this point, totally fictional. Because he has basically been a bad father. A bad father who suddenly, just a couple of years ago, discovered that his son was funny and affectionate and even brilliant. And maybe he thought that if he was capable of—let's say—producing a son with those characteristics, he couldn't have been such a bad father.

Even though he sometimes forgets to call Vicente and tends to stand him up over invented emergencies, León enjoys his son's company, and he especially likes to show him off, introduce him to his friends; he exhibits Vicente as if he were the latest model of a car or a fashion model he was dating. Vicente knows all this, or at least he senses it. He suspects, even, something that León can't even begin to intuit: his father needs him much more than he needs his father.

"You can't be that naïve, Vicente. Do you really think education in Chile will ever be free?"

"That's what they promised," says Vicente with conviction.

"And do you really believe it?"

"That's what they promised."

"You believe politicians?"

"No, but I believe in the people's movement. And in the young representatives, the new ones."

"Those fucking kids don't know anything, they're just starting their first jobs. Their first jobs are going to be as elected representatives. Fucking great! They've never earned a peso in their lives!"

"Who did you vote for, Dad?"

"No one. We all knew Bachelet was going to win. I didn't vote. I went to the beach during the first round, and I was going to vote in the second but I got sucked into watching *Breaking Bad*. Goddamn, it's good, have you seen it?"

"Not yet."

"It's intense."

"I want to see it."

"Did you vote both times?"

"Yeah."

"Did you feel anything when you voted? Did you feel like you were changing the world?"

"I don't know. A lot of my friends didn't vote, they don't believe in the system."

"And you believe in the system?"

"Not much, but Bachelet promised free education and a new constitution."

"A new constitution! No way will they let the old lady do that. Or make education free. Vicente, please! No way. And even if it were true, even if education in Chile really was going to become free and high-quality"—it's better to just omit the scare quotes León employs with rudimentary sarcasm (think Homer Simpson); and anyway, if we were to try to represent his speech that accurately, he speaks so loudly that we'd have to write everything in uppercase letters, and this page would look awful—"even if all that were true and we could believe them, it's still going to take many years."

"How many?"

"At least ten years," says León, with the ease of one accustomed to tossing out numbers. "Maybe fifteen, twenty years."

"That long?"

"Well, in the absolute best of cases, with all possible political will and good luck and positive macroeconomic conditions—because that's really the fucking key—at least five, six years."

"In five years I'll be twenty-three, I'll still be young. I'll be like those wishy-washy students who change their major a thousand times until they figure out what they want to be when they grow up," says Vicente.

"You're afraid of failure. I was afraid of failure too when I was a kid, it's the most normal thing in the world," says León.

Vicente is not at all sure that his father has done anything other than fail, though it's true that it's hard for him to imagine what León understands success (or failure) to be. Of course Vicente is afraid of failure, that's precisely why he is resisting being herded along with the rest of the cattle. To fail, for him, would be to suddenly wake up in the middle of an insipid existence, doomed to serve out a life sentence in a miserable job.

"And you really don't know what you want to be?"

"Of course I do. You know, Dad," replies Vicente, tired of repeating it over and over. "Poetry. I want to be a poet."

"But you don't have to go to college to be a poet."

"That's exactly why I don't want to go to college."

"But you could study literature."

"I want to be a poet, I don't want to study literature. Or I want to, but not yet. I want to start school when I'm more mature."

León laughs and looks at him tenderly, he can't help it.

"But you *are* mature. You're a good person."

"Thanks, Dad, but I mean I'll be more mature as a poet. Less impressionable. Five years would be perfect. I could work and save money and travel and visit different countries and learn different customs and understand—"

Although Vicente is speaking very seriously, León bursts out laughing and gives him a quick pat on the head.

"Oh, my little poet, my Chilean poet," he says.

"Quit it, Dad," says Vicente, angry or offended or both.

"So where do you want to travel?"

"I don't know, places I've never been, there are lots. Temuco, Coyhaique, Punta Arenas. And to the north. Iquique."

"I thought you'd want to go to Paris or Rome or New York."

"That too, but later."

They are silent as they eat dessert: papayas with chirimoya alegre ice cream. They talk about soccer, which Vicente is no longer interested in, but stays up-to-date on precisely for this reason, so he'll have something to talk about with his father. And they drink coffee, they drink maybe too much coffee.

Pru and Jessye met at a master's program at the University of Texas and soon they were roommates, first in Austin and later in Williamsburg, where they lived in an old clothing workshop converted into a gigantic apartment where ten people could live comfortably, but where around twenty were living uncomfortably. They both worked at bars and wrote culture articles for emerging magazines, awaiting the elusive big break from a more prestigious publication.

The only thing they didn't share was a bed. Much of their time was squandered on dates that went nowhere, because they also shared an infallible instinct for taking up with the worst possible candidates: it was as if they intentionally went out with the stupidest, cruelest, most egocentric of men. Until Pru met Ben, a guy in his thirties with startling blue eyes who was finishing a computer science doctorate. Ben was from New York, which made him almost bizarre, because he was about the only person born and raised in New York Pru had met over the course of her five years there. All signs indicated Ben's parents were millionaires; they lived in a fabulous brownstone in Park Slope four blocks from Prospect Park, and Ben lived in the garden apartment that was completely independent of his parents, with whom he claimed to have bitterly fallen out. When Pru asked how he could be estranged from his parents while living in their house, Ben looked at her as if to say: *You don't understand anything about anything.*

Ben tended to spend hours in front of the TV watching stand-up comedy. He'd park himself on the sofa with some beers and a generous portion of mac and cheese, and there was nothing strange about that, but what *was* very odd was that he didn't seem to enjoy his pastime in the slightest. Ben gave the impression that, rather than listening to jokes, he was watching the thriving evening news of some Nordic country or a never-ending golf championship. In real life he did laugh, and his laugh was particularly booming, but when he watched the comedians, at most he would react with a slight curling of his lip that was pretty hard to interpret. At first Pru thought Ben took comedy so seriously because he wanted to be a comedian, and although he flatly denied his new girlfriend's hypothesis, it didn't seem so misguided: it was plausible that Ben wasn't watching those comedians because he found them funny but rather to learn—or maybe, more precisely, to study the tradition and get to know his peers, because he watched giants like George Carlin or Joan Rivers with the same attention he dedicated to contemporaries like Dave Chappelle or Louis C.K., or the brave upstarts who were just breaking into the stand-up scene.

That hypothesis would also explain why Ben was so averse to Pru keeping him company when he was in front of the TV. In the beginning, she would sit beside him with a glass of white wine and slip in witty remarks and laugh hysterically, but Ben ignored her completely, and though he was careful not to say it, it was clear he would rather be alone. The only person with whom Ben shared his hobby, or more like his silent addiction, was his cousin Martha, a forty-something woman who was morbidly skinny and spoke only in monosyllables, except when she was talking to Ben, with stunning seriousness, about the comedians' routines. Like her cousin, Martha didn't laugh when they watched, but unlike Ben she didn't seem capable of laughter in general, or even of smiling. Her pallid face seemed incompatible with expressing emotion.

One night, to celebrate their four-month anniversary—Pru's amorous instability was such that, like a teenager, she tended to celebrate every milestone from the get-go—she planned a surprise for Ben, but when they exited the subway and he realized they were headed for the Comedy Cellar, he pulled up short and said he didn't want to go there, he thought that place was awful. She dragged him in anyway, and he spent most of the time staring at the floor and laughing—it was a different laugh from his usual one, a discreet, uniform laugh, almost mechanical, whose hidden intention was to keep anyone from noticing he was having a terrible time. Pru thought Ben must be sweating so much because he was afraid the comedians would single him out, which she found irrational—Ben's life couldn't offer much in the way of fodder for crowd work (something like, "Where are you from?" "New York," "Oh, okay, sorry, I'm off to find some foreigner and make fun of their country"). After forty minutes it was quite clear that Ben was hating it—one might even say he was suffering—and they left.

That night, unexpectedly, as if he'd needed that unpleasant and erratic evening in order to reach a decision, Ben insisted on talking about the future. He told Pru that his intentions were serious, that he wasn't interested in wasting time, and he wanted to have a lot of children. Pru found this intimidating because, like so many adoptive New Yorkers, when she moved to the city she'd decided she wouldn't have children—she thought that having a baby would force her to put off her career, and although objectively speaking her career had long since stopped being promising and was in fact faltering, the illusion of being at the center of the world continued to work its magic on her.

Pru spent a lot of time at Ben's apartment, which wasn't easy for Jessye, who missed her, or for Martha, who still came over to watch TV with her cousin but had to resign herself to coming less often. One day at the beginning of autumn, as she was leaving Ben's house, Pru noticed Martha staring down at her from the second floor of the brownstone. Although she had asked Ben more than once, Pru still wasn't clear on whether Martha lived in the building or not. In any case, she waved casually; Martha didn't wave back, and she jerked away from the window with telltale awkwardness.

That same afternoon Pru went to Community Bookstore, and she caught Martha spying on her, camouflaged behind a novel by Cynthia Ozick. Pru had read and adored the novel, and it struck her as unlikely that Martha would also be capable of enjoying it. She didn't want to be prejudiced or paranoid, but during the next week the scene was repeated, with slight variations, at the stationery store on the corner and at a sushi restaurant. She wasn't sure whether to tell Ben or not. She was thinking off and on about that question one afternoon as she gazed at the dazzling Argentine parrots perched at the Gothic entrance of the Green-Wood Cemetery. She liked to watch them through her phone's zoom, though their cries sometimes seemed wrenching: it was as if the poor parrots aspired to be heard in the Argentina of their ancestors. That day she went into the cemetery and looked at the oaks and at some of the graves, and she was focused on a majestic maple, fascinated and entranced by the ardor of that almost unreal red that made her so love fall, when she became aware that Martha was there, very badly hidden behind a pine.

She still waited another week before telling Ben, whose reaction was disconcerting.

"We have to fix this right now," he said, as he texted his cousin. "No way can there be family problems. We can't be together if you have any problems with my family."

Pru replied that he himself had or claimed to have problems with his family, and Ben gave her a new look, a look that Pru found indecipherable and that later on she thought she should have tried to decipher, a look in which—and this thought came weeks later, when she was just starting to find the serenity to tell this story—she could read contempt and madness. In the now five months of her relationship with Ben, she had never felt as defenseless as she did then. They were naked, they'd been having sex all afternoon, and although Ben had only had one beer, Pru got the feeling her boyfriend had been drunk for hours or days. There are times, to be sure, when it's advisable or useful or necessary to think that our beloved has spent days or months or years or their entire life drunk.

Pru quickly got dressed, while Ben put on only his underpants. Martha arrived immediately.

"What's the problem?" she asked in a voice that sounded put on, almost a parody of a voice; the few words Pru had heard her say did not correspond to the timbre of that voice.

"Nothing, Martha. It's just, I think you've been following me."

"I'm not following you," she said. "Why would I follow you? Do you want me to follow you?"

"Well, maybe I'm wrong, I'm sorry. I don't want you to follow me, there's no need. We could go out together. We could be friends."

"Do you want me to follow you?"

Martha repeated the question three times, and she came so close that Pru could smell her breath, coffee or chocolate or coffee with chocolate, and maybe a little toothpaste. Pru didn't back away, but she looked at Ben in search of help or at least a hint of complicity. It was a quick look that said something like, *Tell me what to do* or *How should I deal with her*, or *Your cousin is a fucking crazy woman*, or *This is getting out of hand*. But Ben had brought a chair over to one corner of the room and settled into it to watch them. He could have sat on the sofa, it didn't make sense to bring that chair to that specific spot, though none of it made sense; it didn't make sense, certainly, for him not to intervene in the conflict. He looked at the two women with the same inexpressiveness as when he stared at the TV screen. Martha kept repeating the same question again and again, always with her mouth very close to Pru's face, and Pru thought she should defend herself, but the only way to do that was to push Martha.

It was Martha who struck first: she pushed Pru and kicked her three times while she was down. The blows were erratic, like those of a child trying to hit a piñata, or like fake karate moves, like someone who had just seen a karate class and was trying to re-create the movements. Pru got quickly to her feet. Amid the confusion and profuse tears she looked at Ben, imploring, but he stayed seated, gazing at them as if he were enjoying his front-row seat.

Martha pushed her down again. Pru managed to grab her ankles to neutralize her. She didn't want to hurt Ben's cousin, but Martha fell to the floor, and then he did get up and come over to them, furious.

"Let her go. If you hit my cousin, you're messing with my family," he yelled. "If you hit my cousin, you might as well hit my whole family, one by one. You might as well be trying to make me an orphan."

"I didn't hit her, I don't want to hit her. But I don't want her to hit me either."

"Let go of her right now and get down on the floor," Ben ordered her. Pru obeyed immediately.

While Ben repeated his warning unnecessarily, Martha started to kick Pru in the stomach and legs and butt. Ben didn't intervene, he only circled the scene as though marking off the radius of action, as if he were refereeing the fight. Pru was no longer crying, she didn't even scream; she wanted to scream, but she was afraid of infuriating her aggressor even further. Finally, Martha herself fell to the floor and burst into tears. And Ben went over to hug and console his cousin.

Pru ran out of the apartment, ran until she reached Prospect Park, and then she kept on running, passing several people who were running for exercise. She left the park by Grand Army Plaza, and then wandered aimlessly for about fifteen minutes before taking refuge in a deli, where she downed a hot coffee almost in one gulp, as if it were cool water. Only then, with a burned throat and an immediate acid reflux that at that moment felt purifying, was she able to call Jessye. She stayed in the deli to wait for her.

Jessye consoled her that afternoon and that night and the following weeks, the following months, which Pru spent practically shut in. She didn't want to report the cousins. She looked again and again at Ben's laconic Facebook page, not even daring to block him: anyone who saw his photos would think he was a totally normal guy, she repeated to herself, searching for some kind of solace. She decided she would never go out with anyone else, and she thought she would never feel safe again.

Seeking comfort, Pru moved into Jessye's room temporarily, but soon they decided to share it on a permanent basis. They pushed their mattresses together like two teenagers at a slumber party, and, with increasing frequency, they woke up in an embrace. One night Jessye came into the bathroom and saw Pru toiling away with a vibrator (the classic neon-orange rabbit). "I can help you with that," she told her. Neither of them had ever been with a woman before and they liked it a lot—it seemed a superior experience, incredibly full and satisfying, and they thought it was absurd that they hadn't tried it before. Pru, especially, thought so: some nights before falling asleep, she calculated the period of happiness they had missed out on, and she went back over her failed relationships one by one, remembering Ben and reproaching herself for not having known how to read the signs, which in retrospect she found unambiguous. She felt stupid for not having escaped in time, though she also thought that if she hadn't met Ben, maybe she wouldn't be with Jessye now.

She would often recall the bruises on her body, and felt as if they'd never faded from her thighs, her buttocks, her shins. She remembered Martha's idiot face, and she dreamed that the two of them drank coffee and talked about books, and also that they were teenagers and went to the same school and didn't know it: they ran into each other in the library, and Martha looked at her with contempt, or else smiled at her.

Why did she dream about Martha and not Ben?

Only one night did she dream about Ben, and in an incomplete or tacit way. Pru was a comedian, and she was about to go out onstage. It wasn't her debut but she was nervous, maybe it was her first performance before a crowd; she went over her opening jokes, listened in the wings to the presenter's voice, and only once onstage did she intuit Ben's presence. She felt panic and tried to look toward the corners of the bar, because she was sure that her ex was studying her from there, contemplating her with a beer in his left hand, because he was right-handed but always held the bottle in his left.

She woke up still blinded by the spotlights, but she was in her bed, in the middle of the night, in the complete darkness that she didn't like but was nonnegotiable for Jessye. She heard Jessye breathing beside her and brought her face closer, almost to touch. Jessye was sleeping soundly and peacefully, and Pru felt supported and loved as never before. She thought they should buy a king-sized bed and maybe look for an apartment of their own, a place where they could live as a couple, though what that meant was imprecise, because the only new thing in their relationship was the sex. The only new thing, in any case, was very powerful and inundated everything else, thought Pru that night, feeling emotional. She wanted to wake Jessye up to thank her or to ask her to never leave or to get her off. She had the almost unbearably romantic thought that she wanted to walk hand in hand with her. It wasn't that she wanted to shout to the world that they loved each other—she simply wanted them to walk hand in hand down any street.

The next morning they stayed in bed and fooled around for hours on end. They didn't get dressed until the afternoon, when they set off for a riotous pizzeria in Crown Heights. There they ran into Gregg Pinter, a writer friend who had just been promoted to senior editor of a magazine of growing importance, and they drank Maker's Mark standing up while they waited for their tables. It was Gregg, a consummate traveler, who talked to them of the lunar landscapes—so defiant, so incomprehensible, so irrationally beautiful—of San Pedro de Atacama: he really wanted to go and had been about to buy a ticket to Chile, he said, but when he was offered the new position he decided to put off all travel indefinitely. Jessye said that maybe she and Pru could go and write something for the magazine.

"Sure," said Gregg. "I'd love that."

"We're serious," said Pru, excited. "We'll write it together, we've never written anything together before."

"I'm serious too," said Gregg, with a generous smile. Maybe that exists: the smile of a person who has just acquired a certain amount of power and is willing to share it.

They agreed to iron out the details later. Gregg wasn't convinced they should write the article together, he thought maybe it could be two related articles, one about San Pedro de Atacama and another about Santiago or Valparaíso. At their table, while they devoured their pizza, Pru and Jessye googled images of Valle de la Luna and Laguna Verde and the El Tatio geyser and they decided they would go on that trip no matter what.

Two blocks from home on the walk back, Pru took Jessye by the hand, and Jessye hesitated for a second but then seemed to agree it was a magnificent idea. They walked those two blocks in a state of theatrical happiness. The next morning, Jessye found tickets that were a little cheaper than they'd expected and Pru called Gregg, who confirmed the assignment, but warned them he could only pay for one article and he didn't care whether they wrote it together or not. He asked them to make it as original as possible, though he didn't provide many criteria. ("Try to do something no other magazine would ever do.") With the euphoria of swift decisions, Jessye bought the tickets and they began to plan the trip: they would spend Christmas in the north, then they'd go to Santiago and maybe ring in the New Year in Valparaíso.

Then came three months that for Pru were idyllic, virtually perfect: she no longer thought about her misadventures with Ben, and suddenly her life as a whole was simple and solid. Jessye, on the other hand, spent that time tormented by horrible doubts; while for Pru being with Jessye meant exclusively that she had fallen in love with her best friend, for Jessye being with Pru made her wonder insistently if she liked women in general; that is, if she had always liked women, if she had always been a lesbian. Those torturous doubts crystallized into a few fleeting infidelities with other women, and one passionate and much more serious affair with an Italian woman she met at the laundromat. Twenty days before the trip she told Pru that she couldn't go to Chile, claiming she had to go to Arizona to be with her mother, who was sick.

"What's wrong with her?" asked Pru.

"They don't know yet," replied Jessye, who didn't lack the imagination to invent an illness, but thought that a less elaborate lie would somehow attenuate her transgression.

"Is it serious?"

"They don't know yet."

"Do you want me to go with you?"

"No."

Pru pictured Arizona and then the mysterious Chilean desert and she felt it was a bitter and arbitrary coincidence. Jessye disappeared the next morning, and Pru was riddled with suspicion. She had wanted to banish suspicion from her life for good, and she'd thought she had; it hurt her not to trust Jessye. The Chilean novels and movies they were theoretically using to prepare for their trip were there on her desk, but Pru no longer felt like doing anything. The day of the flight she called Jessye ten, thirty times, until Jessye finally answered and told her the truth. She'd wanted so badly not to hurt Pru that everything ended up even more painful. "Thanks to you, I've understood a lot of things," had been her melodramatic opening line, and she returned to it every time she felt the vertigo that creeps in when we know the effect of the next words will be irreparable.

Stunned with disbelief, Pru left for the airport. Her beautiful love story had become every bit as crude as the ones she used to confide to Jessye, and only to her. And maybe it was fidelity to optimism that made her think that, like in a sitcom, Jessye would appear at the airport at the last minute and apologize, but she didn't.

Pru got on the plane, spent the ten hours of the flight drugged, and walked like a zombie through the Santiago airport to catch her connection. She was forlorn as she boarded her second flight, then waited with false patience for the brand-new backpack she'd bought with Jessye one rainy morning just a few weeks earlier, and exchanged a hundred dollars for a quantity of pesos that seemed inexhaustible.

She looked for a bus, but, strangely, none of them were going to San Pedro de Atacama. She approached some drivers who were smoking and watching a soccer game on an immense cell phone. She asked them in Spanish how to get to San Pedro de Atacama, and the men looked at her with lecherous curiosity.

"Me entienden? Do you understand?"

"Sure we do," replied one of the drivers, condescendingly. "You want to go to San Pedro. I can take you to San Pedro, of course I can."

The men laughed, but Pru chose to believe they weren't making fun of her. She got into an enormous van in which she was the only passenger. The trip did not last two hours, as she expected, but a mere twenty-five minutes. By then Pru was already sensing some kind of mistake, but it still took her another hour to assimilate and evaluate it: she was in Hacienda San Pedro, a tiny town in the Atacama Region, and not in San Pedro de Atacama, in the Antofagasta Region. The mix-up wasn't that common, but neither was it rare: instead of landing in Calama or Antofagasta, Pru had flown to the Copiapó airport, which was called Desierto de Atacama—surely the reason for the mistake. All told, she was over eight hundred kilometers from San Pedro de Atacama.

It was Jessye who bought the tickets, thought Pru over and over; this wouldn't have happened if I'd bought them. If I had bought them, I wouldn't be a dumb gringa lost at the ass-end of the world.

León has the afternoon free, so he suggests to Vicente that they stop in at the Providencia bookstores. Vicente finds several books he wants to read, in particular an anthology of contemporary Irish poetry and a book of previously unpublished poems by Enrique Lihn, and although his father offers to buy them for him Vicente won't accept; under the current circumstances, with the application deadline in the immediate future, it would be like taking a bribe. In the end he chooses three very cheap books by poets who are fifteen or twenty years older than him, and who, if they'd been soccer players instead of poets, would be considered past their prime, headed for retirement, but since they are poets everyone still calls them *young poets*. The exercise of poetry doesn't pay, but it does notably prolong youth.

They sit down in a café frequented by prose writers, which Vicente detests—he doesn't detest prose or those specific prose writers, he couldn't detest them because he hasn't even read them (he rarely reads prose), but he knows that his father is bringing him here to see them, which in a way is like going to the zoo, though his father never took him to the zoo when he was little (maybe he wants to make up for that). He eats a piece of orange layer cake that he finds delicious, while his father keeps ordering coffees and also devours, as if he hadn't just had lunch, a chicken-and-avocado sandwich. León coughs falsely again to return to the conversation that Vicente in no way wants to continue, especially in the prose writer zoo, because he knows that his father has it in him to approach one of the writers to illustrate his arguments, so he fakes an urgent call from his mother and says he needs to go home right away. His father unexpectedly offers to drive him, and Vicente tries to resist because he doesn't really want to go home, but León won't listen, and they're already walking to the parking lot.

León wants to use the drive to insist on the matter at hand, and Vicente replies in monosyllables while he searches among the CDs in the glove box and doesn't find anything he likes. He puts in one by White Lion, a band that after a few seconds he finds horrendous. He listens to the first seconds of all the songs on the disc, and there are two that he thinks he's heard on the radio before. In a philosophical mode, he thinks that it's immensely sad that someone named León would like a band called White Lion. He tries to focus on the music, or rather on the image of his father listening to that album once upon a time, maybe with long hair and an outlandish mustache, and the image strikes him as funny, but then he remembers that this album is *currently* in the glove box of his father's car, which means it's likely that he *currently* listens to it, not in order to remember the old days but because *he really likes it*. He thinks how maybe León had listened to the album that very morning and it strikes him as an exasperatingly pathetic scene: his father on his way to work, his receding hairline, the wrinkles on his face treacherously betraying the passage of time (that adverb, *treacherously*, tends to appear in Vicente's thoughts, but not in his poems, oddly), listening to that schmaltzy, trivial glam rock with the window down, cigarette in hand, completely sure of his swagger and that he's nailing that vibe. He thinks that his father was afraid of failure and he failed. What would it have meant, for his father, not to fail? He thinks about that again, and it seems an unsolvable problem, a true enigma.

They're not far from home when Vicente realizes that his father has abandoned the idea not only of a serious conversation, but of any conversation at all, and it's clear that something is wrong, because he's not even talking, as he usually does when he drives, about the traffic or the lights or—and this is particularly irritating—about the very act of driving ("Now I'll turn left," "I'll just get around this guy, no problem," "I'm gonna have to turn on the windshield wipers"). León isn't saying a word, and when Vicente looks at him closely he notices that his father's face has turned purple or green or mustard and he thinks he must be about to have a heart attack, because he has always thought his father was going to die of a heart attack—in general he thinks everyone dies of that, and whenever he learns of a death he doesn't even ask about the cause, he assumes from the get-go that it was a heart attack.

Vicente asks him what's wrong and León replies in a faint voice that he's about to shit himself. And in a still-faint, truly remorseful voice, León asks his son if there's some bar or diner or a trusted friend who lives nearby with a bathroom he can use. Vicente tells him to just drive fast, that he can use the bathroom at his house, but León staunchly refuses.

"I haven't seen your mother in fifteen years, how can you think I would see her now, under these circumstances?" The pain obliges him to take a wrenching pause in the middle of the word *circumstances*.

It's not fifteen years, actually, it's been longer than that. Since they separated, when Vicente had just learned how to crawl, seventeen years have gone by. After the breakup came a long period when León didn't see his son, almost a full year, until he and Carla agreed on the trade-off protocol that we already know about, though sometimes León took his time fetching his son from his parents' house, and it was also not uncommon for him to vanish for the whole weekend and to shunt the responsibility of the visits onto his dull but willing parents.

At various moments of his childhood, but especially a few years ago, at fourteen or fifteen, Vicente became obsessed with the matter: he wanted to know why it was impossible to get Carla and León together. Not *back* together, that didn't even cross his mind; he merely wanted to know why it was impossible to see them at the same time, in the same place: it was like a play where one actor interprets two roles. When Vicente's questions grew insistent he received tedious, seemingly rehearsed replies. It was as if on the day of his parents' separation, instead of doing what normal people do—yell, apologize, wound each other, and cry and screw one last time while considering the idea of a reconciliation, to then, two minutes later, yell and wound and cry again, and so on until giving or hearing one final slam of the door—as if instead of or in addition to or after all of that, they had sat down civilly in front of a Word document to outline a rigorous code of conduct. Something like: "We will never reveal the reasons for our separation, but neither will we foment a sense of mystery. The answers to our son's questions will not be evasive, but direct. We will have no physical contact, since we both wish never to see each other again, but we will not let tension build up about this." Of course, they didn't draft any such agreement, but in practice Vicente felt as if they had.

For the rest of the drive, which isn't much longer, there is no place where they could ask for a bathroom, leaving León no option but to use the one at Vicente's house, which was also once his. So, while his father contracts all the muscles in his body, Vicente takes out his phone and calls Carla, who has Fridays free because the weekly paper she works for comes out on Thursday, but who may not be home, as she sometimes takes the day to wander Santiago's streets taking pictures for her personal projects. Vicente likes the idea of being alone in his house with León, for the first time ever on his own turf, though he understands that his father will spend a good portion of that time shitting.

It turns out that Carla is indeed home and she is scandalized at the very idea of León using their bathroom, and she employs the very Chilean phrase "ocupar el baño," and in this instance the wording seems perfect, because to Carla, León would in fact be *occupying* the bathroom, that is, it would be like the wrongful reconquest of a lost colony. And yet, ten seconds later Carla seems to have changed her mind. She tells her son there's no problem, of course, he should tell his father he's welcome to use the bathroom, it's absolutely fine, and Vicente, surprised, tells León as much, and León is appreciative but still roundly refuses. He is determined to drop his son off in front of the house and then go in search of a bathroom, though he doesn't like the idea of stopping the car at all, because he has the certainty, much more superstitious than scientific, that if he makes the awful mistake of pressing the brake to the floor, he is going to let go and shit all over himself, and the upshot of this is that instead of driving fast, he advances with exasperating slowness, and although the honking horns assail him and he feels them reverberate in his body, like they're shaking him and may just expedite the disaster, it's still better to drive that way, like someone with OCD who slows down to catch all the green lights, than to stop the car. León speculates that the best thing would be for Vicente to jump out of the moving car, like people do in movies—León makes a great effort to convince himself that in the immediate future he will manage to drop his son off in front of the house without completely stopping the car and that then he will find a restaurant or an empty lot, and he thinks that even if he has to act like a monster again . . .

This last thought must be explained, because it has no relationship to a moral judgment; it's not a metaphor about some occasion when León behaved monstrously, but rather a literal image. To wit: Many years ago, when he was in his last year of law school, some months before meeting Carla and getting her pregnant (nearly simultaneous events), León went camping with three friends at Nahuelbuta National Park, and on the way back, while they lunched on some pork sausages and potatoes in Cañete, they decided to extend their trip by camping for a few days at Lanalhue Lake. They didn't have much money left and the cost of setting up a tent at the lake's official campground seemed exorbitant, so they backtracked a few kilometers to set up somewhere on their own, illegally, on a completely deserted part of the shore. It was a great idea: that evening they cranked up the music and smoked weed and got drunk on tequila (which was a novelty for them), looking at the full moon head-on above the lake, and the next day they cooked up some oily noodles with meat and red peppers.

Immediately after lunch, León found a favorable spot for his throne, nonchalantly pulled down his pants, and began his labor straightaway, with a perfect view of the magnificent lake: he could see almost all of it, only the end to his right was outside of his range of vision, but he could imagine the tourists all packed in together, camping like ridiculous Boy Scouts, while the opposite end was completely empty. He could also make out, exactly across from him on the other side of the lake, three dots that had to correspond to three people; the only explanation for their presence was that they had decided to circle the entire lake. At first he thought that, from what he knew of the lake's diameter, they would pass by his improvised hideout in about twenty minutes, but suddenly he realized that those graceful ellipses were moving much faster than a walk, and he also understood that his own evacuation was and would continue to be slow and long, because he was, to use a false metaphor here too, very full of shit. Five minutes later the dots were already on his left, and then very shortly thereafter he could clearly distinguish the blond hair of three women who were jogging; really they were three young girls, around nine, ten, twelve at the most, and they weren't exactly jogging but rather running and taking balletic leaps; soon they would pass right by the place where León was shitting so continuously, so uninterruptably. He felt a supreme anxiety at this imminent confrontation, and he reached out his arms as far as he could to gather some branches to cover himself, and when the girls passed a meter and a half from where he was, a second before they would see him, he stood up a little, and, covering his penis and face with the branches, he let out the howl of a werewolf or some other mythological or cinematic monster. León managed to divert the girls a couple of meters away toward the shore, though he didn't mean to scare them as much as he did—they fled in terror, and their cries, their shrieks, hung in the air for a long time. Poor things, no doubt they remember the monster of Lanalhue Lake to this day; it's possible that the monster of Lanalhue Lake still appears at crucial moments in their nightmares.

So, that's the experience León is recalling when he thinks that if he could find an empty lot he wouldn't care if he had to *act like a monster* again. But he's already in front of the house, and at the gate he sees a woman who, if he'd seen her on the street, would have vaguely reminded him of Carla, but since he sees her in front of the house where they'd lived together seventeen years ago, he understands that it *is* Carla. His impression is that his ex-wife has been, as some books are, corrected and expanded over time—actually, he doesn't think of it like that, because he isn't given to bookish comparisons, but he feels something along those lines: that Carla has been expanded, because she is notably fatter, and also corrected, because she looks radiant, more beautiful, even, than seventeen years ago: the extra kilos (curiously, there are also about seventeen of them) are maybe not extra because they give the impression of a woman in full command of her age, self-aware, indifferent to the juggling acts of diets and tenacious addictions to Bikram yoga that her peers suffer through.

León runs toward the house, greets Carla with a kind of involuntary bow, which with his ass so tightly clenched is about the only possible greeting, and although for a moment he considers using the second-floor bathroom, the very idea of going up the stairs seems crazy, so he locks himself in the main bathroom and Carla can't contain her sarcastic giggle, and now she is sitting in the living room, somewhere between annoyed and amused by the situation: she would like to head out to the grocery store and linger in the air freshener aisle, to then come home and spritz triumphant aerosols of lavender or wildflowers in the bathroom and all over the house until she completely erased the fetid traces of her ex-husband. But she doesn't do any of that. She stays on the sofa, waiting, because it seems almost imperative to make the most of León's unexpected presence (his physical presence, she thinks) in order to talk to Vicente. That's why she changed her mind, that's why she let León use the bathroom: she imagines an uncomfortable but opportune conversation that will make clear once and for all that Vicente needs to study something. Her expectations are optimistic, disproportionate: she imagines that that very night, after a forceful and productive argument, her son will, finally, apply to college.

Vicente sits down facing her, and the living room temporarily becomes a waiting room, and the situation is so strange that the natural thing would be to lighten the mood by exchanging a few jokes, but they both stay quiet, their heads almost pressed together, as if they were waiting for some crucial news of life or death. He is about to see his parents together, which in a way thrills him, even though he is no longer so obsessed with the matter and he doesn't know very well what that thrill stems from—perhaps he would describe it as mere curiosity.

"When your dad gets out of the bathroom, we're going to talk about your college application," says Carla suddenly.

It's a tactical error the size of a barge, because at this clear ambush Vicente loses his excitement or curiosity about finally seeing his parents share the stage, and he immediately tells Carla that he's sorry but he has to go, and he grabs his backpack and shouts in the direction of the bathroom, with a slightly comical familiarity, "See ya, Dad!"

Meanwhile, as he labors, León thinks conventionally about the past, about the relentless passage of time, about the brief period when he lived in that house attempting the tragicomedy of a forced marriage. It had all been so fast and confused; what people usually live in four or five years, they had lived in under two: the pregnancy, the ill-advised whirlwind wedding, Carla's parents' stubborn and authoritarian insistence on giving them the house, Vicente's birth, the annulment. Back when he'd lived there he used to play the harmonica while he shat, which Carla found particularly irritating; though he tried to play quietly to keep from waking the baby, he didn't always manage, because the harmonica is not meant to be played softly, and it's not easy to ration your breath. Maybe I should have kept going with the harmonica, León thinks now, because although he tried to play songs by Bob Dylan ("Just Like a Woman" and "Like a Rolling Stone"), Neil Young ("Heart of Gold"), and Los Peores de Chile ("Chicholina"), he always ended up playing the famous and eternal melody of spider and spout.

Back then the downstairs bathroom had held a magazine rack he'd bought himself at the Bío-Bío flea market, which featured a few issues of *Barrabases* and some *Vanidades* and several installments of *Condorito*. Why didn't I take the magazine rack with me? Where is it now? Can it be that neither my son nor Carla reads in the bathroom? Vicente, who reads everywhere, apparently does not read on the toilet, or else he doesn't keep his reading materials in the bathroom, thinks León. As for Carla, he remembers her reading in the living room, maybe in the lead-up to some argument.

That's how he finds her half an hour later, reading in the living room.

"I'm sorry," says León.

"And here I thought you'd never apologize to me," she replies in a voice a little hoarser than the voice in León's memory.

Of course it's a joke and León laughs, but then, as if he felt the need to withdraw the laugh, he turns serious:

"I'm apologizing for having come in like this, after all this time, to use the bathroom."

Carla looks at him with pointed contempt.

"Still, it's good to see you," she tells him then. "Maybe we should meet up for coffee, to talk about Vicente."

They've already talked about that; in fact, given the situation, their emails have been more frequent lately, though no friendlier or less curt.

"Anyway, he's not going to apply now," says Carla. "It's a lost year."

"Let's at least get him to enroll in the second semester or next year, especially now that things are going well for me," says León. "And for you too, apparently. You're the photography director at a magazine, right?"

"Art director."

"We can pay for tuition."

"You always thought that," says Carla.

"Thought what?"

"That things were starting to go well for you," she says.

It's true. Seventeen years ago, when he worked as an attorney at a firm in Providencia, León felt like he was doing well, that good things were just around the corner. And that Carla and Vicente were added baggage that would only slow him down. He would look at Carla nursing the baby in bed and think of them as one single thing, a single entity.

After work one night, he'd been about to enter the house, but in a moment of inspiration he decided to keep going. Just that: he kept going, walked a few blocks, and stopped at a corner. And he took a bus downtown, got off at a bar, and woke up at nine in the morning, hungover, between two sleepy whores who were drinking Nescafé and watching TV.

"I'm sorry, I couldn't make it back," he told Carla later, over the phone.

"Why couldn't you?"

"I didn't want to."

"Why are you doing this to me?"

"Because I can."

He went home that night, but Carla had changed the locks. León pounded on the door while she paced the house with the baby in her arms, soothing him. He pressed his ear to the door and heard Carla's sweet, nervous voice singing a lullaby. Then he left. León felt like he should get angry, like he should fight back—it was his house too, after all—but he was walking faster and more lightly as he walked away, and he loved that. He wasn't even interested in being right. He just wanted to be single again. He just wanted to play the harmonica in peace, as loud as he could, while he shat.

The mystery that Vicente vaguely imagined didn't exist. There was no extraordinary, sinister, illicit, or spectacular situation that needed to be kept secret all those years, one that would explain the absolute distance they'd maintained for so long. The story was so asinine that it was better to presume there was a secret, but no, there wasn't: it was just that Carla had gotten mixed up with a jackass, and then, when she got pregnant, she had acted innocently and obediently, like the good girl she didn't want to be, in order to make her parents happy and to believe herself that she was in love and that it made sense to try to make a family.

Then came a time of bitterness, assuaged by the heroic saga of maternity. Carla hated León, but it was an abstract hatred, because she hated herself much more: she depended on her parents, who never missed an opportunity to rub that in her face, and every time she heard the word *future* she felt like vomiting. But then she'd watch her son collecting pebbles in the weeds or running with other kids, waving at her, seeking her out, blowing her kisses, radiant, and she found him so intoxicatingly beautiful that sometimes she thought his beauty would succeed in rousing her, would return to her all she had lost. But Vicente's existence also functioned as an incessant, ferocious punishment; a punishment she had chosen willingly, but an incessant and ferocious one nonetheless.

"If things are really going better for you," says Carla as they're saying goodbye at the gate, "if you really feel like things are going well, you should replace that car."

"It's from 2009," León replies, disconcerted.

"But we're in 2014," says Carla.

"It's still 2013," says León.

"Yeah, you're right," replies Carla mockingly. "It's still 2013. Two more days till your car turns into junk."

And they both smile a little: very little.

Hacienda San Pedro was a quiet town of five hundred people that had nothing like a hotel or a hostel. At the walls of the eponymous hacienda, now converted into an olive factory, there was a stand selling churrasca bread. The vendor explained to Pru, in an amiable tone that was not without irony—an irony frequent in Chilean Spanish, but still imperceptible to her—that she wasn't the first tourist to come to Hacienda San Pedro by mistake.

"Mistakeville, that's what this place should be called," said the man, laughing at his own joke.

She talked to five other people who were friendlier, more compassionate. One woman said Pru could stay with her; she lived with her two young daughters and she baked pan amasado. The house was small and made of white-painted brick, and Pru's bed was a tattered but enormous blue sofa that filled almost the entire living room. She took off just her pants, covered herself scrupulously with two blankets, and only when she was sure the whole family was asleep did she break down and cry. Hers were the muffled sobs of the outsider, of one who isn't authorized to cry, a weeping that could be confused with the howling wind or the cries of distant ghosts.

She woke up at five in the morning. Her hostess was kneading dough, absorbed in an unbroken soliloquy that to Pru sounded like a prayer. Then, at six-thirty, the woman asked her to help carry the big baskets of warm bread to the shop two blocks away. It was Christmas Eve and Pru was sorry the store didn't sell anything that could pass for a real gift, but she bought some candy for the girls. She waited for them to wake up and gave it to them, and when she was about to leave they gave her a gift in return: an imitation Barbie, on which they'd drawn some red nipples and a bit of blue pubic hair; they'd even managed to cut its blond hair a little so the doll could sport the same style as Pru.

Grateful, she stashed the doll in her bag and hitchhiked to Copiapó, the nearest city. She could have tried to get on a bus and sleep the fourteen hours that separated her from her original destination, but she didn't want to—her plan was to find a safe place to stay, and she didn't think much beyond that. She checked into a small hostel near the Plaza de Armas and spent the rest of Christmas Eve sleeping.

The next day she talked for a while with a tour guide who was quiet in Spanish but became unexpectedly loquacious in English. Pru belatedly realized the guy had memorized, as if they were lines for a play, long paragraphs of a tourist brochure on the area—an area that, as he repeated with some insistence, was less popular but every bit as good as San Pedro de Atacama. She thought about staying to see those theoretically marvelous places, like Pan de Azúcar or La Virgen Beach, and when she found out they were about to start filming a movie in Tierra Amarilla about the miners who'd been trapped in the San José mine three years before, she thought maybe she could write about that, but the truth is she just didn't know what to do. She spent almost an hour on the La Paz bridge looking down at the Copiapó River, which was completely dry. An older, nearly elderly woman came to smoke beside her, and in a Spanish as slow as her drags on the cigarette, she told Pru how a lot of palm and pepper trees had been planted along the shore, and that the city was building a park called Kaukari that would permanently revitalize this sector. Pru was left thinking about that future park, trying to picture it as intently as she tried to imagine the erstwhile torrent of the lost river. Before leaving, she took one last look at that dusty riverbed where stray dogs abounded and children rode their bikes and skateboards, bearing the sun on their faces joyfully, bravely.

Two days later she left Copiapó, trying to believe it had been a good trip after all, and that all of her mistakes, from Ben onward, would start to make sense over time. On her first night in Santiago, she slept for fifteen hours. The next day she set off on a long walk downtown under the punishing two o'clock sun, thinking obsessively about the street dogs, which apparently wandered not only around Copiapó, but throughout Chile. "They're called quiltros," said a very young waitress, almost a child, whom Pru chatted with at the restaurant where she ate some porotos granados.

She walked toward the city center thinking of proposing an article to Gregg about those stray mutts, the quiltros. The idea was brilliant, in its own way: she would follow some of them at a discreet distance, merely describing their trajectories, and she would take photos and alternate the story with facts and information about the lack of protection for dogs in Santiago and Chile in general, and maybe she could interview animal rights activists, because there must be some, she thought, sitting down on the front steps of the National Library, right beside a beautiful mutt with a pink nose and abundant black fur that was gray around his eyes and on his chest.

She looked at the crowd that filled Alameda in spite of the heat, and she remembered the day when she'd spent a full hour sitting in front of the New York Public Library, waiting for Ben. She'd felt like she was on a stage that day, part of the scenery for the hordes of tourists taking photos, many of them armed with the newly invented selfie stick. Here, on the other hand, though the National Library's neoclassical building was beautiful, no one even glanced at its facade, no one noticed the people sitting on the steps, no one took photos, not even tourists: people walked toward Paseo Ahumada or Santa Lucía Hill looking straight ahead, or really almost always staring at the ground, as if they were afraid of tripping. It was strange and sad but also pleasant, because she had always liked places where she could look without being seen.

Right as Pru was leaving, the dog woke up—it seemed confused, and it took a few seconds to stretch and look around. It stared straight at Pru and gave a few short, intense yawns before trotting off toward Santa Lucía as if it were an executive who'd remembered an urgent meeting at the last minute. Pru followed from a distance, walking fast so as not to lose sight of it. The dog stopped on the corner and seemed to be waiting, like the humans around it, for the green light at the crosswalk. Pru stroked its head and spoke to it in Spanish, and the dog responded with a conventional pant, as if it were necessary for it to say, *I'm a dog.* She went on flattering it in Spanish and then felt stupid, because she remembered that she could talk to it in English. She decided to name it Ben, not in honor of her ex but in order to replace him with someone in whom—she loved this thought—she could actually trust.

They crossed Alameda together and got lost down the side streets. Sometimes Ben jumped up on her, like a child getting tangled up in his mother's legs. They walked for many blocks until they came to a McDonald's, where the service took so long that Pru was afraid the dog wouldn't wait for her outside, and it took her even longer because she had to go to the bathroom to dump the Coke in the sink and fill the cup with water. Of course Ben went crazy at the hamburger smell, but she didn't give it to him immediately, she wanted to find an empty street, ideally one without homeless people, and the dog got anxious and started to bark at her, and although the sensible thing would have been to drop the bag, Pru started to run and the dog to hound her with fierce, menacing barks. Finally they came to a small, charmless plaza, and at the foot of a towering poplar Ben wolfed down his quarter pounder with cheese and his large fries, then spent a little longer finishing off the cup of water with his delicate, elegant lapping. Pru got into a taxi that the mutt followed for two full blocks; he only barked a little, though, accustomed as he was to defeat.

She spent the afternoon in various cafés, trying not to think about anything. It was almost ten when she decided to go into a restaurant; it looked expensive, but she wanted to try the famous Chilean shellfish. Some Brazilians who saw she was alone invited her to sit with them, and they were nice and talkative and possibly millionaires, because they ordered everything, and Pru ate machas a la parmesana, dozens of oysters, locos with mayo, and sea urchin, and she even dared to try a piure, which is like the cocaine of shellfish. She thought she would never get rid of the aftertaste, and she downed a couple glasses of an expensive white wine with the sole purpose of changing the taste in her mouth. The night was shaping up to be a long one, but then the Brazilians stood up and suddenly, without much ceremony, took their leave. Pru walked toward Plaza Italia promising herself that never again in her life would she eat anything that came from the sea, and then she vomited and then she met Vicente and we know what happened then.

She wakes up at three in the afternoon, starving. She orders a pizza that she eats while Skyping with her mother and stepfather. She doesn't go out until six, and it's dark by the time she heads back to the hostel. She wants nothing more than to lock herself in her room to read or think or sleep, but Vicente is in the lobby, with a friend, waiting for her.

Pato is Vicente's best friend and maybe also his worst, because relationships between Chilean poets tend to not be straightforward. A Chilean poet sooner or later finds his true Chilean poet family, but in this case we're not quite there yet: for now, Pato and Vicente listen to and respect each other, they share pursuits, drunken nights, and tribulations, but while Vicente is still stumbling Pato is already on track, he has glimpsed the path to success, a success that is only relative and yet clearly distinguishable from failure. Still, most Chilean poets do write about failure, so one might say that there are Chilean poets who write about failure and succeed, and there are Chilean poets who write about failure and fail.

The promise of definitive success or relative success or non-failure basically consists of publishing some poems in an anthology at as early an age as possible, and then right away venturing a book or at least a chapbook for which you get someone to write a few words of praise for the back cover, hopefully someone important like Raúl Zurita, although by now practically every Chilean poet has been praised, likely with the same adjectives, by Raúl Zurita, the greatest blurb-maker of Chilean poetry and Latin American poetry and possibly the entire world. Maybe saying it like that sounds mean—one could also say that Raúl Zurita is the most generous of the Chilean poets. In any case, maybe true success means that the chapbook, in addition to Zurita—who must be asked for a blurb no matter what—would also boast the name of someone as respected as Zurita but less conspicuous. Vicente, at any rate, would never dream of asking for a blurb from Zurita, for whom he has an immense and timid admiration, or from anyone else, because in this matter and a few others he is very shy. There are so many shy Chilean poets that they could fill an abundant anthology, which might actually be a good idea, because the shy Chilean poets are so shy that they appear in practically zero anthologies. There are people who say it's precisely those poets, the ones who aren't featured in any anthologies, who are the good ones, the ones who are really worth your time.

But the path to success starts even before the first book or chapbook. Excluding school contests and the publication of poems on social media, the first real flirtation with recognition comes with the verdict of the Neruda Foundation, which chooses ten young poets every year to participate in a workshop that includes a small but not at all inconsequential monthly stipend. Vicente and Pato had both applied at the end of last March, and when Vicente found out he'd been passed over he called his friend immediately to commiserate, only to learn that Pato had in fact been chosen. What Vicente felt then was something more complex than what is usually codified in the word *envy*, but still, yes, that's the word.

"Don't worry, you're young, you're two years behind me," Pato consoled him. "You're still learning, finding your own voice."

Emboldened by success, Pato misses no opportunity to display his command of the scene and his generational awareness. His fellowship at the Neruda Foundation has just ended and it could be said that his life is forever changed, because now he knows a ton of under-thirty poets and has even made use of his platform to cultivate friendly relationships with several of the under-forty poets, whom he holds in contempt even while he's aware that that contempt serves him little, at least for now. Vicente, meanwhile, isn't even sure of his own poems. He works conscientiously, starts at least one poem every day, but he's reluctant to show anyone the results because he doesn't think they're good enough. What's more, he suspects his poems don't really fulfill the requirements, that they won't fit in, because if everything Pato spouts can be believed, the truly new Chilean poetry has a duty to be political, the truly new Chilean poetry must fight, head-on and without eschewing literality, against the capitalism and classism and centralism and sexism of Chilean society. And Vicente, though he subscribes to those struggles, is not sure that his poems express a social dimension in a clear enough way. Pato's poems do talk about contemporary issues: they are pointed, fierce, iconoclastic. They are celebrated at the readings he periodically takes part in, and the student leaders of his university congratulate him. He's going places, they say. Vicente isn't crazy about Pato's poems, and Pato himself doesn't even seem to like them much: it's as if he were writing them to satisfy some external need. Still, sometimes Vicente wishes he wrote like him.

Pato tends to hog the spotlight, and that's why it's so hard for him to accept that Vicente is the star tonight. Vicente, for his part, doesn't want to sound like he's bragging, so he comes out with the details little by little, as Pato listens to him with a mixture of interest and resentment, almost as though he were saying out loud, *This should have happened to me.*

"Maybe the gringa will want to sleep with us both," Pato says, after considering the idea a few seconds.

Vicente thinks it's a joke, and the idea of a ménage à trois that includes his friend doesn't strike him as all that exciting, but Pato runs with the idea and tries to convince him they should go to the hostel together to look for the gringa. Vicente wants nothing more than to see Pru again, but he only agrees after Pato promises he won't try anything, that he'll limit himself to acting as interpreter, because Pato does know English, he says.

Halfway there, on the bus, Vicente is already regretting the decision and suggests they do something else, but Pato won't be deterred. Twenty minutes later they're in the hostel lobby. The receptionist is not the bearded hippie Vicente saw the night before, but a skinny, short, blond guy who is *also* slowly strumming a guitar, possibly the same one: perhaps, Vicente thinks, the job description includes the constant, apathetic playing of that guitar. Pru isn't in her room, so the boys wait for her in the lobby, paging through the books Vicente bought earlier.

"Nihil novum sub sole," Pato says pompously and disdainfully, pointing out a poem to his friend. "Pure technique. You can tell this guy knows how to write poems, but he's got nothing to say."

"Nulla dies sine linea," replies Vicente, not to be outdone, and the phrase is a non sequitur, but it's the only Latin saying he can remember.

"What does that mean?"

"That you have to write every day," says Vicente.

"Oh. Labor omnia vincit," adds Pato, without mentioning that this was the motto of his high school.

"Sure," says Vicente, not wanting to ask what the words mean.

Pru appears a half hour later, wearing sunglasses, a bottle of mineral water in her right hand and an iPad in her left. She reacts to the boys' presence with stifled terror. In addition to the shock of seeing someone she thought she'd never see again, she has the sudden impression that Vicente could be underage; the night before she'd thought he must be at least twenty, but she hadn't asked. She imagines the juicy news story of a U.S. citizen accused of seducing a Chilean minor, and realizes she doesn't even know whether the legal age in Chile is eighteen or twenty-one.

She feels calmer when Vicente smiles at her. The receptionist asks, in an English striving to sound British, if these boys are friends of hers, and she nods and asks him to give them a moment alone. The guy takes the guitar out to a courtyard and lights a cigarette while he plays, with feigned fluidity, the opening of "Pequeña serenata diurna," by Silvio Rodríguez—which neither Pru nor Vicente recognizes, but Pato does, and he demonstrates it with an approving whistle before he sets off talking in English that is in fact pretty good.

Pru tries to include Vicente in the conversation, but Pato insists that he is the interpreter and his friend speaks no English at all. Pru sits down on the floor with her back against the wall and covers her face with her hands in real embarrassment, though it looks very much like flirting. She tells Pato to tell Vicente that she acted badly, that she's really sorry about what happened that night—she says *that night*, as if she were talking about a distant event and not the night before—and that she's grateful to him for helping her and for listening and that she had a great time and she hopes they can be friends, but nothing more. Pato translates for Vicente, who in any case already understood, because the lacerating language of rejection is universal.

The conversation hits a dead end. Pru looks at the time on her iPad and says she needs to go, she has work to do. Pato asks what she does. She tells him she's a journalist and that she has to write something about Chile, but she still doesn't know what.

"In Chile we have beautiful views and good wine, but for me personally, the best is the poetry," says Pato. "It's the only really good thing in Chile. The only thing we win the world cup in—two world cups, actually, two Nobel prizes. We're two-time world champions of poetry, it's the only thing we win at."

"I was thinking of writing about the street dogs. What are they called here? Quiltris?"

"Quiltros," Pato corrects her. "Why do they interest you so much?"

"It's just that there are so many, it's shocking," says Pru. "Or maybe I could write about Pablo Neruda."

"Neruda? Better to write about other poets, no one here is interested in Neruda," says Pato categorically.

"Not even the investigation about his cadaver?"

Pru is referring to the recent exhumation of Neruda's body to determine whether he died of cancer, or, as the unofficial story went, was poisoned by agents of the dictatorship. She has followed the news but isn't convinced the magazine will be interested in the story, and most likely more powerful international media outlets are already reporting on it. Nor is she sure she'll be able to find a different angle for the story. She feels the same way about the theoretically hopeful reelection of Michelle Bachelet or the fortieth anniversary of the coup.

"Neruda's death is important, but it's just one more crime of the dictatorship," says Pato. "There are a lot of crimes of the dictatorship that haven't been solved."

"But they still don't know whether it was a crime," says Pru.

"Well, it's just a matter of adding two plus two."

"So, you *are* interested in Neruda."

"I am interested that they clarify all the crimes of the dictatorship. And yes, Neruda is an emblem. He is an important poet, but there are many other poets more important. No one reads Neruda now."

"But he *is* important."

"Of course. In fact, I myself have a grant from the Neruda Foundation."

Pato tells Pru what the Neruda Foundation is, explaining that the workshop takes place in the poet's very own house in Bellavista. He says that all the relevant poets of recent generations have passed through there.

"Have you heard of Paul Walls, Pola Andthecow, Xavier Beautiful?"

"No," says Pru curiously, or maybe just politely. It's very likely that translating those proper names for her is the stupidest thing that Pato has done over the course of his brief and erratic life. And he goes on tossing out names, the list grows much longer.

"What about Hecthor Herrrnandiz, John Sántander Loyal, Leonard Seinhuezei, Germain Karrascou? Do you happen to know them? Have you read them?"

"I'm afraid I haven't."

"William Valinzuella? Alexandra of the River? Ralph Blond?"

"No," admits Pru, now fairly overwhelmed. Although she looks interested, of course she is not. Vicente thinks that Pato is ridiculous, a social-climbing, name-dropping wannabe, and for a second he hates him.

"Not all good poets have been at the Neruda Foundation." Vicente chimes in unexpectedly, in Spanish.

"What?" asks Pru, in English.

"Not everyone has been there. Think of the regional poets, for example" [Spanish].

"Well," admits Pato [English], "not all of them, but a lot."

The two friends are finally showing themselves as what they are, two contentious kids, but thankfully it doesn't escalate.

"You guys are like Bolaño characters," says Pru, for the first time—finally—in Spanish.

It's a compliment, she doesn't mean to offend, but neither Pato, who looks at her haughtily, nor Vicente, who smiles in surprise, likes the idea of seeming like characters, Bolaño's or anyone else's.

"He wasn't a great poet, Bolaño," says Pato decisively.

"You don't like him?"

"I haven't read his novels, but I've read some poems and they aren't good at all," argues Pato. "In poetry you have to give everything. If you are a good poet you can write novels to earn a little money, because writing novels is easier. I myself plan to write novels at some point, but there is nothing sadder than a novelist writing bad poems. I'm sure Bolaño knew he was a bad poet, because I read some of his interviews and there is no denying the guy was intelligent."

Pru looks at Pato with real interest. She's amused by his tone, so arbitrary and categorical.

"And have you read him?" Pru asks Vicente [Spanish].

"You speak Spanish?"

"A little. Have you read Bolaño?"

"Just his poems. You?"

"Yes, but not his poems, just some novels and his stories."

"I liked his poems," says Vicente. "He's no Enrique Lihn, but he holds his own."

"Henry Lihn," translates Pato. "You have to pronounce it like that," he tells Vicente, "or else the gringa will think you're talking about Tribilín."

The clarification is obviously nonsense, because for Pru, Mickey Mouse's friend is not named Tribilín but Goofy, but still, Pato achieves his goal of cutting off the brief exchange between Vicente and Pru. Seizing the moment, Pato invites her to a nearby bar, and it's not clear whether the invitation includes Vicente. She thinks Vicente seems intimidated or jittery or upset, and she thinks that she hasn't been fair, or that she has, because she doesn't want to repeat the scene from the night before. Really, she's not sure she doesn't want to, but Vicente now looks to her more clearly like a kid. Still, she hopes to thank him again for taking care of her, which is something no one else has done lately, and for listening, even if he didn't fully understand. She is also grateful to him for a few orgasms, but of course she won't thank him for those, you don't thank people for orgasms. Pru says she wants to go to the bar, but only if all three of them go. Pato takes her words as an auspicious sign and resets his sights on the ménage à trois, though he also aspires to a hookup without competition from Vicente.

Vicente livens up at the bar, and they speak in a slow, tentative, hospitable Spanish. Pru has trouble understanding them, but manages to express herself fairly well. She orders a mineral water, the boys drink beer, they exchange phone numbers and emails and add each other on Facebook; Pru takes the chance to discreetly check their ages, and learns that Vicente is eighteen and Pato is twenty. In general, smiles predominate, but when Pato takes the floor the conversation moves off in boring directions. Although Pru is loosening up more and more in Spanish and at times talks without pausing, he insists on speaking English to her, now with the obvious intention of sidelining Vicente.

"So, are you going to write novels later on too, to earn money?" Pru asks Vicente.

"I don't think so," he replies. "I think you have to spend a lot of time sitting down to write a novel, and I don't know if I could take it."

"Novels are poetry for stupid people, as Chico Molina said," adds Pato.

"So do you guys know any Chilean poets?" asks Pru, interested.

"We *are* Chilean poets," replies Pato in now-unnecessary English, a little offended.

"Right," she says, "but besides you: Nicanor Parra, Raúl Zurita, Gabriela Mistral."

Pato is scandalized, and explains that Gabriela Mistral died in 1957. (He gives the exact year.) Pru apologizes for her ignorance.

"There's no reason she should know whether Gabriela Mistral is alive or dead," Vicente says with avenging zeal.

"All she'd have to do is look at the five-thousand-peso bill," says Pato. "The people on money are always dead."

"No. Not in every country. There are a lot of countries where the people on money are alive," says Vicente, who doesn't know whether what he's saying is true, but he bets Pato doesn't know either.

"Where?"

"Puerto Peregrino, the Republic of Terramar, Rocamadour, there are lots," Vicente recites very quickly.

"And where did you get those places?"

"From the map of the world, dumbass. Anyway, whose face is on the thousand-peso bill?" attacks Vicente authoritatively.

Pato has never looked closely at the thousand-peso bill. He accepts the blow and is quiet for some five minutes while Pru and Vicente talk. But soon enough he interrupts again, impatiently, always in English:

"Have you seen any Latin American movies?"

Pru replies that she's seen *Machuca*, *No*, and *Nostalgia for the Light*.

"*Nostalgia for the Light* is beautiful," says Vicente.

"What about Mexican movies? You like them?" asks Pato [English].

"I love Mexican movies," replies Pru [Spanish]. "I've seen a lot."

Vicente, who can sense what's coming, closes his eyes to weather the storm.

"And have you seen the movie *Y tu mamá también*, which in English should be something like *And Also Your Mother,* or maybe *And Your Mother Too?*"

Pru nods and says she saw it many years ago and thought it was funny, and for a moment she thinks about Diego Luna and Gael García Bernal and tries to decide which of the poets would be Luna and which García Bernal—Vicente looks more like Gael and Pato like Diego, but she'd seen Gael once at a diner in Harlem and was surprised by how short he was, maybe as short as Pato, while she thinks Diego Luna, whom she has never seen in person, is probably tall like Vicente. Deep in these thoughts, at first it doesn't occur to Pru that the mention of the film holds the proposal of a ménage à trois at its heart, but then she notices Pato's eager, mischievous look; to dispel any doubt he takes her hand, which she instantly withdraws.

She isn't angry, but she thinks she should get angry, or at least seem angry. She stands up, and before leaving she tells Pato that he should sleep with Vicente because he's very good in bed, but she says this in English and very quickly.

"Had to give it a shot, man," says Pato, finishing his beer in one gulp.

"Sure you did," says Vicente, mortified.

"Did you understand what she said at the end?" asks Pato.

"No. What?"

"That you're good in bed."

"Really?"

"Yep. And that you and I should sleep together."

Vicente laughs, while Pato remains very serious and looks straight into his eyes.

"Want to?" he asks. "I know you don't sleep with guys, but we could try. We could have a few drinks and go with the flow, what do you think?"

"No," says Vicente. "I'm not attracted to you."

"How do you know, when you've never slept with me?"

"Do you really like Zurita more than Millán? More than Enrique Lihn? Rodrigo Lira?"

Vicente finds it absurd, this urge to compare poets as if they needed to be ranked. He just wants to change the subject, and attacking Zurita seems like a good out, because Pato gets desperate whenever anyone talks shit about Zurita, who for him is a kind of Maradona or David Bowie, and also a mentor or a father figure, because it was Zurita who not only agreed to read Pato's first poems, but who then wrote him a long email in sparkling capital letters praising the "excoriating audacity" of those first poems, and urging him to keep writing.

"I really do, Zurita runs circles around them all, he's the true people's poet," says Pato in an automatically militant tone.

"You're sick in the head," says Vicente, surprised by the success of his strategy. "Zurita's really good, but Millán kicks his ass a thousand times over."

"Millán is too lyrical."

"Did you read *La ciudad*?"

"Obviously. It's a good book, but I like *Zurita* better."

"Which book?"

"Zurita's book called *Zurita*."

"That fat book that weighs like two pounds?"

"Yeah."

"I'm gonna read it, but I don't think I'll like it at all," promises Vicente, who already read it and found it magnificent, but thinks it's best, for now, to keep that to himself.

For her part, back in the hostel, Pru Skypes with Gregg Pinter, who claims to have a terrible hangover though he's sporting a shirt buttoned up to the neck and looks particularly bright-eyed. Pru doesn't know Gregg that well and her first impulse is to lie, but she decides that in the interest of professionalism she should tell him the full truth, which she nevertheless abridges and adorns a little. He says he's sorry about the breakup, but that things happen for a reason, and then he urges her to tell that story. She refuses flatout but he insists: Why not spice it up with details about those landscapes, in the first person? he asks. Gregg is a little obsessed with the first person. She says no, what for, and suggests a piece about Chile's stray dogs or Neruda's cadaver or about the new Michelle Bachelet government or about Camila Vallejo or Valparaíso, but, just as she'd feared, Gregg isn't interested in any of those articles.

"Our magazine wants weirder stories. More marginal, unexpected ones."

"And a country full of street dogs doesn't seem like enough?"

"It's just that your story is better. Maybe you can include the dogs."

"The story of a stupid journalist lost in a tiny town in the north of Chile." Pru loses her patience. "A lonely journalist who spends the holidays chasing down street dogs."

"I'm sorry, Pru," says Gregg with professional gentleness, "I know this still hurts, and I'm sure it's going to go on hurting for a long time, but it's a beautiful story, and maybe if you write it you'll see that, how it's a very sad story but also a beautiful and important one."

"Important to who?"

"Important to everyone," says Gregg, avoiding the question. "To readers."

"You write it, then," says Pru, with unintentional aggression.

"You want me to write your story?"

"No. I mean, you're a novelist, you write it, you make it up. I don't want to."

Gregg is silent for a few seconds as he imagines that novel, or imagines himself in front of the computer writing that novel and even signing a six-figure contract in a Manhattan office with walls covered in framed certificates that say Pulitzer and National Book Award. Then Pru returns to Neruda's cadaver, and Gregg tells her, as Pru had assumed, that there are surely powerful media outlets already reporting on the story, and that anyway, no one is interested in Neruda because he'd raped a woman and even admitted to it, a fact Pru was not aware of, though since Gregg says it in the tone of a person affirming common knowledge, she pretends she was.

Then Pru suggests starting from there but expanding the report to include other Chilean poets. She talks about Nicanor Parra and the preparations to celebrate his hundredth birthday as a national holiday, and Gregg hasn't read Parra but remembers that Bolaño quoted him constantly, because he *is* a fan of Roberto Bolaño and by extension of the numerous authors Roberto Bolaño cited, authors Gregg hasn't read but feels sure are brilliant.

Pru tells him that apparently it's impossible to interview Parra, but she can try, and she talks about the younger poets, so serious, so contentious, so sure of themselves, whom she has just met. Gregg loves the idea of an article about a literary country, a country where poetry is oddly, irrationally important.

How do the current Chilean poets dialogue with that legacy? What is it like to be a poet in a country where apparently poetry is the only good thing? He asks her to interview poets who are unknown to English-speaking readers, a broad range of them, of all ages—the idea is to capture the atmosphere, the scene.

"We're going to discover a bunch of savage detectives," says Gregg, visualizing the article printed in the magazine, much more enthusiastic than Pru.

The little room outside had long been the repository for all kinds of junk, until Carla turned eighteen and, as she was about to start college, convinced her parents that she needed some independence. They cleared it out, painted it, and repaired its minuscule bathroom, and Carla just knew she would be spending a lot of time out there, in what she referred to with emphatic joy as *my house*. The place wasn't all that independent, because you still had to enter through the front door of the main house, go through the kitchen, and finally walk about twenty steps outside to reach that small, freezing-cold room. A moderately athletic person, however, could take a shortcut by climbing over a low side wall. And that was exactly what León did, on three occasions: the first time for sex without a condom, the second time for sex with a condom, and the third time for no sex, but a desperate meeting to hotly discuss what the hell they were going to do.

The place returned to its condition of storage unit until Gonzalo moved into the house and took over the little room—he bought a desk, covered the walls with shelves, and started pompously referring to it as *my studio* and sometimes *my study*, although mostly everyone just kept calling it "the little room." When Carla started photography classes she decided to set up the little room's bathroom as a darkroom (the "little darkroom," they called it, naturally), but that only lasted a few months, because digital photography was already starting to take over.

A few weeks after the breakup, two of Gonzalo's friends came to pick up his things, which basically consisted of the books filling those shelves. They didn't take the desk, which was beautiful, or the chair, which was pretty uncomfortable, nor did they take the brand-new mattress.

Vicente didn't come out of his room that morning, but he watched from the window as the truck full of books drove away. Then he went running down to the little room, and the sight of all those empty shelves struck him as dismal and bleak. He sat looking at the areas where the paint was whiter, and he had the confused thought that the lost books had been protecting the walls, and now they were more exposed, naked. He ran his hands over the outlines left by the library, noticing how those irregular shapes rose and fell according to the size of the books, like a useless sideways staircase.

Sitting on the mattress, he gave in to the idea that if he rubbed his eyes harder than ever before and let the fascinating, iridescent chaos grow behind his eyelids, right at the moment he opened his eyes all the books would reappear. He immediately regretted the thought, which was too childish for a twelve-year-old boy, and yet the next thing he did was even more childish: he didn't want to open his eyes, so he fumbled his way out of the room like he was blind. He returned in the middle of the night, wide awake, and lay down on the mattress to sleep. That's where Carla found him, at four in the morning: she tried to pick him up but couldn't, so she woke him, and, as if Vicente had a broken leg, she helped him to bed, to hers, to the bed that now was hers alone. He woke up at noon, with the indistinct impression that his mother had rescued him from the little room.

During the following days Vicente went out to the little room often, still without any clear intention of taking it for himself. Sometimes he lay on the mattress and thought about nothing, and others he remembered Gonzalo not with nostalgia, but with something like bafflement. He thought that his stepfather or rather ex-stepfather shouldn't have taken the books: he knew that they were Gonzalo's, that the books had arrived with Gonzalo and as such they should logically disappear with him, but still he felt it was unfair to take them. It wasn't that he especially valued books in general or those books in particular, though sometimes, when Gonzalo was working, Vicente would come into the room and peer at the shelves and think that some-day he would read them. It was a vague idea that was probably tied to a much less vague notion that the library would always be there, because Gonzalo would always be there.

One Saturday morning while he was playing soccer at a field ten blocks from his house, it occurred to him that the first step to making the little room his own would be to remove the shelves. He went on playing for a while but he was just too eager, so he told his friends he had a headache and ran home at a speed that no one with a headache has ever achieved, ready to get his project underway. It didn't look like those knotty pine boards held up by brackets would be hard to take down—they were nothing very elaborate. Suddenly converted into an efficient junior carpenter, he neatly unscrewed a couple of shelves and filled in the holes in the walls with multicolored Play-Doh, thinking it would give the place an artistic air. The result was horrible, though, so he reinstalled the shelves, which turned out to be considerably more difficult than dismantling them—it took him the entire afternoon and all of Sunday.

In the bathroom Vicente found a large box that contained an old vacuum cleaner, the pointy plastic branches of a Christmas tree, and several forgotten toys, including a racetrack that his maternal grandparents had given him years ago. He decided to put it together, not in order to play with it, but so the room wouldn't look so empty. Among the pieces of the track were the books Gonzalo had stashed there on his night of imposture. Vicente paged through the Emily Dickinson first, but he didn't understand much, and then he read some poems from the other book, the one by Gonzalo Millán, which confused him too, though he thought it was funny that there was a poem called "Blaaammm!" He set the two books side by side on a shelf, where they looked like what they ultimately were: the lone survivors of a catastrophe. He set up the racetrack on the mattress and found he did want to play, but it had no batteries.

For several months, Vicente forgot about the little room and the race-track and the pair of orphaned books, but then one morning he woke up with the idea of making a gym for cats. He pictured Darkness and a bunch of grateful stray cats settled into the place, which was perhaps better to imagine as a shelter or even a spa, with unlimited food and dozens of light-up toys, balls of yarn, wall massagers, rattling mice, catnip-filled scratching pads, and many beds for the guests who preferred to spend the whole day sleeping, which would probably be most of them. He thought that instead of removing the shelves he could rearrange them as a cat jungle gym, and he designed an ingenious blueprint for what he proudly called a "zigzag slide." Just then, sadly, Darkness died tragically, not from dental complications but from being run over, in broad daylight, by a police van. Since Vicente had spent nearly three years thinking Darkness could die at any moment, he was in a way prepared. He buried her in the yard himself between the rosebush and the privet hedge, and he offered up an Our Father for her, though his Catholicism was nonexistent. He didn't even know the prayer by heart, in fact, and had to google it.

The mourning period was long and multifaceted: everything had changed, suddenly and in very little time, and although Vicente wouldn't have put it this way, he related Darkness's death to Gonzalo's absence. You could count on one hand the times the cat had entered the little room, and yet Vicente associated that little room with Darkness's disappearance, and, by extension, with death.

The racetrack was still on the mattress. Vicente found some batteries, but he felt silly making the red car compete with the yellow one—he couldn't manage to identify with either. That was on a Tuesday. On Wednesday, he took apart the track and set up the TV from his room on the desk. There was no TV connection by either cable or antenna, but the device could pick up almost all the public channels. He started to watch a Chilean telenovela, which seemed like an intriguing idea, and he decided from the outset he'd keep watching it every day, but on Thursday he got deathly bored and carried the TV back to his room. That night he fell asleep thinking he never wanted to go into the little room again, and yet he went back the next day, and again he saw those two poetry books on the shelf, and again he flipped through them and dismissed them, though this time the solitude of the books struck him as problematic: he couldn't decide whether to place them together horizontally or keep them far apart and vertical, and in the end he chose to lean them against each other in the middle of a shelf in the shape of a triangle, like a teepee for ants. On Saturday he brought all the books he owned to the little room, and he also transplanted several he found scattered around the house, and over the following weeks he stole a few from his grandparents' house and asked León for some of his. Since it still wasn't enough to fill even one of the twelve shelves, he decided to add a bunch of magazines as well.

Though every personal library, like every person, seems strange when looked at closely, that first version of Vicente's library was particularly disconcerting, because alongside Millán and Dickinson there were fantasy novels like *The Neverending Story* and *His Dark Materials* and *A Wizard of Earthsea*, copies of *Reader's Digest* select editions, *Estadio*, *RockTop*, *APSI*, *TV Grama*, *Fibra*, *Vanidades*, *La Bicicleta*, *Condorito*, *Barrabases*, and *National Geographic*, novels by Hernán Rivera Letelier, Salman Rushdie, Agatha Christie, and Lawrence Durrell, byzantine and boring legal manuals, essays by Paul Johnson and Francis Fukuyama, and a fair number of self-help volumes, ranging from bestsellers like *Viva la diferencia* and *Believing the Impossible Before Breakfast* to *Shakespeare on Management* and *She Comes First*. It was hard to form an idea of what the owner of that library's interests were, since it mostly seemed like one of those eclectic collections that grow like mold in beach houses or hotels or landfills.

And that was how, long before he started to like poetry and read voraciously, Vicente became an accumulator of books. As soon as he got a little money he'd head to the Bío-Bío market and buy books as if they were apples or watermelons, though the comparison is flawed because he would have taken more time choosing apples or watermelons, while in this case it was only quantity that mattered: he didn't care at all about subjects or genres or authors, he just bought five or ten of the very cheapest books. His project was merely to accumulate them, though he actually felt that rather than collecting books he was recovering them, restoring the lost library. He did page through them and occasionally read one, but reading or appreciating them was not his goal.

That drive toward restitution reinforced the idea that Gonzalo was something like a library thief. Vicente had spent a year without knowing what to do with the memory of his stepfather or ex-stepfather, who surfaced periodically in emails that were friendly and funny and perhaps overly long, which Vicente read and sometimes reread but rarely replied to, because he wasn't sure what Gonzalo was or should be now, for him. Carla tended to run through elliptical explanations of the breakup that only demonstrated her sadness and reluctance to talk, and Vicente filled in the gaps with his own feelings. Though his mother never uttered a single disparaging word about her ex, Vicente formed an impression of Gonzalo as cruel, disloyal, and selfish. Repopulating the library became an urgent mission that would restore peace or normality or happiness to the household, or all of those things simultaneously.

When he was fourteen, Vicente met Virginia, who became his first steady girlfriend. She was sixteen and much more experienced, both with boys and girls, though she didn't define herself as bisexual. (When Vicente asked, she haughtily replied that she preferred not to label herself.) The first time they slept together was in that little room, and in doing so they unconsciously revived a tradition while at the same time modifying it, because this time there was no pregnancy. In just a few weeks the little room turned into what people used to call a love nest, because Virginia made herself right at home, even contributing a set of gray sheets, a plastic cup for their toothbrushes, and a shower curtain printed with the periodic table of the elements.

"We've got to clean up those bookshelves," Virgina said one morning. Until that point she had only gazed at the shelves in consternation.

"I just dusted them this morning," said Vicente.

"I mean, get rid of all the junk," said Virginia. "Sorry, but I can't believe how bad your taste is."

"Not all those books are mine," said Vicente, imprecisely.

"But the first time I came over you told me they *were* yours," Virginia replied grumpily.

"Yes, they're mine," said Vicente. "But they're not for reading."

"What? What are they for, then?"

Vicente considered making something up, but in the end he told her the truth. Virginia listened openmouthed, not because she found the story shocking, but because she had a cold and was having trouble breathing through her nose. Vicente went to pick some lemons, and when he came back with a mug of hot water with lemon Virginia was already busy classifying the books, which until then had been organized more or less by size and the color of their spines.

Virginia assigned one shelf to the many bad books, and another to the few she considered good. Her decisions conveyed assurance: the self-help and law books were by definition bad, and she recommended throwing them out, likewise the ones that looked like bestsellers, while the literary books were automatically good and worthwhile, and the magazines, of course, were given a separate section. When Virginia found the Emily Dickinson book, the prestige of poetry was added to her memory of the Emily the Strange stories, which she'd loved as a kid, and she lay on the bed and read for a while in silence, and then she also read this poem out loud:

> Love can do all but raise the Dead
> I doubt if even that
> From such a giant were withheld
> Were flesh equivalent
>
> But love is tired and must sleep,
> And hungry and must graze
> And so abets the shining Fleet
> Till it is out of gaze.

"I don't understand anything but I love it," said Vicente, with sincere enthusiasm.

"You can tell Emily was sad as hell," said Virginia. "You really never read her?"

"I read a couple of poems but I didn't like them, maybe I was too young. Like I told you, I've hardly read any of these books, just the fantasy ones and some of the comics."

This happened in the final weeks of his relationship with Virginia. Shortly thereafter she simply got bored with Vicente, who was not at all boring but was falling in love, which appalled her. The day of the breakup, Vicente gave her the Emily Dickinson book. She thanked him, but didn't want to take the book or the gray sheets or the toothbrush cup. She did take the shower curtain, because she was really into the periodic table.

Vicente was crushed, and his retreat into the little room was the best testament to that. He didn't move in officially, he still had the same second-floor bedroom as always, but he preferred the melancholic mess of the little room. He brought his computer out and spent whole days playing online games or watching movies whose endings he almost always guessed. Sometimes he just slept all afternoon. Of course, Carla started to worry. She'd never liked Virginia, but she liked her son's sadness even less.

"You can't spend all day in front of the computer," Carla told him one morning. "You're depressed."

Evoking her long-ago, short-lived studies in psychology, Carla managed to imprint a professional intonation on her words. And Vicente got scared: he belonged to a generation of medicated children, and many of his classmates and friends took pills for depression and ADD, the two illnesses in fashion, and he didn't want to jump on the bandwagon after seeing how his friends suffered. Carla asked him if he wanted professional help, but he said he would rather try to get better on his own.

"How?"

"I'm going to do something," replied Vicente.

"What?"

"I don't know yet, Mom, but something. I have to get past this."

Carla took heart; she knew it was true, her son *would* do something, or at the very least would think about doing something.

The first step Vicente took was to take a break from using the computer, which turned out to be nearly impossible, so instead he tried using it in a different way. In recent months he had immersed himself in online pornography, but he decided, now, to do the opposite. After thinking about it for a while he posited that, given the current impossibility of real-life sex, the opposite of watching porn was watching YouTube videos about Inuit tribes. The plan was successful at first, because it really was hard to imagine those bundled-up people removing layers of clothing one by one so they could get it on at forty degrees below zero in a forest in Alaska, for example. It was hard, but, as it turned out, not impossible: ultimately he did jerk off a few times to those images. In any case, it was more creative than anything porn offered, and it was also better for his self-esteem, because masturbating to porn inevitably led him to compare his dick size with the actors', and though he didn't always come up all that short, the matter didn't even arise in—to put it delicately—Inuit-inspired masturbation. Of course, Vicente knew that this strategy didn't really solve anything, but masturbation without audiovisual stimulation was unthinkable, because the few times he'd tried it he thought about Virginia and his heart was broken all over again as he pictured her shoulders, her green eyes, her millions of freckles, her narrow hips, her thin legs—he pictured her in the bathroom, wrapped in a towel, shaving her head with the razor she always carried in her backpack, as if she were afraid her red hair would grow back at any moment.

The books were still arranged in the order Virginia had given them, and when Vicente started to read them it was essentially a way to remember her, especially the book by Emily Dickinson, a writer whose work no psychiatrist or psychologist would ever recommend for overcoming sadness or depression, but who nevertheless connected Vicente to the power of words, the force of poetry. "A dim capacity for wings / degrades the dress I wear," read Vicente, for example, and he still didn't understand much but the image managed to communicate something, and it transformed into, so to speak, an instantaneous memory, a kind of truth. He spent an entire day reading the six-hundred-plus poems in the book, and although he didn't entirely like any of them, he retained a piece of almost all of them. Actually, there were several that he liked entirely, but he wouldn't have been able to explain why. Sometimes he would read a stanza aloud, trying out different tones of voice as though guessing at Emily Dickinson's tone, at how she would have read the poem—for example these famous lines, which Vicente read as a whisper, then as a lament, and finally like someone sharing a discovery or revealing a secret:

There's a certain Slant of light,
Winter Afternoons—
That oppresses, like the Heft
Of Cathedral Tunes—

He wanted to read more poetry, but he avoided the book by Millán because he was annoyed that the author's name was Gonzalo, and he also thought the title—*Vida*—sounded kind of absurd. So one Saturday he went to the market and paid peanuts for the book *Existir todavía* by Mario Benedetti, and he read it in very good faith, he really wanted to like it, but instead he found it basic and cheesy.

He had no recourse but to read the book by Millán. All the poems sounded utterly strange to him at first, and at times also comical and mysterious:

Giants are composed
by numerous dwarfs
like bunches of grapes

He didn't know whether he liked those poems or not, but he tended to think that meant he did. This short, very strange poem, for example, one day would strike him as grotesque or creepy and the next as naïve or funny.

Sometimes
cats
have
puppies.

It was like a master explanation that worked for everything; it could even function as a saying, a refrain, Vicente thought after mulling over that poem, so deceptively simple.

His favorite poems of Millán's, in any case, were the love poems, so physical and at the same time so evocative ("And you laugh believing I'm biting you"), and also the ones related to home appliances, especially the refrigerator, which was apparently the poet's preferred object. "The refrigerator gives a start / and, hesitating, shifts its rhythm," said Millán, and he even compared it to a book:

> The refrigerator opens
> like a giant book
> composed only
> of blank covers.

There was another poem about a refrigerator with the door open, defrosting, completely empty except for a still-frozen pea, "very small, round, and green." Vicente thought a lot about the solitude of that pea, which seemed like the old solitude of that pair of books in his library.

He read those poems many times, and they changed his relationship with objects and words, or his way of looking at the world, forever—though maybe that wasn't exactly it; maybe it was that he already looked at the world that way, and so Millán's poems surprised him, because he felt them to be close, familiar. The knowledge that those impressions—fleeting, marginal, strange, and to most people useless—could end up in a poem stirred an immense joy in him. And the fact that there was someone, an adult, dedicated to collecting these images, to retrieving and sharing them, and that devoting oneself to that obsessive adventure was something like a job, all seemed astonishing.

He didn't have any faith in his school library, but it turned out that the catalog did include some books of poetry. None by Millán, but there were anthologies where Vicente read poems by César Vallejo (which he found spellbinding and hermetic, though he wasn't sure exactly what the word *hermetic* meant), Nicanor Parra (dark and very funny), Gabriela Mistral (arduous and mysterious), Vicente Huidobro (eminently likable), and Oliverio Girondo (playful). As for the poems of Delmira Agustini and Julio Herrera y Reissig, he thought they were like those songs in Italian or Portuguese that he only half understood but nevertheless hummed and danced to with frenzied enthusiasm. Oddly, the school library had only one book by Neruda, *One Hundred Love Sonnets*, which Vicente found lame.

"Come on, read me your favorite poem," Carla said to him one night.

She'd gotten home early from work and wanted to go out for pizza, which was why she had poked her head into the little room, where she almost never went. She had thought many times of turning it into her own studio, but once Vicente made himself so at home she understood that she couldn't take it away from him.

By this point it was hard for Vicente to decide which poem he liked best, but a few hours earlier he had found the pdf of a book by Carlos de Rokha online, and these stanzas were still echoing in his head:

The dog on the floor conjures blood.

Every morning he comes to my table
and is a dark reminder that settles
onto the rug where I toss him scraps.

He is only the faithful witness who forgives
my meanness, at times, toward him
when I give him water in a dirty bowl.

"That was Neruda's enemy, the one who killed himself?" Carla asked.

"No, that was Pablo de Rokha. This poem is by his son Carlos, who apparently also killed himself."

"Can you read me a poem by someone who *didn't* commit suicide?"

He chose "Message in a Bottle" by Jorge Teillier, a poem he had also recently found online and that was currently functioning for Vicente as the ultimate explanation of his love for poetry:

And you want to hear, you want to understand. And I
tell you: forget what you hear, read, or write.
What I write is not for you, nor for me, nor
for the initiated. It's for the girl no one

asks to dance, it's for the brothers

heading out on a bender, and for those who disdain

people who believe themselves saints, prophets, or potentates.

"Now, that's a great poem," said Carla, surprised. "Awesome. I like it a lot. The end, especially."

"I'm glad you like it."

Vicente read a couple more poems by Jorge Teillier, which Carla also liked, though she was distracted by the thought that poetry was like an illness her son had contracted, an illness associated with the little room, an illness that of course she preferred to his previous illness of sadness, but one that in any case worried her.

Vicente wanted to keep reading poems to his mother all evening. He chose several by Gonzalo Millán, including one that his ex-stepfather had plagiarized, but Carla wanted to leave right away for the pizzeria.

They walked ten blocks, Carla smoking energetically, Vicente counting the squashed plums on the ground.

"So, do you talk about poetry with Gonzalo?"

"I'd love to, but Gonzalo Millán died like four years ago, of lung cancer," replied Vicente, as if he hadn't understood the question.

"I mean the other Gonzalo."

"Gonzalo Rojas?"

"Yes."

"I haven't read him yet, but someone's going to lend me a collection of his poems called *Del relámpago*."

"Oh, you know what I'm asking. The Gonzalo Rojas who used to live with us."

"Why should I talk to him about poetry? I hardly even answer that guy's emails."

"Why don't you answer them? And why do you call him 'that guy'?"

"What should I call him? Daddy?"

"Why don't you answer his emails? Don't you like them? What does he say?"

"He doesn't say anything. He tells me about New York, he tells me stories that are sort of funny. He wants to know how I am, but I don't feel like answering."

A silence fell that was tense but also pervaded with a certain sweetness. Vicente knelt down to tie his sneakers. Carla looked at her son's black hair, long and tangled, and she thought that if he died she wouldn't even wait for the funeral, she would kill herself immediately. She imagined staring down from a bridge at the dirty, roiling water of the Mapocho River, a second before jumping.

"Do you miss Gonzalo?" asked Carla.

"Why should I miss him! You're the one who should miss him, he was your boyfriend, not mine." His words held the failed desire to sound reasonable. "And if I did miss him I'd answer his messages. Your ex isn't the only person who liked or likes poetry. Thousands of people in the world read poetry. Millions. Billions."

"That many?"

"Yes," said Vicente. "Just because you don't like poetry doesn't mean no one else does."

"I like poetry, I love it. I love Blanca Varela, for example," said Carla, to say a name, and she wasn't lying, maybe just exaggerating, because one time Gonzalo had read her some poems by Blanca Varela that she'd really liked.

"But you don't have any of her books."

"Right now I'm reading *The Elegance of the Hedgehog*, but when I finish it I'm going to buy a book by Blanca Varela and I'm going to read it and then I'll give it to you."

"So, do you miss Gonzalo?" Vicente asked while they were waiting for a table at the pizzeria, which was packed.

"I think you and I are fine," said Carla, as though responding to a follow-up question. "The two of us alone in the house. I like that you have your books in the little room."

Later that night, while she was trying to read *The Elegance of the Hedgehog*, Carla got distracted by the thought that Gonzalo was like a wound on her foot; an annoying wound that nevertheless didn't keep her from walking, didn't even keep her from running. She thought intensely about their lost family life, about the first weeks when Gonzalo appeared or reappeared and with him the idea of love as companionship, as the most serious of distractions. The word *family* was revealed in the water with promising slowness: a photograph hung in the sun like a sheet that never fully dries, and that suddenly, from one day to the next, came out blurry, blank.

She left off her reading. Now she just wanted to sleep and get up early the next morning, perhaps very early, with the promise of an entire day ahead of her, so she doubled her dosage of sleeping pills. For his part, in the little room, Vicente had just found some poems by Enrique Lihn online, and he was dead-tired but wanted to keep reading and rereading them, so he made a liter of coffee and stayed glued to the computer screen. When, at 3:34 a.m., one of the most ferocious earthquakes in Chile's earthquake-ridden history began, Vicente ran to Carla's room and put his arms around her—she was so deeply asleep it took her a few minutes to absorb what had just happened.

The house held up, there was only minor damage, but they were afraid the second floor would collapse in the aftershocks, and though the fear was irrational, in those circumstances it wasn't easy to establish the limits of the rational. They decided to stay in the little room, where a few books had fallen to the floor and the shelves had come a bit loose. They took the shelves down, piled the books in a corner, and for four nights in a row, mother and son slept together in the little room, which they temporarily referred to as *the bunker*.

Months later, at the height of spring, Vicente set about redecorating the little room: he painted it a light, nearly white blue, sanded and varnished the wood, and when everything was ready he decided that from then on there would only be good books in his library—he threw out the magazines and all the filler, and he got his hands on more poetry books, Chilean or otherwise. He also started spending a lot of time on Facebook chatting with other kids his age who read poetry. It was during this time that he began going to readings, and he met Pato and other friends who lent him books and urged him to show them his poems. Vicente hadn't even thought about writing poems, but one night, in that same little room, he gave it a shot. Now he was reading Alejandra Pizarnik, Blanca Varela (Carla had kept her promise),

Enrique Lihn, Carlos Cociña, Fernando Pessoa, and especially Rodrigo Lira, but in his very first poem he instead imitated Gonzalo Millán, who was still his most beloved poet. The poem's narrator was a blender who was looking on in trepidation as it was filled with every fruit imaginable, and even some vegetables. "What am I going to do?" wondered the blender, with automatic despair, but it wasn't a comic poem, rather a sentimental one, and it was never stated that the speaker was a blender, only Vicente knew that. He read it in front of Pato and his friends and no one seemed to dislike it, which reassured him.

By the time Vicente turned eighteen the little room was once again the room of a poet. The shelves were not full; the library was only at a third of its capacity, but he'd read all the books, ninety percent of which were poetry, at least once, and most of them around five times. Still, to keep the room from looking so bare, Vicente had put up a series of portraits—Allen Ginsberg, Anita Tijoux, Pedro Lemebel, Mauricio Redolés—and a kind of altar that featured photographs of César Vallejo and Camila Vallejo, as if they belonged to the same family.

And it's that same little room that, during the final minutes of the year 2013, while they stood amid the crowd waiting for fireworks at the Entel Tower, Vicente offered to Pru. He offered it for free, she refused flat-out, and then they negotiated a very modest, almost ridiculous, purely symbolic rent. He told her it was an independent room (true), unoccupied (partially true), that they often rented out (false) to foreigners (false).

"But you know nothing is going to happen between us," Pru warned him, enthusiastic and also cautious.

"Never even crossed my mind," replied Vicente, as if Pru had in fact said something crazy.

"Sorry, I just wanted to be clear," said Pru. "Perdón, solo quiero que quede claro. Clara. Which is it?"

"Say it however you want, I'll understand."

"But I want to say it right. You have to correct me! Promise you'll always correct me."

"I promise. It's *claro*," Vicente told her.

"Claro."

Three days later, the morning Pru came to move into the little room, Carla realized that Vicente had omitted a few essential details in his persuasive argumentation: he had strategically described "a woman your age, more or less," which was not necessarily a lie, because from many points of view a thirty-one-year-old woman compared to a thirty-eight-year-old woman are approximately the same age, and it was even biologically possible that Pru could have a son Vicente's age, though she would have had to give birth during puberty. Carla had found it reasonable to house, for a moderate period— Vicente had talked about "a couple of weeks, give or take"—a gringa who was researching Chilean poetry, although her son had led her to believe, or Carla had believed, that this would be a fusty Ph.D. or postdoc in endearing Coke-bottle glasses, the kind of person who needs a bibliography just to go out for a walk, not a cheerful journalist in shorts and a T-shirt with whom Vicente, Carla had no doubt, was infatuated.

A thin blonde with long legs, breasts on the abundant side, round face, large green eyes, thick lips that revealed perfect teeth: Carla looked Pru up and down and thought it was disappointing or sad that her son would adhere to such a typical, common idea of beauty—she blamed the mass media and beauty pageants and advertising, and then she blamed herself and conceded guilt, because to tell the truth, she found the gringa lovely too.

Vicente immediately became Pru's interpreter, which sounds crazy but really wasn't, because Pru's Spanish had loosened up, and although she still had trouble adapting to the fast, whispered tone of Chilean speech, at critical moments she would combine her English with some fluttering and twisting of the lips that Vicente's amorous impulse allowed him to decipher precisely—he was still ignorant of the language of Shakespeare, but he perfectly understood the idiolect of Pru.

Pato helped too, in his own way: no sooner had he heard that Pru would be writing about Chilean poetry than he chose twelve poets between twenty and forty years old for a speed round of preliminary interviews. The selection was undeniably biased and of course included Pato himself, while excluding Vicente. When Pru asked him why he had chosen eleven men and only one woman, Pato replied, with his usual self-assuredness, that there *were* no more women. ("There aren't many and they aren't very good, but it's not their fault, it's the fault of patriarchal capitalism.") Still, Pru was grateful for his unsolicited mediation, thinking it was a good warm-up exercise, and after all, she had to start somewhere.

The interviews took place at Galindo, a restaurant in Bellavista, on the first Friday in January. The experience was chaotic but useful. Here are some unmethodical, preliminary conclusions that Pru wrote in her notebook. Not all of them have a direct bearing on the matter or refer strictly to Chilean poets, and some of them are particularly arguable or unfair, but still and all they were valuable, in the end, to orient her research:

—"Being a Chilean poet is like being a Peruvian chef or a Brazilian soccer player or a Venezuelan model," one poet told me. I think he was being serious.

—I get the impression that Chilean poets love to give interviews. Some of them told me "write this down" or "this is important" or "you can use this." They didn't even try to hide their attempts to influence my reporting.

—Chilean poets stare openly at my boobs. The only female poet I interviewed also stared openly at my boobs.

—I shouldn't have slept with Vicente. I shouldn't be staying in his house. I shouldn't hope to run into him every time I go to the kitchen for a yogurt. And I shouldn't eat so much yogurt.

—Neruda, de Rokha, and Huidobro hated each other, and apparently they wrote about that hatred and the press dedicated pages and pages to their conflicts. Poets still appear in the press (though there is almost no press here, just two or three newspapers), but not necessarily to talk about poetry.

—Chilean poets are extraordinarily competitive; it's like I'm in New York. It's as if we were talking about the stock market, as if there was a lot of money floating around. But there isn't. There's nothing. Most of them are professors or teach workshops, even the youngest ones give workshops. The government does award some grants, but clearly not enough.

—I feel like some of these poets would be capable of leading a sect if they got the chance. Or of becoming senators, or presidents. Vicente Huidobro and Pablo Neruda, in fact, both ran for president back in their days. Maybe contemporary Chilean poets follow that example.

—Oddly, Chilean poets are more famous than fiction writers, and there are many fiction writers who write novels about poets. Poets are like national heroes, legendary figures.

—None of the poets I interviewed, even the two with Mapuche last names, knew Mapudungun, and they all seemed uncomfortable when I asked. One of them said this: "I suppose you know how to speak Navajo or Cherokee or Sioux?"

—I need to interview two hundred more Chilean poets, ideally all women. I need to find poets who don't want to be interviewed and interview them.

—A lot of the interviewees had severe halitosis.

—None of them work only on poetry. Are there any countries in the world where poets make money? Denmark, maybe? Are there poets in Denmark? If the Danish are really so happy, I doubt it, why would they need poets if they're happy?

—So, being a poet in Chile or anywhere else is like living a double life. It's like having two families or many families. And maybe that's good, they're not shut off, they know what reality is. They're not just sitting in their houses writing pretty things.

—"Some people are better at filling out grant forms than writing poems," said one poet who complained about everything. He was wearing a shirt that said 'I love New York.' I made the mistake of mentioning it, because I thought he'd worn it specifically for the interview. He said: "Go take a look in the shantytowns and you'll see tons of poor kids with runny noses wearing shirts with English words. You think they know what those sayings mean? A person just puts on the clothes they have in front of them, whatever's cheap. Now that I think about it, I have a sweatshirt from the University of Michigan, I don't know where I got it. Try to buy clothes for guaguas with Spanish words on them, they almost don't exist." Vicente chimed in to explain that the word *guagua* means *baby* in Chilean Spanish. I asked the poet if he had a guagua. He told me that question was too personal. Then he insisted on paying for my coffee.

—Vicente tells me that calling someone gringo in Chile isn't necessarily an insult, although sometimes it can be pejorative. Chileans talk about gringos in a general sense to mean foreigners. French, Germans, lots of people are or can be gringo.

—The main character of Bolaño's *By Night in Chile* exists! An Opus Dei priest who writes poems and literary criticism and is interested in avant-garde literature. His real name is José Miguel Ibáñez Langlois and he still says mass, I think in the rich area of Santiago, and he still writes occasionally in *El Mercurio*, though apparently about Tolkien and C. S. Lewis, not poetry.

—Some of the interviewees knew a lot about English language poetry. One poet who looked like a rat asked me if I didn't think Eliot was the best poet of the twentieth century. I said yes, to see what he would say. He looked pleased and asked if I thought *The Waste Land* was better than *Four Quartets*. I told him *Four Quartets* (which I've never read) was by far Eliot's best work, no doubt about it. He looked deeply disappointed, as if my reply had wounded him physically. Then he told me I knew nothing about poetry and refused to go on with the interview. Two other interviewees cited U.S. authors I'd never heard of, and I thought maybe they were making them up just to mess with me, but I googled those names and yes, they're real.

—Maybe they do aspire to be millionaires, because Neruda was a millionaire. But I understand that there are a lot of Chilean poets who died in poverty. The goal, really, is transcendence. Maybe they don't rule out either possibility: becoming a millionaire or dying in poverty.

—I hate the goddamn Oriental plane trees with all my heart. I don't need their shade, I'd rather travel to the center of the sun than get near those fucking trees that are everywhere here. I feel like this allergy has lasted for years, for my whole life.

—I get the feeling Carla hates me. I can't prove it, because she's nice to me, but I don't buy it. I feel like she's making too much of an effort to be nice to me.

—There's a collective of poets who organize "poem bombings" over places scarred by political violence: they throw thousands of bookmarks with poems on them out of a helicopter. They did it in Dubrovnik, Guernica, Warsaw, and Berlin, among other places, and of course they did it first in Santiago, over La Moneda, where Allende died the day of the coup. It's a beautiful, exuberant, meaningful project. The problem is that these same poets also organized a contest to get women to send them photos of their asses. For real.

—Three times now I've seen a bum with a grocery cart selling his handwritten poems. According to Vicente, who has read them, they're great. According to Pato, on the other hand, they're the product of mental illness and that takes away from their "aesthetic value."

—Some of the poets I interviewed, maybe most, think that poetry will save the world; they believe they are revolutionary heroes and it's kind of funny.

And yet I wouldn't dare say that they're wrong. Who knows, maybe they will change the world. Maybe they really *are* revolutionary heroes. Maybe their books hold the keys to it all.

—Everyone gave me their books of poems, like businessmen giving me their cards. I let them all know that I can't read literature in Spanish. I try to read them anyway, and sometimes I understand whole poems. I'm guessing I understand the bad poems and the good ones are the ones I don't understand at all.

—I gave the books to Vicente, so he can tell me whether they're good or bad. He told me they were all good, in a way, but that he didn't really like any of them. Two minutes later he told me he didn't want to contaminate me with his subjectivity. Vicente's great.

—I want avocado on marraqueta bread for breakfast for the rest of my life.

Thanks to those first interviews, Pru feels more prepared to dig into the second part of her project, which begins with a conversation with Professor Gerardo Rocotto, who, according to several sources, is the foremost expert on contemporary trends in Chilean poetry. Professor Rocotto—who in other countries would be called Dr. Rocotto, but luckily in Chile it's considered silly to call someone by their academic title—is fifty years old, though he looks much younger and is short and brawny like a jockey. This guy does look like Gael García Bernal, thinks Pru, he's like a darker, miniature Gael (a miniature of a miniature).

The interview takes place in Rocotto's apartment, where Pru expects to find the customary landscape of a library stuffed with books. But on the contrary, the apartment's spacious living room holds absolutely nothing except a small table and two beach chairs.

"I've just gotten divorced," clarifies Rocotto lightly, anticipating a question that Pru did not intend to ask. His English sounds old-fashioned and put-on, droll.

"I'm sorry," says Pru. "I'm going through a breakup too." It's the first time she has said it, the first time she's formulated it that way, and the sensation somehow soothes her.

Rocotto winds down the short interlude of personal confessions and asks her which poets she has interviewed so far. She recites the list and asks his opinion; he replies that it's an odd selection, and after a few seconds of

suspenseful silence he says he thinks it's terrible. Pru agrees, and tells him
that of course she plans to interview more poets, especially women. Rocotto
says that is indeed essential, and she also needs to include queer poetry and
indigenous poetry, and then he launches into the usual valuable but also
exasperating list of names and bibliographical sources. In any case, Pru's
intuitions are compatible with Rocotto's academic work: for too many years
Chilean poetry was studied as a clash of titans, and those heterosexual
macho men fighting over the microphone were the only protagonists, which
left many poets out, especially women and minority groups. ("Though I
believe the expression 'minority groups' is itself problematic," Rocotto immediately adds.) The current moment, he tells her, is an expansive one of
stimulating disorder.

"I suppose you've read Harold Bloom," says Rocotto.

"No," replies Pru, ashamed. "Should I?"

"No."

Unexpectedly, Rocotto takes from his inner jacket pocket a letter-sized
sheet of paper that he unfolds and rereads attentively before handing it to Pru.
It's a list of around fifty poets, particularly women ("Never call them *poeti-
sas*," he warns her. "Technically it's the Spanish word that applies, but it
sounds terribly derogatory") and indigenous and queer poets—a new canon,
complemented by a bibliography of fifteen articles, all with the byline Gerardo M. Rocotto Contreras.

"It's too much," Rocotto recognizes, surprisingly.

"No."

"Yes."

"Well, maybe a little," admits Pru.

"I'm sorry, sometimes I can be a bit of an ass," says Rocotto.

Pru is charmed by that one-eighty: it's as if he were in fact two people,
an erudite and overblown professor on one hand, and on the other a polite
and cheerful guy living in an empty apartment. The overblown professor
tries to show off and influence Pru's article, which in his judgment would not
be complete without mention of the poets he refers to or the reading of the
numerous articles that he himself has gone to the trouble of publishing in
indexed journals, while the reasonable man understands that Pru is propos-

ing to depict a more generalized panorama that, beyond naming names, communicates the atmosphere of Chilean poetry from a journalistic perspective, and is not an academic treatise.

The reasonable guy blithely crosses some thirty names off the list, and then looks up contact information for the chosen poets on his phone. The conversation takes on a casual air that Pru enjoys enormously. Rocotto suggests they go to dinner, and she searches for a reason to refuse but finds none.

They go to a Peruvian restaurant and order two large pisco sours, and they repeat the dose several times but never reach the point of drunkenness. Sometimes that happens, thinks Pru: when the conversation flows and laughter abounds, people consume an amount of alcohol that should get them drunk, but doesn't.

Rocotto drives her home at two in the morning. Vicente is in the front yard, watering plants. Really he is waiting for Pru, but when he sees the car he grabs the hose and pretends he's been watering for a while. Rocotto gets out of the steel-blue Volkswagen—Vicente has always thought that Beetle model is ridiculous, parodic—opens the passenger side door, and says goodbye to Pru with a casual hug, nothing strange or libidinous about it. Still, Vicente is dying of jealousy. Pru opens the gate and greets him curiously. She asks why he is watering plants at that hour and he replies that any way you look at it, this is the best time for watering.

Pru wakes up at eight in the morning with a major hangover. In spite of her hachazo (she's just learned that marvelous Chileno-Spanish word), she gets up, has breakfast, and tries to continue her notes on the futon, but she falls asleep almost instantly. She dreams she is walking in downtown Manhattan in the afternoon; it's a sunny, perfect day, and the streets look oddly empty. She stops every once in a while to look at the ground as if searching for something, maybe the plaques with famous quotations on Library Way. Suddenly she realizes she is walking with Jessye, who is very bundled up. In the dream Pru feels like she has to rise to the occasion and that, no matter what she does, she can't let Jessye down. They go into a hotel, climb an enormous number of stairs, and reach the top floor. There's a door that leads to the rooftop with a sign forbidding entry, but Pru opens it anyway—an alarm goes off and Jessye says, calm as can be and trying not to laugh, that they have to get out of there right away.

Vicente sits down on the adjacent armchair with his computer muted. His plan is to move up a level in Duolingo (he's just starting), but he gets bored and dedicates the time, instead, exclusively to watching Pru sleep. He notices the tremor of her eyelids. She's dreaming, he thinks, and he remembers that beautiful line by Rosamel del Valle: "I never had more eyes / than when you slept." Maybe feeling the weight of his gaze, Pru wakes up. Her first impression is that Vicente is angry or defeated or depressed.

"Estás *tristo*?" she asks him.

"You mean: estás triste."

"Oh, I knew that!" Pru says, frustrated. "Still, I don't understand why."

"I don't understand why either," says Vicente. "You made the right choice. *Tristo* should be the masculine and *trista* should be the feminine, but the word *triste* has only one gender in Spanish, who knows why. *Trista* and *tristo* sound better. But I wasn't sad, not at all."

"Were you watching me sleep?" asks Pru.

"'Nunca tuve más ojos / que cuando dormías.'"

"What?"

"Nothing. It's from a poem by Rosamel del Valle."

"Rosamel? That's a nice name. Is it common?"

"No, it's a pseudonym. His real name was Moisés Gutiérrez. He based it on the name of a girlfriend he had, Rosa Amelia del Valle. It was an homage. What's your last name? Weird, I still don't know your last name."

"Smith."

"So I should go by Prudencio Smith."

"Except I'm not your girlfriend," says Pru, standing up to get a glass of water.

"No, but it would still be like an homage."

"Were you watching me sleep?"

"Yes."

"Why?"

"Because you are the most beautiful woman I've seen in my entire life," he says, and goes over and gives her a kiss that lasts for three whole seconds.

Vicente goes all in, and his bravery is undeniable. But it doesn't work. Pru tells him about Jessye, she tells him the story all over again, this time in Spanish. She lingers too long over details, straining to convey subtleties, struggling with words in general, and yet that expressive poverty suddenly strikes her as appropriate, even necessary.

"Are you in love with Jessye?"

"I don't know," says Pru, and she knows she should say yes, that it would be the most effective way to brush him off, but she doesn't want to lie to him, nor does she know if she really wants to brush him off.

"What she did to you, you just don't do that to a person," Vicente declares, and it's hard to say whether he sounds naïve or mature.

"I know. It's a bad time. I can't be with you or with anyone else right now. I need to be alone."

They're standing up, facing each other. Vicente hugs her, puts his hand under her shirt and caresses her back; then, with a single, precise movement that denotes a certain amount of experience, he unhooks her bra. She shoves him away and rehooks it clumsily, as if she were doing it for the first time.

They are silent for twenty minutes. Pru decides she needs to move out of the little room. She's determined, and Vicente barely manages to convince her to stay.

Finally she asks if he'll leave her alone, but it translates badly into Spanish. "¿Me prometes que vas a dejarme sola?" she asks.

"Yes," replies Vicente. "I promise I will leave you completely lonely."

Monday morning Pru interviews Tania Miralles, a very young poet from La Florida who says she learned English listening to Radiohead; she quotes lines from *The Bends* and *OK Computer*, laughing hard. Pru thinks she is beautiful, and she catches herself thinking, not necessarily happily, that Vicente would fall hopelessly in love with her.

In the afternoon she interviews Carmen Frías, a seventy-year-old woman who describes herself as a poet-healer. The conversation takes place in a small studio in Bellavista that she refers to as *my consultation room*, where there are no sofas or anything like that, just a lot of cushions embroidered with healing words. Pru sits on the word FEARLESS, and since she's still a little uncomfortable she adds a cushion with the word BIRTHRIGHT.

On Tuesday morning Pru interviews Remo González, a gay poet who resists identifying as gay.

"I mean, I'm gay, but I don't like to bottom, I like to top. Furthermore, no one has ever topped me, so I'm gay and I'm also a virgin," says the poet, as a declaration of principles.

In the afternoon Pru goes to Quinta Normal to meet the poet and essayist Dariana Loo, who does nothing but rail against the heteropatriarchy of

Chilean poetry—although every once in a while she clarifies that her ex-husband, who is also a poet, isn't like that. ("He totally deconstructed his sexism.") At five the ex-husband arrives with an eight-year-old boy, their son. The kid doesn't talk much and his parents tell her he has language problems, which Pru finds paradoxical since he's the son of two poets. Dariana tells her it's a shame she hadn't thought about also interviewing her ex-husband, and Pru, who has some free time, says she can interview him right away. The woman leaves with the boy while Pru interviews the ex-husband, who is named Roddy Godoy and is a strange guy, with eyes like a Siberian husky's and a dopey smile that seems badly drawn-on. Roddy defines himself as an experimental poet and doesn't say anything that seems even a tiny bit interesting to Pru.

While her interlocutor monologues about sonorous preverbal post-poetry or something like that, Pru realizes that Dariana and Roddy planned the whole thing, and she gets distracted by conjecturing about how that went: if the ex-husband pressured his ex-wife to get him an interview, or if Dariana honestly thinks that Roddy is a good poet or a good sonorous pre-verbal post-poet, and as such should be included in her reporting. She also thinks that maybe there is a pact between poets that transcends the amorous pact, which she doesn't think is necessarily good or bad. Pru's own parents, for example, are dentists, and during their marriage and even for some years after their divorce they shared a practice, and they never stopped recommending each other to patients.

"Your dad may be mean and insensitive," Pru's mother used to say, "but he's a good dentist."

The experimental poet is still yammering on. Dariana Loo returns with the boy, who now seems cuter to Pru, maybe because she identifies with him—she thinks maybe being the child of dentists isn't so different from being the child of poets, and it's a silly thought that nevertheless takes a few seconds to disappear from her mind.

The family heads off toward the metro, and Pru thinks she too can remember once walking along holding the hands of her separated parents; she especially remembers a park in North Carolina, her fear of the bees, the terraced gardens, the damp grass under her feet. Later, as she looks at the stunning, ruined Quinta Normal greenhouse, it occurs to her that she identified with that boy because the coming and going from one language to another makes her feel like a child, especially now that she no longer has Vicente's help. Sometimes, as on that very afternoon, she speaks only in Spanish, and she feels happy at her ability to communicate effectively. She even recalls her histrionic Puerto Rican professor of Advanced Spanish and thinks he would be proud of her, though he'd always taken points off when she confused the genders of words, and she's sure he would still find cause to penalize her. In any case, she never stops perceiving communication as a problem; she never stops thinking about words, and sometimes she feels dizzy and would like to fall silent, in Spanish and in English, indefinitely.

On Wednesday morning Pru interviews Hernaldo Bravo, a poet who writes thousand-page books. ("Some people consider him a charlatan and others a genius," Rocotto told her, not specifying his own opinion.) To Pru he seems funny and warm. Ten years ago, when he'd just started college, Bravo had been run over by the son of a multimillionaire, who took care of all the medical bills and also gave him a healthy, off-the-books indemnification that the poet used to found a publishing company and publish all his friends.

"And thus my generation was born," says the poet proudly, with real emotion.

"How come you write such long books?" Pru asks him.

"Better to ask the others why they write such short books," he responds. "They're afraid of poetry."

"Then why do they write poetry?"

"I don't know, maybe they want to overcome their fear. And it's better for them to write. It's better to write than not to write. Poetry is subversive because it exposes you, tears you apart. You dare to distrust yourself. You dare to disobey. That's the idea, to disobey everyone. Disobey yourself, that's the most important thing. That's crucial. I don't know if I like my poems, but I know that if I hadn't written them I'd be dumber, more useless, more individualistic. I publish them because they're alive. I don't know if they're good, but they deserve to live."

"A lot of people say that poetry is useless."

"They're afraid of useless things. Everything has to have a purpose. They hate pure creation, they're in love with corporations. They're afraid of solitude. They don't know how to be alone."

At noon Pru interviews Chaura Paillacar, a poet who writes in a mixture of Mapudungun and Spanish, and who is polite, but approaches the conversation with visible distrust. She loosens up little by little. Chaura had asked her if they could do the interview while walking, it was her only condition. So that's what they do, they walk through Forestal Park, chasing puddles of shade from the trees.

"Paillacar means 'peaceful people,' and chaura is the name of a bush with edible fruit, similar to blueberries. Chauras are delicious and medicinal. Really, Chaura is my maternal last name, but I like it better than my real first name, which I'm not going to tell you. One morning, when I was twelve years old, I wrote a story about my last names and it gradually, over the years, turned into my first book."

"What do chauras cure?"

"In my family they were used to treat acne, but I never had that." Chaura touches her glowing cheeks and smiles. "It has double the antioxidants of a blueberry. But it's mostly used as a substitute for aspirin, because it has salicylic acid. They say it's better than aspirin. It doesn't work on me, though."

"Does aspirin?"

"No. I get really severe, brutal headaches."

Then, as though ashamed of talking about herself so much, Chaura changes her tone and starts talking about police repression, about the drones and helicopters flying over Wallmapu. She says that every time she travels south to visit her parents she comes back with an impression of war and defeat. She also talks about her community of female Mapuche poets in Santiago: schoolteachers, academics, domestic workers, artisans, activists, all united in the evocation of a place of origin that was stolen from them, of a language they reconstruct with patience and tenacity. She says she reads almost exclusively Mapuche poets; she also likes the Chilean poetry tradition, but she gets bored by the grandiloquence, the infighting, the lack of solidarity, and what she calls the "intelli-nonsense" of some Santiago poets.

"For me, writing is a way of returning to a place I've never been and don't know," she says suddenly, with feeling, as if she had just thought of it.

At sunset Pru interviews Maitén Pangui, another young poet of Mapuche origin who, in addition to writing poetry, is a hip-hop artist.

"How do you know if what you're writing is going to be a poem or a song?" Pru asks her.

"When it rhymes it's hip-hop, and when it doesn't rhyme it's poetry," the poet responds, with utter certainty.

That night she dines with an anonymous poet—"He doesn't have a name," Rocotto had written on his list, beside a phone number, and naturally Pru thought it was a mistake, but the professor clarified that this poet insisted on radical anonymity. No one knew his name, and because of that he'd been left out of almost all the anthologies.

Some people identify him by his phone number, which is pretty easy to get, because the nameless poet is paradoxically a pretty sociable character. He has published a lot of books, all photocopied and with no ISBN.

"How did you come up with it?" Pru asks.

"With what?"

"Not having a name."

Pru expects a very long and convoluted explanation, but the man falls silent in a pose of utter solemnity, and then he bursts out laughing for no apparent reason, as if he'd told himself a joke, and right away he turns serious again. He is a fat man, short and robust, fifty-something, with very little hair that he combs back with gel.

"I didn't come up with it," he says finally. "It just happened. I'd gotten the money to photocopy my first book, *Volunteer Work*. I was so happy, and maybe that's why I forgot to put my name on it. I mean, I gave a bound copy to my girlfriend and it was the first thing she said. You forgot your name, dummy! And I'd already spent all my money on the photocopies—the ring bindings were pretty pricey. I was really hard on myself at first, how could I be such an idiot, how could I forget to put my name on the thing. But then I liked it, or at least I got used to it. There are so many people, so many names, it's boring. Better not to have a name. And then I started to play it up. I mean, I kept thinking of more and more reasons not to have a name. It's shameful to 'make a name for yourself' in this country. Especially if you're a poet."

"Why?"

"Because poetry, after the coup, is no longer possible. It's like what Adorno said about the Holocaust. You can't write poetry in this fucking country anymore. But I still keep writing, I can't help it. It's my weakness. I'm like an addict and it's my drug. I don't even realize it and I go and write a poem, or two, or three, or twenty."

"So, you think there's no hope for Chile?"

"This country went to hell a long time ago. All gone to shit."

"But the dictatorship ended, right?"

"It's not over, my dear, of course it's not. Pinochet won, he got what he wanted, he must be laughing like crazy in his grave, that son of a fucking bitch. We're all in hock up to our ears, doomed to work five hundred hours a week. Depressed, jumpy, angry. Half-dead."

"And you don't think things could change with the new government?"

"The only hope is the same one as always, that the people will rise up. But the people are too depressed. We'd have to hand out antidepressants in the slums. Prozac first, then the revolution. No, sorry, none of that. It's just a line. You interview me and right away it goes to my head. It's like I want to talk to you in headlines."

"So then what *do* the people need?"

"I don't know. Yoga, kickboxing, poetry, revolution. Real education, real joy, gardens, pedicures, ceviche. Rhythmic gymnastics, fencing. A lot of avocado, quinoa, cochayuyo. Sharp stones, superpowers, amulets. Good shoes. And especially sex, every day, every eight hours, religiously, like antibiotics. But really great sex, exceptional, cosmic. And good music."

"And what is good music?"

"That depends on the person. I, for one, like rancheras."

Soon the nameless poet winds up the interview. They pay the bill, leave the bar, walk together for a couple blocks.

"Forget about poets, my dear. Go to the sandlot fields, to the shanty-towns, but be careful when you do. Talk about what happens there. Forget about poets. Including me. We're not important."

"Then why did you give me an interview?"

"Because I'm extraordinarily vain."

"You're vain but you don't want to say your name?"

"Right. I'm so vain that I don't want to say my name."

The next morning, Pru interviews Floridor Pérez, who is almost eighty years old and strikes her as a particularly cheerful man. Perhaps influenced by her conversation with the nameless poet, Pru assumes that Floridor Pérez is a pseudonym. He realizes this, and clarifies laughingly that it's not.

"That's just what my mama named me. I think it's good to have weird names. I had to make a big fuss with my first son, because they wouldn't let me name him Chile. I even had to bring in a poet friend who was also a law-yer. It was crazy, there are plenty of girls named Africa or America or Francia or Irlanda and they have zero problems. There was even a soccer player on the Unión San Felipe team named Uruguay Graffigna. But the guy at the civil registrar wouldn't let me name my son Chile. Chile is a very nice name."

"And that's his name? Chile Pérez?"

"Well, he changed it when he turned eighteen. He wanted an average, run-of-the-mill name."

Then they talk about the time Floridor spent detained during the first months of the dictatorship and about the years he was relegated to Com-barbalá, an exile in his own country.

"They took everything from me, but they took much more from others. I'm no victim," Floridor says suddenly. He repeats that. He says he doesn't like to talk so much in first person, that the suffering was collective.

Floridor Pérez has been in charge of the Neruda Foundation workshop for decades and he knows a lot of young poets, so at the end of the conversa-tion Pru asks his opinion about Pato.

"He's a good kid," says Floridor. "He does like his parties."

"Do you like his poems?"

"Not so much, but I'm sure that someday, in the future, I will like them," says Floridor, with a sarcastic or kindly smile.

"And what has it meant for you to meet so many young poets?"

"They're like my children. I don't think they think of me as a father, but I do think of them as my children. Some of them turn ungrateful, others I go on seeing, I read their work, I'm happy when things go well for them."

The self-denominated urban poet Pru was supposed to interview at noon cancels with ten minutes' notice, saying she has a cold. The gay poet she was to interview in the afternoon also cancels: he says it's too hot to go outside. Pru is grateful for the break, and stays home all day. She washes clothes, hangs them up, takes them down, folds them, puts them away. She goes out for a walk, buys some ulmo honey ice cream that she plans to share with Vicente and Carla, but neither of them is home. She eats half a liter while reading the harrowing arguments between Chilean poets on Facebook.

On Friday she interviews Miles Personae (this one *is* a pseudonym), a poet who writes dramatic monologues in the voices of torturers, criminals, and other malevolent figures from the Chilean extreme right wing. The poems, as far as Pru has been able to deduce, are parodic and controversial. He is also the author of some very innocent young adult novels, which sell quite well and which he signs with his real name, Radomiro Robles. Pru was expecting to meet an unpleasant character, but the man turns out to be scintillating, even.

"I noticed that in Chile there are no right-wing poets, as if it were a contradiction to be a poet and right-wing. And then I created this poet-character of the right, who provoked disgust and curiosity. It's hard to find a space in Chilean poetry. And I found that little niche," Miles tells her with unexpected simplicity.

"But are you right-wing?"

"Of course not! But thanks to me people know how dangerous those fuckers are."

On Saturday, Pru has been locked in the little room for hours working on her notes when she gets a message from Jessye asking to Skype. Never, over the course of nearly eight years, had they gone this long without speaking. Pru replies that she doesn't have time, but Jessye insists. Pru signs into Skype but says the signal is bad and she'd rather not use video, but it's just an excuse not to have to see Jessye. She also tells her, she doesn't know why, that she's in Valparaíso.

"Alessandra left her husband," says Jessye abruptly.

The release of two details previously unknown to Pru—the woman's name and the fact that she has a husband, which, more than a detail, is a key piece of information, a start for a scandalous love story, passionate and bold—seems like an unnecessary act of cruelty. The purpose of the call is to let her know that Alessandra had to move for a few days, for a little while, into their room, the room that still holds Pru's things.

"We want to find a place just the two of us, but you know how it is in New York," Jessye says.

It sounds like a prerecorded speech, or as if she had rehearsed it. Pru has the impression that Alessandra is right there beside Jessye, listening.

Pru hangs up Skype and immediately writes Jessye an email saying that she will not be coming back, that she can put her things in storage and go ahead and live in that room until the end of time if she likes. Then she writes another email calling Jessye an idiot for having bought the wrong tickets. And right away she writes a third, which will be the last, saying that it's fine, she's sorry, she doesn't think Jessye is an idiot but she doesn't want to see her for a long time, maybe never again, though she bears her no ill will (which is completely false).

"Now I'm homeless." She thinks that and also says it aloud, to nobody, to herself, to make it real.

She lies on the bed and while she cries she thinks it's been a long time since she cried and that it's the first time she's cried for Jessye, and it seems astonishing that she's made it so long without crying over her, and that thought, which could be soothing, does not soothe her in the least. Quite the contrary, it accentuates her sadness. And then she remembers she did cry over

Jessye, on the sofa at the house with the two little girls and fresh-baked bread in Hacienda San Pedro, and she wonders how she could have forgotten, and she concludes that her brain isn't working right. She takes a sleeping pill, finds the fake Barbie in her suitcase, and falls asleep hugging it to her chest.

When she wakes up she gets into the shower and starts to masturbate without thinking about anyone, but some seconds after her orgasm she realizes she was actually imagining Vicente going down on her, and then she returns to the image and keeps masturbating and quickly reaches another orgasm. She lies down on the bed conjecturing that maybe she hadn't been crying over Jessye but rather Vicente, who no longer seeks her out; at most they chat for a few minutes when they happen to coincide in the kitchen, like two colleagues who occasionally run into each other by the coffeepot or the copy machine. She listens to her favorite playlist on her iPad, all very sad and danceable songs. When "Who Loves the Sun" comes on, she does, in fact, start to dance. She dances to it five times. Then she listens to it again, lying in bed, and tries clumsily to translate the lyrics into Spanish (¿Quién ama el sol?).

On Sunday she has a Skype interview with Rosabetty Muñoz, an endearing poet who lives in Chiloé. Pru is still recovering from her conversation with Jessye, but she manages, unexpectedly, to laugh wholeheartedly at the woman's wise and insouciant commentary, and Rosabetty also tells her she can't leave Chile without visiting the island. She invites Pru to Ancud, promising a place to stay. She asks if Pru is vegetarian, and when Pru says no, Rosabetty offers to kill a pig in her honor. Pru has scheduled a few days in Valparaíso but she's not in any condition to take more trips, especially not so far from Santiago. She has very little money left, and although she's not a vegetarian she's never really liked pork, so she's happy to give that poor pig a few extra days of life.

"You're sad," Rosabetty says, out of the blue.

The interviewee now seems to want to turn the tables. She asks a thousand questions Pru doesn't want to answer, but does anyway, and in the end she tells her the whole story with Jessye. Rosabetty is quiet for a few minutes, focused and pensive, as though consulting a crystal ball.

"Just kick Jessye out. She's got some nerve, the floozy. Who does she think she is?"

"Well, it's not like it's my house, though." Pru doesn't want to sound like that, so disconsolate.

"Breakups are tough. I was just writing something about that."

"Did you have a breakup too?"

"Me? No way, not a chance. Juan and I are great, and have been for years. But a friend who lives close to us just got separated, and his wife took the house and he kept the land."

"What?"

"Do you know what palafitos are?"

"No."

"They're houses built on stilts."

Pru googles the word *palafito* and sees dozens of houses built over calm waters in Venezuela, in Myanmar, and Chiloé.

"There are palafitos in many places in the world, but in Chiloé we also build palafitos on solid land," says Rosabetty.

"What?"

"You stick the stilts into the earth, that way it doesn't matter if the ground is uneven. And if there's a breakup, one person can take the house and the other keeps the land."

"How do they move the house?"

"They put it on some thick trunks and drag it with oxen. They call that kind of move a 'tiradura de casa,' a 'house pulling.' And if they have to move the house from one island to another, they lash the trunks together and make a raft and tow it with motorboats. It's lovely. The house sailing between islands. Plus, it's practical, you don't even have to empty the drawers. You do have to take the pictures off the walls, though, because they can fall."

"Do people separate much in Chiloé?"

"Not much, but sometimes you want to live closer to your kids or your grandkids, and then you find yourself a plot of land and you take the house there. And it's good to know your house isn't stuck to the earth. And that it'll work on land or on water. It's good for a house to have legs, all houses should have legs."

"It's beautiful," says Pru, moved.

On Monday she travels to Valparaíso, where she spends four days interviewing poets Rocotto recommended, three women and two men. The two men do nothing but talk shit about Santiago, though they are both Santiaguinos. Pru finds one of them brilliant and maybe the other one is too, but he tends to conceptualize everything, and he constantly, pedantically cites French and German philosophers, and he talks or dictates to her like a boss to his secretary.

As for the three women, they claim to be friends but it seems to Pru like deep down they hate each other. The one she likes best is named Javiera Villablanca. Every morning, over her first coffee, Javiera reads a poem by someone else ten times, trying to memorize it. Then she has breakfast with her daughter—the two of them live in a small house on Cerro Miraflores—and drops her off at school, and her day is spent working precarious, badly paid jobs. That's until eleven at night, when the poet sits down at the dining room table and writes the poem she read in the morning just as she remembers it. The degree of the divergence varies a lot, but it's always there. The idea is to recall the poem many times over the course of the day, and for life, so to speak, to correct her memory. She's worked that way for almost twenty years, and she's published four books of those versions that she views as translations or distortions of the original poems.

By her last night in Valparaíso, Pru is exhausted. She goes into a random restaurant with the idea of eating some french fries and resting her brain. She wants nothing more to do with poets, but she hasn't even finished the first beer when what should begin but a poetry reading.

Pru feels like the entire population of Valparaíso writes poetry, though she intuits that the people reading at that bar belong to a different circuit, that of the—as she provisionally calls them—amateur poets. One of the amateurs, who has hair down to his thighs, begins his reading this way:

"I want to dedicate my presentation tonight to one of my best friends: Julio, Julio Cortázar."

His poems are horrible but he is nonetheless rewarded by steady ap-
plause. In addition to the overall dedication to Cortázar, each poem is dedicated to another of the poet's friends: John Lennon, Friedrich Nietzsche
(whom he calls Federico), Camilo Sesto, Joaquín Sabina, Jean-Paul Sartre,
and the soccer player David Pizarro.

Pru thinks she might like the amateur poets more than the professional
ones. Later, near midnight, some French tourists she meets take her to see
the singer-songwriter Chinoy, and Pru is fascinated: his strange, falsetto
voice and the fevered rhythm of his chaotic but delicate strumming are permanently burned into her memory.

"Chinoy is a poet too," she's told afterward by a very friendly drunk who
insists on walking her back to the hostel. "Apparently he publishes books
and everything."

"Is there anyone in Valparaíso who isn't a poet?" Pru asks.

"Me. I'm not a poet. But I do write."

"What do you write?"

"Aphorisms."

After finally getting rid of the friendly drunk, Pru flops onto the hostel bed
and starts to look at videos of Chinoy on YouTube. There's one where the
singer is playing guitar while sitting on a wooden staircase—suddenly, between two lines, he says, "Go on, don't worry," to a little boy who wants to
get by but doesn't dare interrupt filming. Without stopping the song, Chinoy
moves aside to let the boy go quickly and carefully up the stairs. Pru repeats
the scene over and over. She imagines herself, years later, looking at this
same video and remembering this trip with wild nostalgia. She falls asleep
thinking about the final lines of the song, which she likes a lot:

> *That voice that asks for my silence*
> *If you go never ask for the change*
> *That voice that asks for my silence*
> *If you go never ask for the change*
> *If there were tracks in the river*

If there was an ocean there was no end
If there were tracks in the river
If there was an ocean there was no end

As was to be expected, during her four days in Valparaíso Pru receives numerous declarations of love at first sight, but it is Valparaíso itself that she falls in love with; it seems to her a very rough city but also a welcoming one, beautifully dangerous, wild, and she even thinks that the omnipresent stray dogs are fiercer and happier than their Santiago peers.

She wants to stay, but she has to return to Santiago for the last of her interviews. When she gets off the bus, the city seems sadder now, and it strikes her as illogical that so many people live in Santiago: it's as though they want to hide from the sea, she thinks.

The next day she spends hours talking with Armando Uribe, a nearly eighty-year-old poet who made a promise not to publish as long as Augusto Pinochet was in power, and had kept his word for the seventeen years of the dictatorship. Since he returned to Chile in 1990, he has published over thirty books. The poet has lived locked away in his apartment since his wife's death a few years back. He smokes nonstop, alternating randomly between various cigarette brands. Pru starts the interview in Spanish, but he insists on speaking in an English that to her seems impeccable, though he speaks with a single remaining tooth.

Uribe had been a diplomat as well as a poet, and later he wrote about the U.S. intervention to topple Salvador Allende's government, a subject in which Pru expresses interest. The poet expounds on the topic, and his storytelling is so impassioned and brutal and overwhelming that she starts to feel real distress.

Suddenly they hear the music of an organ-grinder, who apparently stops every morning in front of Uribe's building.

"Excuse me, miss," Uribe says, and he gets up with almost implausible youthfulness. He opens the window of the second-floor apartment and greets the organ-grinder as he searches his pocket for some coins and tosses them down.

The poet returns to the conversation, which has moved on to Ezra Pound and T. S. Eliot and other English-language poets. The exchange is animated, and in spite of his sententious tone her interviewee strikes Pru as truly kind, but then they're interrupted again by the same organ-grinder's music.

"Excuse me, miss," the poet says again, and again he hops up and opens the window and tosses out some coins.

The poet sits back down and says:

"Clearly he didn't think it was enough."

Pru's penultimate interview is a delirious yet polite conversation in the house of Aurelia Bala, a poet-performer in her fifties, artificially blond and naturally huge, famous for her anti-canonical vocation. ("To me, Neruda, Huidobro, De Rokha, Lihn, and Zurita are like one single macho jackass, overblown and small-dicked.") At one point the poet offers her a white chocolate weed cookie, and Pru eats less than half but she's still overcome by laughing fits and a sudden, acute attack of the munchies. Aurelia makes her a spinach-and-chive omelet; Pru devours it and, satisfied, falls asleep for twenty minutes, though when she wakes up she feels like she's slept for three hours, or five. Her hostess is at her desk writing with both hands in two different notebooks. It's astonishing: both hands write at practically the same speed, or maybe her left hand is just slightly slower than the right. What's more, each hand has different handwriting, and it is hard to say which is clearer or more beautiful. The poet is writing two completely different and simultaneous poems.

"When did you learn to write with both hands?" asks Pru.

"Very young, I've done it almost my whole life," says the poet, with friendly pedantry. "Everyone should be ambidextrous. If everyone knew how to write with both hands, there would be some hope for this motherfucking world," she says, overpronouncing the words with funny theatricality, and then she bursts into tears, but only for a few seconds.

Pru asks if she can take some photos of Aurelia.

"No," says the poet sweetly.

"Sorry."

"No worries, it's just, people need to stop with all the picture-taking, goddammit. It's going to kill us all, it's a real scourge."

"It's just so I'll remember. I like to take pictures to remember."

"You take pictures because you know you're never going to come back. You never want to see me again, because you think I'm too intense, everyone thinks that. And because you want me."

Pru doesn't know how to respond. She just looks at her.

"You want to sleep over, you want to have sex?" The poet offers sex in exactly the same tone as when she'd offered the weed cookie.

Pru smiles, intimidated, and shakes her head.

"Then get going now, I'm working."

Aurelia Bala walks her to the door, and as she's saying goodbye Pru almost asks her if in addition to ambidextrous she is also bisexual. It seems like a journalistically important detail, but she doesn't dare.

The final interview takes place Tuesday afternoon, though it would be wrong to qualify it as an interview, because Pru mostly spends the time playing with the two-year-old twin daughters of Bernardita Socorro, a poet with short blond hair. They talk a lot, but very little about poetry.

"When they were smaller I cried myself to sleep almost every night. And I had to cry quietly so I wouldn't wake them. And I think they picked up on it, and when they woke up they cried quietly too. Even today, compared with other kids, they cry quietly, it's a really weird thing."

"So you taught them how to cry," says Pru.

"Right!"

With sudden enthusiasm the poet jots something down, maybe the start of a poem, on the same sheet of construction paper where one of the twins is scribbling with blue crayon. The other one is sound asleep in Pru's arms.

Around that same time, Pato gets them invited to a party at the house of Eustaquio Álvarez, a poet-editor. Vicente calls Pru to let her know, with the hope of, so to speak, winning her back. Pru says she can't go with him, but he insists, because there's a rumor that Nicanor Parra is going to be there. She tells him there's no way that a ninety-nine-year-old man is going to travel from Las Cruces to Santiago to go to a party. Vicente replies it's not all that unlikely, because Nicanor Parra has a house or a few houses in Santiago, and apparently he's tight with the party's host. She tells him that in any case she's going to meet Nicanor Parra soon, thanks to Gerardo Rocotto, who is friends with a friend of one of Nicanor's daughters. She says they're going to Las Cruces together next Tuesday.

Vicente is left thinking that, in effect, it *would* be very strange for a ninety-nine-year-old man, surely at death's door—because a ninety-nine-year-old man can only be at death's door—to go to that party. And he thinks maybe he could tag along on Pru's visit to Las Cruces. I'm friends with a gringa who is friends with a professor who is friends with a friend of Nicanor's daughter, thinks Vicente, with coy self-pity, but then he returns to his symphony of jealousy centered on Rocotto. And then he hates them all a little, not just Rocotto, but also Parra and Parra's daughter and Parra's daughter's friend. He meets up with Pato, who clarifies that the Parra who is going to the party is the poet Sergio Parra, owner of the bookstore Metales Pesados, and not Nicanor Parra, and he asks how Vicente could honestly think that

Nicanor Parra was about to take a bus from Las Cruces just to go to a party in Santiago. Vicente thinks that if he were ninety-nine years old he would go to all the parties he was invited to and he would also try to dance and get drunk, even if it put his life at risk. And he thinks he wants to meet Sergio Parra, whom he has seen many times in the bookstore and whom he admires, though he's never dared speak to him precisely because of that admiration.

Vicente and Pato get to the party at eleven at night, not wanting to seem too eager. To Vicente's surprise Pru is standing in one corner, surrounded by Rocotto and a few other vultures. Pru explains: she had already committed to going to a party that she thought was a different one from Vicente's. Vicente apologizes and says he got mixed up, that the Parra who will be there is named Sergio and is the owner of the Metales Pesados Bookstore, and that Sergio and Nicanor are not related. And to confer at least a little importance on himself, he says that when Sergio Parra arrives he can introduce her. She tells him she knows Nicanor and Sergio aren't related and that she already knows Sergio, she's been to his bookstore several times now. And he's already here, Pru adds after something like a dramatic pause, pointing toward a corner where, in fact, Sergio Parra is sitting, wearing his trademark black suit and dolphin-shaped ring on his right ring finger. Pru comments that Sergio Parra has an air of Bob Dylan about him, and a poet-critic overhears her and butts in to say that he looks more like the Mexican singer Emmanuel. Pru looks up photos of Emmanuel on her phone and doesn't agree, but she goes on talking about Sergio Parra's look with the poet-critic.

"So, are you a poet too?" Rocotto asks Vicente pleasantly, to make conversation.

"I am someone who doesn't want to talk to you," says Vicente, cup in hand, surprised at his own hostility.

In addition to poet-critics, and poet-editors like Eustaquio Álvarez, and poet-booksellers like Sergio Parra, the party has many poet-professors, poet-journalists, poet-fiction-writers, poet-translators, and several bards dedicated to less literary professions (a designer who works at a liquor store, two pollsters, a preschool teacher, a tattoo artist, two sociologists, two phone operators, two DJs, an educational psychologist, a hairdresser, and a lawyer who is also a firefighter and who has everyone up to here with his analogies between writing poems and confronting a blazing fire). There aren't a ton of non-poets, but there are a few, including Pru herself, who has never even come close to writing a poem, and Professor Rocotto, who, while he did write verses in his youth, had the good sense never to publish them. The male-to-female ratio, meanwhile, is alarming: at best twenty of the nearly sixty people crammed into the living room are women. Pru is also surprised, in this case pleasantly, by the variety in age: forty-somethings predominate, but there are also young kids like Pato and Vicente and people sixty and above. (No one is ninety-nine, though.) In a way it seems like a family party, with grandparents, parents, and kids all crowded into the living room of a house that's not very large or clean, though it is quietly beautified by the shelves full of books, almost all of them with very thin spines, because they are almost all poetry.

Vicente looks out of the corner of his eye at Pru, who is surrounded by eight alpha-poets vying for her attention. He is sad and subdued, while Pato, of course, shines: he's in his element, he talks and jokes with everyone, he speaks in long sentences full of subordinate clauses that allow him to toss out, in passing, a few humblebrags. ("I thought I sent them my worst poems, I was really surprised when they published them!") Though he's in full-on networking mode, he suddenly catches sight of Vicente and goes over to offer his support. Vicente wants to get drunker than ever before in his life; he would like, he tells Pato, for the gringa to move out of his house, he'd like to open the door to her room and find it empty.

"So you can lie on the mattress and cry and rub one out while you think about her?" asks Pato mockingly.

Vicente looks at him with rage, but he thinks that if he did open the door on that empty room he would do precisely that, start to cry and rub one out, of course he would.

A poet wearing Bermuda shorts picks up the guitar and sings a Los Prisioneros song, but in honor of Pru he sings it in English ("Like another skin / another flavor / like other hugs / and another smell"), and then a David Bowie song, but in Spanish (the first lines of "Rock 'n' Roll Suicide"). He is

supposedly improvising, but he does it so fluently it seems like he's been practicing the number for a long time. Eustaquio Álvarez calls for silence, and
when everyone ignores him he asks again, only this time imitating the hoarse,
earthy voice of the poet Gonzalo Rojas. He manages to capture the group's
attention, so he draws out the imitation by reciting "Al silencio," one of
Gonzalo Rojas's most famous poems, which, not surprisingly, loses some of
its beauty in the parody:

> *Oh voice, singular voice; all the hollow of the sea,*
> *All the hollow of the sea would not serve*
> *All the hollow of the sky*
> *All of beauty's cavity*
> *Would not be enough to contain you . . .*

Another poet, who is sporting a pair of ridiculous glasses with a fair
amount of dignity, interrupts the host with an imitation of Armando Uribe
that is so good Pru recognizes the voice of the eighty-year-old poet she's just
interviewed, though the imitation Uribe speaks in Spanish and has all his teeth.
The owner of the house and the poet with ridiculous glasses continue competing with imitations of Pablo de Rokha, Enrique Lihn, Nicanor Parra, and
Jaime Huenún. A third chimes in to imitate Raúl Zurita passionately reading
a grocery list, and then someone imitates Neruda and receives several dis-
dainful looks, because the odious Nerudian drone is too easy to imitate.

Vicente sits down next to Sergio Parra, who is watching the scene in silence, with reserve and contempt drawn in his bloodshot eyes.

"That's what these fuckers are, a bunch of karakoe singers, look how
happy they are, whooping it up," Parra says to him.

Vicente is about to tell Parra that the word is *karaoke* and not *karakoe*,
but really, what for? He's happy just to talk to Parra, who he thinks is drunk,
but then he notices the non-alcoholic beer in his hand. Just then there's an
oasis of relative silence, and Sergio Parra takes the opportunity to stand up
and shout, with contained anger, more or less the same thing he just said to
Vicente:

"What you all do is just karakoe. You all are the karakoe generation."

"Karaoke, asshole!" several people correct him in unison, and Vicente regrets not having corrected him sooner.

"Karaoke, karakoe, same shit. That's what you all are, karaoke poets, you don't have a single idea in your heads."

"Take it easy, Parrita," several people say. That's what his friends call him, Parrita, which Vicente thinks sounds patronizing.

Then comes another interpretation that is apparently an homage: the poet with regrettable glasses launches into a recitation of a poem by Sergio Parra himself, and the imitation is also excellent, though he pillories Parra excessively. Parra endures the impression with good humor, smiling with an expression of calculated contempt that perhaps accentuates his physical resemblance to Bob Dylan or the much less influential Mexican singer Emmanuel or to both, or maybe neither. It seems like things will end there, but then a very fat poet brings his face ten centimeters from Parra's (which is of course a provocation and also quite unpleasant, considering Pru's observation about the tendency toward halitosis among Chilean poets), and he says, or rather spews:

"Your books aren't worth shit."

A skirmish of shoving breaks out. In theory, Sergio Parra has the advantage because he's completely sober, but a sober man fighting a drunk one tends to recognize the futility of the fight, and anyway Parra came to the party alone and he's been alone for a good portion of the night; he's friends with everyone, he loves them all, reads them all, but tonight he decided to stay in a corner and the only person he's spoken to is Vicente, who in any case, in the event of a pitched battle, would defend Sergio Parra, not only because of his innate tendency toward justice, but also because the fact that someone like Sergio Parra had entrusted his comment to him before taking it public stirs an instantaneous fidelity in him, so that, though he is averse to violence—he once, at fifteen years old, seriously considered the possibility of tattooing the peace sign on his chest (luckily Carla vetoed that)—he would be willing to enlist in the paltry ranks of Sergio Parra's army.

In the end it doesn't escalate beyond shoving. Parra goes to the fridge for the alcohol-free beers that he brought himself, and, though people try to stop him, he opts to leave; Vicente decides to go with him out of allegiance, and also because he thinks that this forceful exit will grant him a heroic aura that in effect Pru, who is watching the events a little trepidatiously, perceives. Or rather: she perceives that Vicente seems to form part of this group that could be considered representative of Chilean poetry, which to her is not necessarily a good thing. Vicente doesn't even look around for Pru to say goodbye.

J ust when the belligerent atmosphere is fading, a tall, emaciated poet
bursts shirtless into the living room. Apparently he had tried to shit on the
host's bed. Two forty-something poets are accusing him, and there's a
third, very drunk poet who could be backing up the accusation or not, it's
unclear, because all he does is point to the emaciated poet and repeat, in a
tone that is frankly bullying: "And now, the slippery shadow of Enrique Lihn,
the slippery shadow of Enrique Lihn, the slippery shadow of Enrique Lihn."
The poet with ridiculous glasses takes the opportunity to accuse the emaciated poet of having stolen a book by Nikos Kazantzakis from him at another
party, and, as if this accusation were much more serious than that of having
tried to shit in the host's bed (which, it must be said, the emaciated poet does
not deny; quite the opposite, he claims it was an attempt at performance art),
or that of being Enrique Lihn's slippery shadow (which he doesn't deny either, but merely ignores), the emaciated poet attacks everyone with a barrage
of punches and kicks thrown in every direction.

Pru is in a corner with Rocotto, who puts a protective arm around her.
She is scared, but her journalistic streak wins out: she wants to understand
the fight or at least identify the sides, but that's not easy, because after a few
seconds it looks like everyone is fighting everyone.

"You hogged José Emilio Pacheco in 1999, motherfucker," a poet with
a bushy gray beard says suddenly to Eustaquio Álvarez, who until that

moment had miraculously managed to remain on the sidelines, but now gets a punch right in the snout.

It's an old resentment, totally unrelated to the excesses of the emaciated poet: in effect, in the final months of the twentieth century, José Emilio Pacheco had spent several days in Santiago, and Eustaquio Álvarez was his point person, and it was practically impossible to access Pacheco without first getting a blessing from Álvarez. That wasn't the first or the last of the Mexican poet's visits to Santiago, nor was he what one might call a rock star, but some poets—like the one with the bushy gray beard—were left nursing a grudge, and the rumor that the party's host was a hogger of illustrious visitors (he had really only hogged Pacheco, but we all know how rumors tend toward generalization) was permanently inscribed into the boisterous milieu of Chilean poetry.

Eustaquio Álvarez lies unconscious on the floor for some seconds, a few faithful friends trying to reanimate him. A gay poet rushes to give him mouth-to-mouth, which doesn't seem necessary—the first aid evolves into a tongue kiss and right away Álvarez stands up, the guests fall silent, and Pru thinks the host is going to announce the end of the party. Instead, again imitating the solemn voice of the poet Gonzalo Rojas, he shouts:

"Let the festivities continue!"

And the party does go on, yes, it does: incredibly, the party returns to normal, there is no trace or aftermath of the fight, and there are some ten tardy enthusiasts dancing to "Sympathy for the Devil," but then the Los Prisioneros song "Estrechez de corazón" comes on and the floor is instantly swamped with rowdy dancers. Pru dances and talks with or shouts to everyone, receives advice and book recommendations, which is awkward, because what she wants is to look and listen (and dance), though she does sort of enjoy her starring role. She gets a message from Vicente ("I had to leave with Sergio, sorry"), which she answers right away ("I'm a little sad you left but I'm having fun"). Vicente answers: "You're triste, not trista."

At three in the morning Gerardo Rocotto decides to leave, and he tries to convince Pru to come with him, but she wants to stay, a little out of inertia and a little out of curiosity, but also because she's not sure about Rocotto's intentions, or her own. Rocotto, annoyed, withdraws.

Pru goes to the kitchen with the healthy intention of pouring herself a giant glass of water. The owner of the house is stirring an immense pot, flanked by a woman who is watching him cook with exaggerated attention, as if instead of a vulgar powdered asparagus soup the man were preparing a concoction of the most original or mysterious sort.

The woman's name is Rita, she's around fifty years old, has long white hair, and is extraordinarily tall. Pru stares at her until Rita notices she's there.

"They're all crazy to be interviewed for your article," Rita tells her. "You want some soup?"

"Sure."

Eustaquio Álvarez serves up two mugs and also sips a little straight from the ladle before succumbing to a long yawn. Rita takes a bottle of cola de mono from the refrigerator and pours a glass for Pru. The host returns to the living room, where only a few people are left. Pru thinks it's contradictory to eat that hot soup, which could clear away their drunkenness, along with that cold drink, so sickly sweet and savage. Rita does not share the opinion and alternates timid sips of soup with long swigs of cola de mono, and in fact she immediately pours herself another tall glass. The women go out to the patio. Rita lights a cigarette and smokes looking up at the starry sky. She offers a drag to Pru, who thanks her but says she hasn't smoked since she was a teenager.

"I don't smoke either when I'm not in Chile," says Rita. "But I've never left Chile."

Pru smiles and accepts the drag. Though she knows that smoking again after so many years is going to be awful and will make her cough, she's still surprised by how badly the experiment turns out. She coughs like a tuberculosis patient, and Rita tries to help by giving her some useless little taps on the back. In the absence of water, Pru takes a long gulp of cola de mono.

They go back to the living room. It's four in the morning now, and the owner of the house is sprawled on the sofa, hugging the guitar and snoring like a cartoon character; beside him, two poets are arguing passionately over the word *tenderness*. The poet with the gray beard is sitting on the floor absorbed in a game of *Snake II* on his almost obsolete cell phone. The emaciated poet, ever shirtless, is talking calmly and eloquently with the CPR poet about a film by Lee Chang-dong. Tania Miralles—the poet who learned English listening to Radiohead—has just arrived, and she greets Pru as if they'd known each other all their lives, then lights a giant spliff that she starts to dispatch in eager puffs. An old poet, the only one at the whole party dressed in a suit and tie, is drinking a glass of water and looking out a window in a pose of disillusionment, almost as if he expected to be photographed. A very drunk poet is looking at himself in a small hand mirror and singing, with inharmonious melancholy, the Bunkers song "No me hables de sufrir." Pato is in a corner, the remnants of red wine stamped upon his lips, playing a game of chess in utter silence. Pru goes over to him.

"You're playing alone?"

"Yes, but I identify with black," says Pato.

"And are you winning?"

"No, white is kicking my ass."

Pru sits watching the game and thinks that no, actually the black pieces are winning. Then she returns to Rita, and they drink a little more cola de mono.

"I don't understand why they didn't kick out the skinny poet and the bearded one," Pru comments, still shocked by the fight and also surprised at herself for sticking around. "How is it possible they're still at the party?"

"They're friends," says Rita. "Good friends."

"I can't believe it," says Pru, as though to herself.

"Some people stop being friends for a few years but then they make up and keep going as if nothing happened. Or, well, what do I know, I'm talking just to talk."

Rita wants to leave and offers Pru a ride. It's unnecessary and dangerous, because the woman is visibly drunk, but Pru accepts. The car is a small orange Fiat, and Rita hardly fits in the driver's seat. To Pru she looks simultaneously funny and majestic. A crucifix hangs from the rearview mirror.

"Are you Catholic?"

"Because of the cross? No, this car is my oldest son's."

Pru wants to ask how many kids she has, and if she lives with them, and if her son is as tall as she is. Instead, she asks if Rita is a poet. Rita says no, but she likes to hang out with poets, it's a fun world. They are silent. For a moment the only sound is the engine as they drive along the empty streets.

"It's an entertaining world, but tiring," says Pru, to reanimate the conversation. "They're all really intense."

"But it's a better world. A little better. It's a more genuine world. Less boring. Less sad. I mean, Chile is classist, sexist, rigid. But the world of the poets is a little less classist. Only a little. At least they believe in talent, maybe they believe too much in talent. In community. I don't know, they're freer, less stuck up. They mix together more."

"But they're still really sexist."

"Sexist as motherfucking hell."

"There weren't very many women at that party."

"We have better parties," says Rita. "These can be pretty lame, pretty boring, and they always try to hit on you."

"Men, or poets?"

"Men. Poets too, but I like them better. Poets are more awkward and more genuine. They work with words, but they don't even know how to talk."

"I've interviewed lots of them, and it sure seems to me like they know how to talk."

"They know how to give interviews, they know how to talk about what they do, they'll sell you a little snake oil, but take them away from poetry and they start stuttering. That's why they write poems, because they don't know how to talk."

Pru is about to fall asleep, but she's jerked awake when Rita slams on the brakes at a red light. If I wasn't wearing my seat belt, thinks Pru, I would have smashed my head into the windshield. Rita apologizes. She says she is very drunk and shouldn't be driving, cola de mono should be outlawed, it's so deceptive, so treacherous. She opens the window and tries to light a cigarette, but her hand is too unsteady and she desists. Pru offers to drive, and Rita unexpectedly accepts. They stop the car, change seats. It's been many years since Pru drove, she never did it in New York. She is nervous, but after two blocks starts to enjoy herself, and she also likes that she knows or can kind of guess the way home. Pru thinks about how she hadn't smoked in years, hadn't driven in years. Rita puts a hand to her forehead, still ashamed for braking so suddenly.

"Come in for a while so you can sober up," says Pru.

She asks Rita to be quiet and leads her by the hand through the kitchen and out to the little room, where Rita casually flops onto the bed.

"That's how I like my mattresses," she says. "People nowadays buy these soft mattresses that are terrible for your back. Chileans are all about soft mattresses. This one is perfect."

Then she sets off talking about the time she spent working in the furniture section at a department store when she was twenty-one. She says it was the perfect job, and that sometimes, in winter, they even took turns napping. And she came to know a lot about mattresses, she still knows a lot about mattresses, though the technology has changed a fair amount since then.

Pru lies down next to her. Rita tells her that she's a journalist too by training, but her job is selling life insurance. And that she has three children, two boys and a girl, and the girl is twelve, the middle boy is twenty, and the oldest twenty-two. She says she was never in love with her husband. She says he sleeps with other women, and so does she. And with other men, but only sometimes. She says men don't know how to fuck and that all women, without exception, do. She says that life, for her, is settled. Pru asks what she means.

"Just that," replies Rita. "That it's settled, nothing is going to change."

"Do you want something to change?"

"Yes. I want everything to change, my life and other people's lives. But nothing's going to change."

"I want almost everything to change too," says Pru. "All of it."

Rita goes to the bathroom, splashes water on her face. Then she looks at the books with a frown, as if she were solving a crossword puzzle.

"Who lives in this room?"

"A poet," says Pru.

"Of course."

Rita looks at the photos, lingering over the portrait of Camila Vallejo, and finally kissing it.

"What a hottie," she says.

Pru bursts out laughing.

"So your older son is Catholic?" Pru is thinking about the crucifix again.

"The thing is that almost everyone in Chile is pretty Catholic, in a way," says Rita. "Not me. Or I am, but I hide it well. My oldest son doesn't hide it. That's why I like poets."

"Because poets aren't Catholic?"

"No," says Rita, emphatic. "I mean, poets are poets. They're believers, but they believe in other shit."

Rita asks Pru if she has any cocaine or marijuana or whiskey or beer. Pru says no to everything. Rita drinks a lot of tap water and lies down on the bed again. She falls asleep. Pru curls up beside her and turns out the light. They sleep in an embrace, like classmates or old friends, and their snores play out a weary dialogue of questions and answers. In the morning Pru walks Rita to the door; it seems no one is home. They both know they will never see each other again, and they look at each other with joy or gratitude and they hug without sadness.

As she tries to go back to sleep, Pru decides she is going to buy a very small car and a crucifix to hang on its rearview mirror. She imagines herself driving alone through the streets of a city that isn't Santiago de Chile or New York or any other city she's ever been to. And she thinks that as she drives alone through that unknown city, she will be completely happy.

In the afternoon she gets the urge to see Vicente. She imagines them walking through one of Santiago's squirrel-less parks and looking at the trees in silence, and then starting to talk for hours, about whatever. She looks for him eagerly, but he's not home. She waits for him, sitting down in the living room to read. Carla comes back from the grocery store, offers her some crackers and Brie, opens a bottle of wine, and tells her that Vicente went on vacation.

"When is he coming back?" Pru asks.

"I don't know. It's summer, all his friends are on vacation. I don't even know if he went to the beach or Cajón del Maipo or to the south."

"I want to see him," Pru says involuntarily, as though thinking out loud.

"I guess you want to say goodbye," says Carla, "because you're leaving soon."

"Pretty soon, but I still don't know when I'm going back to New York."

"I know when," says Carla as she pulls her hair back, appearing nonchalant. "You're going back soon, very soon. Tomorrow, or the day after. In five days, a week max."

Pru has just been kicked out and she is furious, partly because she understands Carla's reasons. Her impulse is to leave the house immediately, but after she calms down she decides to stay a few more days, because she has to wait until Tuesday for her interview with Nicanor Parra. She feels like a teenager, and she hates it. She calls the airline and confirms her ticket for Wednesday.

Rocotto is not interested in the work of Nicanor Parra, and he is hugely annoyed by the poet's cult of personality. He trash-talks Parra a lot, it's practically the only thing he does during the two-hour drive to the so-called Coast of Poets, frequented at various points in history by Neruda, Vicente Huidobro, and Nicanor. Rocotto says the latter's work is overvalued, he rails against Parra's friends, who he claims are a Mafia in control of the media. He tells Pru that visiting Parra's house is like a rite of passage for Chilean poets. That many idolize him and others detest him, but they all go meet him anyway, like the faithful making a pilgrimage to the altar of some saint—and Nicanor Parra is anything but a saint.

"For years now, Parra's just been writing little jokes," Rocotto declares.

"But he's ninety-nine years old," says Pru.

"So?"

"Well, if I was ninety-nine, I might like to be able to write jokes."

"But everyone celebrates them like they were words from the Oracle."

"So are you saying Parra isn't the most important living poet in Chile?" asks Pru, a little sick of Rocotto.

"Of course he is, in Chile and maybe in all of Spanish-language poetry, but what does that matter?"

"I feel like I'm forcing you to do something really unpleasant," says Pru.

"No, how could it be unpleasant?" says Rocotto, trying to make his voice sound deeper. "It's always pleasant to be with you."

In front of Las Cruces' Playa Chica, which is packed with sunbathers, they meet up with Pancho, Rocotto's friend who is friends with Nicanor Parra's daughter. He lives in Santiago, but he's spending the summer in Las Cruces. He clambers into the car and directs them to Parra's house, where they are received by Nicanor's maid-nurse-assistant Rosita, a small woman with an occasional smile and a permanently suspicious demeanor. Pancho introduces himself and says he's come to see Nicanor many times before, and Rosita says she doesn't remember him. While the tug-of-war lasts, Pru notices what a small house it is: after all the gossip she's heard about Parra and the Chilean poets, she'd come to imagine he would live in a mansion and that the beach at Las Cruces would be more exclusive than Malibu.

Just then, providentially, the poet's youngest daughter, Colombina, arrives and greets Pancho with a hug, then tells them to wait a few minutes.

"I thought you scheduled the interview," Pru says to Rocotto, who shrugs.

"It's always like this," says Pancho, "don't worry. But remember, it's not an interview, you can't record."

After a while Nicanor himself appears at the gate. His walk is slow but steady. At times it seems he's going to lose his balance, but it's just his way of walking.

"Who is it you're looking for?" asks Nicanor.

"Nicanor Parra," replies Pancho, playing along. Pru doesn't understand a thing.

"Oh, Don Nicanor is sleeping, he sleeps all day long," says Nicanor.

"Well, we were hoping to wake him up," says Pancho.

"Well, he's ninety-nine years old, you know? If you were ninety-nine I'm sure you'd spend all day sleeping too, right?"

"Come on, wake him up, we want to talk to him," says Pancho.

"As you wish, then."

Nicanor opens the door ceremoniously, gives Pancho a hug, greets Rocotto and Pru with a slight movement of his hands and a cordial, distant smile. He walks them to the terrace and disappears for twenty minutes. He returns with an open newspaper.

"That's why you looked familiar," says Nicanor, pointing to a photo of

Britney Spears in the paper. "You're the one who kissed Madonna? I would've kissed Madonna too! Madonna's the real deal, huh?"

"Thank you, Nicanor," says Pru, "but I'm no Britney Spears, sorry to disappoint you."

"But you're not a journalist, right?" replies Nicanor.

"Of course not," says Pru coyly, "I hate journalists."

"I don't hate them," says Nicanor, and then he adds, "I envy them, a lot."

"And why is that?"

"Because it's the ideal job. They ask a bunch of questions, and that's it. No one asks them anything in return. I would have liked that. To ask. And not be asked anything! Questions are aggressive. People should just talk."

Colombina sits down beside her father, and Rosita also comes out with some glasses of red wine.

"This is the true anti-poet," says Nicanor, pointing to Rosita. "I copy everything from her!"

Nicanor doesn't even glance at Rocotto, who is trying to talk to Rosita and Colombina and appears very tense. Only after a half hour of small talk does the poet seem to notice the professor's existence.

"I'd like to ask you for a favor," he says.

"What's that?" asks Rocotto, surprised.

"'Parra's antipoetry is completely obsolete,'" says Nicanor.

It's a quote from an article of Rocotto's, and he is frozen, uncomfortable, but also flattered: he finds it incredible that Nicanor Parra has read an article he wrote.

"What I meant was that—"

"Don't worry, you're right! I'm completely obsolete!"

"Well . . ."

"That's why, Professor Rocotto, I wanted to ask a favor of you."

"Go right ahead."

"Two blocks from here they sell an arrollado that's the best in the area. Go buy one. And if you walk two blocks farther down there's a real small grocery where they sell good tomatoes. I like 'em nice and ripe."

Nicanor laboriously reaches into his pocket and pulls out a ten-thousand-peso bill. Rocotto looks to the others for solidarity, but they're all struggling to hold back laughter, especially Colombina.

"Don't forget the change, please," says Nicanor.

"Sure," Rocotto grudgingly replies, and he has no choice but to go out and buy the food.

The laughter continues but Nicanor, like all good comedians, remains unsmiling. Then he asks Rosita to put on some piano cuecas, and he follows the rhythm perfectly, slapping his palms on his knees. When the music ends, Pru asks the poet if she can record the conversation.

"Of course not!"

"I was told I couldn't record, but I still wanted to ask."

"I mean, you can record me as long as I don't notice it."

"So I can't record."

"You can record me, but in secret. Are you familiar with Auden?"

"The poet? W. H. Auden?" Pru puts her hand in her pocket to activate the recorder.

"That's the one. He was a teacher of mine, Auden was. He was a good teacher. He was against recording too."

"Was he?"

"Sure was. For the same reason I am. If I say something good, something you'd be able to remember, then what do you need a recorder for? If I said something interesting you'd remember it, right? I had a class with Auden; he was a good teacher, Auden was."

Nicanor begins talking about a class Auden gave on a Shakespeare sonnet. He had erased one word of the sonnet and asked the students to guess what it was. Nicanor tells them how he raised his hand and immediately gave the correct word. Auden was surprised and also pretty displeased, because he had planned to build the class entirely around the absence of that word, and Nicanor had gotten it right away.

"And you know how I guessed the word?"

Pru assumes the answer is not easy. She glances at Pancho, who seems somewhere between distracted and entertained.

"Because I had read the sonnet that very morning! Over coffee! I used to read a Shakespeare sonnet every morning over coffee!"

When Rocotto returns, they all sit down to have a lunch of arrollado and tomato. Pru eats only bread with tomato. Nicanor chews silently, slowly, laboriously, and every once in a while he blurts out a question. Suddenly he livens up and talks for a while to Pancho about the many acquaintances they have in common. As the conversation stretches on after lunch, Nicanor recalls Allen Ginsberg and Lawrence Ferlinghetti, and softly croons the first stanza of "Dear Prudence." He also talks about Violeta Parra, whom he sometimes calls "la Viola" and others "la Violeta Parra." He says he thinks it's undignified to remain alive when almost everyone is dead. He says that there's no mystery to his longevity: he's reached ninety-nine years old thanks partly to his addiction to vitamin C, and partly because his mother breastfed him until he was ten. Everyone laughs, but he insists that it's true: since his mother kept having kids, there was always breast milk. He says that sometimes there was nothing to eat, but there was always breast milk.

Pru stands up to get a closer look at the photograph of Violeta and Nicanor that's hanging on the main wall of the living room. Nicanor follows her, and suddenly the two of them are gazing at the photo in silence, like in a museum. The picture shows the siblings wearing identical ponchos, and Nicanor is also wearing a hat. They look serious, and the poet, oddly, looks very old. Of course, he was around fifty years younger than he is now, but the photo shows a fragile, exhausted man. It's an everyday scene: Violeta holds a ladle in her right hand and is serving something to her brother, something that to a Chilean is clearly navegado, but that Pru thinks might be soup, though the mug seems small for soup.

"I liked being Violeta Parra's brother," says Nicanor suddenly, in a whisper, as though to himself. "I was used to it. I liked it a lot."

Pru takes Nicanor by the arm, and she is surprised at her own gesture of familiarity. They go back to the table.

"Are you eating soup in that photo?" Pru asks him.

"We were drinking navegado," Nicanor replies.

"Vino navegado is a hot wine made with orange peel, clove, and cinnamon. It's very wintry, very common in the south of Chile," explains Rocotto. It's his first contribution to the conversation, and also his last.

"Hey there, Pru, what's in your pocket?" Nicanor asks.

"Nothing," says Pru.

"You wouldn't have a recorder in there, now, would you?"

"Of course not. And you, what's in your pocket?"

"I have a handkerchief," replies Nicanor, smiling with unfettered flirta-
tiousness. "Always gotta carry a handkerchief. It's real handy, good for everything, good for crying or for dancing cueca."

And then he takes out the handkerchief that he does in fact have in the
same pocket he'd taken the ten thousand pesos from, and he uses it to wipe
his forehead, though he does not appear to be sweating. Then he announces
he's going to take a nap. He says to stay and wait for him if they want—they
can take naps too, or go to the beach, take advantage of the summer day. Pru
wants to go to the beach and come back to keep talking with Nicanor, but
Colombina says it's better if they go, because her father is very tired even if
he doesn't want to admit it. Nicanor looks at Colombina and smiles at her
as if they had just run into each other by chance in a deserted square.

Before saying goodbye, Pru takes from her backpack a copy of *Poemas y
antipoemas* that she found in the little room. She wants Nicanor to dedicate
it to Vicente, but before she manages to explain this, Nicanor replies that he'll
sign anything she wants, but next time. She says there won't be a next time,
because she has to go back to the United States. The poet replies that he
doesn't plan to die just yet, so there's time.

While Rocotto and Pancho, who are still hungry, eat some chewy locos in
the Puesta de Sol Restaurant, Pru walks along the shore and can't believe
how cold the water is. The beach is packed, but she finds a spot to lie in the
sand. She falls asleep and wakes up to a soccer ball to the head, followed by
some anonymous laughter. No one apologizes.

"Too bad you didn't wear a bikini," says a twelve-year-old boy who approaches and picks up the ball.

"Leave her alone," interjects a girl who's maybe twenty. Pru thinks she
must be the kid's older sister. "She's a tourist, she doesn't even speak Spanish.
Or do you speak Spanish?"

Pru shakes her head, gets up, and walks quickly back toward the restaurant. She's ashamed of having been afraid, of still being afraid. She's ashamed she didn't dare speak Spanish. Pancho and Rocotto have moved on to coffee, and Pru orders some chamomile tea.

"Your first child is the most wonderful experience, enjoy it," Pancho tells Rocotto as he's saying goodbye.

"You're going to have a baby?" Pru asks him.

"Yep," says Rocotto, staring down at the coffee grounds in his mug.

On the way back to Santiago he has no choice but to tell Pru he has a girlfriend and that his girlfriend is seven months pregnant and they've just moved into the apartment that Pru went to. Pru doesn't say a single word during the rest of the trip. Rocotto monologues for a while, tries out explanations, until finally he goes quiet too. Pru thinks she should have stayed on the beach, playing soccer with those insolent kids, eating ice cream and speaking Spanish.

The morning of her last day in Chile, Pru wakes up with the feeling that Vicente is going to come back and she'll at least be able to say goodbye, but it's just wishful thinking. She texts him—she's texted him every day—but he doesn't answer, it's like he's vanished. At ten in the morning she goes out and makes the half-hour walk to Rocotto's apartment. On the way she stops at a pharmacy, and although she doesn't have much money left, she buys four packages of diapers that she leaves with his concierge, with no goodbye note or explanation.

She goes home, packs her suitcase. It's only noon, and the plane doesn't leave till nearly midnight. She looks at her notes for the article. She had decided to start writing it once she was back in New York, but instinctively she launches into a draft, and it goes quickly because she likes the tone that emerges, light, convincing, and unexpectedly personal, partly because it's a multiple goodbye—a goodbye to Chile, and Chilean poetry, and to Vicente, and to that little guest room, which, for now, is the only room she has. And it's also a more indefinite goodbye, because she knows that when she returns to New York, everything will be different. She knows it, fears it, and desires it.

As she writes, she feels a warm assurance; she likes her phrasing, and her conclusions, which are not absolute. On the contrary, they retain an ambiguous, hesitant air, a little like someone thinking out loud. She rereads her first notes and at times disagrees with herself, and she loves that, she has always liked changing her mind, perhaps what she likes most about her work is the moment when she discovers she has changed her mind. She thinks about Chaura Paillacar struggling with headaches and about the unnamed poet's jumpy eyes, and Aurelia Bala writing with both hands and Floridor Pérez with his son Chile, whom she imagines as a teenager every bit as skinny and gangly as the country that gave him the name he wanted to change at any cost. She thinks about Hernaldo Bravo just after he was hit by a car, in a hospital, writing endless poems out of pure boredom, and about the twins scribbling incessantly on the walls of Bernardita Socorro's small, light-filled apartment. She thinks about Eustaquio Álvarez's party and remembers Rita's words and feels like they're true, that the world of Chilean poets *is* a little stupid but it's still more genuine, less false than the ordinary lives of people who follow the rules and keep their heads down. Of course there is opportunism and cruelty, but also real passion and heroism and allegiance to dreams. She thinks that Chilean poets are stray dogs and stray dogs are Chilean poets and that she herself is a Chilean poet, poking her snout into the trash cans of an unknown city—she likes to think of herself as a Chilean poet, a Chilean poet who is neither poet nor Chilean, but whose journalistic pilgrimage in search of a break, her always frustrated dream of publishing in the big magazines or at least writing a noteworthy and resonant piece, somehow unites her with those men and especially those women who skulk in the alleyways of myth and desire. In retrospect, her life in New York seems frivolous, but it's also true that she never wanted to do just anything; she always sought, and continues to seek, *something*, and though she is not sure what it is, she knows it is not entirely tied up with success or recognition. If you look at her right, she really is a pretty heroic figure.

She finishes the draft and still has four hours ahead of her; for no reason at all, she unpacks her suitcase and packs it again, with methodical slowness. She takes a long, close look at Vicente's books. She imagines him organizing them when he returns, and rereading them. She writes him a long message in Spanish, a message that requires much more work than the draft of the article; she resorts to Google Translate and wordreference.com and linguee.com and she isn't satisfied with the result, but she has to say goodbye somehow. It's not exactly a romantic message. She tells him she wishes she could have said goodbye in person, she thanks him for his friendship, but mostly she talks about Nicanor Parra and palafitos and Ben the dog. She asks if he's ever been to Chiloé. She tells him that Chilean poetry seems like an immense family, with great-grandparents and second cousins, with people who live in a gigantic palafito that sometimes floats between the islands of an archipelago, and there are so many people inside that it should sink, but, miraculously, it doesn't. She puts the letter in an envelope and gives it to Carla.

"Of course I'll give it to him. Forgive me. And forgive my son," says Carla, as she helps Pru load her suitcase into the taxi. "He fell in love with you!"

Pru starts to laugh, but it's nervous laughter. She isn't laughing at Vicente, of course. On the way to the airport she thinks that she fell in love with him too, at least a little bit, and the idea of never seeing him again is painful. She thinks that a friend like the Jessye from before would make her see how senseless it was to fall in love with an eighteen-year-old Chilean boy, and in a way she is glad she no longer has a friend like the Jessye from before. She wouldn't know how to explain or deny what she feels. She liked to look at Vicente, liked to talk to him and listen to him. A lot. That's all, there's nothing more to explain, nothing else to understand.

And then Pru thinks about staying in Chile, but her life is not a splendid bad movie, so she gets on the plane, and I would really like to get on it with her and keep her company and follow her everywhere she goes, but at this very moment there are about a million novelists writing about New York, probably while they listen to and hum along with that beautiful song that goes, "New York, I love you / but you're bringing me down," and I want to read their sophisticated novels, which I nearly always like, in fact I'm going to try to read them all to see if Pru or someone like Pru is in any of them. Anyway, I really would like to get on the plane with her, but I have to stay in Chile, with Vicente, because Vicente is a Chilean poet and I am a Chilean novelist, and we Chilean novelists write novels about Chilean poets.

I've seen you in my bookstore a thousand times, but we've never met. I'm Sergio Parra." Vicente knows who Parra is and Parra knows he knows, but Vicente likes that the famous poet introduces himself anyway.

They have just left Eustaquio Álvarez's party, and they've been walking together for a few blocks when Parra hails a taxi with elegant authority. In the taxi he asks Vicente if he's a poet, and Vicente talks about himself erratically, as is fitting to the circumstances. Parra asks how he spends his afternoons, and he doesn't know how to reply.

"I need someone," Parra tells him.

In his drunkenness, Vicente thinks the poet is starting an amorous confession, so he replies that he also needs someone, that he feels very alone. Parra bursts out laughing and clarifies that he needs someone to work at the bookstore a few afternoons a week, and Vicente delightedly agrees, cheered now. He gets out of the taxi with a wide smile but it doesn't last long, because then he remembers Pru is still at the party, and he would bet that Rocotto is going to get what he wants.

He texts Pru and her reply seems promising, but then he gets discouraged again. He goes to his room to keep watch from his second-floor window, and dozes off for a while with his head on the sill. He wakes up to the voices of Pru and Rita, watches them stealthily enter the little room. He sits watching the movements of the shadows on the curtains, feeling a mixture of rage, anxiety, and impotence. He interprets everything arbitrarily and wrong.

While Pru and Rita sleep like the interlaced branches of two separate trees, Vicente speculates on the details of the scene, until, after three long hours of painful and useless vigilance, he falls asleep. Carla wakes him up early, makes him get dressed and eat breakfast. They go to Providencia, she buys him some books and an ice cream, and he tells her he wants to go to the beach. They return home and it's not even noon yet; Vicente stuffs about twenty books and a few articles of clothing into a giant backpack and sets off immediately to meet friends in El Tabito.

On the way there he tries to sleep a little more. The TV on the bus is showing a Jackie Chan movie, and Vicente manages to take a mild interest in the plot, such as it is. Then he pages through a collection of poems by Antonio Cisneros:

> The mornings are a little colder,
> but you'll never have the certainty of a new season.

He likes those lines, likes Cisneros: his assurance, his lucidity, his dry wit. He gets distracted, thinks he is learning something by reading Cisneros, but not necessarily something about poetry. He lingers over some short poems that are simultaneously funny and very sad:

> To forget you and not look at you
> I watch the houseflies on their flights
> Such Style
> Such Speed
> Such Height.

He switches to a book by Andrés Anwandter. He reads and rereads these lines for one or two kilometers:

> You start to write a poem
> whose subject is a deep lake
> the night finds you there
> now you won't know the way back.

In El Tabito his friends do nothing but smoke weed and talk about the imminent start of college. Vicente smokes a little too, and as he listens to them he feels like he loves them and like they're some real idiots and like he is isolated and like he wants to be as far away as possible from them all, and at that moment those are not contradictory sentiments. They're all so hopeful about college, it's like they've already projected solid, solvent, definitive lives. Vicente thinks they're all headed for the slaughterhouse.

In the afternoon he plays paddleball until he's exhausted, and a little before daylight runs out he settles in on the rocks to read *Poema de Chile*, Gabriela Mistral's posthumous and unfinished book. He stops at these lines:

—Because some things are
both good and bad,
as it is with leaves
on one side velvety
while the other side cuts
your palm bloody.
They're almost not leaves at all
They're evil women

He reads that stanza several times. He likes it and thinks it's funny that he likes it—he imagines Gabriela Mistral writing that poem out of spite after a fight with Doris Dana. He looks for photos of Doris Dana on his phone and tries to decide if she looks at all, even a little, like Pru. We're both in love with gringas, me and Gabriela, he thinks. Then he remembers the woman, so tall and gray-haired, who'd gone into the little room with Pru, and since he doesn't know her name he decides to call her Gabriela Mistral. Plus, he has a feeling that Gabriela Mistral really was tall. There are a lot of us now, he thinks: Rocotto, Gabriela Mistral, and me, all in love with Pru.

On Tuesday he heads to Las Cruces. He arrives very early, and everyone in town knows where Nicanor Parra lives, but if there's any doubt, they say, some backpackers wrote the word ANTIPOET in red spray paint on the front gate. There are no cars in front of the house, so he goes down to the beach and tries to lie down to read, but it doesn't work: reading is usually the ideal pastime for people who are waiting, but not for Vicente, who prefers to read without any concrete plans on the horizon. He closes the book and goes for a walk, letting his feet sink into the sand. He sees a cigarette butt and picks it up, then sees another one and thinks it makes sense to kill time that way. He keeps picking up butts, collecting them obsessively; he gathers a few in his hand and then puts them into a paper cone he also finds on the ground, but he keeps counting them as if he had to officially report the number. Eventually he throws the cone with its hundred and sixty-eight butts into a garbage can, and he thinks it seems like too many. Some of them were completely buried in the sand and looked old, like they'd been there for days or even weeks, but still, he thinks, it's too many, people don't smoke that much anymore. A hundred sixty-eight butts is too many, he thinks.

When he gets back to Nicanor's house, there is Rocotto's Beetle in front. He stands there, half hidden behind some cartoonish dark glasses. After fifteen minutes he sees Rocotto come out alone and decides to follow him. Vicente enters the shop, watches as the professor buys the arrollado, then follows him to the grocery, where he takes a full lap around the store in order to meet him head-on, but it doesn't happen, because halfway down the aisle Rocotto stops, obediently, to choose the best-looking tomatoes. While he dissembles by picking out a few tomatoes of his own, Vicente thinks how he hates Rocotto; he thinks that although the man is not precisely his antagonist, he hates him, despises him. They both wait in line and walk back almost together. At no point does Rocotto glance his way.

Vicente returns to his surveillance post. He gets hungry and regrets not buying a Super 8 bar or something, but he eats a tomato. He's never eaten a tomato that way before, as if it were an apple. It's delicious, so he eats another one. (Absurdly, he bought six.) When he hears the visitors' voices saying goodbye, he flees, more like a thief than a spy. When he's far away he turns around and catches a glimpse of Pru's blond hair as she gets into the car.

He feels very silly, because he didn't do anything. He hadn't had a plan, he just thought that when the moment came, he'd think of something. He gives the extra tomatoes to a bum and goes straight back to El Tabito, walking along the highway. It takes him almost two hours because he walks slowly, stopping now and then to pick up cigarette butts. He finds forty-two.

He spends a week lying in a bed reading thin, intense books that fascinate and perhaps also wound him. And he writes, of course. The days are cloudy, the wind seems incessant, and yet the beach is always full of people. Vicente writes about that, and also about involuntary smiles. He'd like to write a whole book about involuntary smiles, but for now he limits himself to a short poem, narrative and sentimental—a dejected person, despondent, disconsolate, perhaps on the verge of suicide, who at some point in the day smiles, because the smile belongs to the innate language of the person's face, or because there was a time, which now seems long ago, when this person used to smile, and they cannot forgo that gesture, even if they fervently want to, and most likely the random moment of the smile coincides with the random moment when they meet someone on the street who returns the smile.

Vicente had told Carla he would be back at the end of the month, but the second Monday in February he wakes up with the fixed idea of returning to his life, so he grabs his things and impulsively boards a bus. On the trip he wants to read and listen to music and maybe go over his new poems, but he stares out the window the whole way.

When he emerges from the metro he discovers he is happy to be going home. He walks along thinking that when he gets there, the first thing he'll do is go to the little room, not because he wants, as Pato said, to jerk off thinking about Pru, but rather to experience her absence all at once, or to erase the traces of her presence as soon as possible. He even imagines himself deep in the rather happy task of transferring his new poems to the computer and printing them on light blue paper, but that project is left pending, all projects are left pending, because when he opens the door to his house he comes face-to-face with his naked mother having sex on the sofa with:

a) Pato

b) Rocotto

c) Pato and Rocotto

d) Rita

e) Gonzalo

(Answer on the next page.)

N one of those options correspond to reality, but they are all more realistic than the correct answer. Because that afternoon, when he opens the front door of the house, Vicente sees Carla going at it hot and heavy with León.

They get dressed immediately, but for some thousandths of a second Vicente is subjected to the sight of that enormous penis, damp and erect, and its abundant gray pubic hair. The scene is objectively comical, but Vicente finds it ominous, and that feeling only grows as his parents, still only half-dressed, try to explain that it just *happened*, and then try to turn the conversation toward Vicente's refusal to go to college, saying they had met to talk about that, and . . .

Vicente runs from the room.

Carla flops onto the futon and León pounces on her, ready to get back to it. Carla shoves him away but he insists, embracing her roughly, hornily. She knees him in the nuts, and León doubles up in pain on the floor.

"Come on, quit whining and get going," Carla says, her voice unintentionally loud.

He leaves in a huff, though when your nuts are in pain, it can be kind of hard to huff convincingly.

Carla chugs a glass of water and thinks how everything is all wrong, but then she goes to the bathroom and looks at herself in the mirror and bursts out laughing, because there is no way to justify what has just happened, and that, in the end, makes it funny.

León had turned up out of nowhere, bottle of champagne in hand, with the excuse of showing her his new car. She found it clumsy and inappropriate, but since León was methodically following a cheesy seduction strategy, she decided to let him continue. She wanted to see just how far he would take this pathetic endeavor—and then, suddenly, the haughty distance from which Carla was observing the scene simply disappeared, and then she was on the sofa moving atop her ex-husband and having a fine time. No one, not even the most oversexed of her friends, would understand that story, which even to her sounds inconsistent. Samantha Jones herself wouldn't understand me, Carla thinks with a smile.

The bottle is still on the table, the champagne now almost flat. She takes a couple sips, turns on the computer, and opens the file where she keeps her photography projects. Some months ago Vicente had given her a book of photographs of people reading, and Carla loved that her son wanted to unite their two worlds. Plus, she loved André Kertész's photos, and she decided to start taking pictures of the people she sees reading on the metro or in public places, with the idea of making a kind of book of her own and giving it to Vicente.

She looks at those files, those photos. There's one of an executive reading a Stephen King novel, a distracted-looking boy in a Batman costume beside him. She loves that photo because it reminds her of Vicente at four or five years old, when they lived, as they do now, alone in the house, and everywhere he went he wore a vampire cape and carried a pirate sword. One day they went out in a hurry and Vicente forgot the sword; he wanted to go back for it, but Carla told him they didn't have time.

"If we don't go back for the sword I won't be able to defend you, Mom," Vicente had told her, very serious and a bit sad.

Carla keeps looking at the files and sipping the bottle of champagne while she tries to devise some decorous or reasonable explanation to give her son. She also considers not explaining anything, a right conferred on her as his mother. She thinks that instead of trying to explain the impossible, she could just print those photos of people reading and give them to him right away, but there are fewer than twenty and she wants to have a lot more.

Then she thinks that there *is* an explanation and it's so obvious it's become invisible: she is, quite simply, lonely. Then she opens her email and replies to a message from a guy who's been asking her out for months. She's interested in him, and doesn't know why she hasn't bothered to reply. She also accepts an invitation from a woman she works with, whom she isn't necessarily interested in, because she's never been into women. But what the hell, thinks Carla, and in a matter of minutes she has arranged a pair of dates for Friday and Saturday nights.

IV. Poet-Ship

When you arrive at the hospital, it will be easy to tell who I am:
I will be the one who most looks like you.

—VERONICA STIGGER, TRANSLATED BY ZOË PERRY

Gonzalo takes advantage of his end-of-summer downtime to leisurely peruse the shelves at Metales Pesados. He feels like buying a long novel and spending the final days of vacation lying in bed with a few beers under a fan, so he goes straight to the fiction section, but instead of looking at recent novels or classics he's never read, he stands there paging through books that he has read before and that once astonished him.

That's almost all he remembers now, just that he liked these books, that once upon a time they fascinated him. Maybe it's strange, but that's how he is with novels, and with fiction in general: he tends to remember isolated phrases and words, specific scenes that his memory distorts, and above all atmospheres, so that if he had to talk about those books he would sound as tentative and unsure as if he were describing a dream. Plus, he used to read quickly, not trying to memorize anything, not even taking notes or underlining—at most he'd fold the corner of a page to indicate passages that were particularly significant or beautiful, but he didn't even do that all the time, because books were sacred to him, even bad books were sacred. Now he respects them less, now he underlines them brazenly and fills them with notes and stick-on tabs, because reading is his job. Maybe he would playfully say just that, if someone were to ask: My job is to read.

He does remember poems, though, because poetry is made to be memorized, repeated, relived, recalled, invoked. There's only a little ostentation when, in the middle of a class or a talk, he flashes on some poem by César

Vallejo or Idea Vilariño or José Kozer and starts reciting it from memory. He knows many verses, many stanzas, many whole poems by heart—though he no longer passes them off as his own, thank god: that regrettable and decisive night when he supplemented his own book with other people's poems seems so distant now. Carla seems distant too. It's only been six years since the breakup, but he feels as if it all happened in a previous life, or to someone else. It's a time he can only picture in black-and-white. He remembers those years like a movie that was either good or horribly bad, he doesn't know anymore. A silent movie, maybe.

Now, nearing forty, he feels younger than he did in those days, maybe because he's alone. Back then, everyone else was alone and he wasn't, and now he's alone and the others aren't. That's why he's alone: everyone else is with someone, but no one is with him. It sounds like a self-pitying thought, but it's not; he's actually pleased with his solitude, he adores his solitude, he safeguards it like an amulet that had been lost for years and he'd had to fight to recover. It's a friendly and noisy solitude, populated by people who go in and out of his life through a revolving door that occasionally gets jammed but in general works remarkably well.

He pages through the final chapters of *Ulysses*, which he'd read anxiously, erratically, back when he still lived with his parents, and he thinks that at some point he should reread that novel honestly, with a real willingness to play the game. He opens a copy of *A Confederacy of Dunces,* and as he reads the first five pages he recovers the laughter and sense of complicity and he even feels hungry thinking of the pizza and garlic bread he used to eat in his minuscule apartment in the days when he read that novel, not long before his reunion with Carla. He reads the back cover of *To the Lighthouse*, a novel he read at fifteen years old during a stormy week, and he remembers having thought or felt that Virginia Woolf's words had the ability to intensify the rain. He reads the first paragraphs of "The Crime of the Mathematics Professor," his favorite of Clarice Lispector's stories, and he recalls the icy counter of the library at the College of Philosophy and Humanities at the University of Chile. He reads the final pages of *The Luminous Novel* by Mario Levrero, which he'd read straight through, as if it were a page-turner of an adventure tale, one long weekend when Carla and Vicente were at the beach.

He lingers over the stories of *Cathedral*, by Raymond Carver: he reads the first lines of "A Small, Good Thing," a story he does remember perfectly because he's read it about fifty times. While his eyes recognize the familiar words, he thinks it's deliciously absurd to read the story standing there like a penniless student, because you go to bookstores to find books you haven't read or don't have, and he has *Cathedral* at home, he's had it since he was nineteen. He's moved house several times but he always takes that book with him, and when he left Chile he'd taken almost no books, but he took that one and even duplicated it: one of the first things he did in New York was go to McNally Jackson and buy the English edition, and he remembers sitting by the Washington Square fountain reading that story for the first time in Carver's language and thinking, though he doesn't usually like translations to Spanish from Spain at all, that "Parece una tontería" ("It Seems like a Silly Thing") felt like a more accurate and beautiful title than its original.

He wants to read a novel, maybe a book of short stories, but above all he doesn't want to read poetry, or rather, he doesn't want to buy a book of poetry, because poetry is his subject of study now and he doesn't feel like working. But there's also a secondary reason, or a reason Gonzalo wants to think of as secondary: he doesn't want to find out that, six years later, the copy of *Memorial Park* is still here. Even so, he's tempted, and he glances toward the poetry section, but from that distance the thin white spine of his book would be indistinguishable among the crowd of books that are also mostly thin and white. Better this way, thinks Gonzalo, better not to know, and he is about to go back to reading Carver's story when he realizes the boy at the counter is staring at him. He meets his eyes, smiles at him, momentarily unconcerned, but as Carver's words line up again before his eyes, the boy's identity crystallizes in his mind.

He hasn't seen Vicente since the night he left Carla's house, eyes red and face burning. It was all so devastating that he felt it would be convenient or fair or even legitimate to leave with no more ceremony than the slam of a door. Instead, Gonzalo went upstairs to Vicente's room to say goodbye, but he carried his suitcase up with him, which was obviously wrong; he should have left that sudden, heavy, badly packed suitcase down by the front door. And while he felt it was undignified to face the boy with tearful eyes and the certainty that he would cry as soon as he spoke, there was no time to prepare a more respectable scene. He looked at Vicente in silence, as though taking a snapshot: Colo-Colo shirt and shorts down to his knees, bare feet, his hair long and gently wavy, and some phantom fuzz on his face—the foreshadow of a mustache and beard that were for the moment out of reach. Vicente was on the floor playing with some Legos, and it was an anachronistic image, because of course at twelve years old it had been ages since he'd played with Legos. But when the shouting downstairs intensified, he'd grabbed a plastic box at the back of the closet and found those multicolored pieces—playing with Legos was really the perfect pastime while he was stuck there, enduring that unexpected scene. He heard the shouts and the unfamiliar adult-male sobbing, and it seemed every bit as unreal as the ill-considered words he didn't want to hear but did. And sure, Vicente was building something with the Legos—an indecisive skyscraper or the bulky trunk of a leafless tree— but he was also staring at the laminate floor, poorly installed and a little lopsided, so it looked like a jigsaw puzzle whose pieces had been forced together. He wasn't sad or scared. For now, the only thing the shouting meant definitively was that he couldn't go downstairs, couldn't just wander down for a glass of chocolate milk or a granola bar. Later, moved by a desire to make the past legible, he more or less invented that he'd seen the breakup coming, that it was obvious things between his mother and Gonzalo couldn't last, but it wasn't true: he understood something was happening that night, something perhaps serious or unusual, but he was incapable of imagining the next chapter.

Vicente intuited Gonzalo's presence, felt him watching from six feet away, and it seemed like he was avoiding meeting his stepfather's eyes, but actually he was afraid of looking up and finding that Gonzalo wasn't really there, because sometimes we're utterly sure we sense someone else and we look up and there's no one, and it's so disconcerting. Five seconds later, he looked up and saw that Gonzalo really was there, and so was his suitcase, and suddenly Vicente understood everything and nothing all at the same time.

Then his stepfather said something that is difficult to record here without any further description; one has to imagine the slow, ceremonious rhythm of the sentence, which was both a question and a confirmation, maybe more of a confirmation than a question:

"I'm leaving, Vicho, but you know that you'll always be able to call me and I'm always going to be there, that I will always be your stepfather. Right?"

He should have started out stammering, should have landed on some initial image that would let him move gradually toward the warm, radical words, compatible with memory-making, that were churning in his head. But it was as if they spoke different languages. Gonzalo was speaking a language made up exclusively of final phrases, a language that wounded, a dark and deleterious language, while Vicente spoke an incorrupt language of words that wavered and lived, a language of tentative sentences that began and then went on indefinitely.

They both cried, hugging, for a full three minutes, without a word. Gonzalo gave Vicente a kiss on the right cheek, one of only a few kisses on the cheek that took place between them in the years they lived together, because fathers kiss the cheeks of their sons all the time, but stepfathers only do it on birthdays or New Year's Eve or when they come back from a long trip—or when they're leaving for a long time, in this case, forever.

"There was a lighted window too high up for them to see inside." Gonzalo concentrates on Carver's words, or more like he takes refuge, hides out inside them: the book is a mask, and that single sentence, chosen arbitrarily, is the elastic holding the mask in place. He remembers nearly all of the story, he could summarize it in detail and cite it textually in both Spanish and English, but that sentence in particular strikes him as new, perhaps because it isn't in itself a memorable sentence, and perhaps because, since it doesn't mean anything precise, it gives him an excuse to remain hidden behind the book a few seconds longer. He has decided to approach Vicente, or it's not even that he's decided—it's necessary, it's natural, it would be unforgivable if he didn't, and above all he wants to do it, he really wants to, but he needs the momentary refuge of that random sentence; he needs, maybe, to breathe through that random sentence so he can then do this right, supposing there is a way to do this next part right. (And what would it mean, anyway, to do it right? To admit that before, that always, for his whole life, he's done everything wrong?)

When he senses Gonzalo approaching, Vicente wants to keep his eyes not on the floor this time, but on the surface that is interposed between his eyes and the floor, which is not a book but rather the counter with the credit card terminal and receipt pad, but instead he looks up and smiles with raw honesty. Their brief hug starts out awkward, precisely because that counter is between them. Vicente stands up and does his best to make the hug less strange.

"So you two know each other," says Sergio Parra, who is just arriving.

At that moment neither Gonzalo nor Vicente remembers the episode with the supermarket cashier; neither of them thinks that in these circumstances the best answer and at the same time the worst, the perfectly parodic reply, as opportune as it is cruel, would be to repeat the words Gonzalo had said then: We're friends.

"We've known each other for years," Gonzalo says instead.

"Many years," adds Vicente, his voice thin and hoarse as though he'd just woken up.

Gonzalo thinks about Vicente's voice, thinks that if he'd heard that voice somewhere else he would have recognized it. It's a confused thought—he doesn't know Vicente's adult voice, or rather, he's just now heard it for the first time.

Parra senses the tension, realizes he has just interrupted something. He goes outside to smoke so Gonzalo and Vicente can talk, and while he smokes he looks in the display window as if he were just a curious customer. He doesn't think Gonzalo presents any kind of threat, but he still wants Vicente to feel protected.

They behave like two timid, polite ambassadors from distant countries. Gonzalo tells Vicente that he came back to Chile a couple months ago, and that he's about to start teaching classes at the university. Vicente tells Gonzalo that he finished high school, and he talks about his refusal to pursue higher education, and about his interest in poetry. When he finds out that his stepson or ex-stepson writes poems, Gonzalo feels a kind of pang or shudder that he wouldn't know whether to describe as a jolt of warmth or a shiver. He buys the Carver book as if he didn't own it already and for a second thinks about giving it to Vicente, but he doesn't, because it's weird to give a salesman the thing he has just sold you, though of course the books don't belong to Vicente, he is just an employee—an employee who, at that moment, does his job: he takes the money and puts the book into a bag that he hands back, along with the change and the receipt, to the customer.

Before leaving, in an overly friendly tone, Gonzalo invites Vicente to visit his class, which starts in two weeks, adding that maybe it could help him decide about college. Vicente nods with the slightly forced smile of a good kid. Gonzalo turns over the receipt and writes down his email address, which is the same one Vicente has had for years, and his phone number. He adds that in any case, whenever he wants, they could get coffee. Vicente replies that yes, he'd love to, anytime. There is no goodbye hug and of course no kiss on the cheek, just your garden-variety handshake.

I n New York he got used to walking long distances. Once or twice a week, instead of taking the subway, he'd walk the hour and a half to the university from the room he rented in a Carroll Gardens brownstone. He's kept up the habit since he returned to Chile. He likes to feel the real distances, he even finds the resulting tiredness pleasant, and it's a pleasure that includes the satisfaction of wasted time: while others advance automatically, caught up in the muffled fury of an eternal Monday, he can wander the streets, looking, thinking, meandering. He likes to know that the walk from his new apartment near Plaza Ñuñoa to downtown Santiago is also an hour and a half. Sometimes, walking down Irarrázaval, he imagines he's approaching the Brooklyn Bridge and he feels like an idiot and a foreigner and he laughs, because in Santiago he is not, could never be a foreigner, quite the opposite: he looks at the new and horrible buildings he finds along the way like someone finding brutal changes in their own skin, like someone inspecting bruises and scars on their own legs and arms.

This afternoon, in any case, walking is more of a necessity than an exercise or a pastime: he moves forward at an imprecise speed, as if looking for an address, as if he wanted to stop but didn't know where, as if the city were new or he were new to it; he dawdles at crosswalks, as if he didn't entirely understand how traffic lights worked.

Maybe there's a word to designate the opposite of mourning, what we feel not after someone dies but when they reappear; what we feel when we suddenly recover someone who had been absent even from our dreams. Words like *rebirth* or *resurrection* are so inadequate, because what Gonzalo feels is more complex, more specific: the opposite of mourning coexists with mourning, it's something like an elegiac joy. What's more, he is the one who has just reappeared, though he thinks of it as the reverse, as if Vicente were newly arrived. Vicente was always there: the one who left, the one who abandoned him, was Gonzalo, and it's Gonzalo who is returning now.

"I didn't disappear, I was thrown out. I wasn't his father, I was just his stepfather," he says out loud, while he walks.

He misses that about New York: there were so many crazy people talking to themselves on the street that he got in the habit of tossing a few words to the wind himself, especially on those long walks: suddenly he'd say a phrase aloud and no one so much as glanced at him, and he could savor the Spanish, which sounded so exuberant, so alive, so genuine. He doesn't know whether there are fewer crazy people in Santiago or if Chilean crazy just tends to be less expressive, more self-absorbed. He gets distracted thinking about that, but it's a false, self-induced distraction. At all costs, he wants to keep the figure of his grandfather from emerging in his head; he repeats, as if it were necessary to recap everything in order to understand it, that they have almost nothing in common, because that old motherfucker abandoned every one of his numerous children, while Gonzalo doesn't have children, nor is it possible to accuse him of having abandoned that non-son or stepson or ex-stepson that he did have (it's not even clear that one could say he had him, at least not the way a father "has" a son), because he didn't abandon him, he was thrown out. Nor am I like my own father, thinks Gonzalo—his father, who never abandoned him, who was always there, who is still there, something for which Gonzalo has never thanked him and probably never will.

"I am someone who was lost and who returned," he says in a whisper. He doesn't want to speak loudly, because in Santiago people do stare at crazy people who talk to themselves in the street. "I am someone who has just returned after a forced disappearance."

But that's not true either, because he chose to go. He chose to disappear and then he did. He liked disappearing, he had a great time doing it. He managed to disappear, he triumphed. He managed to leave, he triumphed. He managed to forget, he triumphed.

"Come to my class, come see me in my class," he says now, out loud again; he wants to review his words, imagine what Vicente heard, imagine him listening, receiving his words. "Come see me in my class. I abandoned you, but come see what a good teacher I am."

It's night by the time he reaches his apartment. He opens the door as if he were in a hurry, as if he were just returning for ten seconds to grab his passport or turn off the heat. But he's not in a hurry, and though he drinks four glasses of water in a row, he's also not thirsty. The apartment consists of two spacious rooms, plenty for a single person, though the accumulation of books and especially of boxes gives the place the air of a storage room or warehouse. There are around twenty boxes all sealed with packing tape, plus a few half-open ones. He should have bought some bookshelves right away but instead he put everything off, as if he were still arriving, settling in, getting the lay of the land.

An immense suitcase full of shoes and winter clothes acts as a coffee table, piled with twenty or thirty books and an empty flower vase. Gonzalo makes a cup of tea and drinks it fast, like medicine. It's only eight-thirty, but he feels like he wouldn't be able to read or watch TV, like the day is already over. He tries to read a random book anyway, but then he starts doing a math problem right there on the first page, as if there were no time to find a blank sheet of paper, though it's a calculation so simple he could solve it in his head. He wants to take his time, go step by step; he hasn't written out a math problem since he was in high school.

$$6 : 18 = x : 100$$

And then

$$600 = 18x$$

And then

$$x = 600 : 18$$

And finally

$$x = 33.333333$$

33.333333 is the percentage of time that Vicente lived with Gonzalo—"A third of his life," murmurs Gonzalo, who does not calculate the percentage of his own life that he spent with Vicente (15.78). Then he realizes the calculation is wrong, because they didn't live together from the start, and then he thinks Vicente might have already turned nineteen—he is sure his birthday is in March, but he can't remember if it's the third or the thirtieth, and today is the third, meaning maybe his birthday was, is, today. The possibility that their reunion has coincided with Vicente's birthday strikes Gonzalo as awful, and not just because he forgot to wish him a happy birthday, but also because that coincidence would turn him, his reappearance, into a kind of surprising and awkward birthday present.

But no, Vicente's birthday is March thirtieth, he remembers it now with certainty. His familiarity with March third is tied to the earthquake of '85—he thinks about that earthquake, when he was nine years old, and then his memory turns to a much worse earthquake, in February of 2010, which he didn't experience because he was in New York, asleep. He'd gotten up at nine, eaten some pancakes for breakfast at the diner on the corner, and only on his second cup of coffee did it occur to him to look at his phone, and when he saw the many missed calls from his friends and parents he immediately wrote Vicente, who didn't answer. Some hours later he received a devastating reply from Carla that he would prefer not to remember, but still, he opens his computer with the intention of rereading that message—he types his password very fast, without thinking about it, because we don't think much when we type a password, we're used to the frenetic movement of our fingers over the keyboard:

****

It's important to change your password every once in a while, for security, though many people, maybe most, remain faithful to some kind of formula, because the fear of forgetting one's password trumps the fear of theft or online fraud. Experts recommend using passwords that combine upper- and lowercase letters, numbers, and symbols, and of course it's important that there are no personal details, so it's impossible to guess the association that led to the creation of the password. From that perspective, the password for Gonzalo's computer, which is also the one for his email and acts as the basis for his iCloud, Netflix, and Spotify accounts, is perfect:

..VicentE50

Experts recommend not using names of children or family members as passwords, but they don't say anything about the names of stepchildren and especially not the names of ex-stepchildren. Still, it's heroic that this password has survived all these years through all the periodic adjustments, because the original password was vicente26 (the number alluded to Colo-Colo player Humberto Suazo's jersey) and then, when he had to change it, the uppercase letters and periods started appearing, and he also had to change the numbers. It's a password from the past, a survivor password, and surely with the passage of time it will continue to change and the reference to Vicente's name will be lost entirely. And it's very sad that Gonzalo types it automatically precisely tonight. It's sad that he writes Vicente's name without realizing. It's sad that he sees nothing but eleven asterisks.

There are few people who would associate Vicente's name with Gonzalo's personal information, although it's true that until not long ago he would often reveal Vicente's existence and importance in his life to the new people he was meeting, an importance that seems arguable in light of the facts; one might even get the impression that he told his sporadic girlfriends about Vicente in order to demonstrate that he had once been something like a father; one might even think he'd used Vicente's existence to announce or imply or proclaim that he wasn't just another one of those bachelors joyfully stuck in an endless adolescence of cartoonish instability—just another one of those thirty-somethings who walk around the Village believing them-selves the protagonist of some more or less good novel or some charming independent movie.

During that time he would say he had a stepson with whom he kept in contact, and it was true, even if the contact was rare, though perhaps that wasn't Gonzalo's fault, because he did try. In reality it was excessive to say, even if only in passing, that they were in contact: the correct thing would have been to explain that he didn't want to fall entirely out of touch, that he was trying not to disappear from Vicente's life completely. His very simpli-fied version of the story was this: the boy's mother had broken up the family. (He said it with restraint, measuring his words, but he said it.) Since he seemed willing to answer any question—sometimes it was clear that he wanted, even needed, to talk about it—people tended to ask if he missed the boy, and he said yes and it wasn't a lie: he missed Vicente, in fact, much more than he missed Carla, whom he had managed to demonize and forget.

"You can't call him your ex-stepson," said Flavia, an Argentine anthropolo-gist he sometimes went out with.

They were at a bar in Harlem drinking red wine.

"What should I call him?"

"He's your stepson, that's it. He was your stepson and he's still your stepson. You and Carla never wanted another child?"

"We did," said Gonzalo. "She lost a baby."

"Your baby?"

"Well, it never actually became a baby."

"But was it yours?"

"Yes."

"Then you lost a baby too, Gonza. You don't know how to talk."

Gonzalo was going to say that it felt illegitimate to give himself prominence in the story, but he didn't, because she was right, he had also lost that
baby. He'd never thought about it that way before. He'd never thought of
himself as someone who had lost a child. They went to Flavia's apartment;
it was a long trip, by subway and on foot, out to Bushwick.

"So, chilenito, you want to screw or not?" she asked when they went into
her room.

Sometimes they slept together, sometimes they didn't; they'd been playing that game for a while. That night they lay down in bed and kissed while
they fell asleep. When they woke up, they both sensed they wouldn't see each
other again.

That was the only time Gonzalo talked about his lost baby. From then on,
he changed his answer too: when someone asked if he had children, Gonzalo
no longer mentioned Vicente—he simply said no, and when he did he felt a
bitterness that took a while to dissipate, a bitterness that lengthened out and
manifested as the feeling that he had lied, that he did have a son and that
unnamed son was Vicente, and without ceasing to be Vicente it was also the
baby he had lost. Over time the bitterness would pass more quickly, maybe
as long as it took to down the first whiskey, and the physical sensation gradually lost intensity, until it became a slight twinge that lasted only as long as
a cough. The twinge never entirely disappeared: even now, when he's asked
if he has children, the twinge, the cough, reappears.

Gonzalo should have spent the months before his trip to New York shaping
a new relationship with Vicente—Carla probably would have accepted some
kind of temporary visitation agreement—but instead, he frittered that time
away. He felt hurt and disappointed, he thought Carla was the stupidest
woman in the world (he avoided naming her, but when he had no choice
he called her "Vicente's mom" or simply "that dumbass"), and he missed

Vicente in many ways: he missed, especially, the constant sensation of play, the possibility of launching into a song or a joke at any moment, the overwhelming joy of being important to someone.

He tried to hate Vicente's mom and he was resolved to work out with Vicente a relationship like that of friends, or of brothers, yet instead he spent those months hiding behind his professed wounds, ultimately getting lost in beery conversations with indulgent friends who were just as far from understanding anything as he himself was. Then, during the whole time he was in New York, nearly six years, Gonzalo never wanted to return to Chile: he saved up money to travel around the United States, and he went to conferences in Marseille, Salamanca, São Paulo, and Lima—it would have been easy, he thinks now, to pay for a ticket from Lima to spend a few days in Santiago and at least get ice cream with Vicente.

He should be banging his head against the wall—sometimes that'll do a person good, it's not always inadvisable, and in fact it's occasionally the correct, sensible thing to do. But instead he is on the floor with his laptop on his knees, going through his email, looking for some shortcut, some alibi. He still won't renounce the method, the sequence, the story: he's looking for messages in his email as if he could find in them the answers to questions he hasn't even bothered to ask, because he knows they would be insipid, simplistic: am I good or am I bad, did I change or did I not change, did I ruin everything or did I not ruin everything.

He reads the long, funny messages he wrote Vicente from New York, and he rereads the boy's occasional and generally laconic and elusive replies. He pauses on the message Vicente wrote him after Darkness died. It was just a few lines, written with endearing formality, trying for the detached tone of serious messages:

> Dear Gonzalo, this morning Darkness died. She was hit by a car, we buried her in the yard, I'm telling you because I know you loved her a lot.

Then he rereads forty times the message that not Vicente, but Carla, wrote him from Vicente's email, a few hours after the earthquake:

Hi, I hope all is going well in your life.

I heard you wrote Vicente to ask how we were after the earthquake.

We're fine. Nothing happened. It was like the world was ending, but the house held up no problem. It's a shit show here, especially in Concepción, but I guess you watch CNN.

I'm saying this with the best of intentions, but please, don't write Vicente anymore. Why go on confusing things?

Hugs, take care, C.

He also reads the reply he sent Carla, which is the last of the whole series:

OK.

Can you reread a message that consists of a single word? Can it be said that you *reread* a single word over and over, as if it were necessary to rest your eyes on it, as if it were impossible to simply remember it? It seems you can, because that's what Gonzalo does now: he rereads, fifty, a hundred, two hundred times, the word *OK*.

He dreams he is at Sit and Wonder, a Prospect Heights café where he used to meet up with his friend James Hey, who suddenly appears and casually sits down across from Gonzalo without greeting him, as if he were just coming back from the bathroom. Right then, a goateed guy about six feet tall comes over and asks how old they are. They laugh, thinking the guy wants to know their names. The stranger clarifies that he isn't interested in their names, but rather their ages. James says he is thirty-five years old, but Gonzalo has a much harder time answering. I'm more young than old, but I'm not at all young, not *really* young, thinks Gonzalo, as if reading a clue in a crossword puzzle. The guy is still waiting for an answer. Over thirty, under fifty, Gonzalo thinks then. I'm younger than my father and older than my son, he finally replies, and in the dream the phrase is not absurd, but almost luminous, like a revelation.

"I am thirty-eight years old," he says when he wakes up.

Maybe he says it while still in the dream, asleep: it's a shout, at five in the morning. He gets up and thinks about the obvious interpretation of the dream, but he also thinks that the meanings of dreams are never obvious. Over coffee, he copies the phrase in a notebook and tries for a poem:

> I am younger than my father
> I am older than my son

And over my chest a shirt
is washed clean in the rain.

He hasn't tried to write poetry in years, and maybe that's why he feels
ridiculous and abandons the draft. Some hours later he heads to Home-
center, where he buys six tall shelves made of particleboard, neither elegant
nor particularly sturdy. He pays for transportation in a truck whose driver
is a taciturn, agreeable twenty-something named Mirko. He looks familiar,
and Gonzalo thinks he reminds him of Vicente, the new Vicente: maybe it's
the shape of his body or his large eyes, the indecisive waves in his hair. He
asks Mirko to help him put the shelves together, and between the two of
them they finish the job in under two hours. They order pizza, drink some
beers. Gonzalo offers a little more cash if Mirko will help him organize his
books. Mirko says he has to go, but he still helps unpack the first few
boxes.

"Did your girlfriend make you do this?" Mirko asks.

"Do what?"

"Organize."

"I don't have a girlfriend," says Gonzalo. "I just got the idea to organize
them, I don't know why."

"And how do you organize them?"

"By genre," said Gonzalo, but in Spanish the word for *genre* and *gender*
is the same, so he felt the need to clarify: "By literary genre."

"Of course, I understand," says Mirko. "Poetry, novels, stories, essays.
You think just because I work as a mover that I'm ignorant?"

"That's not what I thought, I'm sorry."

"Anyway, it wouldn't make sense for you to classify them by gender,"
says Mirko. "Almost all your books are by men."

"You could probably say that about most people's libraries, men's or
women's," says Gonzalo. "Used to be almost all the books that got published
were by men. Luckily that's changing."

What he says is what he thinks, but it sounds like a prepared and practiced speech, studiously categorical. Mirko looks at him with renewed distance, with irony.

"Easy, teach," he says. "You really don't remember me?"

"No," admits Gonzalo, surprised. "Have we met before?"

"I was your student for a whole semester."

"When?" asks Gonzalo, with growing enthusiasm.

"A long time ago."

"When?" Gonzalo insists. "Ten years ago, something like that?"

"Almost ten, in 2005. It was the only semester I went to college."

"And after that you couldn't afford it anymore," says Gonzalo, in the tone of one who has heard the same story a thousand times.

Mirko nods.

"Was my class good? Tell me the truth."

"Truth is, I don't remember."

"Just in case it was bad, I'm going to give you some books."

"But you're not going to give me the ones I want. You're going to give me the bad ones, the extras. I'd rather you just gave me a tip."

"Which book do you want?"

"The one that hurts you most," says Mirko with a smile. "Your favorite book."

Gonzalo gives him the brand-new edition of *Cathedral*.

"But this book is new," says Mirko.

"It's new, but I have another copy, so it doesn't hurt that much."

"Your class was good," says Mirko unexpectedly.

"You mean you do remember?"

"It was the only class I liked," says Mirko, his voice dry, neutralized, avoiding any hint of emotion. "You were like me, from Maipú, and sometimes you talked about Maipú. You were like an older brother. You knew everything, and how to explain everything, even the weirdest poems, in simple words."

"Thank you."

"You shouldn't teach at a university," adds Mirko, who has a slight stutter. "You should teach four- or five-year-old kids, in Maipú. That would make sense."

"I'd like that," says Gonzalo, who is taken aback and is being sincere, though he thinks he sounds flippant.

They talk a while longer. Then Mirko has to go, and at first he resists accepting a tip, but finally he accepts it and departs.

Gonzalo lies down on the floor as if trying to cure back pain, and dozes off for a full hour before returning to his task. He dusts off the books with a dish towel and also shakes them, in case there's anything between their pages. He proceeds with robotic indifference, but halfway through he realizes he is looking for something specific, that the sudden need to organize his library responds to the desire to find papers, documents, photos—above all, photos—stuck between the pages of those books. And he does turn up some of Carla's—photos Carla took, that is: when she started studying photography she would often give him the assignments she was pleased with, and Gonzalo kept those photos in his books, inspired by vague or literal associations: a butterfly in *Speak, Memory*, by Nabokov; a ladybug landing on a branch in *La ola muerta*, by Germán Marín; some strange bleached-out clouds in *Ciudad gótica*, by María Negroni; a man in shorts and a T-shirt in line at a bank in *Bartleby & Co.*, by Enrique Vila-Matas; the sea reflected in a pair of sunglasses in *The Beautiful Summer*, by Cesare Pavese; a solitary fly in *Writing*, by Marguerite Duras; a bride adjusting her dress in *La nueva novela*, by Juan Luis Martínez; a corner of Providencia adorned with jacaranda flowers in *Cartas para reinas de otras primaveras*, by Jorge Teillier.

Those aren't the kinds of photos he is looking for, though. What he wants is the more casual record of daily life—he wants to recover images of Vicente playing with Darkness in the yard or blowing out candles on a birthday cake or walking in the park; he wants, above all, to recall the afternoons of boredom suddenly animated by the temptation of posing for the camera, for the future; that bold assurance, that blind and audacious wager on a future that is compatible with the present.

Carla had the camera around her neck all the time, and theirs was a family, so to speak, that was amply documented. Gonzalo can't believe all those photos were lost—he was sure he'd kept at least some—but now he admits it's also possible that he threw them away before he left for New York. He remembers having thrown things in the trash, and it's possible that in a fit of spite or indolence he decided to get rid of those family mementos. It would have been easy—correct, even—to cut Carla out of those photos and throw her into the trash, like a double of a worthless baseball card, while keeping Vicente. He also could have cut himself out of the pictures, thrown himself into the trash, shredded or burned himself, but kept Vicente. He focuses on that imprecise, conjectured scene: his past self burning and throwing away photos like someone disposing of evidence, maybe the very day he packed these same boxes of books and left them in the attic at his parents' house.

When almost all his books have been organized, Gonzalo finds, between the pages of a book of poems by Wisława Szymborska, a photo of Darkness the cat with her complete set of teeth:

Carla had tried to take that picture so many times she came to think it was impossible, but she followed the cat around until finally convincing her to look straight at the camera—it's a resigned pose, like for a passport photo or mug shot, and her stunned, innocent gaze communicates what is perhaps a certain disappointment.

He reads "Cat in an Empty Apartment," the poem of Szymborska's he had marked with that picture, and then he remembers the poem "Black Cat in Sight," by Gonzalo Rojas (the real Gonzalo Rojas). He looks for it and intends to reread it, though he's not sure he likes it, and as he is flipping through the pages he finds another poem, "Rodrigo Tomás Growing Up," which the poet dedicated to his three-year-old son. He is left paralyzed by those verses, which he already knew, but only now, in the threatening clarity of the present, does he isolate and absorb them:

> For your freedom, I gave you glorious snow and guiding star.
> I was your sentinel watching over you at dawn.
> I see me still, like a tree, breathing for your nascent lungs,
> freeing you from the chase and the seizure of beasts.
> Oh my son, son of my arrogance,
> I will always be atop that Andean scene,
> a knife in each hand to defend you and save you.

Would he have defended Vicente with a knife in each hand? Would he have given everything to save him, to protect him? Of course he would have, he answers himself. He did, in a way. He devoted himself to raising Vicente, to caring for him, but then he let time and distance do their work. He would still defend him, would still take a bullet for him, he would still rather die himself than let Vicente die. He would sacrifice himself. Wouldn't he?

He remembers Carver's story "A Small, Good Thing," and the game of coincidences and asymmetries makes him dizzy and sadder still. He thinks of phone calls, of solitary people baking cakes or crying in the shower, of children breathing their last, of fathers dozing off in the hospital waiting room. If Vicente were to die, if he had died, or if he'd been hit by a car and lay dying like the boy in Carver's story, would Gonzalo have gotten on a plane? Would he have flown eight-thousand-plus kilometers to Santiago? And if he had taken that flight, what would he have done when he got there, other than cry? And what would his crying have sounded like? A prudent, embarrassed sobbing, the cry of a secondary character? Or a wrenching and honest cry, one whose decibels would compete with the wails of Vicente's mother and grandparents and friends? Crying as a pose, or a pose of crying? He would have donated a lung to Vicente, a kidney, his liver too, of course he would. He would have given it to him, he'd give it right now, and maybe that would be a good way to ask for forgiveness, an unquestionably concrete way. I'm sorry, here, have a kidney.

There are people who in moments of desperation pick up the Bible or the *I Ching* or *The Tibetan Book of the Dead*. Gonzalo does the same but with poems. He looks for poems; that is really his job. If he had to define his job precisely, if he had to explain it honestly, he would say that it consists of trying to understand the world through poems other people have written. That's why he needs to organize his books: the alphabetical order grants him certainty, familiarity, peace of mind. It's good to know, for example, that filed under *L*, for *Lihn, Enrique*, is the book that features this poem:

> Nothing to lose by living, try it:
> here's a body just your size.
> We made it in the dark out of love for the art of the flesh
> but also in earnest,
> thinking of your visit as a new game, joyful and painful;
> out of love of life, out of fear of death and of life,
> out of love of death
> for you or for no one.

Then he comes upon a poem by Matías Rivas in which a beleaguered and self-critical father apologizes to his son, and then he finds another by Fabio Morábito where a man, with persuasive tenderness, somberly accepts that his son is too big to pretend his father is a horse, because his feet can touch the ground now. He also reads "A Prayer for My Son," by Yeats; "Catalina Parra," by Nicanor Parra; "El dios de los mamíferos," by Pedro Mairal; "Imagen y semejanza," by Germán Carrasco; "Universal Father," by Julián Herbert; and fragments of "You're Going to Be a Father," by Henri Michaux, and "El paseo," by Silvio Mattoni.

He reads those poems as though preparing to apply for the impossible position of father, the father of a double son, half-abandoned and half-dead. He doesn't know if he is exaggerating or dissembling. He doesn't know if he's falsifying his experience or not. But he's applying, that's clear. He fills out imaginary forms, constructs an image of himself, a fiction that, like all fictions in the history of humanity, is based on a true story. For example, he knows a bit of Italian, very little, but he could carry on a conversation, he could try to read a poem by Valerio Magrelli, or at least *La Gazzetta dello Sport*, so he doesn't get nervous when, as he's filling out an application, he declares that he speaks and understands and writes Italian fluently, and he knows he is lying but he also knows he will never have to demonstrate his dominance of Italian, and that even if he did have to he would come out of it for the most part unscathed. He would claim he had lost his voice, maybe, as in fact he did a couple of times in New York when he needed a rest from English. He would simply excuse himself, waving his hands and tapping his throat. That's been his method, forever: cling to those two or three things he does know, the few things he has mastered, and leave for tomorrow the conquest of true knowledge; trust in his intuition and good luck, and if things turn dicey, get out of Dodge with relative elegance, or at least cunning.

At the same time, it's true that he had been a father for some years. He'd been a father in the fullest way possible for someone who is not a father. His alibi coincides with the truth. I wasn't allowed to go on being a father, he could argue: I was about to learn the language of paternity, I studied it with discipline, with zeal, and no one forced me to, I signed up for classes all by myself, I paid my monthly tuition punctually and that school cost an arm and a leg, there's no state funding to study something like that, and I did all my homework, I was top of my class, but I stayed humble, I knew I still had a lot to learn, and I spent all my free time plugging away, but one day they just closed the school on me: one Monday I showed up for class at five to eight in the morning, as always, and it was closed. And time passed and gradually I just forgot that language. Because languages have to be spoken, you forget them if you don't practice. I gave it my all, I did my best. And there were mistakes, lots of them, of course there were. Trusting Carla, for example. Falling in love with her. Deciding to fall in love with her. Because I must have decided. At some point I must have decided and then I forgot, I conveniently forgot. At some point I decided I was in love with her and that everything made sense and I would die for her and for her son. At some point I decided to buy a few knives and I decided I would take those knives and climb all the mountains and all the hills in my country and defend Carla and Vicente with my life.

He finishes organizing his books, devastated by those intense poems that depict a beauty he cannot participate in. He keeps trying to adapt them to his own life, keeps imagining his own poem, the poem he should write as an apology or homage or indictment. He remembers when he thought he could affect other people with his poems: he thought he could be loved, be accepted, be included. It would have been easier to be disillusioned by poetry, to forget about poetry, than to accept, as Gonzalo did, that he'd failed. It would have been better to blame poetry, but it would have been a lie, because there are those poems he has just read, poems that prove poetry is good for something, that words can wound, throb, cure, console, resonate, remain.

During the following days Gonzalo puts extra effort into planning his classes, animated by the possibility that Vicente will show up. He imagines him arriving late, in the middle of class, and sitting down discreetly in the back row. He writes Vicente to remind him of the invitation. Two days later, Vicente replies. He asks Gonzalo to repeat his schedule, since he lost the receipt it was written on. Gonzalo sends it immediately, gives him all the directions to reach the university, as if Vicente were coming from another city or country. Vicente replies that he will come to the Tuesday class at 11:20, Gonzalo's very first of the semester.

Gonzalo starts class completely convinced Vicente won't come, but he does, and not halfway through, but practically on time. He does sit in the last row, a little sheepishly. He smiles from the back of the room, pulls out a notebook, takes notes. A few hours later the two of them are walking along the median strip on Alameda under the indecisive March sun. In six years, the speed of Vicente's steps has changed: they walk at the same rapid pace, but at times Vicente tends to go even faster, so every once in a while he takes a short step, staying in almost the same place, to wait for Gonzalo.

If someone were to look closely at them, they'd think these two were either father and son or teacher and student. But if in addition to looking that person were also to listen, they would think these were two scholars or nerds or hyper-informed journalists, or else exactly what they are: two Chilean poets from different generations discussing their readings.

"So have you read Yanko González?"

"Yeah, almost everything."

"And Bárbara Délano?"

"Just some poems in an anthology."

"And Bolaño?"

"Not the novels. It's just, everyone says you have to read them, like it's obligatory."

"Well, they're pretty amazing," says Gonzalo. "What about Lihn's novels?"

"*La Fiesta de Cristal?*"

"*La Orquesta de Cristal.*"

"Right. I started it, I liked it. I'm going to keep going. Still, the truth is I almost always get bored with novels. So many pages. As if a poem wasn't enough."

"That's what Pound thought," says Gonzalo. "In a letter to William Carlos Williams he says he only writes the good parts of novels. And that everything else, the other four hundred pages, are just filler and tedium."

"I agree."

"I do too, sometimes. But there are good novels out there," says Gonzalo, with a pedagogical inflection.

The conversation goes on considerably longer, and it sounds like an interrogation yet it flows, it works; they bring up names, which is the favorite or perhaps the obligatory sport of poets, and it's fun, but above all it allows them to talk a lot while saying practically nothing: they make contact, get used to the words, instate their own particular signals. Gonzalo leans toward recommending authors he thinks have been forgotten, but Vicente is well informed and navigates effortlessly through the tradition of Chilean poetry. And he also talks about younger, unpublished poets whom Gonzalo doesn't know.

"What's this Pato's last name?" asks Gonzalo.

"His name is Patricio López López, his mom and dad have the same last name."

"And he's already published?"

"His book is about to come out."

"Is he going to use that double last name?"

"Yeah, he likes for people to think his mom was a single mother."

"Sure," says Gonzalo, thinking of his own pretentious deliberation over his name.

"I don't know if you'd like his poems."

"I'm still going to read him. Seems like you're the one who should be recommending books to me, you've read everyone," says Gonzalo, and he's being indulgent but is genuinely impressed. Vicente feels a little deceitful, a little guilty, because he hasn't read even half the authors he's just said he has. He wants to read them, and he's going to, that's for sure, because he wants to read everything.

"I read you too," adds Vicente, in a very low voice, as though practicing the words.

Gonzalo is stunned. He looks at Vicente with frank incredulity and doesn't know what to say. All the poets they've mentioned thus far are ones he envies a little, because they managed to exist fully: if Vicente knows them, there can be no doubt that they have found their readers, which is a good deal more than he could say for himself. He is not part of that improvised list, he never was and he thinks he never will be. He doesn't appear on any lists, unless there is some record of failed poets. And yet, Vicente says he has read *Memorial Park*. He had not even considered that as a possibility. He *could* have thought about it—he did mail a book to Carla, and the kid could have come across that copy. Or Carla could even, for some reason, have shown it to him, Gonzalo thinks now, with hesitant gratitude.

"Seriously, you read that book?" Gonzalo doesn't say my book, nor does he say *you read me*.

"Yes."

In truth, Gonzalo hadn't thrown away any photos or burned anything: days after their final fight, Carla went to the little room and spent the whole afternoon shaking the books one by one, precisely in order to gather up all the photos of her or Vicente. She didn't do it out of cruelty, it just seemed unfair for Gonzalo to get to keep them. She put the photos of Vicente alone or with her into a drawer, while the ones of her alone or with Gonzalo she put into a trash bag that she stored in the closet in her room, the way we might store an old coat we're never going to use again, one that doesn't fit and that we don't like and is all tattered, but even if it weren't, we still wouldn't give to anyone. When she received Gonzalo's book, after reading the printed dedication ten times ("For Carla and Vicente") and the handwritten one twenty times ("You'll never know how much this book owes its existence to you"), she stashed it away in the same bag.

So Carla's copy of *Memorial Park* was not the one Vicente read. Three years ago, the first time he went to Metales Pesados, he'd looked through the entire poetry section and glanced at the book, but it didn't catch his attention. He'd paged through it moved by the same voracious curiosity that led him to page through any book of poetry. He didn't read the dedication, and if he had it wouldn't have occurred to him that this particular Carla was his mother and this Vicente was him and this Rogelio González was his ex-stepfather.

The day of Vicente and Gonzalo's reunion at the bookstore, Sergio Parra had searched the shelves for the copy of *Memorial Park* and given it to Vicente.

"I suppose you've read your friend's book," he said. "It's been here for years. He brought it in himself when he published it."

Vicente paged anxiously through the book. Now he did read the dedication.

"That Vicente must be me, and Carla is my mom," he said, showing Parra the names with an emotion that was simultaneously childish and somber.

It was as if he'd just appeared on TV by chance; he felt exposed or used or spotlit.

"Is he your dad?" asked Parra, surprised.

"No, but he was my stepfather."

"You've really never seen this book?"

"I didn't even know he'd published a book," said Vicente, who was still impatiently turning pages. "Why'd he use the name Rogelio González?"

"Probably so people wouldn't confuse him with Gonzalo Rojas," said Parra. "There are a ton of Gonzalo Rojases who use pseudonyms. You can have that."

"What if someone comes in to buy it?"

"No one's going to come in to buy it. And I have another one at home, I'm pretty sure."

"What did you think? Did you read it?"

"I don't remember much, but I liked it," said Parra.

It was a lie, or a half-truth, because, in effect, he didn't remember much. At the time, except for a handful of poems, he'd found the book trivial and fairly pretentious; he'd liked the idea, but felt Gonzalo lacked audacity. He preferred to tell Vicente, for good measure, that he'd thought the book was good.

They walked together that night, after closing up. Vicente hadn't even been working two weeks at the bookstore, but Parra sensed that his new employee needed to talk. They went into a bar, where Vicente ordered a dark lager and Parra his usual non-alcoholic beer.

"Beer has alcohol in it," a young waiter around Vicente's age told Parra.

"What? You don't have non-alcoholic beer?" asked Parra.

"We have a lot of beers, all kinds of them, but they all have alcohol. Beer has alcohol," replied the waiter, like someone explaining the planet is round. "But we have juice and soda, we have everything."

"Non-alcoholic beer has existed for years," said Parra, indignant.

"Personally, I doubt such a thing is possible, sir," replied the waiter, imperturbable.

"There's also decaffeinated coffee," said Vicente, trying to be helpful.

"All right," said Parra, "since non-alcoholic beer doesn't exist here, let's go somewhere it does."

They found a table at a restaurant that did have non-alcoholic beer. Vicente ordered one too, but he thought it was terrible and immediately asked for his dark beer instead.

"It's crazy," said Vicente. "Six years. In six years no one bought his book. He's a failure."

"It's not so strange," said Parra. "That's poetry for you."

"True."

"Was he good to you?"

"Yes," Vicente said without hesitation. "But then he left."

"You became a poet, just like your stepfather."

It was a joke, one Vicente received with bewilderment.

"Seems that way."

"And your dad's not a poet?"

"No, not at all. He's a lawyer, but he doesn't work as a lawyer anymore. So, do you really think it influenced me?"

"What?"

"That my stepfather, or my ex-stepfather, was or is a poet. But I didn't even know he'd published a book."

"But did you know he wrote poems?"

"Yeah, but I never really thought about it," said Vicente. "I knew he read a lot and wrote poetry, but not that he'd published a book. Plus, when we lived together I wasn't interested in literature. I was a late bloomer, I started reading at like fifteen."

Parra bursts out laughing and Vicente looks at his fingernails, as though intending to bite them.

"We always end up like the people we live with," Parra said then. "Our partners, friends, even the people we work with, even our cats. I know I look more like Truman every day."

"Your cat?"

"Don't tell anyone I have a cat."

"Why not?"

"I don't like to talk about my personal life," said Parra, irony flashing in his eyes. "I think you're going to be a better poet than your stepfather."

"Thanks." Vicente smiled. "Maybe he's not a poet anymore. Do you know if he's published anything else?"

"I don't think so. But if you publish a book, you're a poet. Maybe you end up regretting it, but once you publish a book of poems you're screwed, you'll always be a poet."

"And if someone was your stepfather for a while, does he stay your stepfather forever?"

Parra was silent a few seconds before replying:

"I think so. Yes. If you want him to, he does."

He lit a cigarette and managed to take three quick drags before a waitress came to ask him to either put it out or leave.

"I'm a foreigner, you see," said Parra, putting on some kind of French accent. "I didn't know."

"We are not from here," Vicente said in English, and it sounded pretty good.

They walked as far as Alameda and said goodbye. Vicente walked for a few blocks looking at the windows of the buildings. He especially liked that hour when windows started lighting up and announcing a return, and sometimes two or even three panes, in different parts of the building, lit up simultaneously: he loved to imagine those unconsciously synchronized lives.

He sat beneath a streetlight on the sidewalk of Calle Santa Isabel to read *Memorial Park*. He wasn't looking for poetry, really, but rather clues or messages, signals; he confronted the book like someone reading through a file, advancing very slowly, returning to previous lines as if he were afraid the text would change from one second to the next. He had enough light to read by, but he used the flashlight on his phone anyway.

When he finished reading, he thought he had liked at least one poem a lot. It was this one:

GARFIELD

Every time a plane crashes
anywhere in the world
Chilean newspapers report
on whether there are Chileans
among the victims.
But my four-year-old son
doesn't ask if any Chileans died
he asks if any children died
because children belong
to the country of children
just as the dead belong
to the country of the dead.

That's what I think as I walk
with my son through the cemetery
and I see him run off
toward a gravestone
where a paper pinwheel
and a stuffed Garfield
attest to a recent visit
from disconsolate parents.

My four-year-old son plays
with a dead child's stuffed toy
and I'm afraid he'll want to take it home

but he says nothing, doesn't want
to keep it: a few seconds later
he sets it respectfully back
in the same place
and says goodbye, either to the toy,
to the gravestone,
or to the dead child.

Vicente only had to read it two or three times to learn it by heart. He never tried to memorize poems, but sometimes it happened that the verses stuck in his memory with no effort on his part and stayed there, like flies that happen to land on flypaper. It was a beautiful poem, very different from all the others in the book, thought Vicente—still, he wasn't sure about his judgment, it was hard for him to evaluate the text as such, because he was thinking insistently about that four-year-old son in the poem; he figured the kid was invented, but he also thought it was possible that Gonzalo had a son. He didn't think the son was him, though when he was little he did have a stuffed Garfield.

He asked Carla exactly how old he'd been when Gonzalo appeared in their lives. She said he'd been six, which fit with Vicente's calculations and feelings and memories. Carla asked why he wanted to know. He told her he was just curious. He also asked whether Gonzalo had other kids.

"No, not that I know of," said Carla, surprised. "I don't think so. You mean, did he have a kid afterwards, recently?"

"Or before."

"Not before. After, I don't know, I haven't heard from him in years. But I don't think so, I don't think Gonzalo is really father material."

"Why not?"

"No reason," said Carla. "I don't know if he had kids, to tell the truth. Why are you thinking of him?"

"No reason," replied Vicente.

He didn't want to tell his mother about running into Gonzalo. During the days that followed he reread *Memorial Park* many times, almost always lying on the mattress in the little room. The thought that those poems had been written in that very place at times seemed pleasing and at others disturbing. He wasn't sure whether to go to Gonzalo's class or not, for reasons that were hard to put into words. He himself didn't understand them or know what they were, but while he put off the decision he reread the poems over and over. He felt like rereading the book was preparing him for the encounter. He soon became the person who had read *Memorial Park* far more times than anyone else. He didn't—couldn't—know that, of course.

The day of the class he got up very early so he could reread the book once more, and he even went back over it on the bus, as though cramming for a test. Only then did he think about how it was the first week of classes and there he was, on his way to the university. Gonzalo's class wasn't for freshmen, though: it was a seminar on literary analysis for juniors and seniors. It was a long class, two blocks in a row, three hours total. When the first session ended Gonzalo looked for Vicente, but Vicente rushed out to the patio, bought a cup of coffee, and drank it in one corner of the snack bar. Gonzalo thought he wouldn't come back, but he did. In the second session they analyzed the lyrics of "Maldigo del alto cielo," by Violeta Parra. The professor asked if they knew the song and the students surely did, but none of them nodded, so he started singing it—he wasn't bad, and he even mimed playing the guitar. The students celebrated his interpretation with approving giggles of complicity, and at the end they all clapped, except Vicente, who was frozen in the fog of a new memory: Gonzalo singing that song and bobbing his head to the rhythm, in the kitchen, while he made pesto.

Vicente thought the class was extraordinary, very different, of course, from the tedious hours of Language and Literature in high school. Gonzalo moved freely among references that were not always familiar to Vicente. He talked about Roland Barthes or Virginia Woolf as if referring to familiar, close, approachable people. He jumped from Sylvia Molloy to Viktor Shklovsky or Elvira Hernández and then turned to Marcelo Mellado or Yorgos Seferis or Haroldo de Campos, and yet he never sounded pompous, quite the opposite: as he listened, Vicente thought Gonzalo simply loved literature, and had devoted himself to it with steady dedication, perhaps even humility.

He thought Gonzalo knew a lot, that maybe he had always known a lot, that they would have been able to talk for hours on end about poetry or about the world, and he even felt he had wasted those years they'd lived together. He thought, with straightforward melancholy, that all those students in the classroom, though they had just met Gonzalo, would have the privilege of getting to know him more than Vicente knew him or would ever know him, though he had spent years as his stepson.

After the class, several students surrounded Gonzalo and peppered him with questions, which he answered with veiled impatience while he looked at Vicente, who was still sitting in the back row, his head brimming with newly unearthed images.

S eriously, you read that book?" Gonzalo says now. He doesn't say *my book*, nor does he say *you read me*.

"Yes."

For a couple minutes there is only the noise from cars and buses. Vicente is no longer sure it was a good idea to tell Gonzalo that he read *Memorial Park*. He'd said it just because, with a spontaneous lightness, but now he feels a responsibility to formulate an opinion.

"I liked it," says Vicente, and he rushes the question: "Are you going to publish another one?"

"No. I don't write anymore. I mean, I write papers, essays, sometimes reviews. And I have to finish writing my dissertation. But I don't write poetry anymore. Did you really like it? You don't have to tell me you liked it if you didn't. I wasn't going to ask you."

"I did like it. It was weird to read it, but I liked it."

"I dedicated it to you."

"Yeah, I know. Thank you."

Here, they both burst out laughing. Because it's absurd, it's comically anachronistic for Vicente to thank him for that dedication.

"My favorite poem was 'Garfield.'"

"I'm so glad you liked it. I think it's the best poem in the book. Really, I think it's the only good one."

"I know it by heart," says Vicente, and he launches into a recitation.

As he is reeling off the poem, Vicente feels he is behaving like a baby just learning to speak who imitates all the words he hears, or, more precisely, like an insufferable kid who loves to show off playing the piano for guests. And he also feels he's being excessively generous, and Gonzalo doesn't deserve his generosity. He likes the poem a lot. But praising Gonzalo is strange. It's unreasonable, and possibly a betrayal.

While he listens to his poem in Vicente's voice, Gonzalo looks at his stepson or ex-stepson as if he doesn't understand what is happening. He feels pride and a dense, intricate sorrow. When he pictures Vicente memorizing that poem he finds a complex beauty in the scene, bitter and piercing. Vicente's voice is deep and young—it's the voice of a son, not of a father. It's the voice of someone who has not had a child, thinks Gonzalo, his mind wandering now, adrift. Then he figures, correctly, that Vicente must be the only person in the world who has memorized a poem from *Memorial Park*. Not even Gonzalo would be able to recite it from memory, precisely because he has tried, over the years, to forget that book.

"I can't believe you know it by heart."

"I just have a good memory," says Vicente, almost as an apology.

"That's the one your mom liked most too," says Gonzalo. "It's the only one your mom really liked."

The reference to Carla changes something, spoils something: until then, Gonzalo hadn't even asked Vicente about her. It's like the voltage lowers. It's as if they had agreed not to touch on controversial subjects, and Gonzalo has now violated that pact.

They've been walking for forty minutes now, and they stop on the Arzobispo Bridge to buy water and some Super 8 candy bars. There's a gentle, cold wind blowing that perhaps heralds the end of summer.

"I like that poem a lot, but I don't like the book," says Gonzalo, a little to fill the silence.

"I feel the same way," says Vicente. "I like that poem, I'm fascinated by it, really, but I don't much like the book."

He immediately regrets it. The criticism was okay coming from the author's mouth, but not from that occasional reader who, don't forget, has also just said he liked the book. He tries to backpedal, but Gonzalo reassures him, saying he doesn't really expect anyone to like the book, though that's not true, because for a few minutes he thought, just now, with understandable naïveté, that Vicente had liked not only that poem but also the whole book, and he'd even started to feel the elusive caress of recognition.

"I'm a one-hit wonder," jokes Gonzalo, to lessen the intensity, "and not even that poem was a hit."

"Well, you have to put out another album," says Vicente as they start walking again. "So did that happen?"

"What?"

"The stuff that happens in the poem."

"One night I sat down and wrote it all at once, as if I were living it. As if, while I wrote it, I was experiencing it. Or as if I'd just experienced it. And I had, in a way. You remember how you and your mom went with me a few times to Memorial Park?"

"No. To a funeral?"

"No. I used to go to the cemetery to take notes."

"I don't remember that." As soon as Vicente says this, he thinks he feels the spark of a memory.

"One morning the three of us went, you, me, and your mom, must have been a Sunday. I saw some kids running toward us, yelling and teasing each other. And they were jumping really lightly over the headstones. They were like athletes leaping hurdles. It was a sunny day. I remember I put sunscreen on you, and then we walked around the cemetery looking at the trees."

"Did I jump over headstones too?"

"No. You weren't so little anymore. You stayed with me or you wandered off to look at the stones. You'd read the names of the dead out loud, the dates of birth and death. And I think you did look for graves of children. Or maybe we just stopped in front of the grave of a child and you read two dates that were too close together and you were disconcerted. Something like that."

"So I'm the four-year-old son?"

"In a way, yes."

"But I wasn't four years old."

"You were eleven, I think. Maybe twelve by then."

"And you put sunscreen on me?"

"Yep."

"At twelve years old?"

"Yes. You hated sunscreen. Putting sunscreen on you was my job, my responsibility. Your mom almost never did it. And you resisted, you always resisted. Sometimes you'd say you wanted to be darker than me."

"But we're almost the same shade."

"You're still a little lighter than me."

It seems too intimate to Vicente—Gonzalo's hands on his face, his arms, rubbing in the sunscreen. It's hard for him to picture the scene.

"And was that Garfield mine?"

"Yes. People leave stuffed animals on children's graves and they get ruined by the rain and the sun. But in the poem it's a stuffed animal that the parents left on a recent visit."

"Right, and the pinwheel is recent too," says Vicente, as if they were still in the literary analysis class. "Or else it also would have been ruined by rain or frost."

"Yes. I was imagining that stuffed animal of yours, which I gave you. It was pretty much the first thing I gave you. I wanted you to like Garfield the cat."

"How come?"

"Because I liked him. I still do. And lasagna."

"Who doesn't like lasagna?"

"Absolutely no one."

"And why'd you talk about a four-year-old son?"

"That's how I imagined it. I pictured a four-year-old son who wasn't exactly you," says Gonzalo. "But also was you. When you were six years old and I'd just met you, we saw a plane crash on the news, in Colombia or Peru, I don't remember. The newscaster said they still didn't know whether there were any Chileans among the victims. And you asked me if any children had died in the accident."

"And the poem was better if you said it was your son than if you said it was your stepson," says Vicente, in a tone that in no way could be interpreted as a reproach, but was more like he was completing an unfinished sentence.

"It all happened, but in a different order, in another way," says Gonzalo, who prefers to pretend he didn't hear Vicente's words. "The poem just came out, all at once. The other poems I had to make myself write, through sheer will, sheer brainpower, forcing myself, or like someone was forcing me. You're right, the book isn't good. I should have written an essay or something. I wanted to talk about those cemeteries that disguise death, that try to dress it up, rid it of tragedy, and take such pains to avoid the macabre, the funereal."

"The sepulchral," says Vicente, for the mere pleasure of adding that weird word.

"The augural." Gonzalo smiles.

"The portentous," says Vicente.

"The tenebrous."

"The sinister."

"The calamitous."

"The enigmatic."

"The sibylline."

"The inscrutable."

Their laughter is long and their steps short, as if they were competing to see who would arrive last.

"We pay tribute to the dead by cleaning their headstones with wax," says Gonzalo, when they turn serious again. "And by sticking carnations in the grass or leaving a vase with white roses. That's what I wanted to talk about. A weepy woman frantically waxing a gravestone. Bent over, honoring her dead, working. When you try to write a poem there's something that either works or it doesn't. Something you can't force. And that time, with that poem, it worked."

Unexpectedly, Gonzalo sits down on a bench as if he were tired, though he's not.

"And you really stopped writing?"

"I really did. I haven't written in a long time. I'm not a poet anymore."

"No, you published a book of poetry, so you're a poet forever. You're screwed."

Gonzalo smiles and looks out at the horizon, as if he were trying to catch sight of someone.

"What's your dissertation about?"

For a second Gonzalo considers replying to that question in detail, but he doesn't want to bore Vicente. Or maybe it wouldn't bore him, but it would make him see how that is the end; how if he did study literature he would have to keep studying for years just so he could write five hundred repetitive pages that would end up marooned on some library shelf. It doesn't seem like a very enticing prospect.

"I have a better idea—tell me about your poems."

"They're no good yet."

"But what are they like?"

Vicente doesn't answer. They start walking again, and it's four in the afternoon but neither of them gives a thought to lunch. For the first time it is possible that the encounter will come to an end. They haven't agreed on anything, and neither Gonzalo nor Vicente really knows what the immediate present consists of. They stand there on the corner of Providencia and Pedro de Valdivia. It seems like a goodbye. They both feel like there's a lot more to talk about, but it's also possible that, in a way, there is nothing more, or that everything will turn difficult, that the words will stop flowing. They walk a few steps more, and, almost without deciding to, they go into a bookstore.

T his place gets nicer every time," Gonzalo says to Joan, a Catalan who's lived in Chile for decades.

"Hombre, thanks," replies Joan. "And you get fatter every time, man."

While Gonzalo and Joan tease each other, Vicente inspects the shelves. The first thing he looks for is *Memorial Park*, which of course isn't there, and never was—it's not anywhere. Then Gonzalo comes over to the same section, and for a moment they look like two strangers with their heads cocked to the side, trying to stay out of each other's way. Gonzalo chooses several books to give Vicente. He thinks it's only fair, they're all the gifts he never gave him, the ones he owes, and there is something freeing about that thought, but then he realizes his impulse is dumb and offensive: it's like reparations, like compensation for damages. So then he decides to just choose one. He thinks he'd better not give him poetry, because Vicente seems to have read everything. He considers *Youth*, by J. M. Coetzee, but then thinks better of it. It's a stupid, literal choice, because while it is a beautiful, hard book about a person confronting more or less the same dilemmas and desires that perhaps Vicente is facing, giving him that book would be invasive, parodic. And maybe Vicente's dilemmas and desires are different, thinks Gonzalo; maybe Coetzee is talking about a world that's been buried by now, for better or for worse. He decides to give him something more current, more befitting but not explicitly so, and he thinks about it long and hard, because basically he is choosing a gift for a stranger whom he refuses to think of as a stranger. He ends up buying *The Magic Mountain*, which is almost the opposite of what he's looking for, since it's not at all contemporary. And that's fine, old people give the classics as gifts, thinks Gonzalo with merry resignation.

"Let's get a cup of coffee," he says to Vicente as they leave the bookstore.

It almost sounds like an order. It's not, of course, but that's what it sounds like. Vicente feels like he should leave, but he couldn't do it smoothly, he'd just take off running, and one of the few things he is sure of is that he no longer wants to run away from anywhere ever again. Gonzalo takes him by the shoulder naturally, the way a father would. He's not fatter, thinks Vicente, remembering Joan's words. In no way could Gonzalo be described as a fat person, but he is clearly no longer thin. Nor does he have wrinkles, or just on his forehead when he smiles, and it'll be some time before he goes gray or bald, thinks Vicente, who then tries to decide which of the two of them is taller. He himself is five-foot-nine, and he senses that Gonzalo is too.

They sit down in a café, and the service is slow.

"So you don't smoke anymore?"

"I quit a couple years ago."

"And didn't you wear glasses?" Vicente suddenly thinks he remembers Gonzalo with glasses, but he's not sure.

"I wear contacts now."

"You did wear glasses before, right?"

"Just to read. Now I need them all the time."

"I thought you were going to take me to the fiction writer zoo."

"What's that?"

"Café Tavelli."

"Right, that place is always full of writers." Gonzalo gives a belated guffaw. "Though I haven't been there in ages. I don't like Tavelli. But their orange layer cake is exceptional."

"I really like it too."

"Then let's go and have ourselves a piece of cake, and then we'll come back here."

"Okay."

And they do. At Tavelli, there are indeed several writers, and Gonzalo and Vicente sit in a corner and look at them as if they really were animals in an exhibit. They scarf down identical slices of cake and go right back to the café next door, where Gonzalo gives Vicente the copy of *The Magic Mountain* he just bought for him.

"How come you're giving me this book?"

"Because it's amazing. Especially the chapter called 'Snow.' I don't really remember why, but there's one page I transcribed and hung up on the wall and read over and over."

"Yeah, but that's not what I'm asking. I'm asking why you're giving me a gift."

"Because in two weeks you're going to turn nineteen. On March thirtieth," says Gonzalo.

"Right. Thanks. I have some books for you too, but they're not gifts, they're returns."

Vicente takes the books by Gonzalo Millán and Emily Dickinson from his backpack.

For a fraction of a second, Gonzalo doesn't realize these are his books. Once he recognizes them, he touches them and flips excitedly through their pages, as if he wanted to be sure they were real. He didn't underline books back then, but he did write his name on the first page: he recognizes first his name and then his handwriting, though his writing hasn't changed since then. He flips through the pages, which now have been underlined by Vicente, who never thought he would be returning them—he doesn't want to return them, to tell the truth: he's betting that Gonzalo isn't going to accept them, and it's a risky wager because it's based on the idea that he knows him, which is not at all certain. But he bets right:

"They're yours," says Gonzalo.

"No, they're yours. I'm sorry I underlined them."

"They're a hundred percent yours. Happy birthday, Vicente," he says, with a faltering smile. "Happy early birthday."

"That's three gifts in total."

"But I owe you a lot of gifts. Birthdays and Christmases. These books aren't early gifts, they're late, very late."

"True enough," says Vicente, satisfied.

They look through the books, pausing over certain lines. He'd bought the Emily Dickinson at the Ulises bookstore, which is right there, just steps away. It was really expensive, he remembers. He'd gotten the Millán in a trade that had shades of a con job: when he was in his second year of college, he'd befriended a freshman whose father was a reader of Chilean poetry, and the father had owned this book, which was almost impossible to find. It had been published in Ottawa in 1984, while Millán was in exile; apparently the book was a gift from the author himself. Gonzalo proposed a trade to the freshman, the Millán for a novel by Roberto Ampuero that had just come out. It was an asymmetrical deal—it didn't make sense to exchange a bibliographical rarity for a recent book that Gonzalo hadn't even bothered to read, a birthday present from the typical misguided relative. ("I heard you like to read.") Years later, his victim wanted the book back. He wasn't interested in Millán's poetry, but he'd learned that with the money he'd get for the book he could buy about twenty Ampuero novels.

"And you didn't give it back."

"No. It was his own fault, the dumbass."

"In the end, poetry books are worth a lot more than fiction," says Vicente, philosophizing.

"True."

"Did you ever meet Millán?" Vicente asks, in a tone of candid, perfect innocence.

"I saw him about five times, at readings. We talked one night and I thought we would talk again, but he died suddenly."

"In 2006."

"Yes."

"Did you miss the book?"

Gonzalo says he did, but it's not true. He had never read Millán again. He did read Emily Dickinson. It's unfair. After his imposture, he'd been ashamed and he'd punished Millán, so to speak, but not Emily Dickinson.

They spend about another hour in the café talking about poetry, Chilean poetry, and drinking espressos. At times they talk as if they'd just met, as if they were on a blind date. There are silences, but they never grow uncomfortable, perhaps because the books remain on the table. Every once in a while Vicente rereads a poem, and at one point he also opens *The Magic Mountain* to a random page and reads:

> Barely twenty years old, but already graying and balding, the patient was emaciated, his skin waxen; he had large hands, large ears, a large nose; grateful to the point of tears for this diversion and their encouraging words, he actually wept a little out of weakness as he greeted them and accepted the bouquet.

Vicente thinks that he likes the excerpt and he's going to read the entire novel, he's going to start tomorrow, though he doesn't know whether it'll be lying in bed in pajamas or in the front yard with his first coffee. He gets distracted over that dilemma, as if it were necessary to decide right now.

Then they walk back the way they came as if returning to the university, as if they'd just been taking a very long break. They wander without a clear route, and now it does seem like the encounter is going to end, but then Vicente launches into a retelling of his story with Pru, starting with the night he met her all the way to the end, though he omits the scene of Carla and León going at it. Gonzalo doesn't know what to say. He tries to console him, the way a friend would.

"What's New York like?" Vicente asks, in the same guileless tone he'd used before to ask if Gonzalo had met Millán.

Gonzalo could describe New York for hours on end, but he understands that Vicente is going to relate those images to Pru, that he's going to imagine Pru on that stage. He understands that Vicente is not interested in New

York, but rather in Pru in New York. He remembers that poem by Ernesto Cardenal, so maudlin and exact:

> If you are in New York
> in New York there's no one else
> and if you're not in New York
> in New York there is no one.

Vicente didn't know it, and he thanks Gonzalo. He thinks he could write Pru and send it to her, though he would rather send a poem of his own. And really, he's not sure whether Cardenal's poem is appropriate. He doesn't know if he wants to—and he thinks this word in scare quotes—*woo* her; it would feel ridiculous. He's wanted to write her for weeks now, he's read and reread the letter she left him a hundred times, but he still hasn't answered.

"But, what's New York like?" Vicente asks again.

Gonzalo tells him about some of the bookstores, about the dense orange of a tupelo tree in Central Park, about the extravagant library he amassed just by collecting books every Sunday from the sidewalks of Brooklyn. About his attempts to learn to ice-skate in Bryant Park. About the buzz of the radiators in winter. About the view of Washington Square from the windows of Bobst Library. About the endless summer battles against water bugs. About a day when he spent around five hours collecting iridescent bottles in Dead Horse Bay. About his obsession with some drawings of Goya's displayed at the Frick. About his unshakable fear of squirrels. About those rare few days of silence when even the fire truck sirens seemed to have abandoned the city. About the slow sunsets in East River State Park. About the ice cream from Morgenstern's. About a trip to Amherst. About the letters people leave on Emily Dickinson's grave. About the afternoon he spent reading those letters.

Vicente assimilates these possible scenes, and indeed he doesn't picture Gonzalo walking around New York but rather Pru. Suddenly he gets the idea they know each other—that Gonzalo met Pru in New York, or maybe more recently, that she could have interviewed him. Alarmed, he imagines they are friends, or that they slept together at some point. He visualizes the scene, panicked and resentful: Pru rocking atop Gonzalo, the two of them very serious, concentrated.

"Do you know Pru?"

"No."

"Seriously, tell me the truth," says Vicente, "do you know Pru?"

"I'm telling you no. Why don't you believe me?"

Gonzalo perceives Vicente's distress, but doesn't understand it. Vicente accelerates, and for a second Gonzalo has the feeling it will be impossible to keep up with him: that Vicente will walk faster and faster until he disappears over the horizon.

"My mom slept with my dad," says Vicente.

It's such a comical and bizarre sentence, one that almost any human being would be in a position to utter . . . Vicente feels silly, but he maintains the intention of wounding or at least shocking Gonzalo, so he goes on. He talks more about the day he went to Las Cruces, the last time he saw Pru, or at least Pru's blond hair as she got into Rocotto's car, and about the walk back along the highway to El Tabito. He is quiet for a few seconds, as though deciding whether to keep talking or not, and then he rushes onward: he talks about those useless vacation days under the miserly sun of the February coast, and about his abrupt decision to go back to Santiago, where he was met by the grotesque surprise of his parents in the nude, fucking.

Gonzalo can't believe it, and even gets retroactively jealous. He asks Vicente what he felt in the moment, and Vicente says nothing, because he thinks that any possible answer is somehow a betrayal.

"My dad is an idiot," he says, and immediately regrets it, but he doesn't take it back; he doesn't know how to.

"So are they together now?"

"No. They say it was a onetime thing. And I don't think they could be together anyway. They have nothing in common. What about you?"

"What about me?"

"Are you interested in my mom?"

"What?"

"Anyway, I'm pretty sure she has a boyfriend now." Vicente is about to say that actually his mom has a girlfriend, but he doesn't know that definitively, it's only a suspicion.

"I'm sure she does," says Gonzalo. "She must have guys beating down her door. Your mother is very pretty and charming and talented. I don't think she'd be interested in getting back together with me."

Neither is Gonzalo interested in getting back together with her, but of course he doesn't want to say that. And Vicente understands, in any case. He wouldn't want Gonzalo to get back together with Carla, but maybe he does want Gonzalo to exist again. For Carla and Gonzalo to exist in completely separate, parallel worlds, just as they do now. And to have access to both of those worlds. No more than that, no less.

Time has flown, it's now seven o'clock, and most people are heading home. They reach Plaza Italia, and Vicente looks at the bus stop where he met Pru and thinks about her—or rather tries to think about her, because it doesn't work. He's still brooding over what he said about his father, and he still wants to take those words back, defend León, but it's almost impossible to defend him, it always has been. What the hell am I doing? wonders Vicente. Why do I want to defend my dad and why am I talking to Gonzalo? Why do I listen to him and accept him and believe him? Suddenly he has the brutal vision of his mother abandoned by these equally mediocre men; he thinks that León and Gonzalo are the same, they're both good for nothing, they were both incapable of transcending the narrow circuit of their interests, of giving real love, real companionship.

"It's true that my dad is an idiot," he says, with a slight tremor, "but so are you. And you're worse. You made us think you were better, but you were worse, you are worse."

Gonzalo receives those words like a deserved and expected punch in the nose. It's a punch that should knock him out, but right now he can't afford the luxury of hitting the mat. A sadly opportune reply emerges in his head, which nevertheless he refuses to utter: *I don't judge you for judging me.*

"I never wanted to hurt you," he says instead.

"You didn't hurt me," Vicente replies automatically. "I'm fine. I'm strong. It's not so easy to hurt me."

"Are you hungry?" Gonzalo asks, as if he hadn't heard.

"What?"

"I asked if you're hungry."

"Yeah," replies Vicente, disconcerted.

They go into the **Fuente Alemana** and order two lomo italiano sandwiches, which they devour in a couple minutes.

"Do you know Gerardo Rocotto?"

"Sure do."

"Do you like him?"

"I mean, I know his work. As a person he seems unbearable." Actually, Gonzalo does like Rocotto, but he wants to show solidarity.

"Did you read Pru's article?" Vicente asks.

"No," says Gonzalo, surprised, but then he understands that he could very well have read it, since it is after all about Chilean poetry. And then he thinks he remembers someone telling him about an article that must have been Pru's. Vicente looks it up on his phone, shows it to Gonzalo.

"Have another sandwich while I read it," says Gonzalo, and Vicente agrees.

"Sometimes I'm not hungry, but then I eat something and it just makes me hungrier." He downs all of his peach juice.

"I know what you mean," says Gonzalo. He likes when Vicente comes out with these fresh, quotidian comments.

Pru's article came out a week ago, and the whole big little world of Chilean poetry is talking about it. There are those who say the reporting is deep, tough, and restorative, others who consider it spiteful, biased, superficial, incomplete. They accuse Pru, above all, of being feminist and foreign. Someone suggests that Gerardo Rocotto is the article's real author, and he dictated it into the journalist's ear. Pato says Pru mistreated him, Aurelia Bala says she is a repressed lesbian, Rosabetty Muñoz thinks the article is very good but should have been much longer, Miles Personae considers it deficient, Javiera Villablanca is surprised by her unexpected prominence, Roddy Godoy reads it five times looking for his name, unable to resign himself to being over-looked, but then he consoles himself with the thought that truly experimen-tal poets have always shared that fate. In short, as always happens in these cases, the poets who were left out are offended, and the ones who were in-cluded adjust their level of approval or contentment to the number of times they were mentioned, and can't stop sharing and discussing the article on Facebook. Gonzalo has never been on Facebook, and maybe that's why he hasn't read Pru's article. There are some mistakes, not many, which the de-tractors point to as unforgivable and which he notices right away, but he likes Pru's perspective and her language. He also likes that she mentions Vicente, that she thanks him for his help warmly or possibly flirtatiously ("*It was Vicente Aspurúa—a very young and thus far unpublished poet whose help in writing this article was invaluable in more ways than one—who told me the story of . . .*").

"It's really good," says Gonzalo. "It's different, it's alive, it's original. Pru's a good writer."

"Yeah," says Vicente. "The first time I read it I didn't understand much, but then I translated it in Google and I understood more."

"Do you remember we used to study English?"

"No."

"Do you remember there was a year when you almost failed English? And you had to memorize 'Sweet Child o' Mine'?"

"I don't remember, but it makes sense," says Vicente, as though thinking out loud, "because that's the only song in English I know by heart, and I don't even like it."

"I don't either, but we sang it about a thousand times."

"Was that the year I repeated?"

"Yes," says Gonzalo. "You repeated, but not because of English."

"Thanks," says Vicente jokingly, and then he asks seriously, probing Gonzalo's memory: "Do you remember which classes I failed?"

"Math and science," says Gonzalo.

They leave the Fuente Alemana, and neither of them wants to go home. They walk to La Terraza and order two draft beers.

"Do you drink beer with or without alcohol?" asks Vicente.

"With alcohol." Gonzalo thinks the question is funny. "Non-alcoholic beer is awful."

Vicente rolls up his sleeves and part of a tattoo on his left forearm is revealed. Gonzalo thinks about whether the other day, at the bookstore, Vicente had that tattoo or not, and he's almost sure he didn't. He decides not to bring it up, but he does ask to see it.

"It's nice. Why'd you pick it?"

"That's why, because it's nice."

"It looks recent."

"Yeah, it's new."

"Do you remember we had one of those on the refrigerator?" Gonzalo asks, and for a second he is sure the reply will be affirmative.

"No, I don't remember. A ship?" says Vicente. "When?"

"A tangram. A long time ago. A red, magnetic tangram. I bought it myself at a store on Merced. We always played with it, I'd put together a figure and you'd go over to the refrigerator and take it apart. Maybe it wasn't there for long, the pieces got lost."

"I don't remember that. What shape did you put together? This ship?"

"I didn't always make the same shape. Maybe at some point I made that ship."

But he's lying, he did always make the same shape. He always moved the pieces of the tangram around until he arrived at the classic image of a house, and then Vicente took it apart. He lies now to keep that memory from turning against him; he lies because he can't bear so much irony, such bitterness.

"I'm sure you remember things that I've forgotten, and I remember things you've forgotten," says Vicente.

The words hang in the air like something imminent, like an atmosphere, like a mantra.

The beers come, and maybe it's always like this: the beers come and the first sip is immediate, and the subsequent pause is for smiling or looking at your phone, and then comes the second sip, which is a little longer, and then suddenly there's a silence of a different sort and there are no more smiles, because after the second sip of beer no one really knows how to behave. Vicente, for example, retreats into the foam of his beer, watching the minuscule bubbles disappear, and then he closes his eyes and rubs them vigorously.

The place starts to fill up, because that night there is a Copa Libertadores soccer match between San Lorenzo and Unión Española. The waiters hurry to deliver pisco and cokes and chacarero sandwiches, the game starts, and every once in a while Vicente takes another sip and looks Gonzalo in the eyes and looks down again at the thinning head on his beer.

Then Gonzalo talks a long time, uninterrupted, for almost an hour—he apologizes multiple times, hastens to take all the blame for himself: he doesn't litigate, there are no excuses or alibis or euphemisms. He talks about family, failure, love, the future, absence, inconstancy. He talks about memory and the power of memories. He talks about selfishness. He talks, above all, about selfishness. Vicente looks at him the way he would look at an incomprehensible painting in a museum. A strange and rather ugly painting that nevertheless he would like to understand. Gonzalo blinks fast and keeps talking and repeats a few things, trying to reformulate them, to find another emphasis and other turns of phrase that are even more accurate, more convincing and honest—wordings that may or may not exist.

"I'm going to the bathroom," Vicente interrupts.

He comes back quickly, his face and hair wet.

"Go on, then," he tells Gonzalo.

Gonzalo doesn't go on; he stays quiet. He takes a napkin and crumples it a little, as though playing a slow-motion game of destroying it.

"You ran out of words," says Vicente.

"What?"

"Nothing."

"Tell me. Tell me whatever you want."

"Tell me what you want," Vicente mimics him. "You brought a prepared speech. I didn't prepare anything. I'm naked here."

"I didn't prepare anything, this is all improv," says Gonzalo, trying for a joke.

"But in order to improvise you have to know how to talk. And you know how to talk," says Vicente, speeding up. "I didn't remember that. I didn't remember you talking so well. I listened to you talk for many hours, many years, and I didn't remember that. But me, I'm just now learning."

"You speak very well."

"That's not true. I don't speak well and I don't remember anything. And I don't want to be like you or like my dad or like anyone I know. I don't want to talk like you. You didn't teach me how to talk. I learned on my own. I'm learning on my own. I'm still just okay. I've got a ways to go. I need to learn to talk about the things that matter. I'm learning, still. But I'm going to learn how to talk better than you."

I'm learning how to talk too, thinks Gonzalo, but he doesn't say it, because he understands that Vicente is asking him to learn, rather, to be quiet.

They order another round of beers and again come those first two sips, and Vicente watches the final minutes of the game and then is about to sink definitively into the foam on his beer, but Gonzalo takes a napkin and draws a number sign and marks the center box with an *x*. They play many times, tie many times. They use more than twenty napkins, until Vicente wins:

"So, are you going to go to college?" Gonzalo asks then.

"Come on," Vicente says, laughing. "You mean your college?"

"Any college."

"Do you think universities are ever going to be free?"

"I hope so," says Gonzalo, thinking of Mirko. He's thought about Mirko several times over the course of the day; he imagines him paging through the Carver book while he waits for customers in the mall parking lot. He imagines him carrying TVs, bicycles, microwaves, kitchen furniture, bookshelves.

"What would you do if you were me?"

Gonzalo thinks, is quiet, tries to let an honest answer ripen. When he was eighteen, he'd been so clear on everything. He'd thought he was brave for defying his family. He'd thought he was smart because he read the Greeks, because he was learning Latin, because he cited Derrida. Even before, much younger than eighteen, at ten, twelve years old, he'd had a plan: speak in a different way, live in a different way, think in a different way, break all the mirrors in the house until he joyfully, definitively forgot his own face. All his childhood friends from Maipú had failed, none of them finished college, they'd all met the same fate as Mirko, but he had succeeded, he became the exception, the diligent young man who made the most of the few opportunities he had. And there'd been a long time when he was proud of that. Not anymore. Now he is ashamed. Now he thinks that he failed too.

"So, what would you do if you were me?" Vicente asks again.

"What you're doing."

"I don't believe you."

"I'd study something else."

"What?"

"I don't know, Japanese. Physics. Entomology."

They order more beers. The TV is replaying the goals from the game over and over, and there are still some office workers finishing their last drinks before going home.

"All right, then," Gonzalo says. "Come on, read me your poems."

Vicente demurs a little, but he wants to, and of course, like all Chilean poets, he's come prepared; he takes a sheaf of light blue paper from his backpack and launches into a reading:

> If you ever can come back here just remember:
> it's the round key that fits in the garden gate
>
> the key that fits the front door has been painted
> with a neon yellow bright enamel paint
>
> the door is old but sturdy and has two locks
> but we only ever lock the bottom one
>
> any other keys that you might find are just extras
> the lights in my house have twelve light switches

there are ten double outlets and a triple
and two extension cords that don't go far

the password for the wifi you'll remember

my house is full of cracks that are unseeable
and contumacious cats prowl on its roof

its walls are full of stains my eyes are blind to
and there's a lemon tree that's full of bitter fruit.

Vicente wrote it for Pru, naturally, but Gonzalo also feels part of the poem, because he was the one who had the idea to put paint on the front door key—he did it many times, touched up the paint every few months, and apparently Carla continued the tradition. Or maybe it was Vicente, thinks Gonzalo, while in his imagination he swiftly revisits every one of the rooms in that house, to visualize and count those outlets, those light switches.

Gonzalo feels the desire to write, to start writing again, even if it's just to show Vicente the results. He asks him to keep reading and he doesn't have to twist Vicente's arm; he reads about fifteen more poems. Gonzalo likes them, he thinks they are full and personal; they are all very different from each other, and that's perhaps the best part: Vicente's voice is the sum of all those voices, all those poems, all those poets. He's multiplying himself, thinks Gonzalo. There are verses in classic styles where an enveloping and messy rhythm suddenly emerges, an inconstant music with images that are tentative, bold, turbulent, and warm. He especially likes a long poem that talks about houses floating from one island to another, about planes hanging indefinitely in the air, unsent messages; a poem that talks about someone who is looking out at the waves and who records a video on their phone and then travels many hours while it pours down rain, but during the whole trip doesn't look out the window, doesn't watch the fat drops of rain sliding down the glass, but rather stares at that video of the waves on the phone, over and over, over and over.

The last poem Vicente reads is also different from the previous ones, and it's the one Gonzalo likes the most:

> In my mother tongue the word for earthquake
> is masculine
> (Though I may disagree)
> The word for tattoo is too
> The mole on your skin—that's male.
>
> But a freckle is female
> Like a scar, like a wound
> Like the rain and a raindrop
> But a leak, now that one is male.
>
> The wind is a he
> Same as thunder and lightning
> But the snow (which I've never seen) is a she
> And the frost (which I have) is also a she
> And so is the drizzling rain
> And the storm
>
> The word for lamp is a she, naturally
> And likewise the word for table
> And the word for word
> And the word for chard
>
> In my language the words for winter, summer, and fall
> are all male
> Only spring is a female season
> I may disagree, and I do
> But those are the words that we have.
>
> A fingernail (she) and nail clippers (he)
> A bottle (she) and its opener (he)
> But a foot and a kick are both he

night and midnight, hers and hers
day and midday, his and his
But shadow and sun, hers and his

body and space are his

hand and blouse are hers

But foot and footfall, his and hers

And the desire to never play with words again
(is all mine)
And the desire to never play with words again
And the desire to never play with words again

"I like it a lot," says Gonzalo.

"Really?"

"Yes."

Gonzalo talks about the virtues of the poem as if it had been written by someone else, an absent third party, a poet they both admire, and Vicente smiles, with relief and restraint, but he also asks about specific passages, asks Gonzalo to please point out what he doesn't like, what he would change.

"Should I send it to the gringa or not?" he asks then.

"Go on, send it to her," says Gonzalo.

"I still think it's missing something. I don't like it. I mean, I don't want to write like that."

"Like what?"

"Love poems."

"What kind of poems do you want to write?"

"True poems. Honest poems, poems that make me change, that transform me. You know?"

"Yes."

"I'd better not send it."

"Send it to her. Anyway, if you think my opinion could help you, we could get together again to reread it, or edit it. Whenever you want, any day. Or to read other poems or talk about whatever."

"And you'll read me your new poems," says Vicente.

"I'm going to start writing again just so I can show you my new poems," says Gonzalo.

"Try to make them good."

"But if they're bad you have to tell me."

"I will," promises Vicente.

It's almost midnight, the TVs are off, a waiter cranks up the reggaetón, and Gonzalo and Vicente have to raise their voices in order to keep talking. They have a good time, they laugh hard, neither of them knows what's to come and right now they don't really care. I don't know either: maybe Gonzalo gets into it and goes back to writing poems, goes back to fully being a Chilean poet; maybe Gonzalo and Vicente become friends who get together every so often to talk about poetry. Or maybe Vicente goes off to find Pru or to find no one and never comes back, or he stays in Santiago forever, same as Gonzalo, and they meet up or fight or lose track of each other and don't see each other again for seven or twenty years, or they never see each other again. Maybe they get together every once in a while, every other year, or they happen to run into each other at book launches, at protests, at concerts, in classrooms, and those encounters are always awkward and sad, until one day they simply stop acknowledging each other.

Hopefully they don't lose touch. That would be the closest thing to a happy ending, and I'd like to go on writing until I reach a thousand pages, just to be sure that at least for those thousand pages Gonzalo and Vicente don't lose touch, but that would be to condemn them, rob them of life, of will, because it's possible that they want to stop seeing each other, and that for one of them, probably Vicente, or maybe for them both, it would be for the best.

I don't know, we're never going to know, because this ends here, this ends well, the way so many books we love would end if we tore out their final pages. The world is falling to pieces and everything almost always goes to shit and we almost always hurt the people we love or they hurt us irreparably and there doesn't seem to be a reason to harbor any kind of hope, but at least this story ends well, ends here, with the scene of these two Chilean poets who look each other in the eye and burst out laughing and don't want to leave that bar for anything, so they order another round of beers.

Mexico City
February 21, 2019

Text Credits

Grateful acknowledgment is made for permission to reprint the following:

Page vii: Fabián Casas, "Técnicas." From *Últimos poemas en Prozac* (Emecé, 2019). Reprinted with permission of the author.

Pages 137, 216, and 217: Gonzalo Millán, "Kamasutra," "A Happy Bedtime Story," "Fears," and "Libro Blanco." From *Strange Houses* (Split Quotation, 1991). Reprinted with permission of the author's family.

Page 218: Carlos de Rokha, "Interior." Reprinted with the permission of Fundación de Rokha, Santiago de Chile.

Pages 218–19: Jorge Teillier, "Message in a Bottle." From *Cartas para reinas de otras primaveras* (Ediciones Manieristas, 1985). Reprinted with permission of the author's family.

Pages 256 and 314: Gonzalo Rojas, "Al silencio" and "Crecimiento de Rodrigo Tomas." From *Contra la muerte* (Editorial Universitaria, 1964). Reprinted with permission of Gonzalo Rojas's representation.

Pages 249–50: Chinoy, "El Rayo." From *En Cada Esquina Vol. 3*, 2008. Lyrics reprinted with permission of the musician.

Page 280: Antonio Cisneros, "Cuatro boleros maroqueros." From *Como higuera en un campo de golf* (Instituto Nacional de Cultura, Peru, 1972). Reprinted with permission of the author's family.

Page 280: Andrés Anwandter, "Comienzas a escribir un poema." From *El árbol del lenguaje en otoño* (Ediciones Dossier, 1996). Reprinted with permission of the author.

Page 281: Gabriela Mistral, "La tenca." From *Poema de Chile* (First published by Editorial Pomaire, 1967). Reprinted with permission of La Pollera Ediciones.

Page 289: Veronica Stigger, from the novel *Opisanie swiata* (Cosac Naify, 2013). Translated by Zoë Perry. Reprinted with permission of the author and translator.